Praise for Leslie Hall Pi

"[Pinder's] writing takes chances that are poetically vivid...this is a brave work."

–*The New York Times*

"[A] forceful piece of writing...the book is tense with a body-in-the-cupboard kind of chill, and it manages to convey a sense of the Canadian mid-west without being provincial or sentimental. Pinder is a lavish and intriguing writer."

–*The Times Literary Supplement* (London)

"[A] very original first novel...Pinder's prose is suspenseful and held taut by striking images."

–*The Independent* (London)

"Pinder's prose is stark and subtle—with barely a description of people or places she creates a chilling and claustrophobic picture of the sinister side of family life."

–*The Sunday Times* (London)

"[A]n astonishingly accomplished debut...in the course of a technically complex and assured narrative... and in the slow unfolding of her absorbing tale Ms. Pinder has the reader eating out of her hand. A major talent."

–*The Metropolitan Magazine* (London)

"[T]his is crisply poetic, powerful fiction...Pinder clearly registers as a writer with a future."

–*Kirkus Reviews* (New York)

"Intense and compassionate, Pinder's story skirts sensationalism by focusing on character. It is a powerful tale."

–*Publishers Weekly* (New York)

"[E]verything exists on more than one level, and nothing is quite what it seems. 'Under the House' is a striking and engaging debut."

–*Chicago Tribune*

"*On Double Tracks*, an intriguing, densely written novel about covert angst and overt anger...an interior novel in the tradition of Faulkner... [Pinder is] a master at depicting the fictional unconscious."

–*Quill & Quire* (Toronto)

"Pinder...has both an elegant, fluid style that resonates with quiet emotion and a genuine appreciation for the eerie..."

–*Vancouver Sun*

July / 2012

For Satya –
On the day
of our wonderful
meeting

Lalee

BRING ME ONE OF EVERYTHING

Other books by Leslie Hall Pinder:

Novels:

Under the House

On Double Tracks

Poetry

35 Stones

BRING ME ONE OF EVERYTHING

A NOVEL

LESLIE HALL PINDER

Publisher of Fine Books
Marblehead, Massachusetts

First Trade Paperback Edition: February 6, 2012
Published by Grey Swan Press
Marblehead, MA 01945
www.greyswanpress.com

100% acid-free paper
Printed in the United States

Trade Paperback
First Edition

Library of Congress Control Number: 2011941177

ISBN: 978-0-9834900-1-2

0 9 8 7 6 5 4 3 2 1

For Lorita Whitehead and
Kim Baryluk
the shape-makers, the authenticators, the loves

“Oh voices, sublime voices, high clear voices, how you make one forget the words you sing.”

Opera; or, The Undoing of Women
by Catherine Clement

1

THE TAKING OF THE WEEPING WOMAN TOTEM POLE

A tree is brought down slowly, unlimbed, unbarked, laid bare but not barren. Sap, blood of cedar in the hot pitch-perfumed air. The careful flensing of the adze skimming long curls, urging out what's within: mouth, tongue, widening eye, we become—miracle—a totem. A shape that's wooed, wished, wound out of wood: the Watchman. Underneath the Watchman in the mandated order of things: the Weeping Woman who is neither weeping nor woman. Eyes reach down passed Bear to give birth to children of sight itself, sight giving in to blindness and back to sight, a blink.

The menagerie awakens the stories in us, told, retold, clan, family—being of this place, watching over this place—to this place we belong.

We are enhanced with such colors from the earth so as to command all attention, the red, the black, the green, meant to fade weather-worn, a return.

Even if you forget the stories, even if you forget to pray or sometimes even hope, even if you cannot speak, we're here. Bow to the boughs become bold and holding the bones of the sacred dead in boxes, holding your song. The birds sing for the glory of it, especially in the morning. No mourning, aging ageless, seeing sightless, a cycle, a necessary order in the spinning planets.

Come listen.

Listen!

The grating of hard-soled boots against the small pebbles still becoming beach.

A man in strange clothes, looking at us like an artist, assessing us like a merchant. A butcher knife in his hand.

Alarm! Alarm!

Spluttering, coughing, the sodden unsparked sound of the ragged-toothed machine and then hand-saw—maiming. Back and forth, relentless hypnotic heartbeat a deathbeat, back and forth—a blade that severs through, not a chisel or an adze, not a bow for a stringed wind, but a hack and gnaw, pain beyond telling, oh if we could but flee the ram of it, the hated horror of it, the teeth eating into and cutting out all the stately order of us, lined up to pierce the sky we find ourselves pierced. Men below hack and hurl, rack and saw, back and forth dismembering, unremembering, not knowing us at all, but wanting what we keep, what we are bidden to keep, to hold, our promise. They steal. Our songs bloodied, they hew and chop and rip us, spoiled. Unpardonable.

Shamed.

It should take forever, a slow decline that teaches as much in the leaving as in the arrival. But not this. The forest entangled in our head, entwined, reaches out, clutches to hold us up. Too late. Now leaning—now tipped terrible, interminable, all things held upright falling.

The ground comes closer, these butchers are not meek or gentle, the blessed ground our bed our home come to meet us.

We've fallen.

Felled. We are all felled.

AUSTIN HART, WEARING street shoes caked in mud, drew from his pocket a handkerchief, pushed back the collar on his shirt and wiped the sweat from his neck. He pointed. The crew took axes to the next pole. "We'll have to section them before they're crated." Hart paused, looking at the third pole to be taken, then walked towards it.

2

INTRODUCTIONS

Austin Hart killed himself when I was nineteen years old. Although we'd never met, I later found myself making such calculations, measuring dates and events against the pylon of his death driven hard into the bed-rock of our lives.

I was just home from a trip to Europe after my final year at college. Sophia, my mother, came into my room at 7:15 a.m. with a cup of coffee. The coffee was black, the way she liked it; perhaps she'd run out of milk or had forgotten I took cream; or she might simply have decided, that morning, I should start to drink my coffee black.

Would I drive out with her to Aldergrove, before the heat of the day, and pick up some bedding plants, begonia and blue danube? We could have lunch.

She acted cheerily oblivious of my state of exhaustion. Sophia didn't like anyone to be asleep in the house if she were up. It wasn't that she wanted company; it was just that if she were awake, re-establishing order in the household, and someone was still asleep, a minor disharmony made its way into her sense of well-being.

On the way to the suburbs, with Sophia driving, I hadn't been paying conscious attention to what was on the radio. It was a satisfactory sound which excused our not talking to one another. Because of this when mother said, "Oh, no," it was her shocked, empathetic tone that caused me to retrospectively hear the news: a famous anthropology professor, renowned for salvaging Haida totem poles on the Queen Charlottes, had been found dead in his office at the university; he shot himself; used a rifle; survived by his wife and two children.

I asked Sophia if she'd heard the man's name. Austin Hart; wife was Mary-Anne; the children's names weren't mentioned; no, she didn't know him. Her sympathy for this person she didn't know was uncharacteristic.

That was all that was said between us.

HE WAS A SUICIDE. A noun. He suicided. A verb. Suicidal thoughts. An adjective. I played around with the variations of the word, rather than think about the calamity of the action, until the phrase "my own bout with suicide" repeated in my mind. It had happened nine months earlier. Really, describing it as a "bout"—as though it had involved a contest and a struggle—wasn't correct. At the time it felt two-dimensional, flattened out, almost entirely lacking in tension.

The idea of taking my own life seemed to seek me out. It arrived like a guest. Once in, there was nothing to be done but welcome it and be a good host: to follow through with its wishes carefully and with a calmness that confirmed its inevitability. I was going to kill myself. Except for the planning, that's all there was to it. Through dint of self-preservation against my mother, I'd managed in my life to limit my emotions and enhance my discernment. I felt nothing. The only thing that disturbed my almost languid tranquility was a dream one night that I was standing in a barn, surrounded by the dusty-sweet smell of mown hay, when a hawk flew down from the rafters, getting its wings caught in my hair.

I BOUGHT A NEW DRESS. I had a young, healthy body with which I found fault. I never believed the pictures which showed an attractive young woman. The camera was a deceiver. Mother was the beauty in the family, admitting no rivals.

The dress was purple satin with a chiffon top. I liked the look of it on the hanger, and imagined someone else wearing it for graduation or a first date.

I told my friends I was flying home for the Thanksgiving weekend. The extravagance of such a trip wasn't a surprise to them. When I was in residence the previous year, my mother had caterers deliver twenty turkey dinners to my floor. As was her way, she'd forgotten my birthday a week earlier.

I made a reservation for 6:30 p.m. at Le Loup, a fancy restaurant in Halifax. Before then I would pack up my apartment: take the posters off the wall, wash my hair, put my sheets and pillows, my books and kitchenware in my steamer trunk. I'd already wrapped my journals in plastic bags and put them in the garbage can.

By five p.m. I was ready. I'd booked a couchette on the train that left at 11:55 p.m. I sat quietly at my desk, waiting for enough time to pass so I could go to dinner.

The empty space between my chair and the bed contained what I wanted: to be nothing. Once on the train, I would tell the porter I didn't want to be disturbed. It would take four days to go across the country from Halifax to Vancouver, where my mother, sister and step-father lived. On the evening of the third day I'd swallow a bottle of sleeping pills. I'd arrive dead. It sounded melodramatic but I meant it as practical, a matter of common courtesy. I didn't want my mother to come and take me home. Despite her consummate self-absorption, she'd taught her daughters to be polite.

In point of fact I didn't want to die so much as I never wanted to have lived. I couldn't easily undo what had happened.

When I arrived at the restaurant, I suddenly felt conspicuous, all dressed up in my purple chiffon, as though I should be going to a wedding party. The elderly, genteel maitre d' frowned a little, perhaps perplexed that I was unchaperoned. Although illogical and not quite reassuring I said, "I'm going back to the west coast later this evening."

When I confirmed to the waiter that I'd be dining alone, he removed the extra dishes, napkin and charger plate on the other side of the table. As he picked up each piece of the cutlery I counted: two spoons, three forks and two knives. The white expanse of the linen table cloth across from me was reassuring.

I had a double sense of time, looking at that vacant space: I was watching and I had already gone. I had no feelings except my intention to get to midnight and then into a white and dreamless state. After the flat expanse of the prairies I'd climb through the blessed cold of the snow-capped Rockies; I would be emptied out while the train took its zig-zag course through the valleys along the Fraser River until I was deposited onto the shore. The landscape of myself would be a film unwinding to the edge.

Even though I'd never tasted one before, I ordered a whiskey sour, a drink Sophia sometimes had.

I'd have wine with dinner.

I chose the set menu, and, within the choices, simply asked for the first one in each of the categories without even looking at what they were. Scallop carpaccio arrived as a starter; I swirled the pieces in the olive oil mixed with cilantro. My arms looked thin. Duck confit with couscous came as the main course. The food seemed not to have much taste.

I realized I had a sense of enormous relief. My birth had been an accident, my mother had always intimated that. I was the result of a one-night stand during the war. She didn't know the man who got her pregnant, had never seen him again. Her subsequent marriage to Russell provided her with wealth, security and respectability. My relationship to the world had been half in the shadows: illegitimate, an accident, a nameless shame, an unspoken debt. I was a poacher, a tolerated visitor in Sophia's otherwise perfect household. These unwanted things would be corrected; I'd correct them. Nothing would be wrong again. I was being led, inexorably, to this extended blank and I wanted to stay awake until it struck me, like chloroform. I saw the future as clearly as through a washed window. I'd occupy the space of nothing.

I didn't even need to leave a note.

I didn't hate her, I simply didn't trust her. I couldn't say I loved her either. Anyway, Sophia considered love to be a rickety emotion. She was a good story-teller, maintaining the right to be the only one in the family who was; but her tales were inconsistent, contradictory. There seemed to be planned obsolescence built into the very structure of whatever she recounted. Some of the stories disappeared entirely, never to reappear despite my prodding, while others hardened into a kind of veracity I could rely on, even if they'd never happened. All of this gave me a good nose for truth-telling. As a teenager, I'd become a self-appointed triage officer of what she said—of what everyone said—always sorting according to degrees of believability. Yet every fact was a potential casualty to truth. My distrust of my mother leached into our morning greeting and into the thin embrace of good-night. I left as soon as I could, going east to Dalhousie University in Halifax for my Bachelor of Arts degree, 3,000 miles away from her. My sister, Peg, went north to Prince Rupert.

Within all of this I believed, eating the citrus sorbet after dinner—my arms were like sticks—that my mother would understand my decision because it was what she wanted. In any event, it would be—finally something would be—unalterably true.

For the first time in my life I felt for Sophia something which might have been akin to love.

Despite the cost of the dinner, I had plenty from my monthly allowance. I left a large tip.

It was a short but cold walk back to the old three-story house overlooking the harbor. The whiskey-sour and wine had had little affect on me.

I climbed the wide, winding staircase. It would be nice to say good-bye to someone, but everyone was out for the evening.

I entered my apartment at the top of the house.

I ordered a cab for eleven o'clock, asking the dispatcher to please have the driver come and help me with the trunk.

The apartment looked the same as when I'd first moved in, except I'd painted the walls white—four coats to cover the dark green, an improvement for the next occupant. One window was flush against the slant of the roof and I opened it by pushing out the lever and securing it three notches from the end. The sea air was moist and over-ripe.

I sat at my desk. The watch hanging loosely on the wrist of my right hand said 8:05 p.m.

I'd gone to the restaurant too early.

Three hours was such a long time to wait.

I stared at the bare wall where there'd been a poster of the tapestry of "The Lady and the Unicorn," the pleased Unicorn regarding himself in the mirror held by the Lady, with the somewhat gangrenous lion looking away.

I waited.

8:22

I leaned back in the chair, drifting.

The telephone rang.

My head jerked back.

I didn't know who would be phoning at 8:24 on a Sunday night. The train station didn't have my telephone number. There was no reason for the cab company to ring. My friends knew I was away. I'd been silent for hours, not talking to anyone at the restaurant except to order, and then to make the arrangements with the taxi. The telephone on the side-table near the couch was making a noise that seemed excessive.

It rang six or seven times. Then stopped.

I stared at the phone, willing it to stay silent and inanimate. Ten minutes passed, and I'd succeeded.

Again, ringing. 8:36. Twelve, thirteen, fourteen. It wasn't a telephone, it was a tormentor. Eighteen, nineteen. Please stop. It wasn't going to stop. It seemed to be getting louder.

Twenty-three, twenty-four, twenty-five.

This wasn't my plan. On and on—I broke.

The ringing ransacked the vacated rooms of my brain, down

the empty hallways, into closets, carrying a searchlight whose beam ran up and down the walls, over the ceiling, into every corner. Why don't they know there's no one here? Why don't they leave me alone?

The sound, wearing me down, wearing me out—as I picked up the monstrous, vibrating thing and moved it as delicately as a sulphurous bomb. The cord was stuck behind the couch where it was wired into the wall. I dislodged it, opened the closet, slowly pushed the line under the door, and placed the phone inside. I sat on the couch staring at the door behind which the ringing continued, unmuffled.

"There's nobody here." My own voice, calling out. "There's nobody here." My own voice yelling.

Taking the small key from the inside pocket of my purse.

Turning it in the lock of the trunk, the clasp banging.

The lid resting against the wall.

Emptying the books, papers, a saucepan, and a bag of cutlery, reaching the layer of sheets and blankets, hurrying.

Some mad person was calling me, someone unmerciful. No one could persist so long in letting a phone ring when there was no one answering.

I opened the closet door with one hand and with the other placed the blankets on top of the phone, careful not to jostle the receiver. Nothing—blunted—the sound. Returning with sheets and towels and then with all my clothes, heaping even my books on top. The entire contents of my trunk were now mountained over this monstrous, harsh, blaring, incessant, cruel ringing that went on and on and on.

I couldn't answer it. I wouldn't answer it. My tightly wound resolve would unravel. All I had left in the world was my large midnight purpose, my decision—my careful, simple uncomplicated plan that wasn't going to hurt anyone, that would leave everything ordered, all things finally straightened again. The wide swath of my intention which had led me through these last days, had calmed me and given me such contentment, such confidence and faith, this intention was becoming narrow because I couldn't—stop this ringing.

It became so small, this purpose, this desire, this needle-pin of certainty—

—somehow the receiver in my hand.

My mother's voice coming through the thick black instrument.

"Alicia. What's going on? Alix, are you there?"

It was all over.

"Alix, darling, are you there? Answer me. I know you're there. I just felt that something was wrong."

I STAYED AT SCHOOL and finished my degree, graduating cum laude. We never spoke about that night. If ever again I planned to end my life, it couldn't be while my mother was still alive. She'd somehow manage to intercept me. I wasn't sure how, but she would. My fear was as non-rational as her uncanny knowing to call me starting at 8:24 p.m., Sunday, October 13, and not stopping.

AFTER THAT, I WAS NO LONGER host to the suicide visitor. Even the recollection of its presence slipped away. I went west to Toronto and found a job in the publishing industry, eventually creating my own company. It became the imprimatur for authors who were required reading. My own books were amongst them: two collections of short stories, three of verse, the most recent of which had won the Governor-General's Award and the Brennan prize for poetry. I had a long-term relationship. I was at the top of my game.

Then, like the insidious creep of water through the pores of something as solid as concrete, the accumulating disturbance began again, first signaled by a headache I couldn't dislodge, and then by a migraine which split my sight. The migraines were prelude to a much more disturbing and inevitable thing: all color evacuated my vision, putting me in a burnt-out house, the gunmetal light offering no promise of dawn. Something was terribly wrong and a higher dosage of Prozac® wasn't going to solve it.

I left the company, not because I was afraid but because I was in a godless state. In that condition, twenty-five years after the newscast about his death, I heard the name Austin Hart again. Time disappeared like a false floor collapsing.

3

A BROKEN GLASS AND MELTED ICE

I was listening to a message from a Vancouver composer, Brett Morris, about possibly writing the libretto for an opera about a notable anthropologist—when the telephone rang. I could see from the call display that it was my mother. Ten p.m. in Toronto, seven p.m. in Vancouver. It was late for her to phone, and unexpected. Generally, we spoke once every few months, and I had just talked to her the previous week. She'd been concerned about my leaving the publishing company. Maybe she was calling to badger me.

I clicked off the answering machine to talk to her.

She'd been making herself a drink, felt fine, and the next thing she was on the kitchen floor. She lay there for fifteen minutes, trying to decide if it was serious enough to go to the hospital, and when she couldn't decide, she managed to pull the phone over to call me.

"I'm sure it's nothing, but I can't seem to hoist myself to my feet." Even in such a state, her voice sounded the way it always did: deep, melodic and almost languorous. She took her time when she spoke, and didn't mind long pauses; she always managed to prevent even the uninitiated from interrupting her.

I contacted emergency at the Vancouver General Hospital,

her neighbor, Rachel Epstein, and Air Canada. When the medics arrived I was told she seemed to have a fractured hip. I left a brief, probably too brief, note for my partner, Richard, who was still at work. Within an hour my mother was in the hospital, and within two hours I was on board a flight to Vancouver.

As the cab pulled up to the hospital, I noticed a long chimney stack beside it. Some black corruption—it looked like tar—had drizzled down the length of the bricks.

I was calm.

The reception area was spacious, even a bit theatrical. There were the tiny lights on the ceiling, imitating stars, as though infirmity could be buffered, made to wait off-stage.

There was no one at the desk. I went farther in and found a woman in hospital greens behind one of the glass cages. I leaned over to the mouse hole opening, asking for Sophia Purcell who'd been admitted during the night.

"Emergency ward. Follow the path."

I left my luggage in the reception area, not really caring if someone might take it.

The hallway, swilled by an attendant with the grey strands of a long mop, was not clean. Behind me, the sound of a cart. Two male orderlies wearing large light blue shower caps were gossiping as they pushed a bed down the hall; the front wheels gyrated harshly against the forward motion. A bag of blood was hooked above the head of an old woman, and as they passed, I looked hard to see if it were my mother. She was too ill to be my mother.

The yellow line ended; I walked along the red stripe and followed it left, then right, then left again. The red line disappeared on me, and I was, for a moment, bewildered. I picked it up again across the hall.

Patients in trolley-beds lined the halls, different parts of their anatomy raised. I looked discreetly at each person.

Finally I reached the emergency reception area at the end of the red line. The sallow-complected nurse turned the pages of a computer print-out. Without looking up and before I could speak she said, "Have a seat."

I joined the others. Some were clinging to their coats placed back to front over them like straight jackets. They all stared blankly, immobile as chairs. A sickly man in hospital wear was sitting in a wheelchair. His thin legs, leaning against one another, looked incapable of motion. On the wrist of one hand was tattooed, in crude lettering, the word "HATE," then a misshapen heart followed by the word "LOVE" underneath.

I touched one of the plants to determine that it wasn't real, although there was soil. I waited forever. Again I approached the glassed-in nurse. She was on the phone, and when she saw me, she held up her hand. I persisted. "I'm looking for my mother, Sophia Purcell." She shook her head. I remained standing.

Finally the caged woman said, "Sophia Purcell—your mother?—she's in there, station four in the right-hand corner. Don't have a room for her yet."

I went through the double doorway. I hadn't seen her for two years yet my childhood fear of the penetrating glare of her eyes was still prologue to every visit. I found her amidst a shanty-town of beds. To my relief she was sleeping. Her dyed auburn hair, which instead of seeming counterfeit and an obvious attempt at cheating age, made her look fifteen years younger. I'd never known its natural color.

She had on amber clip earrings and a matching necklace which I had given her for her seventieth birthday. Her head and jewelry didn't belong to a body wearing a washed-out blue nightgown covered by thin, fraying bedclothes. The tattered yellow blankets looked flammable.

She opened her eyes wide and quickly. It took her a few seconds, not more, and then her face sloughed its fear and confusion. A loving smile blossomed, as if she were a mother who adored her daughter and always had. I stepped back.

"Alicia, I sure am glad to see you. I thought you wouldn't be able to find me."

I had the urge to run.

I expected her to wink at me, her tricky invitation to collude with her deceptions. I made myself take her hands in mine, hoping, in the gesture, to locate a feeling which wasn't either of suspicion or fear. "Have you seen the doctor yet?" She shrugged.

SOME TESTS WERE DONE; others were required. Mother's blood pressure was so low they didn't think she could stand without falling. She would be in hospital for some time. A metal pin would repair her hip.

I stayed with her until she was put in a private room. Then I took her keys.

Beside the main door of the hospital I noticed a room which I read as "Scared Space" instead of sacred space. I went into the chapel.

The air was dank and cloying, as in a thrift store. I sat in one of the chairs and put my head back, closing my eyes against a sabotage of tears.

The fingers on my right hand went numb around five p.m. each afternoon, as though set to an alarm. I'd shake them out and rub them until the momentary relief of a tingling thaw followed by the sense that I'd touched a tray of ice-cubes. My grandmother had developed a rare nerve disease and was crippled late in her life. I remembered her as an old woman at the window, her wispy grey hair tortured into curls caused by a home-permanent given to her by her husband, my grandfather. She'd push up her left arm at the elbow with the stronger right hand so as to be able to wave to me as I came up the walk. It wasn't really a wave, but more like a nod with her hand, as though she animated a puppet.

I worked my thumb up and down the outside of my fisted hand. Gradually feeling returned.

What a long haul it had been to reach this now.

Meaning for me had always hung on a line, to be reeled in like freshly washed clothes smelling of the outside. The next day everything might have fallen to the ground, trampled and irrevocably soiled; I was never sure why. I had now chosen to clothes-peg, side by side, three events: quitting my job, the call from the composer, my mother's illness. I'd shoved them out on their course to wait for significance. And there was also a fourth event: I'd left Richard.

What was I doing?

I retrieved my luggage and hailed a cab.

As we drove into a kind of mildewed dusk, I felt myself slipping into the clutter of illogical associations which were the hallmark of the transition between awake and asleep. If the body accepted the mix-up which the mind offered, it would be conned into silence and the dreams would begin. I followed the stages in the drift...my mother was dressed like a road-worker, wearing a bright, nicely fitting vest, darts at the bosom, hot pink with silver stripes so that the headlights from the car I was driving shone—

"Ma'am? We're here." It was the cabdriver.

WHEN I OPENED THE FRONT DOOR, I knew this was going to be more difficult than I had imagined.

In the front hall, I faced the portrait of Russell, my sly step-father. Beside him were all of his ancient relatives. Only Oliver, Sophia's brother, belonged to my side of the family. In one photograph he was striding up Oxford Street on his way to Buckingham Palace, supposedly to receive the Victoria Cross for bravery in 1944. I met him once, I think, or someone very much like him.

I was ensnared by the pictures in the hall, just as I had been as a child. While this was the only place I ever remembered living when I was growing up, I didn't think of it as home. I was unassuming about the wealth and privilege with which I had been raised because it came from my step-father and wasn't mine. Only my Uncle Oliver, with his bravura walk and his large quantity of heroism, was there to shoulder me. I knew his name was Oliver—because my mother had said so and that was the name on the back of the picture—and that he was walking up Oxford Street, because I could see it written on the corner of the building.

The living-room was as immaculate as ever. The furniture, the wall-to-wall carpet, the cushions: everything was white-on-white. I used to imagine that guests would be in danger of going to sit down and miss the couch, foreground blending into background.

Next was the dining room with its dark and gleaming oak floor. The third fireplace in the house was here, the logs neatly placed and ready to be lit.

The rooms were as Sophia always had them: a stage set for a long running play, with all the parts scripted and ordained. But not this part.

In the vast kitchen with its bounding stainless steel surfaces, I saw the only thing that was out of place: an ice tray on the center island had melted water in it. On the floor was a broken glass, and liquid from the glass had soaked into the Persian carpet which was in the walk-way next to the counter near the window. Someone, probably a medic, had taken a broom and swept the glass into the kick space.

On the outside of the fridge were small photographs and lists: a recent picture of my sister Peg standing beside her husband, Jeremy, on their boat, forever sailing around the world, snapshots of garden flowers, notes of appointments, groceries to buy. Sophia had always hated cooking and, as a strategy of avoidance, never had a plentiful fridge. It was now full of food. There was an almost empty box of Cadbury's chocolate bars at the front of the center shelf.

I moved into the solarium. Its roof and two walls were of glass so that the outside pond, with its long grasses, and the entire abundant garden, seemed part of the inside of the house. Along the common wall with the library was the ubiquitous liquor trolley which Russell always moved into the solarium in the summertime. Mother had continued this practice.

That was enough. I couldn't manage going upstairs to the bedrooms. I felt drained like a pool.

Except for the contents of the fridge, at least on the ground floor there was nothing to indicate that my mother had been in trouble before she fell.

I spread the sheets and the duvet onto the couch in the library. Although I was exhausted, I didn't want to surrender to sleep. I should call Richard. Instead, I phoned the number for Brett Morris, the composer.

He answered.

He was so happy he'd located me. Someone who was familiar with my writing (I couldn't quite understand who) had suggested he track me down, knew about my winning the Brennan Prize—maybe I'd be interested in writing the libretto for the opera he was creating, shaping the story, that sort of thing. It was just in its formative stages and—actually it was fairly urgent that we meet soon, if I was at all interested—

The composer overcame anxiety by raising his voice and acting as though we were already friends. He spoke rapidly, halted and abruptly changed course, uncertain of the best strategy. I thought I'd probably like him because he was nervous and over-excited. Despite my apparent reserve, I was drawn to people who might crack.

He explained the work was classical, based on an important story—the life of the renowned anthropologist, Austin Hart, had I heard of him—

Yes, many years ago, I said.

Inside me something shifted and aligned, like a compass.

We arranged to meet.

I POURED MYSELF A GLASS of *Mercurey* burgundy from the solarium trolley, and wrapped myself in the covers.

Had my renewed connection to Austin Hart happened through a cheat? The poems that had won the Brennan Prize were culled from a file on my computer which I called the cutting room floor. In a dry spell, it was all I had to offer. It was one of those literary and publishing ironies that these once rejected lines were the dropped crumbs that led me back to Hart.

And from a collapsed house, it's easier to see the moon. I drifted to that night in Halifax, before the phone rang. I was someone who'd wanted to disappear, as from a crossroad, vanish without being noticed, traffic continuing to flow in an orderly fashion, everyone yielding and going about their way. I had so thoroughly failed there was nothing to do but carry on. Yet the major event of my life, my intended suicide, was one of which only I was aware, and which I had not fully escaped.

Austin Hart had succeeded. At a crossroad he disrupted everything, killed himself in the middle of his life. I wanted to place myself at the scene, triangulate the events which intersected at his putting a gun to his head and pulling the trigger. I wanted to find out what a person thought and how a person felt at that settled point of no return. More than anything, however, I wanted to know how he had disentangled himself from all his commitments.

This was my cool, cerebral desire.

However, this opportunity to discover the mechanism of Austin Hart's suicide also posed a risk to me. I only had to stay alive as long as my mother did.

Blessed sleep coaxed me away from any further attempts at certainty.

4

STYX MANSION

The hospital became a familiar place, a community of isolates whose members disappeared without explanation and new ones joined. Patients installed in their rooms looked up as I passed. They'd been captured, now bed-ridden, and were either bored or afraid. What the visitors shared was our lonely preoccupation about another's body. We went steadfastly to our designated patients, walking the yellow line and then the red line, tunneled in our distracting worries. I was the one heading for room 444. The native woman and her partner went to room 424. We had locations in mind, hoping the room would still be inhabited by someone expecting us.

We left tracks of mud in the hallways.

Within the week, my mother's most obvious problem, her fractured hip, had been operated on, and an unknown one revealed. In all likelihood she had fallen because she had uncontrolled diabetes. Dr. Riddell sat with me. Sophia had probably had the disease for a decade, a product of "toxic excesses in the system."

"She'll have a predisposition to all types of infections, heart disease and—the greatest worry is blindness. Glaucoma steals the sight without warning. She needs intensive insulin treatment under medical supervision, physical therapy for her hip; being in a home." The doctor gave a series of karate chops to the future.

I went to my mother, reluctantly carrying the diagnosis like a plank under my arm. As the triage officer of veracity, I was being forced to deliver the ultimate truth.

Mother had had me bring some of her jewelry and seven of the scarves from her dresser drawer. This morning she was trying to complement her blue hospital gown by wearing a Hermes tied loosely around her neck and draped over her shoulder. Turquoise earrings and, in addition to her wedding rings, a sapphire on her right hand, completed the valiant fashion statement.

She looked so diminished. This was not how I wanted to prevail in my lifelong battle with her. Mustering a neutral tone, I reported the information Dr. Riddell had given to me, leaving out the possible deterioration of her eyesight.

She countered the diagnosis. "I always gave to the diabetes society, put out clothes, you know, and electronic things, probably half a dozen blenders in a decade—how could I buy so many avocado green kitchen aides?—but I didn't expect they'd give back to me. We've never had diabetes in my family. We die of heart."

Falling into the rut of our habitual engagement, I took her on. "You've always said that, but over the years, from what you've told me, our relatives succumbed to many causes, and mostly of brain, not heart: tumors, strokes, encephalitis—"

She interrupted. "What will you do with me?" She seemed surprisingly cheerful. "Does this mean that I'll go home and you'll stay on—you'll leave Dick."

We were matching one another, diversion for diversion, and now she'd topped me. I couldn't let it pass. "Mother, his name is Richard, not Dick."

"No matter. I've never much liked him. I don't think you should have fallen in love with anyone whose name is Dick."

"I fell in love with Richard."

"He's still Dick to me."

I tried not to laugh.

I told her that her medical condition required she be put in an extended care facility. It was too abrupt, and she looked terrified, as though I'd pushed her and she was falling. I had to find a ripcord. "I won't leave you. I'll stay in Vancouver." The parachute opened.

"We'll be all right then." She closed her eyes. "Come back later, dear. I'm just tired for the moment." I got to the door. "Find me a nice rest home with smartly dressed people, will you? Everyone around here is so poorly attired. But you're looking swell these days, wearing my clothes." Not bringing enough from Toronto, I'd put on a pair of her jeans and a sweater. "I'm in pretty good shape for an old girl, don't you think?" I turned the door handle.

"I'm scared," she said quietly. Although her eyes were still closed, she sensed my looking back to her. "No, you go. But come again soon."

I closed the door.

I had made a promise to an old woman, my mother. I had done something I hadn't intended to do.

I HAD BEEN SLEEPING on the couch in the library for a week. The only time I'd gone to the second floor was for the limited purpose of finding mother's scarves. I hadn't looked around.

I didn't want to see my bedroom still unchanged from how I'd left it when I was eighteen. I hoped my mother had put it to another use, or had chosen it as the object of one of her renovation projects. Over the years the house would stay the same for long periods of time and then, without notice, she'd remodel it, sometimes in dramatic ways: take out walls, put in walls, repaint everything, find new fixtures for each of the four bathrooms. After Russell died, she made a bay window in her bedroom so that it extended over her garden.

I went upstairs. I opened my bedroom door. The room was a museum.

Why hadn't the chatelaine of alterations changed this place, absorbed it into the rest of the house—made it a spare room? It wasn't as though there was anything worth saving from the almost uninhabitable terrain of my youth. The desk in the corner had been too large for me as a child and too small when I was a teenager. There wasn't a time when it was right. I felt almost sick looking at the narrow bed with the familiar bedspread which had ribbed my face, trapped me in sleeplessness. The child in this room didn't have words for the huge boulders of emotion which leveled her. Maybe these feelings were sourceless—or maybe it was some ancient and inconsolable discontent; whichever, they had bred here.

I closed the door. I would sleep on the couch.

I'D ONLY HAD A FEW short conversations with Richard. Finally I called to tell him I was going to stay in Vancouver. We had a run-on sentence of miscommunication.

Does this mean we're splitting up? he asked, more aggressive than hurt. I have to be with my mother, I said. You never liked her, that's what you've been telling me for the last ten years, isn't it? It's more complicated than that. I think you're telling me we're splitting up; why can't you say so directly, Alix? All right then, I guess we are. You guess we are? he repeated, more bullying than dismayed. It's broken, Richard.

As soon as I said it, I knew it had been so for some time. Then he was angry.

Broken?—that's just one of your poetic declarations.

We really haven't been very happy together for a while, you know that. What will you do, just hang around and be the nursemaid for your mother? Someone here has a project he wants me to work on. What kind of project? It has to do with an opera. But you don't know that much about music. I'd be working on the libretto. What's that?

Now I fell silent.

Alix did you have this set up before you left? Before I left?—my mother collapsed on the kitchen floor, I didn't plan that. Just tell me how this guy found you. Brett's his name; his friend knew me from winning the Brennan Prize. That's pretty obscure. You're about as encouraging as my mother. Okay, sorry—what's the project? It's based on the historical story—

You have no sense of history, you lose your way getting home—Alicia, how can you do this to us?

His sincerity grounded me at last. I'm sorry.

I thought maybe he had hung up, until I heard: Are you still having those strange visions? Not since I've been here. Get your eyes checked—or something—Love you, Alicia. Then he did hang up.

I immediately reached for the phone to make amends, to soften my resolve, to calm the beast so fearful of change. I hadn't said that I loved him, as I had dozens—thousands—of times before. Actually, he hadn't said it either. It was "Love you"—the sentence structure which lacked a subject, that had no "I." The subject, the lover, had gone missing. Perhaps another beast had consumed the forthright ability to say: I love you.

In my new state, these word-wrangles deflected something much simpler: I wanted to follow the clues to an unknown world. I was being offered the possibility to find out what the hell Austin Hart was doing in my mother's empty kingdom, and why I still remembered him from an uneventful ride to Abbotsford with my mother so long ago. Thinking of Richard, I sickened a little. I had falsely allowed him to treat me as if I were slightly ill and he, my only remedy. There was also the most recent, disturbing vision.

A month before I quit my job, I'd been at a poetry reading where I was to present with a number of other writers. I watched the audience filing in, finding their places. As they did, the color bled from peoples' faces, their clothes, from the paintings on the walls. The spectrum shifted to sepia tones that held gold, then to grays that held soot. I watched it go. I was left in a room of Van Gogh's Potato Eaters gathered around a dull light at their smoldering, vengeful meal, food enough for them to survive but not enough to flourish.

They didn't know how ugly they'd become.

Dutifully, as if they were my relations, I read to people marked by death.

It wasn't my failing relationship with Richard, but this disquieting projection of my inner state in a cafe at the end of the road, that made me realize I'd lost track of myself again. Nothing was wrong; nothing was ever wrong until the entire world went to ash.

When the distressed phone call came from Sophia, I was only a location—drifting; all the lights were out.

I should have told Richard these things, but he was on one side of my brain and all of this was on the other. On his side, when a canvasser came to the door I wrote large checks because I felt stingy.

I'd fallen in love with Richard once, but I couldn't quite remember why or how. I thought I'd look back at the love poems I'd written to him in the early days, but I neglected to do so.

I didn't want to dine with the potato eaters; I didn't want to dine alone.

For twenty-five years I'd managed to elude the pull into the space of nothing that had been a siren to my early life. Austin Hart had been the cap to that dark time; now he was back. The synchronicity was as rousing as the smell of fire.

THE RESIDENCE I FOUND for Sophia wasn't on the doctor's list because it was scheduled for destruction, so a place was available on short notice. It was an old mansion on Point Grey Road overlooking the water of Burrard Inlet. The driveway swung off the road in a satisfying curve up to the front of the house. A massive wrap-around veranda was supported by large, textured granite blocks. While the garden seemed run down, the house was fine. Part of the upstairs and main floor had been divided into small bedrooms for patients, but all the common rooms were the original, unstinting size.

Visiting my mother at what she called Styx Mansion required fortitude and hypocrisy, especially making it past Mrs. Askew, always stationed near the front door. She sat in her wheelchair with her head tilted to one side, looking at me as if through the mail-slot in a door. When I entered and when I left, she held out her blue-veined, darkly pigmented hand to touch me. If I made a wide berth around her, she'd perilously try to extend her reach. I learned to always stop and say hello, placing my hand on the thin hair of her skull.

"Take me home," she would say. "Please, take me home."

I BROUGHT MY MOTHER tulips from her garden, gathering them quickly and dutifully. As I went down the hall, her neighbor's door was open. Mrs. Griffin was sitting in a wheelchair, watching television with a doll on her lap. She called "go away, go away." I stepped into the room. "Are you okay, Mrs. Griffin?" She stared angrily at the television. "Get out of here." On the screen was a woman looking in through a glass door, somewhat menacing. Because the film was shot from inside the house it did look as though she were trying to enter.

"Mrs. Griffin, it's a movie."

"Tell her to go away. I'm going to have a baby, and all she does is knock and pound. Don't let her in. I have to have this baby."

I found one of the nurses.

MY MOTHER WASN'T in her room. I eventually located her on the front veranda, sitting by herself. I presented her with the bouquet.

"I love these tulips. The Prinses Irene are my favorite, but they must be over now. Would you bring me some Maywonder next time? Tomorrow. They're like a peony."

"What does a peony look like?"

With an equal mixture of derision and disbelief, she said, "Alix, surely to goodness you know what a peony is like."

But I didn't. Her garden had simply looked like a lot of work. "I'll find some. Where are they in the yard?"

"Yard? What a tepid word for my only solace. Haven't you been sitting out there in 'the yard'?" It was as though I'd called it a prison ground. Her voice strained with mounting accusations. "Unless, of course, you haven't watered them and they've died." The badgering mother of my youth had resurfaced. When I was eight she'd found a poem I'd written. She called it "a load of bosh." We were again primitive and unevolved.

I didn't rise to the challenge. "I'm not sure if I've seen them." My strategy was always to appease her and disappear.

"The Maywonder are near the front of the beds on the east side. I planted some Garden Party tulips last year. Did they come up?"

I was about to become ensnared again. "I'll describe the garden for you next time, all right? I'll bring you one of everything that's still in bloom."

I tried to divert her by mentioning the phone call with Brett Morris.

"Surely you can find a proper job. You don't know anything about music. You wouldn't even take piano lessons after you were seven. You simply refused."

I ignored her belittling remark. When I told her that the central character in the opera was Austin Hart, her predacious eyes, set a little to the sides of her head—like one who hunts and was hunted—narrowed and she squinted a little. "Really? How curious."

"Why?"

"He's been dead a long time." Her mood had shifted from sardonic to confused.

"You remember then, when we both heard—"

"Of course I remember, dear. April 8. The Feast of the Assumption—the celebration of the fact that there is a union between body and soul."

Her formal education had been interrupted by the war and her unwanted pregnancy with me, but she had taken night classes throughout her life and was well-read. Still the extent of her knowledge on many subjects always surprised me.

"Let me know how it goes with this work." She was being guileful.

"Of course I will. I'm here every other day, sometimes every day."

"I know you are." She was almost appreciative. "Funny how

this is all working out. I fall down, you come home, now this job offer." She cottoned on to my own sense of the strangeness of it. "You'll have to be careful, though, if you take this job."

"Why?"

"You can get caught in an undertow of waves that have broken against the shore a long time ago."

5

THE OVERTURE

Through the glass paneled front door of the house, I could see that Brett Morris was tall and his face was handsome, but I was a little startled by his appearance. As he aged I imagined he would come to resemble a woman. Some internal resolve—he was in his early thirties—barely kept him clear of seeming effeminate. The idea both attracted and repelled me. As I watched his jaw set with the waiting, and his head turn away, I wondered if others also saw him like this the first time. He ran his fingers through his thick, curly hair, impatient.

It seemed he would have preferred that I own the expensive real estate where I served him tea, because he looked a little disappointed when I told him it was my mother's house.

Light filtered through the petals of the daffodils I had picked from the garden. It was Good Friday and Brett Morris was telling me about Austin Hart.

"He was a great man, there's no doubt about that. By the time he died, so young, tragic, he'd left the legacy of a giant. Just think if he'd lived." He shook his head and with the small finger on his right hand raised delicately, drank his tea. As on the telephone, I again wondered if he were also considering his strategy with me. He continued in the same vein. "Not only had he published dozens of books, all important, he had a pile of real degrees and honorary degrees from around the world—invited to conferences, friends with the French anthropologist Claude Levi-Strauss—Levi-Strauss was a visitor in his home. You know who he is?"

"Yes. He was the renowned anthropologist who became so absorbed with northwest coast native people—long before it was fashionable. I tried to read *Triste Tropiques* at school, but I didn't understand a word of it."

I hadn't intended it but Brett seemed impressed. He admitted, in a quieter tone of voice, "I didn't know any of this stuff before. About structuralism—the search for the underlying patterns in everything—well Austin, in turns out, anticipated structuralism, Chomsky, all that. He was way ahead of his time, way ahead. But this guy wasn't just a towering intellect, he virtually discovered native art, as art—not the museum's pigeon-holing but, you know, he declared these artifacts important masterwork that could, I don't know—rival Picasso. What a debt we owe to him." I believed he was sincere but quoting someone else.

He leaned back against the couch, intense, self-assured and wanting congratulation. I would have obliged but I knew so little. My silence roused him to go on.

"He didn't just write and talk, like most intellectuals. He actually did something useful. In the 50s he went up to the Queen Charlotte Islands. Then the thing was to go into an area and take out the artifacts—they were all deteriorating. It was called salvage anthropology, or something. Thanks to him hundreds of thousands of visitors have been able to see—well you've been there, right?—the massive totem poles he saved, just in time. When he went, Ninstints hadn't been looted. He led the expedition that preserved the largest remaining stand of totem poles in the world—in the world. Totem poles that represented—I don't want to sound corny but they represented the divine—he rescued them. They put some at the Museum of Anthropology. Hart had his office there. That's where he ended his life. This is just the best theater: everyone praising him, wanting to be his friend, a hero just seven years after the expedition—then he shoots himself. This is the mystery we're working with. It's a great vehicle for my music."

I was a little taken aback at his ordering of the world, a little embarrassed. I changed the subject and asked if he understood why Hart killed himself.

"How would anyone know?" Almost for the first time, he seemed authentic. "Of course, there's the obvious guilt he must have felt about taking the poles."

"Yes, although none of that is very straightforward." He frowned, not seeming to understand me. "I mean the moral issues, they're complicated. But then I really don't know much about the Haida and their culture."

He'd done a lot of reading to prepare himself for this work. "The Haida go back thousands and thousands of years living in their territory—on the mainland and on these remote islands. It was a stratified matriarchal culture. Transformation was the key, right?—of wood into totems, of animals into gods. Of course they were decimated, by smallpox, residential schools, the usual stuff. We'll work with native dancers, musicians. It's eventually going to be a great collaboration."

He seemed to be a medley of opposites: naive and savvy; innocent and scheming; suspicious and disclosing; generous and acquisitive. I so wanted to be impressed by him. Yet, I had a feeling he was overly ambitious. My step-father was the first greedy man I'd ever known. It made him exceedingly unlikeable.

"Of course I know what a totem pole is, but do you know how they function within the Haida culture?"

Brett looked blankly at me.

"Is that a dumb question?"

He smiled and seemed almost pleased. "No, that's a good question. Great question. It's like one that Austin would ask, everyone else too full of themselves to make the real inquiry. You know what? I don't know. But I want you to find out."

What a strange man.

"You'll have to look out for diversions in this work. Mary-Anne, Austin's wife, is a diversion. Another place where we shouldn't get lost. They weren't living together when he died. My friend Trevor, Trevor Crane—he was working on the libretto, he got lost."

"I didn't realize there was a failed librettist in the works." I said it a little too crisply. Brett didn't seem bothered.

"We need to focus on what happened in those months before Austin killed himself. That's the deal."

The path that led to that day had grown over and the reasons for his suicide were obscure. Hart gave a controversial lecture at a conference in Vancouver three months before he took his life.

"His death shocked everyone. Just imagine this well-adjusted man in his prime and all that, doing himself in. Impossible. For instance, Claude Levi-Strauss sent Françoise Le Brun—young and beautiful—from France to study under Hart. She was on a field trip to one of the Gulf Islands on the day of his death. She woke up to the clacking of ravens. There were so many outside her house, making such a racket, she was almost afraid to open the door. Then she received the phone call about Austin."

Brett said someone else had a dream about a hawk getting its wings caught in her hair.

My habitual reserve dissolved—it didn't dissolve, it sizzled like water spritzed on a burner. This had been my dream when I was at the university.

He couldn't remember who had told him. "Everybody thinks Hart must have left a note, but if he did it's disappeared."

Because of my absorption with the hawk, I forgot to check myself. "I understand about not leaving a note."

Brett looked at me quizzically, then continued. "The daughter—her name is Paige—told me after his death she went back into the house, up to her father's bedroom, expecting to find a good-bye letter to the family, or even to his friend Tom Price—nothing. You must know of Tom? He's the great Haida carver who Françoise later married. He was on the expedition to Ninstints with Austin, but as a newscaster. He didn't even know, until later, that he was Haida, which wasn't so unusual because natives were trying to hide their ancestry then. He's fully in support of this opera, but he's quite ill now with Parkinson's. Hart's family, they're all behind it. You'll be able to speak to them."

"Are they okay with the idea of an opera?"

He looked at me askance. "Why wouldn't they be?"

"He died quite a while ago. It might be painful for them to revisit all of this, especially if they have to dig back into old memories—to help explain what happened."

"No, no, I don't think so. Not at all. They'll talk. In fact, Paige has been approached by a bunch of other people wanting to do biographies and things about her dad's life. But she's interested in a dramatic piece. An opera's perfect. So we're in. But I warn you, she's a little impatient. We can't lose any more time."

He now talked expansively about the staging. "When Austin's death comes in the opera, it'll have the emotional equivalent of the gouging out of Gloucester's eyes. In a heartbeat, we will convince the audience there's merit in being blind."

I couldn't really say—because I didn't know Brett at all—but such hubris made me wary. "I know he shot himself. What are the details?" I wanted to water-down my alarm.

"He was in his office at the museum where some of the poles were kept. He put the barrel of a rifle in his mouth and pulled the trigger."

I could almost feel the coldness of the metal.

Brett got up. Our meeting was abruptly over.

We stood at the door.

"How awful for the family," I said.

"Look, we'll want to pursue the notion that Hart believed he was the reincarnation of Edward Shawcroft. Austin was obsessed with him. He was the first Haida commercial carver. Collectors flocked to him in the 1800s. I'm pretty sure Hart thought he was Shawcroft. Hart sometimes lectured as if he were Shawcroft. Anyway, it would make great theater. Think about it. And about whether you want to work with me. You seem to like to listen. I mean that's great. Look, to be honest the other librettist, Trevor Crane—my friend—I told you he read your book that won the prize—and suggested I call you. He says your poetry is fantastic. I trust him. This is a poetic exploration of a very dark subject. Trevor says you're very internal but your poetry is on the money. You'll have to decide whether all this external stuff interests you. There's a film of the expedition you should see. I'll arrange it. For some reason this project didn't work out for Trevor. It's not easy, this story. And we've lost a lot of time."

"You mean because Trevor quit?"

"Uh huh." Brett gave me his business card, explaining that he lived on a small acreage on Vancouver Island, but he'd come to the city whenever we needed to meet. He also handed me a book titled, somewhat dryly, *Latent Structural Symbolism*, by Austin Hart. I flipped to the back. It was a library book, overdue by eighteen months.

"Oh, yeah." Brett was embarrassed, "I forgot to give it back. They seemed to have forgotten, too. I never get notices." He smiled. "The producer has cash. No experience, but lots of capital. He can raise whatever we want. I'll get him to call you. He's formed a society and is contacting the important people to lend their names to the work. Then we'll need a director, someone big."

He seemed to have offered me the job.

"I'm very glad you came," I said. "This is an important story for me." I had the clear, unmistakable and happy image of a newly washed shirt hanging on a line.

"Why?"

"I'm going to find out."

6

TWO FILMS

I stared at Hart's photograph at the back of the book of his essays Brett loaned me.

I made myself try to describe him—his pomaded, slicked-back hair. It was strangely difficult.

In running the publishing house, I functioned with high-octane, administrative efficiency that left me a little cold. I could spot a punctuation mistake in a page-proof across the desk, but being introduced to someone, I couldn't remember afterwards either their name or what they'd worn. Yet without being told, I might nail it that the person was an only child, raised by in-laws, still hated their father. The color of their hair wasn't so obvious. I seemed to have an ingrained distrust of information given to me by others, even if offered by their appearance. Unless I was running the ship, I didn't know how it worked... . Until I got home and slid into the arms of the abundant winged-back chair and closed my eyes—then I knew things. It made for a gap, a kind of loneliness difficult to describe.

I wasn't even quite sure what I looked like. When Richard moved in with me ten years earlier, he complained that in all the bathrooms there were paintings above the sinks, not mirrors.

Sometimes he'd buy clothes for me and put them in my side of the walk-in closet, as a test. When I came downstairs in the morning, ready to go to the office wearing one of the outfits, he'd say, "You look good, is that new?" And then I'd glance down at what I had on and say, "I'm not sure." He claimed never to have met anyone who lived so thoroughly an inner state of being. It was hard to be really breezy, being like that; caution was in order, for fear I'd do some crack-pot thing, like getting lost on the way home. I'd not notice and then I'd be on a street which didn't look quite right. "Some day: 'All the kings horses and all the kings men,'" Richard would say. He meant it as a sweetness, a tease. I worried that our love couldn't survive my myopia. In the end it didn't survived the tease.

Now I was being offered a place in the world, not to make it run more efficiently, but to make the death of this brilliant man exultant. To find my way, wide-eyed, across an inconsolable gap. If I took this job, I'd be required to notice things outside my vaporous self.

This was my difficulty in studying the photograph of Austin Hart. Immediately, I thought of him as a surgeon. It was his hands, the way his veined right hand rested on top of the long fingers of his left, as if it were a friend's hand and not his own. Some profound detachment was there which would enable him to scalpel out the truth... . But that wasn't good enough. I had to describe the surface of him, the commonplace projection of his features, not some off-base description of his psyche that would leave others, once they'd listened, a little confused, wondering what he looked like.

In the photograph: thirty-nine years old, a year after the Ninstints expedition, six years yet to go before he kills himself. His somewhat hooded eyelids drooped a little over his dark pupils which smoldered, not with fury but with intention. He could have been a hawk. His hawk-like face was nonetheless sympathetic, likable, because whatever he was thinking was interesting; his ordinary kindness cut against his simmering thoughts, so that if you interrupted him, he would be sure to acknowledge you, apologize, come back willingly, be available. His face was round, like my own. Had he grown into old age, he'd probably always have looked younger than he really was. He had put a stop to all of that. He had blown his face off with a shotgun.

WHEN THE DIRECTOR searched through the museum's holdings, he discovered there were two versions of *Salvaged Shadows*, the black and white film of the expedition made more than 30 years earlier. One film was the silent out-takes, still in 16 mm format. The other was the official, edited copy, which had been transferred to video with the voice-over of Tom Price, the now famous, palsied Haida carver. The director offered to show me the video. I asked if I could see the out-takes.

I went down to the basement of the museum into a room marked "Ossuary." The projectionist set up the film. Along the floor, leaning against the walls, were clear plastic bags. I looked closer and saw that the bags were filled with bones.

The lights were turned out. The silent film wheezed, black letters flickered on the screen, then the numbers 5-4-3-2-1.

An occupied native village with a fishing boat wrecked on the beach, the intact hull resting on its side as though some personal catastrophe had occurred and no one had recovered from it. A child, perhaps seven years old, climbed on the driftwood surrounding the marooned boat. Then to a small house with a diminutive native woman on the porch, her thick grey hair pulled back into a braid. She wore a dark dress with a flowered pattern and was sitting at a table which came almost to her shoulders. Her right hand rested on a cane. With the other hand she turned the pages of a book that had photographs of totem poles. She looked up, seeking some clue as to what she should be doing or saying. Her thick glasses reflected the sunlight and made her seem purblind. A small girl behind her in the doorway, hand in her mouth, looked at the camera, anxious, her face in shadow.

This wasn't Ninstints because that island had been uninhabited for over a hundred years. This must have been one of the small reserves at Massett or Queen Charlotte City that the Canadian government had set aside for them out of the natives' vast traditional territory.

The film shifted to a lowering sky over a turgid sea. Six men, crammed into a row-boat, approached an island. Because of all the rocks and the beached logs there seemed to be no place to land. Then a shot of twenty, perhaps thirty, totems crowded together on the shoreline, leaning this way and that—so many of them—facing the ocean and the arriving boat.

Anthony Island, as marked on western maps, or Ninstints, the name the Haida had for it. Over a hundred kilometers out into the ocean from the mainland, on its own.

Two of the men struggled with a box, carrying it to higher ground.

I called out to the projectionist in the dark behind me. "Excuse me, do you know—is that a munitions box? I wonder why they'd need ammunition."

"Don't know. Never seen this film before," he said.

"Bears? Or maybe it's just a storage box. An old hope chest. Probably. Thanks."

Another rowboat filled with lumber, containers of food. They started to erect army tents. Three anthropologists, two Haida, a carpenter. There was a close-up of Austin Hart.

"Could you stop the film there? I'd like to get a better look at them."

He couldn't hear me over the sound of the projector, and I raised my voice. "Could you go back, so I can see these men? Can you stop the film?"

He rewound it, and the crew undid the tents, packed up the boat, rowed backward into the horizon. Then started forward again.

"There, stop."

The film flickered and the faces bounced and blurred.

Austin Hart was clean-shaven with short hair, wearing a white jacket over a dark button-down shirt. He had on light dress pants, leather shoes with laces, city shoes. He looked like a member of a wedding party. His clothes were so obviously inappropriate to the place it could have been a protest, but I couldn't imagine why.

"Thanks, fine, go ahead."

The camera panned across the poles reflected in the water. A deer ran between them and then into the forest.

There was a shot of boot prints in the sand.

Austin Hart walked towards the totems, his head bowed.

Something glinted at the top of the poles. I'd read that the Haida buried their dead in boxes and placed them at the top of... These were mortuary poles, 50 feet high, and they held grave boxes in the cavities at the top. This was going to be a desecration.

The men waded through the long grasses. Every now and then Hart would run his hand over the lower portion of a pole, touching the ovoid shape of an eye or the long, bared teeth of a killer whale. He was scouting for the best totems to take.

More poles rising from a bed of thick salal bushes—and always those same huge, impassive eyes on the animals, as wide as planets. The long beaks of a raven or hawk, sharp teeth on a crooked mouth, and wings enfolding human figures. The pole of a weeping woman had long streams of wooden tears, with people born at the ends of them. The camera followed the line of the weeping woman to her hand which held a bush; a tree had grown in her lap, another tree was growing out of her head. The frog totem had a crown of evergreens, a forest in its mouth. Above her was the figure of the Watchman.

They came to the remains of a building. The roof and sides had rotted and fallen in, claimed by moss, but the smooth corner posts and structural beams stood. Weathered to the appearance of granite, tall and straight, was the frontal pole, the opening to the house. The fantastic totemic animals mounted one on top of the other, towered above the apex of the roof beam. At its base, human legs protruded from the mouth of a grizzly bear which was the entrance.

Austin stood beside it, diminished. Then he reached into the mouth of the bear.

Was he testing the strength of the wood in order to decide whether to salvage it? What was left of the structure surely stood because this pole had turned to stone against the elements. If he removed the pole, the house would fall.

He pointed. They were going to take this one.

One of the Haida embraced the pole with a rope and flung it out to be anchored to a nearby tree. The other Haida, armed with a chainsaw, cut through the base. Chips of wood showered from the saw as the men used all their strength pulling against the weight of the pole. Slowly it descended until it came to rest on the ground.

The men smiled, were pleased, chuffed one another on the shoulders and chucked one another on the chin.

It started to rain. The rain became a thunderstorm. Everyone escaped to their tents, looking despondently at the lakes growing around them. The poles became streaked with black and receded farther into the trees.

Water ran down the long teeth and tongue of a mortuary pole, down the face of the Watchman. The weeping woman and her children wept.

The men waited inside their tents. Their tents flooded.

It was apparent they couldn't hold off any longer. In the downpour a Haida used the branches of a tree, as easily as if it were a ladder, to climb beside the weeping woman and then cross over to the pole itself. He rested, spread-eagled against her vast eyes. On the ground the carpenter tried to start the chainsaw, pulling the chord to no avail and finally dropping the machine in frustration. They picked up axes, each one, even Austin Hart, and they started in, hacking at the base. They used hand-saws to gnaw through the pole, two, sometimes three people on a saw, pushing and pulling the blade. The wide-bellied eyes of the totem, alarmed.

The carpenter had lassoed the pole and men were holding the ropes guy-wired around her. Finally they had cut away enough of the foundation so that it leaned. It started to sway. Hart was pulling on one of the ropes; he yelled something, called for help, as the pole shifted and swung—from behind the careening pole one of the Haida ran to Hart's side, grabbing at the line, but was no good. The massive pole broke loose and fell flat on its face.

As if a body had been exploded by a grenade, everyone ran away from this catastrophe.

One of the Haida was angry. He wheeled around, punched his fists against his legs and walked away. They were all upset.

This silent film was a loud and blaring nightmare.

Austin went over to the pole, knelt and touched it. He pointed to a cedar tree. The men limbed some branches and set the boughs down on the ground, making a bed where the length of the next pole would fall.

Suddenly the rain stopped. The sun came out.

The sun was on the hunt; it strafed through the trees. It found Austin Hart—

In that brilliant daylight Hart walked, purposeful, trying to glean something from the search that propelled him, testing a pole for rot, putting his hand deep inside it, tilting his head back, listening like a doctor.

More poles were felled the same way, hacked with axes. One after another they came down. A mortuary box snapped off and flung into the air. Bones flew out.

NOW THE CAMERA FOUND Hart sitting on a rock at a point of land away from the felled poles. He had his head in his hands. The carpenter went to him. They spoke. Hart pointed. A man brought down an axe on the remaining pole. They took it.

The poles were sawn into 12 foot sections, the bear separated from the killer whale, the raven from the beaver. They hammered crates together for the dismembered totems. It looked like a hapless task. The Haida checked the lashings on the crates.

With strenuous effort the men pulled the cages along the shore where they were lined up, waiting for the tide. On the slats of wood, in large letters—the alphabet looked foreign and domineering—was marked "BC Provincial Museum."

Hart stood on the beach, his face unshaven, haggard and older than at in the beginning of the film. His leather shoes were muddy and ruined.

A tugboat pulled the long arc of caged poles linked together through the water, making the shape a fishing net does. Hart, in a small rowboat, followed behind. He kept looking back at the island. In the sky above the foreshore, now emptied of totems, was an unkindness of ravens. A freighter waited out at sea.

The final shot was from the boat after it arrived in Victoria. One of the slatted wooden crates held aloft by a hook attached to a crane, dangled perilously over the ocean. The crew was trying to stabilize its awkward swing. The crate wasn't secured properly, and it was lowered back into the ocean. It bobbed and banged against similar containers half-submerged in the water. The camera zoomed down between the slats and onto the wooden head of what seemed to be a man in repose—the Watchman from the weeping woman pole—his capacious eyes unlidded, filling his forehead and half his face, quiescent, abiding.

It was incongruous. These towering statues meant to part the air had been sawn into pieces and were floating in the water. After such dwarfing, no real victory celebration could follow.

I thanked the projectionist and left the museum. I felt glum and shell-shocked; I had witnessed a massacre.

I WENT TO MY MOTHER'S house. Closing the drapes in the library, I watched the second film on the plasma screen, the edited sound video meant for public viewing. In a sonorous voice, serious and monumental, Tom Price narrated the valorous salvation of the poles from their certain demise. The high-spirited purpose of the expedition was lauded. It was a commercial.

This film didn't show the confused old woman on the porch, the taking of the frontal pole—the only remaining support for the house—or the disastrous felling of the weeping woman. It didn't show bones flying through the air from the mortuary box or a distraught Austin Hart, sitting alone, and then giving directions for the removal of the final totem. Nor did it show the disquieting image of the caged, wooden coffins jostling in the water of Victoria harbor.

I called Brett to say I'd take the job. He assumed I already had.

7

THINGS THAT DISINTEGRATE

I've had a disagreement with Bernadette Verspoor, the librarian at the museum archives. My visit had been approved by the director, and I had called ahead for the appointment, telling Mrs. Verspoor I would like to see the Hart material.

When I arrived, the largest table in the center of the library had six cardboard boxes on it. Three more were stacked beside her desk, all with "HART" written on the side in the same large, neat black letters.

I thanked Mrs. Verspoor for getting things prepared, but she continued to stand between me and the boxes. She was much taller than I, and very thin: a thin woman uncomfortable in her body, wearing a black sweater, too large for her, a skirt and black stockings. Her grey hair was pulled back tight against her head. The aggressiveness of her stance, so close to me, was embarrassing. We seemed to be mixed up with one another in an awkward way and for inexplicable reasons.

Almost as a diversion, she lifted the lid on one of the boxes. Folders were marked "Spirit Dancing"; "Black Notebooks"; "Pole Acquisition." She touched the files, which made her thoughtful, as if helping her untangle the twisting of an old, unresolved problem.

"You understand you can't just look through this material. You have to have some legitimate purpose. We don't encourage people to roam through the files."

"As I explained on the telephone, I do have a purpose—"

She interrupted me. "They are very fragile. Every time they are touched they deteriorate to some small degree. When Dr. Hart wrote all this, he didn't think it would be looked at, not in this way, by a stranger. I am, therefore, reluctant... ." Her voice trailed off.

She was pale; she looked worn out. I wondered if there was some pre-existing bureaucratic snare that had settled on this material, stirred up again by my request.

I controlled my annoyance. "As I said, the research is for an opera about Hart, centering on his relationship to the natives—the significance of his work."

"He didn't think these notebooks would be looked at," she repeated.

"I'd always understood that anthropologists' notes were records, to be read by others—"

"Looked at, but not for an opera. Kept here, protected. Only opened if it is for research, for a proper purpose. Not for art. For science, not curiosity."

I ignored her slur. "You've read the files?"

She looked away; she looked around imperiously, confirming her dominion. The room was small, windowless, airless. It could well have been that she's never read Hart's notes and papers. It wasn't the actual contents she was protecting, but the man.

"I knew Mr. Hart. He was a gentleman. I've catalogued the material leaving it the way he had it organized," she said enigmatically.

"Could you help me then, given that the director has granted me access to the materials—"

"He's only the acting director. He's never seen what's here. I have a complete history of who has had access to the files. I control who goes in there." She pointed to the boxes.

"Hasn't this material been reviewed by other anthropologists or historians?" I ventured. "Given his reputation, his original field-work—"

"The material is very fragile." We were circling back around the subject. She took one of the journals from the box marked "Black Notebooks" and opened it at random. "This was when he was up in Masset and the Queen Charlottes—in Haida Gwaii. That's what they call it now, but not then." She was scornful.

I read the beginning of a sentence: "The lost glory was made visible in their art... ."

"These pages are over thirty years old. The lawyer for the museum told me that legally they are considered to be ancient documents. They have a unique status. Actually, I think the public should not be allowed access any more. It won't be long before they will have to be kept in a special place, with temperature controls. Otherwise they'll disintegrate, just by our touching them." She turned the page.

The parallel between the fate of the poles and Hart's journals was not lost on me, but didn't seem apparent to this taciturn gate-keeper. I stood a little behind her, trying to read quickly, fearful this would be my only glimpse. "...H.S. drinks too much...White people are inconsistent and that disturbs him... ."

Perhaps realizing it was odd for her to be lecturing me that the pages should not be touched, while she was fingering them, she stopped. "Well, you're lucky. You might be the last person to see these in the original." She moved back. "Go ahead, they're yours. More over there." She pointed to the boxes in her office.

Her crusty attitude dissolved with a kind of flourish of defeat. I had the feeling she was lonely.

She left me.

I didn't know what to expect from the files. I had read most of Hart's work published before and after his death, but other than seeing the films and talking to Brett, all I knew about this trip was that Hart was then the curator of the museum and he had gone to explore the islands to decide whether or not there were totem poles worth saving.

The two films of the expedition had left me with a discomforting attitude towards Hart. I so wanted to admire him, and really had to admire him in order to do this work.

At the time of this trip he was 37. Married, with two children, a rising star. Out to salvage the totem poles of a dead or dying civilization.

His journals had black covers, lined pages, probably bought in a drugstore along with the pencil he was using. The very ordinariness of the books brought him closer. I started with the journal Bernadette Verspoor had picked up, marked "Massett, Ninstints." I had never read anyone's journals except Virginia Woolf's.

I turned to the first page, the inscrutable, erasable letters, tiny, enduring, written in his own hand.

June 10

I arrived in Masset about 2:30 and took a walk through the reserve. The government moved the Haida from more remote locations to put them closer to the Indian agent and the church. The houses built by Indian Affairs are made of clapboard. Sometimes three or four families live in the space meant for a western married couple. It is difficult to fathom how a stable family life can be managed in these circumstances.

Tonight I had beer in the hotel with some of the native men. Until now I have known these people only from the works of other ethnographers—Boas, Barbeau—who were fortunate indeed to be amongst these people at a time when their society was still intact. At present it is, more or less, in ruins.

The lost glory of this society was made visible in the totem poles carved with such incalculable mastery as to reveal both the inner and the outer life of the spirit. I will travel back through time and contact the ancestors through the art they created. I will salvage the poles before they give way to the putrefaction of time.

Their art rivals the finest in the world which, for the small price of admission, we can view in galleries in London and Paris. I want to make this be so for the natives' work, to shock mankind into the realization that always, amongst these savages, these hunters—their art.

I'm told there used to be the continual sound of singing on these islands and now silence.

I was sitting ramrod straight, my hands tense and tight, as though clutching onto a rock outcropping.

In my upbringing in Vancouver, the native Indians were kept out of sight—or chose to hide—assembling at the rough blood and urine hotels along Hastings Street. I knew nothing about them: where they were from, what they cared about, and especially what had happened to them that they should be in this forlorn state. The child in the first film I'd seen, climbing on the driftwood surrounding the shipwrecked boat, was the remote equivalent of their urban disaster.

The image of Hart sitting on a rock at the point of land away from the felled poles, holding his head in his hands and then giving the direction for the removal of the final pole—that picture was side-saddle with my current perception of this gentle, brilliant man. I would try not judge him.

Hart wrote that at the time of first contact there were fifty Haida villages and a population of over 30,000. In 1915, as a result of traders giving blankets to the natives which were infected with smallpox, and because of other diseases, they numbered 588. *Those remaining engorged with grief.*

I tried to absorb the enormity of the deaths for the Haida. Nobody had died on me in a long time: only my step-father, ten years earlier. I'd never even visited his grave; I didn't remember where it was. To experience, in a generation, most of your family, your friends, dead—how could anyone get up in the morning, or even stand? They showed courage even to be drunk on skid-row.

> *I have been staying in a room above the bar in the only hotel in town. It is dismal indeed, and the sound of the juke box comes through the grimy floorboards until all hours of the night. Living here gives me access to the men of the tribe who spend a great deal of time in the bar. I am out walking a lot...*

Gradually, I relaxed into the sound of his voice recreated in my mind, as clear and immediate as if he's been here only a few minutes ago. Then he got up from the table, and I sat in his place while he was away.

> *The thick fog every morning is almost like rain. Voices come across the water from the natives' boats which are invisible to me. When the fog burns off, children play all day in the water or at its edge, and their laughter mixes with the sound of crows and gulls beachcleaning in the sun. How cool it is in the evening. The music from a clarinet drifts out of an old house as the light fades and a girl walks by, singing.*
>
> *My position here is still as a foreigner, especially for the women. How I miss the company of women.*

It was manly of him to acknowledge his attraction to women. I had never heard such a statement: the unvarnished, inopportunistic longing for the company of women. I half thought Richard was afraid if he showed he loved me, his power would leak out somewhere.

The Chief gave Austin permission to move into a house on the reserve while the family was away fishing. He was making inquiries about native masks and had learned that many generations earlier there was a mask which was *"danced in the winter ceremonies."* Although that was the phrase he used, I gathered that a native dancer wore the mask and so it was danced by him. It was made of stone; it could "see." *With these people the wondrous was part of the everyday. Austin hoped to locate the mask.*

Excitement was enhancing my task. No one had known the

particulars of Hart's search—perhaps only Verspoor. I was thrilled at the very look of the words he wrote on the 5" x 8" pages. I felt the privilege of my position. In my family even the most straight-forward things resulted in a mix-up; now Austin Hart's very thoughts were available to me. I relaxed my anxious grip on the world.

H. and I spoke into the night. He said 'We are ashamed of our traditional ways. We have tried to blot out the past life entirely.' Although H didn't know how the stone mask could open and close its eyes, he is the only one left of his tribe who knows the secrets of how some of the ritual performances were actually done—where a topsy-turvy world is created: performers die and then are brought back to life. The cheating of death is worked out in theater and the miraculous. When order is re-established, underneath the formality of the roles, is the mask of the authentic self.

To find the words precise enough to bring Hart alive in the libretto—that tough grappling with the language that I so loved, searching for a word that might be just right, hoping it would be the abracadabra for his life. To push language to its edge and then have Brett's music come under the words and lift them on an unerring vector. I could not believe such good fortune had come out of the ashen vision of the potato eaters. To use art to resurrect a dead man. For the first time, in a very long time, I felt the simplicity of happiness.

The Haida were divided into two basic groups which were "separate but equal", the Raven and the Eagle clans. Potlatches were given to re-tell the stories of the past and to celebrated things in the present (and thereby create new stories). For example when a daughter reached puberty, or because a chief of the Raven clan had fallen out of his canoe and was saved by a low-status man from the Eagle clan. How attractive this strange world was to Austin, and to me.

Haida society had functioned on the self-evident principle that women are the creative center. All property was passed on through the mother. This, I fear, has been obliterated to such damaging effect by the Indian Department. The government anoints only the men as Chiefs. Ironically, emasculation is the result.

The library was empty, and then one or two people came in the room, carrying books, speaking in hushed voices. Bernadette Verspoor had her office door open. I decided to ask her if I could photocopy some of the diary.

Without looking up from her writing—in a very large book she was putting lists of things in columns—she said, "You've got to be kidding."

I was dismissed.

I would write out his notebooks in longhand.

Spoke to T.M. who had been told by the elders of the first contact between the Haida and the white man. This would have been in 1774 with the arrival of the Spanish who reached the west coast before other European nations. Of course T.M. couldn't give me a date for this as the natives do not construct events within a time frame easily understood by me.

The oral history is that one summer afternoon a huge structure appeared on the ocean's horizon. The people gathered on the beach. They didn't know what this apparition was, whether dangerous or friendly, material or spectral. They sang songs, asking the power to make it go away. It didn't. Some courageous ones went out in their canoes to face it. They sang as they approached it, and opened their arms to welcome it, spreading feathers on the water. It was a huge sailing vessel. They got aboard and called back to the others on the shore: 'These are people, real people; they have features much like ours. They are like us.'

What a staggering response to the unknown—to what was an invasion of their territory by a foreign element. They welcomed it.

They knew this land like the sight of a friend's back which they were following. Everything they did mattered, had real consequences, revealed itself through tangible cause and effect. They had to stay alert. They lived in an environment which required all their attention. Not that they were afraid, because fear diminishes with self-knowledge. They knew the land as their friend, and knew what he required and could provide—they gleaned the future by sensing a minute shift of wind, the changes in the tides...

Brett said Hart believed he had been reincarnated as Shawcroft. I found Austin's first mention of him.

When the missionaries and traders came to Haida Gwaii (in the 1870s) they wanted pipes, walking sticks and other artifacts. From the coal-like argillite Shawcroft made "pipes that won't smoke from coal that won't burn." He was adaptive; he made these useless things for the brash newcomers. His masterworks ended up in the great cities of the world. But one strategy followed hard upon another. He died in unfortunate circumstances, by his own hand. Having a double purpose is a tricky kind of business...

The people watch me all the time. I, too, have dual purposes, but I must gain their trust.

In the past anthropologists gave descriptions of the indigenous peoples' society as if it were the whole thing. Because they were mostly men, with their informants being mostly men, it was only half the world. Even as an outsider, I must find a way to support the reinstatement of the enduring place and power of the women in their world, which the outsiders have eroded.

To sum up my life here: physically, I am in a kind of paralysis; socially, I am in exile; spiritually, it is a feast.

Bernadette Verspoor was standing beside me. Even when I noticed her it was more as a stillness, or even an emptiness.

I put my arm over my notebook.

"I'm closing the library now. You missed lunch."

"May I come back in the morning?"

"The library isn't open tomorrow. You'll have to check again with the acting director." Before she turned to go, as though she'd been brooding on it all day long, she said, "Anyway, what business do you have trying to make Mr. Hart's life into an opera?"

I was sufficiently emboldened by what I had read to say, "The cheating of death can still be worked out in the theater."

"You're quoting him now, are you? Quoting him against me is not going to help."

My approach had backfired. Remaining as pleasant as I could, I left the building.

8

HOW MANY TULIPS ARE IN BLOOM?

I had been neglecting Sophia. She'd moved into the nursing home located on Point Grey Road, which she called "No Point-Gray Point-Gray," a sort of hyphenated name, in addition to its first moniker, Styx Mansion, indicating a slight improvement in her sense of well-being. Her hip was healing; physical therapy was helping. The fear surrounding the change in her life had abated and she was now, for the most part, bored. I wasn't visiting her enough.

While she seemed to be cordial to the other residents, she said she couldn't find anyone to be her friend except the woman in the next room, the thoroughly disordered Mrs. Griffin of whom Sophia said, "She doesn't know me from a bale of hay." Although her ravings alarmed my mother, she somehow took comfort in them the way an insecure, upper middle-class woman is culpably appeased by the sight of another woman pushing a shopping cart full of bottles through the street, as though the presence of this future self would forestall her own decline.

Her affection for Mrs. Griffin—she always called her Mrs. Griffin instead of Abigail (she said Mrs. Griffin's mother should not have named her daughter Abigail and she wasn't going to abet that wrong-doing) was real. When her relatives visited they were wrenched with the anxiety that Mrs. Griffin would increasingly fall below the lucidity grade and have to be moved to a tougher, more institutional place, a move that would make her even more deranged. My mother calmed them and ran interference with the nurses, always saying that Mrs. Griffin was actually much better today than yesterday.

Sophia's eyesight was declining. On one of my visits, she announced she knew full well one day she might be blind. Dr. Hall had informed her.

"I'm sorry, I just couldn't tell you earlier, when it wasn't certain. Are you all right?"

"I asked you a long time ago to describe my garden? I'd like you to tell me how many tulips are in bloom. After which, I'd like you to tell me about your work on this opera. I worry."

"I'm sorry, mother, I forgot."

"Forgot what?"

"I forgot to go out there and check your garden. I've been pretty busy with—"

"But you sit in the back, beside the pond, don't you, I mean the evenings are so beautiful, why don't you just take a peek at it?"

"Fine, mother."

"I mean it, just notice it and come and tell me."

"I said fine."

"No need to be angry. You'd better phone the gardener to come over."

"Fine."

"Not 'fine', just do it. He's Mr. Strange—his real name—he likes being called mister. His number is—"

"In the Rolodex®."

"Yes. The Rolodex. Under 'Strange.'"

I did spend most evenings writing at the glass and wrought iron table on the patio. Not knowing the names of the plants, they blended together. One night at dusk, determined to really look at the garden, I went out with a pen and paper, intent on writing down what I saw. I was quickly overwhelmed by the variety and detail. I was accustomed to learning from books.

"Now how's the project? If you're going to be a chronicler of this new family, you have to be able to faithfully describe them. Who knows, maybe this is your real work."

"'Real work'?" Coming from Sophia, such a sentiment was unheard of. I understood that illness could focus one's life as never before, and I wondered if her comment were projection rather than insight.

"I'm just trying to help you. Also, you need a haircut. Go see Daniel at Tech One."

I raked my hands through the hair at the back of my head, checking its length.

"The project?" she repeated.

Happy to change the subject away from my sense of dowdiness, I told Sophia about the research I'd been doing.

"Mr. Hart had a family, a wife and children, have you encountered them yet?" she asked.

"His son and daughter—and sister—are still alive. The daughter, Paige, lives on Vancouver Island. I finally reached her this morning. She was about to take a group of children on a hike to look at some cedars—she acts as some kind of guide. She'll meet with Brett and me next week."

"Was she pleasant, is she willing to tell you about her father?"

"Apparently she's keen on helping—the whole family is."

"And what do they do?"

"Paige writes poetry."

"How many poets does this story need?"

"Two, apparently. Her brother is in metallurgy—" I stopped. "You always ask what people 'do.'"

"Of course. And the wife?"

"She died a year after Austin."

"How really tragic." So singular was her expression of unadorned sympathy that it drew me back to when we first heard of Austin Hart's death, driving in the car.

"They were separated but were still married. Hart always wore his wedding ring."

"An estranged couple who never divorce?" She had recovered her scrupulous, suspicious self. "You're walking into a packed graveyard, you know. Are you sure you want to do this, write about a dead man? You have to be sure."

She was pushing me into a pleached hedgerow, but I was practiced at protecting my face and eyes.

"I want to find out why this renowned anthropologist, who was privileged to be taken to native ceremonies most of us don't even know exist—who was at the top of his game, loved by everyone—why he killed himself."

"Sure, I'd like to know that." Almost as an aside, she ventured, "I suppose you'll manage. You've always coped with what you've been given. Ever since you were little. It's not that you thought the world was against you, it's that you thought it didn't take account of you one way or the other."

This toss-off left me gaping. She was saying such surprising things, but in a detached tone, as if I weren't present. I felt hopeful and dispirited at once. I wanted to ask, "Why are you telling me things about myself now, as though I were a new found thing you've suddenly remembered?" I was determined not to. She wore her candor like a shield of thorns.

Then she lowered her head and said, almost in a whisper, "Get me out of here, will you? Take me home. Ask them for an overnight pass. I'll even cook for you."

As a little girl I was always left twisting in the coolness of her disregard. Now I was rocked by her desperation for me to give her something only I could give.

I told her I'd take her home after I came back from Alberta where I was going to meet Claire Tomlin, a friend of Austin Hart's.

As I was leaving Sophia said, "Why do you look so exhausted?" It was a moral weakness to show fatigue.

I'd been working late into the night, reading anthropology, listening to opera, studying librettos, both classic and modern. I had to teach myself to fly without a pilot's license or really without a plane. Early that morning Brett had called, waking me up. He said that Trevor Crane had worked for six months on the opera and didn't produce anything: no draft outline of the plot, no lines for the libretto. But he'd interviewed everyone. He was living in Prince George now; he'd take my call.

In response to mother's question, I simply told her that the composer had phoned at 6 a.m.

"Why so early? What's on his mind?"

"It was mainly to say that I should contact the previous librettist."

"There was someone before you?"

"Someone who didn't work out."

"Careful, dear. Things he hasn't told you are worrying him."

"Maybe he's just been testing me to see what I could find out from the family on my own."

"Comrades don't test one another, do they?" She then re-established her usual sense of self. "Do I look tired? I've been dreaming a lot lately, usually in color. But there are never any animals in my dreams."

It was one of Sophia's hair-brained, intuitive statements, so crazily on the mark. She could have been referring to an island clear-cut of the totems, which continued to haunt me.

She added, "You'll have to tell me what you think of Austin. But not now."

I wondered if I wanted to share him with her. Maybe that's what Mrs. Verspoor felt as well.

9

ONE IS SIGHTED

Claire Tomlin lived in a small cabin at the foothills of the Rockies where she had lived alone for many years. Although she was still writing books and lecturing, she was not in touch with any of Austin's friends. She was now 71 years old, and her good health seemed to go beyond the physical. She moved the way a child does, slightly darting and erratic. Her enthusiasm was so pronounced I felt a little protective of her.

Before my rental car had even stopped kicking up a turmoil of dust in her long driveway, she was walking towards me. I rolled down my window.

"Look what I found." She opened her fisted hand which held the treasure. "A projectile point—an arrowhead. Right out back where I was weeding. It's a humdinger." Her petite frame seemed almost too small for the cowboy slang. "Come in, come in."

As I followed her to the cabin, she continued talking about her first excavation at the Katzy dig, near Vancouver, as though we were already friends. When she opened the door she stopped, turned on the top step, and said, "I do hope you're Alicia Purcell," then paused, laughed and shook my hand. "It's just that I haven't had anyone to show, or tell, all day long."

She led me into an outmoded but orderly kitchen, dishes neatly arranged on a drying rack and the dark, wooden cupboard doors closed. It smelled like a spice-box, with the enticing scent of rosemary dominating. The room overlooked a massive garden that filled the sight lines. Unlike Sophia's garden, I was relatively certain I could name the things in it because they were all vegetables.

Claire took the kettle to the sink, talking. "My first projectile point was when I was 26. So beautifully fluted. I was in touch with the man who'd made it twenty centuries earlier. He went out hunting, got a deer, used the hide, fed his children. All of that was in the palm of my hand." She unfurled her fingers again to expose the arrowhead of today, as if it were the same one she'd found decades earlier. "The object was no longer catalogue number 1338, sitting on a shelf in the archeology department." She straightened her shoulders, as if her back were strained or her thoughts required her to be more erect. "After that, artifacts came to life. Shells form a midden. People ate fish which gave them sustenance, gave the women strength to go out and pull the cedar bark for clothes." She turned to me. "If you hold these things, a fish hook, a basket, you'll understand them. You're interested in the technology of the people, what they needed in order to live. But it's not just that these are tools to get food. It's the way they've shaped these instruments. The curve of the bow is a harp."

I sensed that her consideration of any question I might ask—and I hadn't had to ask any yet—would be a portal to another world. But the making of tea wasn't being advanced. She was still holding the kettle.

"I can make the tea," I offered. I could assume this mundane task while she continued to bring the past into our midst.

"Oh, yes. Tea up there, cups in the next one. Whatever you'd like."

Although her competence at any worldly or other-worldly task was not at issue, I wanted to shield her from something—I imagined a cougar taking a child for its prey. It was so strange and bracing a thought I wondered if it were a projection of a submerged fear.

There was an unnerving array of herbal teas on three shelves, some beyond my reach. I took fresh mint leaves from a glass jar and steeped them.

"You have a little knowledge about something, and you want more. I guess it is a kind of acquisitiveness, but to want to possess knowledge, rather than things, is better, don't you think? How sophisticated these cultures, how integrated they were. Back then I would drive all over the country to give lectures, to tell others what I'd learned just because it excited me, and I wanted them to know. This was even before I met Austin." She turned her considerable intensity on me. "But you, you're the important one. What are you learning about my friend?"

"What am I learning?" I begged a little time because of the sudden shift. "One thing is that people who didn't even know Austin remain haunted by his death. An anthropologist called me this morning who'd never met him. He'd heard about the opera. When he reads Hart's work, he feels he's trying to communicate with him directly. He said, 'I'm not a man who would ordinarily think such things.'"

Claire's more practical nature surfaced. "Surely that's why people write, isn't it, to communicate? Even after they're gone."

"Is that all it means?"

"I think so."

We moved into the living room where an abundance of cedar baskets displayed over an entire wall. "You are a collector, then?"

"Only of baskets. Or things I find in my garden. I stop there. Or my bank account does." She was wry and undefensive.

Unlike the sometimes disconcerting wooden masks, the intricate majesty of these round and pliable shapes, made by the hands of women, was comforting. They were for carrying things.

I told her I'd been looking at Austin's unpublished journals in the archives from his first trip to Haida Gwaii. "Lots of things I don't understand, but especially his reference to functional tools the natives used which became dysfunctional." I wanted her to help me grasp the potency of the material world which had so absorbed them both.

"Not dysfunctional. I don't think that's what he thought happened to them. Let me think for a minute. I should make us lunch." But she remained seated.

The magnetic spin of her memory was working hard to get the idea right. "No, Austin would look at an object, like the hand-hammers used for driving wedges—he saw there was something in them that was on the move." She was speaking slowly and precisely, her voice directed to a location somewhere behind me. "Over generations the people reshaped the form of such a tool, again and again. Sometimes it evolved into a thing which stopped having any practical purpose. Yes, that's right." She picked up the pace. "Yes, it was that aesthetic shift, from the pleasing, functional thing to something that was stunning but not functional any more—that shift presented Austin with a real paradox. You've reminded me now."

"Was that also the paradox of his life? That he lost his sense of purpose?"

"Interesting. Really interesting. Maybe." She looked directly at me. "God I miss him. I miss having these talks with him. He used to say that this shift, having a useful tool be transformed into an object of beauty, only to be looked at, was so remarkable—as remarkable as a culture going from having round wheels to no wheels at all. He used to wonder if some things were meant to be kept just for their own sake, as objects emanating power. Power which could be received by its owner." She paused, as though hitting up against an old debate. "I'm not sure he was right about that." She seemed uncomfortable, struggling to change the subject, yet still enmeshed in it. "Collecting involves maintaining scholarly authority over artifacts, and that means staying on your side of the line. It's a tricky business."

It was then she mentioned the stone masks.

"Ever since we talked on the phone, I've been thinking mainly of these masks. For you to get this story right, this is the part you need. It's crucial to understanding Austin. There are two of them—twins—that were taken from the natives before the turn of the century. Taken—I don't know—purchased, acquired, received from them. Whatever the word is. One is sighted and one is blind. But they were separated in the late 1880s. It's an opaque story. We do know that one ended up with a priest who passed it along until it was acquired by the Museum of Civilization in Ottawa. The other was sold by a doctor living in Masset. It went to Paris." She spoke with a new urgency. "You see, the potlatch and dancing were outlawed by Canada. This was in the 1880s. The dancing—well, there were many native groups with all sorts of different practices that came under the category of 'dancing.' There was the ceremonial and the spirit dancing. With an ungloved fist, the government outlawed them all. The church—this is utterly shameful—the church obtained hundreds of ritual masks and regalia."

"Imagine a society where the true sign of wealth is to arrive at dispossession by way of generosity; where to be wealthy meant to give away your wealth. The family hosting a potlatch gifted absolutely everything they had. I've seen photographs of these great potlatches. Stacked outside a house before the celebration starts are 300 bags of flour, 400 bags of sugar, 900 blankets, sewing machines. The gifting went on for days. Stories were told; lineages were confirmed; family boundaries reinforced. The spiritual realm was right there in the thick of it, because, you see, the real source of riches was in songs, in the stories, dancers wearing the masks. This, passed down through the women, the foundation of their world. All of this: outlawed. People were sent to jail."

"What did the natives do—how did they respond?"

"Many went to abandoned villages to hold the feasts, so as not to be caught. There were tremendous protests, too. A Chief of the Kwagut'l, south of the Haida, told the anthropologist Franz Boas, 'We will dance when our laws command us to dance, and we will feast when our hearts desire to feast. It is a strict law that bids us dance. It is a strict law that bids us distribute our property among our friends and neighbors. And now, if you come to forbid us dance, be gone. If not, you will be welcome to us.'"

"You've memorized it."

"Yes, a riveting speech. 'Be gone; if not, you will be welcome.' Such breadth of spirit. It's all so ugly what happened. But the government didn't succeed. Of course, it's legal now. New gifts have replaced the old. Television sets instead of sewing machines. In a really big gathering, which takes the family years in the making, microwaves are given away, tables, chairs, beds."

I was overawed that Claire had seamlessly turned the next page from where I had left off reading Austin's journals at the library.

"When it was criminalized, half the ceremonial objects removed from this area in the north were taken by the missionaries, some of whom had a mail-order business selling them. Just think. They ended up in museums because of this sanctioned thievery. Divorced from their function in the feast, these extraordinary expressions of spiritual capacity, galactic in depth, became—curios. There are reports of whole boxes of masks being burned at midnight in Bella Coola, by the natives themselves, caught up in the frenzy of believing what the church told them, that the masks were from the devil. Then the priests, themselves, secreted a lot of them away, kept these objects meant for the fire. Well, it's beyond telling." Her anger changed into a calmer, somewhat ironic observation, "But, you see, the twin masks were stone. They wouldn't burn."

"So was this part of what came to obsess Austin? That the stone masks represented immortality and the everlasting?"

"We don't really know, but it could be," she said cautiously. "And I've diverted us." She sat down, righted herself, began again. "We did an exhibition together. Austin managed to reconnect the twins; for the first time in one hundred years, they were together. You've got this already, that the artifacts carved from stone held a special fascination for him."

She rolled her hands, as though unearthing the past. Her gestures shaped the physicality of her thought.

"In the early days of the late 1800s, ethnographers turned entire villages upside down to get artifacts. They would say to the natives 'bring me one of everything.' And they did. Austin and I weren't like that, but still we could have been criticized I suppose, for our thorough-going determination in collecting for the exhibition. Anyway, the Paris museum had always refused to let the sighted mask leave the country. Austin pleaded to be allowed to bring the two together for just a short time. To us—I hope you'll get this—they aren't really masks, in the sense of hiding and revealing. It was more like rejoining a shattered self. After all his effort finally the telegram from Paris was 'Agree for Vancouver but not for a roving exhibit entailing too many risks.' The insurance on the masks—it was unbelievable. They were worth millions. So Austin went to Paris to get the sighted mask. It was his first trip. He returned to Vancouver, came back from the airport, walked into a dark house, turned on the lights, and, oh boy, we were all there—all his friends and colleagues waiting there in his house. It was a great welcome. He was really quite a shy and humble man."

"How did you get in? Was Mary-Anne there?"

"No, I had a key." Almost dismissing my question, she then returned to it and explained further, "They'd been separated for a long time. I never met her. He lived in the family home, and she had an apartment. There were no photographs in his house, not of anyone, his friends or even of his family. I always thought it odd. Anyway, he was downright excited, coming back from Paris, finding us there. He talked about meeting Claude Levi-Strauss, about what he had seen, the Champs-Élysées, the Eiffel Tower—and we're all waiting—the box with the mask is sitting there on the table, and people are whispering 'why doesn't he show us the mask.' Finally someone said, 'Austin, the box.'

"So he put it in the middle of the floor, and he kneeled down. Out of his pocket he pulled this little screwdriver. He handed it to me and said, 'I'd like you to open it.' Austin's beaming face. All these important people. They were startled that he would choose me. So was I. You see, I was an outsider. No one knew about us. So it was his oblique way of disclosure, I guess. Anyway, I took the screwdriver, opened the box, removed the stuffing and I looked at this mask, the sighted one. Well—" she was freshly surprised—"all the books gave the overall dimensions of both masks as being the same—so we thought they were two separate masks, but right away I noticed that the features of this one were smaller and more refined than in the blind mask. I pulled it out. There were perforations through each ear, something that didn't show up in the photographs and were lacking in its blind twin. The two were going to fit together. We had champagne. And I thought, 'the blind mask covers the sighted one.' I knew this was part of the message of the art."

"Because the message is about spiritual insight?"

"Good for you." She seemed genuinely delighted that I had been following her. "So the unsighted mask, which we'd brought from Ottawa, was already in the vault in Victoria with all the other stone objects for the exhibition. Austin asked me to take the sighted Paris mask to Victoria. I didn't know where to store it that night so I hid it under my bed. I got up early in the morning, put it in the backseat of my car, and went to the gas station, the place I always go. The attendant had a funny idea about archeology. He thought I was looking for fossils. He asked, joking, 'what do you have in the box back there?' I said it was a Halloween mask. It wasn't even close to Halloween, but that's all I could think to say. I got on the ferry. I thought I mustn't dare leave this in my car when I go to the upper deck. But I did.

"I drove to the museum, went down to the vault, unpacked the two boxes and put the masks on the table. Finally rejoined. No one had ever seen them together, except the shaman. I carefully put a piece of tissue paper over the sighted mask, so as not to scratch it, lifted the blind one on top, and—they nested snugly together. Perfect. You understand?"

"I think so. This was why the ordinary people thought it was one mask."

"Yes, exactly, two masks in one. I went to the phone, walking as slowly as I could, and I called Austin. 'You must come over now.' He did. I let him make the discovery. Please don't make an issue of this; I don't want to take the credit. He deserved it. Still he was somewhat—I guess shaken is the only way I can describe it. An interesting reaction. It made me care for him even more. He was so obsessed about the meaning of the masks, and now I guess his intuition was confirmed. That's what he said, 'It's oddly destabilizing when you find you're correct about something and not perpetrating a fraud.' He talked in that formal kind of way. It was so sweet."

Her enthusiasm in recreating this time vied with her loss of it. She looked troubled. I thought of Sophia's expression: someone just walked over my grave. I wanted to distract her. "What a thrilling period it must have been."

"It's hard to explain what was at stake here. Austin said it was like getting the news—I don't know if this gives the sense of it—that the earth is round—something like that—we accept that now, but to know the world is flat and then, bingo, finding out it's round—that it's possible to travel out, beyond your home, your limited circumstances, and not fall off the edge of the world. What a liberation, what a thrill, to have blindness not be a disability but the absolute precondition for sight."

"It is odd, isn't it? It's counter-intuitive."

"Exactly so. The feminine, having sight, is covered by the masculine that is blind. But that oddity disappears when you know they are worn by one dancer as his mask. They are danced."

"How does that dispel the contradiction?"

"Because they aren't fixed. The inner and the outer change places, constantly. You can't understand unless you've experienced it."

I was a little dispirited, thinking that I'd never really get the meaning of all of this. "How did you know that the twin masks would have been worn by a single dancer? I mean other than how they fit together."

"Because the masks didn't make sense to me; otherwise they would have been collectible statements of beauty, about the obvious polarities: darkness and light, seeing or blindness, or even male and female. They weren't that. They weren't really works of art. The really startling thing, if you can understand this, is that they weren't even material things. Because they were to be enacted, experienced.

They were relied upon as unstable, then gliding back into balance and externalized. Danced, they actually represented a single, fulfilled self. Made of stone and yet the opposite of stone—and, you see, also the opposite of certainty and immortality. They are an object lesson in the evanescent. They are a masterwork of illusion." She added, somewhat sadly, "It was another paradox he banged his head against."

"If that's so," I ventured, "what business did he—did anyone—have in keeping them in a museum?" My tone was more assertive than I'd intended, but she didn't take offense.

"Yes, that's what we came to realize: they had to go back to the community. But what community? And how? We would have figured it out, eventually. We tried what we could to get the Paris mask to stay here with the other. Austin suggested to Paris a trade for something else that they might want. The answer was 'no.' He was upset. He really went into a slump."

I waited.

"He withdrew from me. This was about two months before his suicide. He didn't answer the phone, never returned my calls, and when he did, he put me off, said he was busy writing his Shawcroft book. I shouldn't have believed him."

"You think this decline had a lot to do with not keeping the masks together?"

"Yes, I do, definitely."

"That's hard for me to understand, such caring for—things," I confessed.

She seemed disappointed in me. "Then I haven't adequately explained their power." She turned the responsibility on herself. "They are masks of transformation. For Austin to be able to bring them together was a God-send. I now think—well, I've actually thought this for a long time, that more than personal success was at stake for him in keeping them together. He thought of the masks as a trinity. There's the sighted mask, the unsighted one, and the person who wears them both. When they were separated, when he failed to keep them together, he fractured as well as they." As if following my thoughts, she said, "That word seems terribly diagnostic." She changed focus. "They worked on a mythical level as well. Austin called them 'The Thief,' that they had to do with Raven stealing the light. Shall I tell you that story?"

"It's a Haida creation myth, isn't it?"

"It starts before the beginning of the world." She was comfortable again, and became animated. "There's Raven flying around in pitched darkness. An old man and his daughter live in a house where he is hoarding, in boxes containing more boxes, all the light there could ever be in the universe. Because it's so black, the man has never seen his child. Raven transforms himself into a grandchild. He finds the box. He cajoles the grandfather and connives and wheedles and eventually he gets into the boxes and down into where the light is. He transforms back to Raven, takes the light in his beak and as he does the grandfather can, for the first time, see his daughter. Raven flies up through the smoke hole of the house and into the sky. Then he makes a mistake—so many native myths have the beginning of the world starting with a mistake. Raven drops the light. It becomes the sun and the moon. The world begins."

My fear of disappointing her once more was not as strong as my wanting to know. "How are the twin masks related to this myth?"

"They are the moment before and the moment after Raven steals the light. The question for the Haida, and for us was 'How can a stone mask open and close its eyes?' You see the Haida culture, as with all west coast cultures, had transformation at its center. It's the opposite of what we do in the western world, fixing all sorts of notions, all beliefs—fighting for the immutability of the written word. How absurd. The west coast peoples didn't try to intellectualize the notion of transformation, they enacted it. Such change is excruciating, so difficult, a rebirth. Which was like death. But you must stop me—"

"I don't want to stop you," I said, surprised at her command. "To the contrary." I was a student at her feet.

"About the stone masks, then. We believed they were the apex of the transformative, on every conceivable intellectual and practical level. Our thinking was that because the sighted mask had drilled holes in the earlobes, it was the inner one, as I've said. A willow strap through the ears was clenched in the dancer's teeth to support the weight of it—a twisted willow is very strong. Let me demonstrate." She sat forward on the couch. "Imagine the darkness of the longhouse, with the fires burning. The dancer is brought out from behind a screen. He has on both masks, holding the blind one on the outside."

She put a pretend mask over her face, her eyes closed.

She turned her head away from me. Then she turned back. Her eyes were open.

She tapped her face. She turned away, then back, her eyes were closed. She tapped her face. She turned away. Open, closed, open.

Finally she stopped and put down the invisible masks, inhaling deeply. "Stone can see. Some academics said, well maybe yes, maybe no. But we knew how it was." Abruptly, she got up. "I was going to get us something to eat."

10

ONE IS BLIND

Claire had created a dependence in me, as between audience and actor, and although I wanted to follow her out of the room, I assumed she needed to be alone. But she didn't. She called me to join her in the kitchen where she was making us tomato sandwiches with sprouts on homemade bread.

"I'm afraid Austin was propelled into some very abstract, speculative thought." She was setting the table. "The problem was it became a brain-child, only endless possibilities. Sometimes he would take things quite far, and the local academics would mock him. Until he'd publish an article on the subject in an acclaimed international journal, receive rave reviews, and set them back on their heels." She poured more boiling water into the teapot.

"And his relationship with Shawcroft? The composer, Brett Morris, is keen that we use the idea that Hart believed he was reincarnated."

"Shawcroft reincarnated as Austin? Good heavens." She was more bemused than scandalized. "Certainly there's room for such a notion, but if Austin believed he was a 'come-back' as the Haida call them, some talent was lost in the rebirth. I mean Austin loved to carve masks himself but—" she see-sawed her hand in the air, "so-so in the master-carver department. Sit, eat."

I did, she didn't.

"Have you heard of Austin's lectures. They were legendary, multiple screens, big theaters, always packed. Sometimes he came into class and spoke to his students as Shawcroft, saying 'Austin Hart cannot be here today.' I always thought of it as a brilliant teaching technique. I don't know. Austin studied Shawcroft's work, especially the Raven Rattle he found on Ninstints, which went missing and has never been found. If I write about people who are dead, it doesn't mean much to me. To him, it mattered. Eventually, he was always, completely, someplace else. You have to stay here on the ground, that's all you can do." I was struggling to follow her darting thoughts, and then she landed on something I could answer. "Strange, I've forgotten now, the date of his death. I thought I would never forget, and now I have."

"April 8th. Did you know that he was in trouble?"

"Was he in trouble? I mean of course he was, how stupid of me. But I really didn't know at the time. I just thought he was brooding over the parting of the stone masks. He was going to write the forward to my new book. So from time to time that summer—he died in July was it?"

She hadn't heard me. "April," I repeated.

"I'd call, leave a message, ask how it was going with the preface. Eventually he'd phone, say he'd been busy, that he hadn't gotten around to it yet, but soon. That was fine, I didn't need it right away. Then one day he came to my place. So it was in April?"

"April 8th."

"Then this would have been about April 5th. It was a very brief visit." She now spoke rapidly, soldiering through a rough terrain of memories. "As I said, I hadn't seen much of him for a while. Anyway, he stood on my doorstep and wouldn't come in. He said, 'I'm bringing back your manuscript. I haven't written the forward. I'm sorry, I really can't think of what to say.' Then he was gone. That's the last I saw him." She was finished, like closing a book.

I was surprised. I thought she'd either be slighted by his actions, or take them as a signal there was something seriously wrong with her friend. I suggested as much.

"In retrospect, of course. I let it go because, although he came alive in his writing, he had to fight for every word. He once said it was like giving birth to axes. I just let it go, that he couldn't write the forward. I shouldn't have." I apologized for sounding critical, but she waved it off. "His memorial service, god it was hard. It was held at the museum, right in the midst of the poles taken from Ninstints. So many natives were there. There wasn't enough room; people were standing everywhere, all around the poles and outside on the lawn, looking in through the windows. Then the Haida procession came in dressed in their regalia. It's really something to see these people some assume are just dissolute alcoholics who don't look after their children wearing fringed blankets as artfully designed as the totems and the paintings—the blood red colors of the capes with black and white on top, so dramatic. Fifty men and women, with the drummers all around them. Austin's wife arrived late, just after the speeches. Most of us didn't know who this woman was, although it wasn't too hard to figure out. She stood beside her children, a black veil covering her face, even though it wasn't a formal service. She left without talking to anyone. I walked away from that place, down the long corridor with the Ninstints poles on either side—" Claire started to cry. "After all these years, it's still hard to bear the memory of it. Funny isn't it?"

I reached across the table and lightly put my hand on hers, and then withdrew. "I'm not surprised. You've summoned that time. For both of us."

She wiped the tears with the back of her hand and squared her shoulders. "I went to a lecture he gave in the early days. It was astonishingly good. He talked about gathering the poles. I'd just come back from my first trip to the Charlottes, and I had photographs of what was left. All you could see were the moss covered stumps where they cut the poles. I went up to him after the lecture. I said I'd been to Ninstints that summer and had taken photographs. He asked my opinion about the poles, whether they should have been taken. I said no, they should have stayed where they belonged. To haul them off and put them in carpeted museums with construction beams up the back of the Watchman so he won't fall over—it's wrong. They put the poles in stairwells with floodlights shining on them, and that just destroys their value and meaning. If you'd ever been to Ninstints, you'd know what I'm saying. It's difficult to get there. This abandoned village where so much happened. Someone who'd been on the expedition, maybe Tom Price—someone said 'It wasn't the right thing to do.'"

"I've learned that some of the poles are still in crates after—what—forty-four years?"

"Where?"

"In a warehouse in downtown Victoria."

"I didn't know that. I don't think the Haida know that. They'll be angry. Some of the poles were mortuary poles. The Haida say nobody ever got permission. I can't see Austin doing that. God, had I been there, knowing what I know, caring as I care, I would have fought them tooth and nail. I would have stopped them. How I would love to walk that village and see it as intact as it could be, pole after pole."

Something dropped into a slot, like a coin. I would use her as a character in the libretto.

I mentioned that in the unedited silent film of the expedition it showed that the chainsaws wouldn't work when they tried to cut down the poles, that it seemed auspicious.

"Well, I suppose sometimes chainsaws work, sometimes they don't. Still, you must be a little careful. Maybe not about chainsaws, but certainly strange things happen with these ancient artifacts. When I was in the vault with the twin masks, suddenly the lights wouldn't come on or from time to time the camera just didn't work, and then it did. I don't know why."

"What do you do with that?" I asked. "How do you understand it?"

"It's just part of the story. Make sure not to leave these things out. They have meaning because they happened. Just report them. If something is left out of the story, truth hardens. It's easier to get hold of, to become pedantic, but you actually don't know what you've got. Really, the story is everything, especially for an oral culture, but it is for all of us."

"I've heard something about the last lecture—"

"Oh, yes, the last lecture," she said, speaking in italics. "Unfortunately, I was away at the time, but I certainly heard about it. It caused quite a stir. There used to be an audio tape of it floating around. You should see if you can find it." She mustered her thoughts. "He'd taken a new direction, so out of people's realms. He didn't believe any more in provenance, in needing to know, or even in trying to find out, where the artifacts came from, their history, who made them, what the tribal affiliations were. These were all the things that interest me and his peers—and, of course, the audience. None of that mattered to him. Before he had painstakingly put his ideas into a journal article, well received. The last lecture was improvisational, raw. He was knocked off base by the audience's response."

I had agreed to this project without hesitation, and now I hesitated. Being with Claire was generating a sense of uncertainty in me. I remembered Trevor Crane. "Do you think there's a danger in trying to find what really happened to Austin? Supposedly the previous librettist—"

She interrupted. "You don't have to go where he went. You're not Austin Hart; you are somebody else with your own path. Don't spook yourself." I felt she was comforting and cautioning both of us. "That blouse I wore on the night of the surprise party, it was—what do you call it? A method for painting or dying clothes. Tie dye, that's it. Anyway, I tore up that blouse just the other day—to make dusters. I said to myself 'this has to go.' Funny, isn't it? And now you're here." She laughed. "I guess I should take my own advice and not spook myself either."

A dual purpose was overtaking me. I wanted to be a sympathetic friend and felt I was becoming that. I was also formulating her as a character for the opera. I was in Austin Hart's dilemma: to have his informants trust him when he wasn't entirely trustworthy. I decided to leave rather than stay on this moral fault-line.

She drew me a map showing where Austin Hart's ashes were buried, under a cedar tree behind the museum at the university.

Had Austin Hart loved her, and I hoped he had, I understood why. Austin Hart was survived by this vibrant woman who was like a solar flare.

She had the key to his house.

I was left wondering about Claire's response to Austin the last time she saw him, and her confusion over the date of his death. There was something she couldn't tell me, perhaps because she didn't know me yet. She had a raw, unnamed sorrow. But she had given her approval, a kind of blessing to the opera.

11

WAKE UP THIS FAMILY

I had to build muscle, my capacity to accept Claire Tomlin's generosity. She wanted me to get the story right. An interloper, I now belonged to a cause. My life had made an about-face.

I was unused to speaking intimately with anyone. Richard and I, with our hammering schedules, would find one another at the end of the day, too worn out to do anything but sleep. I couldn't rightly recall what we had ever talked about except how tired we were.

Claire had been the pilot. She'd taxied us down the runway through the Katzie dig, gained lift by knowing the past through holding an arrowhead in her hand, climbed above the clouds to find a stone mask which could open and close its eyes, cruised back to the beginning of the world, tipped into the turbulence of Austin's last visit, barely rose above the tree-line of his funeral, down into that valley, and then, after a few bumps from my double purpose, we were on the ground again—where she drew me a map—and I was gone.

It was quite a ride. And I had to be ready to meet Paige, Hart's daughter, the next day.

BRETT AND I MET PAIGE at a local pub. I watched her come towards us, weaving in and amongst the tables, floating on a cushion of air. She didn't seem at all like her father, who had a dapper, stylish appearance. Her clothes were so against fashion as to be fashionable. Mainly she was in black, with a toque pulled tight around her face hidden by sunglasses, a scarf around her neck. She was wearing a black cape with red lining. As she strode, the cape revealed baggy pants—dark green battle fatigues. Laced-up, oxblood Doc Martens went mid-calf on her legs. She was shorter that I, maybe 5'3" but she dressed in long flowing things the way a tall woman would—a tall woman in winter, and not this warm spring day.

Without any greeting she took my hand, as if I could help her over a pool of water. It was endearing.

"Let's order." She assigned Brett the task of getting hamburgers and beer.

Paige removed her sunglasses. Her eyes were heavy with make-up. Thick black eyeliner winged out to her temples at a sorcerer's angle, smoldering the intensity of her eyes.

"You look familiar," she said to me, "like I've met you before. You know how it is sometimes. Do people say that to you?"

"Some people have said I look like H.D., maybe that's why."

"Hilda Doolittle? But you have a round face, like mine, and H.D.'s wasn't."

Although I didn't intend it as a test, I was glad she knew who H.D. was.

She abruptly pulled off her toque, like removing a mask. Her long black hair, parted in the middle, tumbled around her shoulders and tangled in her scarf. "You're getting to know about my father, so I feel like I know you."

I smiled. "Not so logical but still a happy thought," I said. I liked this odd woman.

Brett returned from managing the food and drink. Paige pointed to the first page of an outline he'd prepared. She read: "'Austin Hart believed he was the reincarnation of Edward Shawcroft.' My father didn't believe he was Edward Shawcroft. I'm really amazed you'd want to portray him in this way. It's not on." Brett started to defend himself but she wouldn't let him. "This is the first thing I've seen about the opera. It's an oversimplification to make this assertion about reincarnation. And, furthermore, it's in bad taste."

She'd come loaded for bear. I'd never met a woman who presented herself with such self-assurance. If I'd had a father, I'd also want to protect him from bogus categorizations which might diminish him.

Brett, defensive, reminded Paige that sometimes her father pretended he was Shawcroft when he lectured.

"That was a just teaching ploy."

As she continued to scold Brett, I kept seeing her as the one who went into her father's bedroom to search, as at an archaeological site, for evidence as to why he had abandoned her.

She turned to me. "You seem like a nice person, although I don't know yet—but you're the librettist, and I don't want you to endorse this business of reincarnation for the opera. Maybe Brett can put transubstantiation into his music, but not you." She was the poet making an alliance with the writer of the words.

Brett raised his eyebrows and inclined his head toward me. He was telling me I was on my own in this. Paige followed the signals, watching the traverse of a ball she'd tossed.

"I can't say I've ever believed in reincarnation." I hadn't quite returned the serve; she waited for more. "Most of us don't have a system of values or institutions around us to give depth to such a belief."

Paige nodded. "Exactly." She seemed happy I'd underscored her position. "If the Haida believe in it, I'm sure my Dad respected that. They had the institutions. But this opera isn't going to be a kitschy ghost story which makes a mockery of my father. He was Austin Hart, not a stand-in for anyone else."

As seemed to be her approach to everything, she ate with a focused attention until she was finished. I thought she mustn't have eaten for a while.

She pushed away her plate, ready to talk.

"In the springtime, three months before he killed himself, I was looking for a place to stay because I had a nine month old baby, and I was a single mother. My Dad lived in our family home, three bedrooms, three floors, a spare room in the basement. So I asked Dad if I could stay with him for a while. He wrote me a letter saying, 'with regret'—that was his phrase, 'with regret, no.' He didn't phone me, he wrote me a letter. I should have known something was wrong, because that wasn't like him. He was a generous guy. I should have just landed on his doorstep anyway, but instead I pouted. It was a pretty costly pout."

I was relieved this had all happened so long ago and the burden of finding an expression of comfort and condolence was mitigated by time. Still I had to be able to shoulder this story and her on-going, mixed-up sorrow. "It must seem—" I began.

Paige held up her hand to stop me. "That's the terrible thing about losing him to suicide—odd phrase—he still has a hold on us. Like looking out to the ocean and seeing him there, and I think he's swimming alone, that's okay swimming alone, and so I turn away to look at something else, but he's not swimming he's drowning." She regarded me intently. "We're still grieving the way families do when the dead body can't be found so the loss doesn't stop." She measured the considerable impact of this statement on me. "Do you know that through this opera you have the possibility of getting through to others—to completing my Dad's work? That's why I'm here and not going with those people who're on me for permission to write his biography. We have to wake up this family—we've been asleep. His death was too much to take, so we all fell asleep. We have a kind of familial narcolepsy."

I was drawn to her self-disclosure, which she used to serve both her passion and her irony, yet I couldn't quite get a bead on her. So long after her father's death, she seemed hounded by a sense of urgency. "Do you feel, somehow, that time is now running out for your father's story to be told?" I asked.

She looked at me the way a fisherman looks at a finely crafted hook. "Yes, it's time." She looked at Brett. "We must talk about Trevor Crane. Alicia is replacing him. He had to quit the project because he started to absorb my father." Now she turned to me, having tossed even more balls into the air. "You didn't know that, did you, about Trevor? Did Brett tell you?" Without waiting for a response she looked back to Brett. "You should have told her. She needs to know what happened to him."

"I don't know if he was absorbing Austin," Brett finally said.

"Yes you do."

"I don't even know what that means."

They were facing off, close to the net. "It means just what it says." She was back to me, a juggler masterfully keeping all the launched balls from dropping. "One death brings in the others. His death puts out a call to all those in your own life, including yourself."

Her comment was alarming. I decided to resort to practical considerations. "There's something maybe you can help me with. I've been to the archives to look at your father's papers. For some reason the librarian's being difficult. Clarence McNabb has told her to give me complete access, but still—"

"I don't want to think about him, he's so foul."

"Mr. McNabb?" I worried about a misstep. I told her I hadn't met him yet.

"You will. You should. He hated my Dad."

"Really? Why?"

"Speak to him. You'll find out."

"Okay. I just wondered if you might endorse his letter to me as well, indicating that you agree—"

"I'll send you my own. I'll tell them to let you see my Dad's papers, on behalf of the family. Everyone wants this opera to happen, even my brother, Jason, although he's pretty shut down. You have to be sure you look for Dad's files on Salish spirit dancing." She was now engaged, less frantic. "He took me to one of them when I was very young. I didn't know what was going on. I fell asleep in his lap, I was that small."

I imagined she wished she could find that place again with an uncomplicated father who wouldn't ruin her life.

"Make sure you see the originals of his papers, not copies. See the real things," she added.

I told her that so far, I'd been allowed to see the originals.

"I had to go to the police station because the cops got to the house before I did. They'd confiscated things. So I was standing there at the counter, and they brought me a note my Dad had written—not a suicide note, but a list he'd made the day he killed himself. It had the date on it. It was things he had to do, making sure he'd paid the insurance, the taxes, that he'd cleaned the eaves. Maybe this was the last thing he wrote, this 'to do' list. So I'm there at the counter, and they hand me the last thing he wrote and it's a photocopy. Bring me the original, I said. The duty officer said no, I could only have a copy. I raised hell. What good was a copy to me? I needed the original. Don't let them pawn a copy off on you."

"I don't quite get the significance of—"

"You will." Seemingly not wanting to be coy she clarified, "The originals are the artifacts."

Paige asked if I wanted another beer. We'd finished two pints each, and I couldn't drink any more. She got up.

"I hope I can talk to you again soon," I said.

"Any time. My Aunt Candice, Dad's sister, is expecting you to go and see her." I wrote her number in my notebook.

As we stood outside, Brett said, "Paige, I'm sorry about this reference to reincarnation. Alix, you figure out where I've gone wrong. I'm not stuck on the idea. But something pretty remarkable was happening in Austin's mind about Edward Shawcroft, that's all I was trying to say."

"Well, that's true. Shawcroft carved the Raven Rattle, my father's talisman, his grail."

We left the pub and I got into my car. I started onto the highway and then I didn't know if I were going the right direction. Either Paige's intensity had disoriented me, or Richard was right about my sense of place.

12

FROG WOMEN

I tried Trevor Crane's number early in the mornings but there was never any answer. Finally, late one night, he called me. His speech was slurred.

He said he had a few pages of something he once wrote as the plot. The word "plot" sounded particularly leaden. He couldn't remember where it was, Brett must have it, nothing very good. I asked if he had come to any conclusions about Hart's suicide.

"He could hardly wait to go."

I expressed my surprise.

"That's what I like to think. Anyway, be careful of that one Françoise, Tom Price's wife, because she'll mesmerize you. What a beauty. Careful of her. The others are frog women. Frog women go into anthropology. Wanting transformation. None of them liked me. Except maybe Hart's sister, Candice. She's an easy like. But who knows what time zone she's in."

"And what about Mary-Anne? What did you learn?"

"Who?"

"Austin's wife, Mary-Anne?"

"The one who died right after he did?"

"Yes."

"She died."

"Yes, I know." I was caught in the inebriate's cats-cradle.

"Well, she followed right behind him, eh? I guess she was still crazy about him. Then there's Hart's shrink. Robert T. Longfellow." He remembered his full name, the way that old people and drunks, lost in a field of forgetfulness and uncertainty, could suddenly become precise and find their way. "He gave Hart drugs."

"Interesting that Paige didn't mention that."

"That's a daughter for you. Loyal."

"Do you think Longfellow would talk to me?"

"I dunno. I talked to so many people, but man it's hard to figure out what's what. Listen—I got all your messages." He had become serious, making an effort to order his thoughts. "I had to wait to get back to you." Then he trailed off. I asked if he was okay.

"You've got to listen." He was scolding me.

"What's up?"

"It's a pretty grim story, eh? Got me down. You chop away at this underbrush, then look around and Christ, it's grown back thicker than before. Anyway, Brett says he's got you guys a producer with money. That's good. But I've changed my mind." If he'd been driving, he would have run into something by now.

"About being the librettist? You're sorry you quit, or—"

"Oh, Christ, no. No way. Listen, like I only know you from your writing, then I told Brett to hire you 'cause you're damn good and now I'm sorry." He abruptly stopped talking again. His engine wasn't firing. We'd have to take it one step at a time.

"You're sorry because you recommended me to Brett?"

"I am. I really am." He seemed genuinely remorseful for having betrayed a complete stranger.

"Okay. And that is because—"

"Look, Brett's my friend. He'd kill me if he knew I was talking this way to you. What's he going to do without you, that's what I keep asking myself. What's he gonna do? I mean he doesn't have to go to the center of it, not like us. It's not right, nope, not right. Just hang on for a sec—I gotta get a drink." He dropped the phone and immediately picked it up. "Sorry, that musta been loud." Then he was gone again. I hoped he'd find his way back.

When he did, he was diverted again, telling me he liked a story I'd written. "That one about the girl who goes out riding on a horse—on the day of her wedding and she cracks her skull—"

I had to keep him on track. "Trevor?"

"—and has to wear a wig to the ceremony."

"Trevor, what are you worried about? Did something bad happen to you?"

"You're not going to come out in one piece."

His stark decree netted my own latent fear that there was too much darkness in my own history to safely be able to follow Hart.

"You need winged shoes." He was caught in the underbrush again.

I thought for a minute. "Hermes?"

"Yeah, a guide. Listen to me, this work—it'll pull you down. I've been where you're heading." Abruptly, he said, "I'm sick. Maybe I was sick before, but now—something doesn't want this story to be told. I got kinda spooked. Austin Hart. He's a 'come-back', you know from the big boundary. He doesn't want it told. Or maybe the natives don't. Somebody doesn't, that's for sure. If you continue, don't go out anywhere, don't talk to anyone. Just lock yourself in a room, write up a storm and *voilà* the libretto, your poetry—I really like your stuff by the way, especially that horse story—Brett'll put your words to music and puff the magic dragon, all's right with the world. Poof. Puff." He was enjoying the moist alliteration of the words. Then he realigned himself. "Okay, so we're all interested in why our dreams fail us, and they do. But Austin's dreams devoured him. Now everybody wants to make some money off this guy's death. I feel sorry for him. All the booze and the pills, his hands probably shook so bad he had trouble pulling the trigger. Like in the movies. Did you see *Leaving Las Vegas*? You must've—"

For fear I'd lose him again I asked bluntly, "What's made you so afraid?"

"The natives are pissed off about what happened at Ninstints. They've got power. More than us. But hey, this isn't a tragedy about the natives, right? It's just about this white dude. Who's a 'come-back.' First as Shawcroft, and now—I dunno, he's around and he's not quiet like a dead man should be."

"Did something specific happen?"

"I can't sleep. My wife made me quit. What's Brett gonna do without you? He'll find somebody. Or make a musical—that'd be good. A nice, light musical. He could do that. Like I mean no disrespect. What's wrong with a musical? Poof, puff, nice kitschy stuff. Hire a few native dancers. It'd be like taking a weekend workshop, find your inner self, your guardian spirit, your soul mate. Wanna past life regression? For a few hundred bucks you, too, can time travel, discover you've been Napoleon, Mary Queen of Scots, Mickey Mouse. Pack up your troubles, come on get happy. Poof. No time for a weekend? We have a one day special on a fast-train to god—"

"Hold on, hold on. I'm pretty sure that's not what Brett has in mind."

"Safest route." He sank again. "Hart was a spiritual obsessive who knew god but couldn't manage to boil a three-minute egg."

He was ricochetting around. I believed he was really afraid and smothering his fear with alcohol, but I had no idea why.

"So, Hart takes these mortuary poles. Bang, seven years later he's the cock-of-the-walk, everybody's darling. Bang, off with his head. People blow their brains out, right, to stop the thinking that's going bloody nowhere. What about the heart, eh? Put the gun right there, middle of the chest, that'll work. No, he had to stop the thinking. But what's he thinkin' about? Somebody—can't remember who—somebody's told me Austin used to go to these winter spirit dancing things, but I can't find anyone to take me or they're putting me off 'cause white-folks can't go or something, so there's a reserve near where I live and I hear they have a sweat lodge. The young native kid tells me I can come. It's f'ing cold outside. I'm hoping no one wants me to jump into the river 'cause I'm not up for that. I go into the sweat. You know what they look like? Just a kind of domed thing made of branches with rugs or something over top. Dug into the ground, with hot coals burning right in there inside. Shit. There's eight of us. I sit near the opening, near the native kid. It's dark, a little hard to breathe, but I'm okay. Then the kid pulls down the flap at the entrance to the dome and I don't like it. We're in the hot of hell. Somebody's saying something or singing. I can't breathe. Like I'm being crushed by a boulder. I was going to die. I called Austin to help me. Get it? Then I'm sobbing, just in my chest, because this thing's going to kill me, and I hear Austin's voice. Loud and stern. 'Go away.' Next thing I'm standing outside, shaking like an earthquake, and I start to run. I run to my car, drive my car to the house, run into the house, run into my bed. I cried for three days. My wife couldn't help me. Just held me. She wouldn't let me go back. I told Brett I wasn't any good for the project. That's all. I told him I'd find somebody else for him. Sorry, I found you." He was holding down the re-created fear as if it were a convulsing child. "I've gotta go now. Brett's mother was a suicide. He doesn't tell anybody. Too many friggin' deaths. Don't following that one." He hung up.

I stopped myself from redialing his number. He needed to be left alone.

Sitting on the couch in my mother's library, I didn't expect, much less could I account for my reaction, a strange cocktail of terror and excitement: I was elated. Not, of course, about what Trevor had been through. Yet I was in a state of exaltation, raised happily aloft. What was wrong with me that I felt this way after hearing a more than cautionary tale from a man who was in real trouble, who said I should run the other way? "You're not going to come out in one piece."

I paced. I couldn't figure it out. It didn't seem like the healthiest response.

AUSTIN HART REINCARNATED as Shawcroft and now coming to stop this story. To believe in reincarnation wasn't a question of faith, but experience, the experience of recognizing someone from before, someone who had come back from the most impenetrable divide between here, mortality, and there, eternity. I'd never felt it and so couldn't fear it. I was being drawn again by the lure of finally knowing the truth of some's life as well as their death.

But what did it all amount to so far? Hart's expedition removed the largest remaining stand of totem poles in the world, even those holding the dead buried in boxes at the top. It was ominous that the chainsaws wouldn't work; in the rain, the men cut down the poles by hand. Claire said that in the presence of the artifacts, lights went out, cameras wouldn't work. Twin masks made of stone, with eyes which could open and close, were brought together by Austin, and were now separated. The previous writer heard Austin Hart telling him to go away, and he quit the project, terrified—still terrified. People were come-backs from the dead. Where was the mysterious Raven Rattle, Austin's grail? Above all else, there were villages of suicides: Hart, Brett's mother, Shawcroft, in the native communities. The trail of dropped clues were made of every sort of thing: wood, stone, even blood. Which lead was I to follow?

Claire's solid, practical advice: I had to follow all of them, and leave nothing out; they had meaning because they had really happened.

I'd call Trevor again, I wasn't sure when. I would continue with the project, but I was alarmed enough to know I'd need a guide for this trip.

THE NEXT DAY I told Brett I'd spoken to Trevor, but nothing more. I asked if he thought his friend was okay.

"Oh, sure. He's great."

"You should give him a call."

When he asked how the writing was going, I told him there were so many leads to follow I didn't feel ready to start writing the libretto just yet. He was alarmed. "Please stay on track. Send me scenes. I'm getting the music ready for you." He was ravenous for words, no matter what their sense.

That day, I received the letter from Paige which she had promised:

To whom it may concern:

This is to authorize, on behalf of the family of Austin Hart, that Alix (Alicia) Purcell is to have free and unrestricted access to my father's papers.

Yours truly,

Austin Hart's Daughter, Paige Hart

I called to thank her.

13

THE INTERNMENT

Mr. Strange came to tend the garden. The nurse at Styx Mansion said my mother was fine, that she'd let her know I'd visit in a few days. I phoned Richard when I knew he'd be at the gym and miss my call. I escaped to the archives, rejoining Hart on Haida Gwaii.

Armored by Paige's letter, I also felt better able to face Mrs. Verspoor's hoary battlements. She wasn't there. Her assistant said she had taken ill that morning and gone home. As with the first visit, the boxes were set out for me on the table in this bomb-shelter of a room.

I found the place in his journal where I had left off.

I know so much about these people, their ancestors, their traditions, and thereby all that has ~~been~~ lost. I intentionally lure my informants with my detailed knowledge and consequently, by degrees, I am gaining their trust. They almost think I have this knowledge as a gift, or ~~because~~ I have ~~been~~ sent. While not fostering this idea, still I don't disabuse them of it. It is by indirection that I will be able to achieve my objective which, were it were not laudatory, my method would put me to shame. I want their permission to take the poles. I went out walking tonight, passing the verandah where native women sit outside on armchairs whose stuffing is bulging at the sides. The one who usually waves at me gestured that I should join them.

They gave me tea and I sat quietly in their midst. They didn't know much English and so our conversation quickly lapsed. They talked amongst themselves. Having learned the Haida language from Boas's writings, I was able to comprehend most of what they said. In all honesty, I can understand more than I can speak, and so my deception in not revealing that I knew what they were saying, is, perhaps, to be excused.

A young mother, Elsie, had her new baby with her. Because of their belief in reincarnation, the women were asking one another "who do you think he is" and saying the names of people, I assume, who had passed away. They looked so intently into the newborn's face. "Who are you now?" asked Masie, as if the question would invoke a gesture in the child which would give her a better clue. "Grandfather, is that you?"

To treat a purblind baby with such respect because he's much older than they and comes to them from before, with all his wisdom and experience intact—is a wonderment. And a wonderment that an unborn soul might choose their parents.

While the women were talking to the child and to one another, they also speculated, amongst themselves, why I'd come. One of them said they must be careful of me, whereupon another looked at me and laughed. They all ended up laughing, and I laughed with them.

It seems, with growing clarity, I must extend my stay here in order to understand how I should direct the fate of the totem poles. I don't yet know the people well enough, and what would be best for them. I am in a quandary about their future, and if they really have one.

In the next entry the tone of Austin's writing had markedly changed.

As I have long conversations into the night with the men, and now some of the women, this place has changed. I think of my experience in the war. This is, in reality, an internment camp.

It started with a visitor who came into your house, sat at your table, ate the food that you offered and at the end of the meal, said—working at his teeth with the toothpick you gave him—'Now to the business at hand. This is not your house. You must leave.' He starts to clear the dishes away, but instead of putting them in the sink, he's putting them in a box and into a truck in the yard where there are many more people just like him. They remove the remains of the food, the pots and pans, and put them in the truck, then the chairs and eventually the table. The man drives off calling 'we'll be back, we won't tell you when but we'll be back to take the rest, because everything is ours. There will be more of us next time. You don't belong here anymore.' You are stunned. Your sister is stunned.

One day your children go out to play in the morning and they don't come back at night. You learn that your son and daughter have been put in the truck and taken away. You sit in the corner. They come to get you as well and you are brought here to this barren place. You can't find your children.

When the children are returned they are speaking a different language. They are taken away again by the man who is no longer a stranger to you. Each time they come back, your children understand less and less of what you say to them. Everyone sits alone at night in front of wet, blackened logs soaking in the rain. You don't have a shelter. You cannot make a fire.

Something like this happened to these people.

This is where I am.

Tomorrow H.S. takes me to Ninstints. I don't even know if the poles are still standing, although H.S. assures me they are. It may well be they have fallen and are beyond reclamation.

The remainder of the notebook was unremarkable except for a note in the margin of the text:

> *The process of enlightenment for a non-shaman can be achieved through the use and possession of their artifacts. My quest is to cross from one state to the other.*

I had been struggling to understand what mysterious changes were taking place in Austin's thinking, and here he was declaring a desire—more than that, an intention—to cross over to enlightenment through using and possessing a native artifact. That a shamanic state could be realized in this way seemed more than illusive. A shaman could travel between the visible and invisible worlds, and in this sense the twin masks were the very essence of the shamanic, moving between being sighted and being blind.

I wondered if this was a darker, more personal reason he wanted to keep the masks together.

I also glimpsed something of what Claire meant about Austin keeping artifacts "for their own sake." It may have been he was trying to acquire a power in some illegitimate way. But I had to stop—this was way over my head; I was out of my depth.

I returned to his journals, where there were technical descriptions of how to move the poles, crate them, get them to Victoria. This was written after his first visit to Haida Gwaii when he was planning the expedition for the following year. Which supposedly meant he didn't write anything about his trip to Ninstints that summer. I knew he would have. I spent two hours vainly searching the box for the missing journal.

I found a page entitled "Owners of Ninstints Island."

> *After thorough-going inquiries, I have discovered that ownership of the poles is more difficult to ascertain than I had predicted. It requires the telling of stories. As with all great oral traditions, such as those which produced the Odyssey and the Mahabharata, even the shortest ones take many days to finish....*

Doubtless the claims to the totems could be ascertained in this fashion; regrettably, there isn't enough time. In these circumstances the decision must be left to the governing Band council.

Hart attended a meeting of the Band council. These were what he'd described as the "emasculated" leaders, appointed by the government. No women were there; no real consensus could be reached without them. Council approved his request to pay for the poles and remove them the following year. The natives would later establish ownership in a public gathering with the elders present.

Further down in the file was a formal petition by the Council opposing the taking of the grave-poles the next year. They'd changed their minds.

While my job wasn't to wander through his journals and treasure-hunt what he had done, I was afraid there was an ethical time-bomb hidden in the works.

I went to a pay-phone and called Brett. "There was trouble over the ownership of the poles."

"Alix? Where are you?"

"I'm at a phone just outside the archives. It's almost closing time. Hart had Band Council agree he could remove the poles before ownership was established at a public meeting. Which would be too late to get consent."

"Except to determine who got the money. There was money offered, I hope."

"Two hundred dollars a pole. Twenty dollars for each section."

"Which meant they could take part of the pole and not the whole thing. They could chop off what they didn't want."

"He wouldn't do that."

"Alix, what is the problem then?"

"Something's not right. He paid maybe $4,000 for poles whose value is inestimable."

"Only because he saved them. Weren't they willing to sell?"

"But who is 'they.' He was talking to a very select group of people which didn't include the elders or the women. Then before the project even got started Band council opposed the removal of the mortuary poles. Hart knew all these things. I don't get it."

"I'm sure you'll figure it out. By the way, this business of reincarnation—you went over to Paige's side pretty quickly, so I had to back down. But reincarnation is a respectable belief. It gives comfort."

"Apparently not to Paige."

"Let's work together, eh?"

I was more concerned about Hart's morality than his reincarnation. There had to be an explanation in his diaries, and I was bent on finding it.

As I hung up the phone Bernadette Verspoor walked passed, going into the front door. "Hello, Mrs. Verspoor." I startled her. "How are you feeling?" It seemed only appropriate to continue to try to be friendly. She stopped but seemed not to recognize me. "Alix Purcell, you remember?"

"Yes, I know who you are."

"Thanks for having Mr. Hart's boxes ready."

"Fine." She didn't move.

"I hope you're feeling better."

She looked even paler than the last time, her skin the color of sour milk. "You know there was lots of talk after Mr. Hart killed himself. Have you found out whether he thought he could communicate with the dead?" Before I could answer she said, "The dead should be allowed to rest," and turned away.

Everyone had a different, changing relationship to Austin. I wondered if that's what the resurrection meant.

14

A GLAUCOUS TIME

Before I visited Sophia again, I had to take on her garden so I could bring her a description which went beyond saying it was in full bloom, but the tulips were now only nail-like spikes of stamen—or whatever they were called—on the end of green stalks, the soil littered with red and yellow petals.

In the library was a shelf of mother's gardening books. I selected a dozen and spread them on the kitchen table, searching for the pictures which most attracted me, then looking through the windows of the solarium to try to find the plants. I identified the common flowers, the quotidian names young children learn proudly as a way of laying claim to the world—daisy, daffodil, pansy—but I was insecure even about the names of flowers used to learn an alphabet.

I had half-remembered lines from poets. "The thorns of the rose, my only delight"—a bush of red roses was in the south-west corner of the garden. "They called me the hyacinth girl...I could not speak and my eyes failed." Hyacinths were in the book but not in the garden. "I am the rose of Sharon and the lily of the valley"; in the book the aphrodisiac lily-of-the-valley was called *convallaria majalis*, but I couldn't see it.

I thought of The Lady and the Unicorn Tapestry poster which had traveled with me, as if the unicorn were my familiar. The *mille fleurs* covered the grass and the walls and became the sky, but they were so tiny I hardly remembered their particulars, and in my mind everything was, in any event, overshadowed by the unicorn seeing itself in the mirror, his large hooves gently resting on the long blood-red pleated dress of the Lady.

In the gardener's encyclopedia I looked up *mille fleurs*. I laughed. The Unicorn Tapestries had been stolen by peasants during the French Revolution and were found decades later being used as potato sacks. Oh my unabashed potato eaters.

I was also sidetracked by the unfamiliar phrases written by these passionate gardeners: umbels of exciting acid-yellow; the scrim effect of the blackish-mahogany leaves; casual swags of two-toned flowers; the magnolia stunning even in death. The glaucous patina on the breathtaking, monstrous hostas. Bulbs for winter forcing. Even the wisteria was made exotic because it had random racemes. A whorl of modified leaves became petals, the inner envelope of the flower. Florescence, the time of flowering.

One book explained that the stigma and style made up the female part of the plant. Stigma and style, an apt definition of the feminine. Could these double entendres have been chosen intentionally by the botanical Adams? I entered a world of etymological delights and I hadn't even stepped outside. If a flower has functioning male and female parts it is called a complete flower, a perfect flower.

A mind-image of the masks, masculine and feminine in one, loomed as the perfect stone florescence. Not abstract concepts carved in granite, but the integrated spiritual beliefs of a nation.

My approach was taking too long. Having gathered these tiny seeds of knowledge, I went out to cut flowers for Sophia but was stopped by the thought of Hopkins's Binsey poplars—"we hack and rack the growing green"—and decided to go to the most expensive florist in the city. I asked for three stalks of The Queen of the Night, requesting the attendant to display the near-black tulips within the sensuous yellow trumpets of—looking at my notes—*Brugamansia versicolor*. She understood me.

It was early afternoon when I reached the mansion. My mother was asleep on her bed, fully clothed and lying under her green pashm shawl. There were beads of perspiration along her hairline, mottling her powdered forehead. I sat near her in the chair holding the paper funnel of flowers like a reluctant suitor. A muscle of her left cheek twitched three or four times. Then she opened her eyes wide and startled, the way she had that first morning in the emergency ward; her look resolved again into pleasure and a smile.

"I'm so glad you're here. You haven't come for a long time."

My imbedded wariness of her was almost comic because when she was sweet to me, I had the urge to turn around and see to whom she was talking. My distrust of her had hardened into the rigidity of steel tracks, the most inflexible means of carrying the rolling-stock of affection.

"Just a few days, Mother. I was in Alberta and Victoria. I was here Monday. It's Thursday today."

"I know what day it is, dear, and the approximate time. Don't 'Mrs. Griffin' me."

Mrs. Griffin as a verb. The scrim effect of a defensive, ailing woman. The glaucous bloom of her love for me. The not yet friable soil of our relationship.

She was, however, still smiling when she looked at the bouquet. She said the names of the flowers like friends. "Now where did you get these? Not from my garden—I wish, from my garden. The inmates will think I have a lover." She was more grateful than coy. With her hand on the bedside table, she stood with difficulty. I would have helped her but she'd taught me not to try.

"Put them in the Harlan House vase you brought last time. It's in the bathroom, behind the toilet. These are lovely. I'm going to plant The Queen of the Night and *Brugamansia* this fall when I get out of here." She looked at me for my reaction, but I remained mute. "Why didn't you bring me flowers from my garden? I do still have a garden, don't I? You haven't sold the place."

That's what she had wanted, for me to bring to her part of her garden, to reassure her. "I was reluctant."

"Reluctant? Why reluctant?"

"Because of Hopkins."

"Who is he? Didn't he want you to bring your old mother her own flowers? How nice, a new beau to replace Dick. But he shouldn't be jealous of me, I'm your mother."

"Hopkins is a poet."

"I expect this of poets."

I couldn't tell if she were being witty or thick. "I should have cut your own flowers for you. Some idea got in my way, I'm ashamed to say."

"Ashamed? That's too grand. It's wasted on me." Then she turned on a dime. "Take me home, Alicia. I don't need their permission, I'm your mother. Let's just go. I never thought I would end up in a dump like this."

Everything I thought to say was false: mealy cheerfulness; mulched stoicism. She had nailed it.

"Me neither."

"Get me out, just for overnight, okay?"

She'd never asked me for anything much. I felt so unsettled by her vulnerability I looked away. "Listen, I have to arrange one of those cabs that are geared for wheelchairs and—"

"I may be falling apart, but I can still walk, for God's sake."

"It'll be easier if we have a chair. Anyway, I have to go to Victoria again tomorrow to interview the head of the museum. I'll come first thing Saturday morning, and you'll stay overnight at the house."

"Put the flowers in water. You're clutching them like there's no tomorrow."

"I'll see if Mrs. Epstein can come and visit while I'm away."

"Who?"

"Mrs. Epstein, your neighbor." She looked confused. "Your neighbor—of forty years."

She saved herself. "Oh, you mean Rachel; you mean Rachel Epstein. I never think of her as Mrs. Epstein."

The first sign of an addled and fibbing brain.

Behind the toilet, where I found the vase, was mold from a leaking pipe. A soggy post-it note was on the floor.

"What's this, mother?" I read: "Children should know which side of the fence their bread is buttered on."

"Oh, that's just to myself."

"You were being funny?" She looked at me with a querulous frown. "I don't think there's a fence in the saying."

"I always have a fence in there."

"What's this about?"

"I was reading the Lives Lived column of the *Globe and Mail* yesterday. They're really prosaic eulogies written by the children. It said something about the deceased's health after such-and-such a year was dogged by kidney problems, and she died of a brain tumor. Now something's gone wrong there in what the family wrote. Some lacunae. Anyway, the column went on to say that this dead woman had been a good enough mother. That annoyed me."

"I think it was meant to be a compliment. It's a theory of child-rearing."

"A theory about being 'good enough?' It would lead to good enough people. Not much for a mother to be proud of."

"Well, darling, I'll never say that of you." I immediately regretted my sarcasm but fortunately she missed the sling.

"That's nice, thank you."

"I'll see you Saturday morning."

"You have to bring me my tweezers from home. These hairs on my chin spring up like mushrooms overnight. They're ugly and miraculous. During menopause is one thing, but I'm way beyond that. Have they done studies on this phenomenon, or do they only study men's beards?" She was talking quickly to defer my leaving. "How's the opera? What are you learning about your Austin Hart?"

I told her I'd met Paige, that she seemed a little eccentric, but that I liked her very much.

"What does she look like?"

I was surprised at Sophia's detailed interest.

"She's a little thrown-together, like accidental art."

"Is she like her father? Well, how would you know? So you've found another family."

"What do you mean? Mother, I'm not leaving you."

"No, I know you aren't. It's taken you a long time."

"For what? Sweetheart, you are my family." I had never made such a sumptuous statement of my relationship to Sophia, and I was afraid, as I always was, that she'd find me mawkish, reject us both as sentimental. I also deflected her because I didn't really understand what she was getting at.

She let the subject drop. "Go now. They'll come for me soon. Physio. You seem happier than I remember you. Take the *Globe* column to read, it's over there. You might get some ideas. Why do people say things like 'he's gone to rest?' He's not resting, he's dead as a doornail. Don't say that about me."

Before I left I talked to the manager about the leak in my mother's bathroom and the state of her bathtub.

I was relieved Mrs. Askew was not stationed at the front door.

15

NOT ENOUGH AIR

Brett and I sat in the reception area of the Royal British Museum in Victoria. He insisted on coming to the interview with McNabb. Our waiting had the uncertainty and alienation of a couple wanting news of a pregnancy. To some extent, I understood Brett's worry. The plot of the opera hadn't yet taken seed in me. I told myself I had to control these roaming metaphors. I felt a little lightheaded.

After Hart went to the university, McNabb, whom Paige loathed, took over his position as head of the museum. McNabb, Randall, Hopper—the people who were Hart's colleagues—they were all still there, secure, tenured, most of them drinking pals who'd started out in Fish and Wildlife. I had the same sense as in the archives: Hart got up and left us.

A native man passed in front of Brett and me. He was wearing green pants and shirt, emasculated in custodian's clothes. His braided hair was thick and black even though, from the lines on his face, he appeared to be beyond middle age. He nodded at me.

Then McNabb arrived. Physically he was so unlike I had imagined him. I'd expected someone older, somewhat domineering. He wore a plaid shirt, jeans and thick-soled shoes, like walking boots. He looked as if he'd aged rather than matured. His hair was combed forward into bangs to cover a bald patch, which was more pronounced by the effort. He stood in front of us and sighed, more an announcement of resignation than a greeting.

He led the way down a narrow hallway with a ceiling so low it felt like a crawl space. We passed rooms called Invertebrates, Vertebrates, then Rubbish. Most of them were empty.

McNabb took us into a large office with a short, orange partition. An analog clock behind him on the wall read 10:07.

To my right was a filing cabinet ribbed shut with glossy moving-tape. The tape had been partially ripped off, just enough to allow two of the drawers to open. The cabinet was bandaged and mutilated at the same time.

He sat heavily in the chair behind his desk. He wasn't overweight but there was a thickness about him. As he slowly swiveled around to face us, he said, "Well, you'd better start asking me your questions. I don't have much information."

I thanked him for the letter to help me with Mrs. Verspoor. He shrugged. "Paige Hart has sent me one as well."

"So the family is behind this?" His meaning was ambiguous.

"In support of it, yes."

Brett took the lead, "You probably think doing an opera on Austin Hart is kind of strange?" McNabb nodded in agreement.

Then for some reason—perhaps because of Brett's empathetic skepticism—his reticence dissolved. McNabb started to talk.

"I don't want to be negative, he had a world-wide reputation—he was way ahead of Levi-Strauss. So he was bright and forward-thinking and all of that. Sure. When he was working with the material culture, he got some really good insights. Hiring natives to work in the museum context, paying them to carve, to rekindle what they once knew—a brilliant move. There were problems with it, of course, big problems, but I handled them. Through his recording of native history, he was able to anticipate the future, what has developed with the land claims—that they'd need all this ethnographic information for the land claims cases—he knew all that way before anybody else. But when he left the museum, he began to dabble in art. It was embarrassing. He lost all credibility with us. We were still at the hard-nosed slogging of ethnography. Our work isn't about *l'art pour l'art*, it's about culture, meaning, societal values. When you want to know which artist in the 1800s made a particular piece, that's when the slogging pays off. Austin? He let the pieces 'affect' him."

McNabb had trouble with his breathing, as if there wasn't enough air in the room. As a result, he seemed edgy, slightly panicked.

"He charmed people, that's all I can say. He cast a spell, even on me for a while. I'd call him up for help on the provenance of a piece. Then he goes to the university and gets this international reputation. Everybody loves him. He's gone beyond us."

McNabb seemed petulant and cranky, a son left home in a small town, abandoned by his father. The strange quality about him was that he was waterlogged. Like something immersed in moisture for so long it became heavy, dank, unpliable. The pattern repeated itself: He talked and then at a certain point his throat constricted, he tried to clear it with a series of little coughs, his voice went low—and then he was breathless. In trying to get air he almost growled.

"He was spoiled by all the recognition he was getting. He was leaving behind the problem Indians, the troublesome genius, the Indian boy who's an alcoholic at fourteen. Austin didn't go for them any more. They didn't have the glamour he needed. Then his really big humiliation, the last lecture he gave. People just rolled their eyes." McNabb re-enacted the derision. "He turned everything into sex. He was out of control. Really—he was perverted."

I hadn't expected this. "How odd."

"You've got that right." He nodded slowly, as though there were depths to Hart's depravity he couldn't reveal.

"Can you explain more?"

"The hall was packed. Two thousand people. They had to open up an extra lecture theater, and those people didn't even see him on stage, just heard his voice piped in from next door. Still they stayed. Standing room only. He hadn't given a public lecture for a while, and there were rumors he'd made some big discovery. Everyone expected the inspirational man. Instead, Hart stood up there talking about pornography—in these iconic works of native art, for God's sake—'sexual fun' in a panel pipe. This guy, our hero, was out of it. People walked out, and he still talked on—about the necessity of 'unmasking the feminine.' Undressing was more what he was up to."

McNabb's own crudity now embarrassed him and silenced us. He was a little creepy. Once again he was on the verge of choking.

I noticed the clock was still at 10:07. It had stopped, as though a major element was resisting this conversation. It was such a large, obvious metaphor, yet like McNabb's breathlessness, it promised to disclose more than it delivered. I wondered if there was a duplicity here in which time itself was participating.

Even though I wondered if McNabb had the capacity to be an honest witness, I asked him to tell us about the exhibition of stone artifacts, where the twin masks had been reunited. I thought it might divert him, dry him out, deliver him from his grudges.

With a false note, he replied, "The pieces were interesting, but the show was boring." His breathing constricted. "He created a black market in native art."

I wanted to say: you'd dunk an angel into a crude oil slick.

Brett, however, was cheery. "How did he do that?"

"This is how. Although these pieces were mainly in museums, some were also in private collections. There are laws about buying and selling these objects and moving them out of the country; they belong where they are found. There was no known value to this work. Hart had to take out insurance on the pieces in the exhibit so a valuation was required. Reluctantly, we put figures on them. Austin gave the figures to the Museum of Civilization in Ottawa. They 'let it slip.' The dealers went after the private owners. They said, 'See what the museum says this is worth; we'll give you more.' Austin created a market. Pieces were bought and sold. That has had continuing repercussions."

"This wasn't his fault though." I didn't want to collude with him.

The telephone rang. McNabb swiveled around in his chair to answer it, his back to us. I looked at Brett with wide-eyed incredulity, but he shook his head, wanting me to behave.

McNabb called out, "Joe, phone." There was another person in the room behind the orange partition. I hadn't known he was there.

McNabb picked up his coffee cup and leaned towards us. "Where was I?" He seemed eager.

"Black market," I prompted. He was enjoying himself.

"Austin figured by possessing something like the Shawcroft Raven Rattle he could connect to its creator, find the answer to the meaning of this art and their way of life. Austin Hart was Shawcroft." Brett gave me a quick glance, making sure I noted the score. "But this is just bar talk. Who knows? With Shawcroft, his work was a last fierce flowering."

The phrase sounded thoughtful but worn out. McNabb had now said too much about almost everything. Coughing a little, he returned to Hart's obsession. "He was infatuated with women. You can tell, reading his notes. It's completely transparent. He always wanted to be with women. I think that's very strange, for a man."

McNabb may have read the journals just enough to turn a poetic inspiration into a salacious misdemeanor.

The person behind the partition leaned around the corner. "I'll be back at one o'clock." It was the native man who had nodded to me when we were in the foyer, a silent witness to everything we said. McNabb didn't acknowledge him.

I asked McNabb how he learned of Austin's death.

"I can't remember who called me. I thought, well it's part of the business. I know maybe four hundred people who have died. Ethnology is the business of death. The native elders, their knowledge, dying off every day."

For the first time he seemed thoughtful and not embittered.

"Sure, I admired what he'd done. Of course I've worried that we added to his existing distress, maybe pushed him over the edge. I led the crowd that walked out on him during his lecture. I've worried about the effect on him."

"Who was to know?" Brett was being comforting.

The shadowy presence of the native man led me to ask about the problems he had to resolve around hiring natives.

"It came to a head because of this Shawcroft business. Hart had collected the Raven Rattle when he went to Ninstints, but it wasn't properly catalogued as a Shawcroft, I don't know why, just one of those things. Then it went missing. It could have been missing for years, because we have thousands of acquisitions boxed up in the basement. I was doing some research on Shawcroft and went to get the rattle. Couldn't find it. I phoned Austin. I knew he'd be upset because this most prized possession, which he had acquired, had gone. He pointed out that it must have been an inside job because no one, other than people working at the museum would have known how valuable it was. There was an internal investigation. Like I said, it wasn't properly catalogued. We concluded probably one of the native artists we'd hired stole it—nothing was proven. Anyway, I fired him. It was his form of 'repatriation' of his people's artifacts. We now make sure the natives we get are artists, not militants who're gonna steal what the museum has paid for with taxpayers' money. Besides, the native communities can't look after these things. Look at the Ninstints poles. They'd be feeding termites, long gone, without Austin."

"Hart's absorption with Shawcroft, do you think that somehow led to his tragedy?" I asked.

"No, I wouldn't follow that lead. Some of us here have been working on a book about Shawcroft. It's legitimate."

"Austin was also working on a Shawcroft manuscript before he killed himself," I said. He must have known this. McNabb abruptly brought the meeting to a close.

"My book certainly isn't about Shawcroft's reincarnation." McNabb sounded annoyed. "That's all." He stood up. "Sorry. I have another appointment in my office in a few minutes. I don't suppose I've given you what you wanted."

Brett reassured him.

He walked us to the door, past "Vertebrates," "Invertebrates," past vacant rooms.

"Why are there so many empty offices?" I asked.

"Asbestos. The place has asbestos in the walls. We have to move."

I wondered if that was the source of McNabb's respiratory problem.

In one room there were two men working on a long table surrounded by cases filled with spears, knives, bows and arrows. I paused to look at what they were doing. McNabb explained, "We've discovered a lot of the weapons the aboriginals used for warfare, even hunting, have poison on the blades which is still active. We've had to get all this stuff out of storage and clean it. One of our staffers nearly died when he touched an arrow acquired fifty years ago."

He left us at the entrance. "Maybe we can talk another time when I'm not so pressured."

Outside was sunny. Brett had forgotten his hat and went back to retrieve it. I walked slowly toward the harbor where the boats bucked and jingled in their moorings, as though wanting to up and away.

I wasn't watching my step, and I stumbled on the pavement, nearly falling onto the grass. It seemed inviting, so I put down my jacket and sat to wait for Brett.

McNabb labored under some old affliction. It caused him to be vengeful in a resistant, indomitable way. A fire had gone out in him. There had been some active spark and flame and then a disappointment fixed deep inside him. Hart had let him down. I wondered how it had been for Jason, Hart's real son.

Brett returned without his hat. Despite McNabb's statement that he had a pressing meeting in his office, it was empty and locked.

We went to a restaurant down the street from the museum.

I opened my notebook.

"God, you've written a lot. You're most of the way through that book. All about this project? Trevor Crane didn't take any notes."

"Say it's a good sign." Yet McNabb's soggy, misbegotten portrait of Hart was a weight on both of us and what seemed to be our formidable task, to make sense of it all.

We ordered lunch but neither of us was hungry.

"I've been thinking about the native man we saw first in the reception area—Joe. I wonder what he will say about what he heard."

"Maybe he wasn't listening."

Brett and I parted, both gloomy and a little worse for wear.

AFTER I ARRIVED HOME that evening, the phone rang. To my surprise, it was the moribund Clarence McNabb but with an urgency to his voice. He apologized for calling so late.

"The theft of the Raven Rattle. There's a bit more to it."

I would have thought he'd choose Brett to talk to. "Okay."

He started slowly and built momentum. "Background. Austin hadn't been exactly forthcoming about giving over his files when he left the museum. Basically, he took everything with him, all the research he had done, everything—not one scrap remained. So we decided we could take him to court. I wrote him on the advice of our lawyers. The material belonged to the museum. Finally Austin sent me a letter and a few things, not much. I mean after he died there was more that came from him, but it was too late then, wasn't it? The point is that because I knew about Austin hoarding his research, I got to wonder if he knew more about where the Shawcroft was. I just showed up at his house one night. I'd confront him, right? I needed the Raven Rattle for my work." He seemed displeased he'd allowed his self-interest to protrude. "That wasn't the important thing. Anyway, Austin answered the door. I more or less accused him of taking the Shawcroft. He just stood there, looking at me. As soon as I said it, I knew I was off-base. He just stood there. I apologized and I left. This was maybe two weeks before his ending, so I'm bothered that maybe going there, suggesting such a thing, added to the stress and mess he was in. Like I didn't know anything about that at the time, but it's always been on my mind. I needed to tell someone. I guess I've wondered if I pushed him over the edge."

Although I'd figured McNabb wasn't trustworthy—and was suspicious he could be using this disclosure not to unburden himself but to continue to blotch Hart's reputation—I believed him. He had redeemed himself.

"Thanks for telling me. It took some gumption."

"Yeah, sure, no problem." He hung up.

I TELEPHONED BRETT. "McNabb just called."

"Hold on, I'm putting the kid to bed, hold on." I waited. "So what can I do for you?"

I particularly disliked that turn of phrase, as though he were a ticket-seller. "McNabb confronted Hart and accused him of stealing the Raven Rattle two weeks before he died."

Brett was eating an apple. "That's interesting. Anything to it?"

"He backed off, realizing he'd made a mistake. But he has worried the accusation may have put further strain on Hart, and that he's partly to blame for his death."

The sound of Brett's crunching apple was loud in my ear. Then he stopped chewing. "Maybe we could use this."

"What do you mean?"

"Have a scene where Hart steals the rattle. It would add a dramatic element."

"That would be—a little irresponsible of us, don't you think?"

"Just a thought." He resumed chewing. "It sounds to me as if it has possibilities. You'll have to struggle with that one."

"Paige would really be upset if she knew about this. We didn't really defend Austin in the meeting."

"If we had, we wouldn't have gotten this part of the story."

16

STRINGS TOO SHORT FOR SAVING

I called Sophia early Saturday morning and explained that her visit to Pine Street would have to be delayed until Sunday because I was going to see Austin's sister, Candice Setter. Mother didn't believe this appointment was necessary that day. She threatened to go home by herself until I finally promised to pick her up later in the evening after my meeting.

Candice lived in a large house in West Vancouver, overlooking English Bay and the Lion's Gate Bridge. The view was distracting, almost alarming, as we were perched on a ledge cantilevered from the mountain, ungrounded in the vast expanse of sky, city and water below us.

She still blamed herself.

"I'm selfish. I knew everything about him, because we were so close. So why didn't I know he was planning this? I could have stepped in? I have my own family—that's my focus. The worst thing is that now he can't come over to my house. I can't call him on the phone. He used to ring up and say 'hi, sis.' He called me 'sis.' He always wanted to know about me and my family, interested you know. He always said 'keep in touch, won't you.' How can I? Why did he do it, do you know?"

"I'm sorry. Not yet."

"The previous person—what was his name—the writer before you? He seemed to dwell on the fact that our father had two shots of rum when he came home from work, maybe more. Maybe he got drunk every night, I don't know. Still it's odd, this preoccupation with how much anyone has to drink."

Despite the seriousness of the discussion, there was a quality about her which seemed on the verge of doing something naughty in a very ordinary way.

"I suppose when I was growing up, our family wasn't any worse than others. But I really wanted to get out as soon as I could. So I got married. Austin felt the same, but he eventually went to college. His idea was better. Whenever I complained to Austin about our father, he would always say 'well, he was a good provider.' He was, even though we didn't have much money. I was bound to marry a good provider. Bill was that."

There was lack of immediacy, a pastness about her husband. Even though it was late afternoon, I never expected he might come home from work. I found myself considering the possibility she was a widow. Finally she said, "Well, Bill will know that. Maybe ask him. He probably wouldn't talk though, unlike me. Paige wants me to tell you about Austin, like I did with that other writer. I would have anyway, without her asking. She thinks this opera is going to fix us up. Paige was a strange, intense child. Not unpleasant looking, you know—you've met her. Just strange, probably because of those clothes she wears, oh well. She has on scarves even in the summer, like she can't get warm." She veered away from the subject. "We found out that Austin went on a binge of buying up native art the day he died. You've probably heard this already?"

I hadn't, but she didn't seem to need confirmation one way or the other.

"Paige is living off the avails, selling the native art my brother collected, mostly on that last day. Anyway, I mean she has to benefit somehow, right? The family decided she should have all the art, being the neediest one and all. Nobody else wanted it, to be honest. It would have been like wanting to keep the gun. I won't say anything more about that. Now you, you're an artist. I like artistic people. So did Austin. You know this already, that he carved masks in the native style. Some of them were pretty good, at least I thought so. He wanted to be an artist when he was younger. Probably he could have made it if he'd developed his own techniques. If I was going to be an artist I would write, but it's too late now. I'm too disorganized."

I asked her if she had any of the masks Austin made.

"Oh, no, Paige kept them all. I guess I shouldn't tell you that. Oh well. I can't help but tell the truth about Austin. Some of the family don't like that. My nephew, he was only 10, and he wanted to know what had happened to his Uncle Austin, why did he die. I said he'd taken his own life. My brother-in-law—this is on Bill's side of the family because—well you know this—there was only Austin and I—so the boy's father was very upset. I am always getting into trouble."

I asked her if she'd tell me about Mary-Anne's relationship with Austin, especially because no one else seemed to want to.

"Oh, good, I hoped you'd ask. The other writer didn't. So there's a letter—the children must never know about this. Mary-Anne wrote to me before they got married. Her handwriting was uneven so I figured she was writing it during a rough ride. She didn't think it'd be a good idea for her to marry Austin. We were friends, you know—do you know this? I introduced her to Austin. Anyway, in the letter she said that—I remember exactly, that she didn't think they should get married. I figured I knew why." She looked around to see if anyone else might be listening. I imagined her doing this even when she was alone, talking out loud to herself. "You see, there was someone before Mary-Anne."

"A girlfriend? Someone important—"

"Oh, yes. I knew about the woman but never met her. Something bad happened, I'm not quite sure what. I think she must have been pregnant and miscarried, or died or something. Whatever. Austin was pretty backed up about it for a long time and then wouldn't talk. I guess Mary-Anne figured he wasn't over this other one, so she had doubts. It would upset the children if they knew about the letter. I destroyed it only a few weeks ago, after twenty-four years. I don't know why I kept it, and I don't know why I destroyed it only last week, or the week before, I'm not sure."

"Do you think they ought not to have married—that in some way their lack of companionship was a cause of his distress and suicide?"

"No, I don't think that."

"I was wondering, because of the letter she sent you, and the previous—"

"Oh, no, you're exaggerating now. You're taking it beyond what I meant. You'd better forget this part. Anyway, Mary-Anne—she had asthma, you know, difficulty breathing. But it was only in the springtime for a few months. She loved the summers. So did I."

I wondered about the complexities of a household where not being able to breathe properly for a few months could be prefaced by "only."

"How is it that no one talks about her much?"

"No, they wouldn't."

"She seems omitted from the story."

Candice looked perplexed, not understanding what I meant. "What story is that now?"

"I just mean—I keep wondering why you're the only person who knows about her."

"They separated—well, she left him—when the children were still young, nine and eleven. She came back into the family though, later on—sort of. Well, not really. I don't know. This opera. I'm not sure. Will it stir up the family, do you think? You know I remember getting a call from Mary-Anne, now this is really going back. So it's before they split up. Some things stay in your mind, especially on the telephone because people are talking right into your ear. She says, 'I have to get out of town.' Just like a cowboy says in a western when there's trouble, like the sheriff is after him. So I asked her. She and Austin had been out somewhere the night before, at a restaurant with other people. She found herself saying, out loud, 'I gotta get out of town.' Then she said, 'No one was listening, not even me.' I don't know what that was about. Anyway, the two of them had a tough time loving one another on this earth. But there really isn't any other place to do it is there? Like with Bill, even if our relationship isn't going well—and I'm not saying that—I would never leave him."

It was as if her bag of marbles had spilled and she tried to gather them up.

"Our father was an electrician. His father, our grandfather, wanted to travel around the world, but he ended up just being a boat-builder. I mean, he was a very good one, in Liverpool. Why am I telling you all of this? I guess because you're a nice listener. They're hard to come by. Dad didn't believe in medical intervention. He didn't even believe we should be inoculated. I guess the worst intervention is to take your own life." She paused for a moment, claiming something rolling away on her. "Of course Austin's death is not related to our father. Strange though. Our Dad didn't really want us kids to do better than him, you know how some parents are, it's a kind of stinginess, as if kids doing better is like spending the family fortune. Austin felt he'd let Dad down by not becoming an electrician. But he was the only one in the family who was ever famous. How could you be famous as an electrician? Dad thought Austin should know how to fix things, cars, machines, but Austin'd rather whittle away on a stick. He did love cars though, foreign ones, expensive. He just didn't know how to fix them. Even when Austin made it, Dad didn't think anthropology was a real profession, nothing you should be able to make money at. He used to say—Dad that is—that we had to take responsibility for our actions. 'You weren't born with a silver spoon in your mouth.' He'd look at Austin meaning it especially for him. Dad could be pretty sour, like he wouldn't allow us to play cards or anything like that, God knows why. I think he was sort of hoping Austin would fail. I shouldn't tell you this. Austin didn't fail. Until the end, if you consider his death was a failure. I suppose it was, although I don't want it to be. I'm pretty sure Austin wouldn't have done it if Dad had still been alive. Austin would have stuck to the order, like parents die first. He would have thought it created a paradox otherwise, or something. He was always noticing paradoxes." Despite being entirely ditzy, she was adept at scrabbling her scattering thoughts back into the bag. "When our mother died we found in her kitchen drawer a box labelled 'strings too short for saving,' and it was a box full of strings. He said to me, like he finally had the right example, 'this is a paradox.'"

I asked if she had a picture of Austin when he was young. She went to the hall and removed a framed family portrait from the wall. She held it in front of her. "Look at this, don't we all seem normal, proper?" implying that they weren't.

She named her relatives and pointed to herself, a little girl of perhaps 8 years old. "And here's Austin right there beside me." She put her fore-finger on the glass of his face, where it had been smudged before. Nothing in the bright, confident photograph of him could unpack the future that he chose. She placed it carefully on the couch beside her. "You know Austin left a note for some people but didn't leave one for me. That will always bother me."

"I'm not sure anyone received a note."

"They didn't? Really? I don't know if I feel better about that or worse." She got up. "I guess that's all I can help you with for now. I'm a little tired."

I thanked her and she showed me to the door. I stood at the top of the outside stairs "You know before he left—he was so thoughtful—he made sure that his car was serviced; he renewed the house insurance. He even had the gutters cleaned. Funny, eh?"

"A defiant paradox."

"Anyway, the only thing I worry about is Mary-Anne's letter. I wish I could wipe out that part that I told you. The children must not know. Austin loved his children, and he loved Mary-Anne, too."

I had more access to Austin's past than to my own. I asked if I could come and see her again. I hadn't quite gained her confidence.

She was closing the door. "Me? Sure, I guess. I guess so."

WHEN I RETURNED to Pine Street, three dozen roses blocked my way into the house, all dressed up and nowhere to go. Richard had commenced a floral assault. "See you in a few days" was written on the card.

17

HOW I ALMOST KILLED MY MOTHER

Mary-Anne [to Austin]:
This maul must grind food
not your soul–
It must grind nourishment
not your life–
not your family.

Alix's Lines for the Libretto

I had taken two boards from the garage and placed them down the front steps to form a ramp so that I could wheel Sophia into the house.

On the way to Pine Street, she fell asleep in the specially equipped taxi. When we arrived, she nevertheless insisted I immediately take her into the back garden. As I pushed her through the living-room, on the way to the solarium, I saw that I'd forgotten to hide the roses from Richard which were beside the couch. I pointed Sophia towards the library and, chattering about spider-webs and dusting, I quickly picked up the enormous vase in both hands, whirled like a dervish searching for enlightenment, and finally put them in the fireplace.

The water in the pond, filled with lilies, circulated over the rocks and comforted her. While she was staring out at the garden, and nodding her head as if to some inner conversation, I went into the kitchen, bruised a lemon, and from the liquor trolley in the solarium, poured her a drink from the half full bottle of Hendricks gin. Just a little tonic, the way she liked it. I had a scotch on the rocks, my first hard liquor since I'd come back to Vancouver.

She quizzed me about Candice, correctly guessing that she was a few years younger than her brother and not academically-minded. Although stingy in sharing her perceptions, Sophia had always been intuitive; recently she seemed to have developed a long-range receiver.

She then started planning changes to the location of most of the bushes and flowers in front of us. "I'm so glad you brought me those tulips. I'd forgotten how silken The Queen of the Night is. We'll plant them together. That will help you."

"Help me?"

"Be more interested in flowers. A grouping of them will go nicely over there. It will fit like a hand in a dove, just as I'd figured when I was thinking about it at Styx."

I couldn't resist. "Is the dove alive or dead?"

"What are you talking about?" She looked at me scornfully without turning her head, her big and wide right eye, magnified by her new thick glasses, was like a horse's eye from the perspective of an uncertain rider.

"You said 'a hand in a dove.'"

"Hand in a dove...Hand in a...how does that go?"

"Glove. Hand in a glove. You seem to be succumbing to the malaprop."

"Is malaprop a noun? Isn't the noun 'malapropism'? How about another drink to clear my pate." She actually winked at me, an odd gesture at the best of times.

"Drinking is going to mess with your medication. You shouldn't have any more."

"Alicia, I'm old. Who cares? Another drink."

I did her bidding, for both of us.

"My garden seems dim. Is it the failing light?"

"Your books say it improves a garden by planting flowers that blur it, make it impressionistic. Umbel-like flowers can do this."

"Don't patronize me, Alix, especially using the bits of things you've skimmed from my library."

This was the mother I recognized: curt, excluding, unkind. I stood up.

"Don't leave." She was somewhat panicked. "I'm sorry. You always leave."

"I'm going to turn on the garden lights."

"No, you aren't. They'll come on automatically."

"All right then, I'm going to get a wrap for both of us."

When I returned and put a shawl around her, Sophia immediately launched into a lesson on the history of tulips.

"Do you know that in the 1600s in Holland, one bulb of some of the prized species was worth something like $160,000 each—each—in current Canadian money. One poor sod sold his family owned brewery for a single bulb. But the flowers had a trick. They could 'break'—that's what it's called—so a red tulip might come out the next spring with the petals feathered and flamed into really intricate patterns. White and red. You know what causes this?"

"I haven't read deeply into tulips." I didn't want to be as abrasive as my scotch, so I smiled, a hesitant smile.

"A virus spread by aphids." She was triumphant. "People are avaricious. The virus is the joker in the tulip bed."

"Like a mistake. Claire, Austin's friend, said the world begins because of a mistake. Generally caused by Raven."

Sophia was mainly intent on her tulip lesson. "Hold on to that, we'll come back to your idea." I nursed my drink. "So once the bulb has broken it remains broken and the—what are they called—right, the offsets have the same characteristics. But the virus gimps the bulb so the offsets are not so vigorous."

"Like marrying for money gimps the children." The liquor had gone directly to my brain, by-passing discretion.

She heard my step on the out-of-bounds creak. "Marrying for money?"

I directed her back to the virus in tulips.

"Well, the virus partly suppresses the laid-on color of a tulip, so the underlying color, which is always white or yellow, shows through. The contrasting red or purple of a broken tulip looks as though it has been painted on the petals—with a fine brush. You saw that, didn't you, when the tulips were in bloom while I was in that so-called home?"

"I wish I had." I was making up to her.

"The best aphid is the peach potato aphid. Are you interested in this, or am I talking to myself? Now that I think of it, I don't know what a peach potato is, but we'll have to get some. Maybe we can eat them while the aphids do their trick. Imagine, it's a plant disease which increases the value of the infected plant." Unexpectedly she then said, "What's the daughter like again?"

Sophia was skittishly preoccupied with the Hart family, using my work as a distraction. "She's very intense, perceptive, a little impatient."

"A little like you, I think."

"Am I impatient?"

"With you I'd have to add clever, very clever." If a mother could flirt with a daughter, she was flirting with me. For her next drink I'd add more tonic.

As a non-sequitur I said, "I did support her in what she was saying to Brett about reincarnation."

"Reincarnation? Is she in favor or opposed?"

I laughed. "It's not like a plebiscite. Brett thinks Austin believed he was the reincarnation of a native carver who lived in Haida Gwaii at the turn of the century."

"Oh, I doubt Austin believed that," she said knowingly. "If he did, he'd have killed two people, right, in killing himself? Maybe it was a mistake, maybe he was just cleaning his gun. I don't like to think he'd kill himself." She withdrew a little from her caring and her bold conjecture.

"He called the campus police and said, 'This is Austin Hart. You can come and get me now.'"

"Oh, I see. Pretty definite." She'd had enough of that subject. "Peg's going to call," she declared.

"Peg? But she's still off-shore, in the Solomon Islands."

"I just think she'll call. In the meantime—" She held up her glass.

When I returned, she was ready with another question about Austin Hart. "You're my scout. I can't go out into the world so I have to send you. Did he have any love interests?" It was a quaint inquiry, like a guidance counselor's.

At which point, as though on cue, the phone rang.

"That'll be Peg." Sophia said. And it was. I brought the telephone outside and talked to her in front of my mother, to keep me honest and to keep Mother from jealousy or paranoia. When I handed the phone to Sophia, she immediately started to cry. It was the first time, since her hospitalization, she had cried. Her tears started mine.

"Now, Peg, I'm going to pull myself together." She squared her shoulders and the shawl fell away. "There, fine, I'm fine. Tears are not good for the skin. You pull yourself together too, and Alix. No, dear, you don't have to come home just yet. Where the hell are you anyway? Vanawatu? That sounds Norse. I saw a film—oh never mind. Will it be in the atlas? No, I'm really pretty good. The other night at this place Alix put me in—it used to be a stately, old home but it's gone to rack and ruin, needs a lick of paint—a few licks. Anyway, I woke up and looked at the digital clock near my bed—I must look at it a dozen times a night—and it was flashing 12-12-12. I got onto my walker—no, I just use it sometimes—anyway, every clock in the joint was flashing 12-12-12. I thought my time was up. Taken at the midnight hour. Yes, exactly. The power had gone out and then come on again. Anyway, your sister and I are into the booze. She has to pour me another. We're not on our lips yet, but they're flapping. Goodnight, dear heart. Alicia will tell you my number at the mansion. I'll give you back to Alix. Yes, darling, I love you too. Don't start, I've had enough of crying. All right, here's Alix."

When I'd hung up, Mother said, "This is fun. I wish someone else would call."

"Why did you think Peg would phone? Was that intuition or hope?"

"Intuition I guess. It's sort of in the family, but about pretty useless things. Never did anyone much good. Women have stronger intuition than men because they have to be able to understand what someone is saying who can't speak. I mean their child. Come on, Alix, you know about this."

"I suppose. I seem to know when something is broken."

"You see?" I looked at her askance. "You're so pretty. I should have told you that long ago. But you could change your hair-style, grow out your bangs so you can pull your hair off your face."

"Ever the mixed blessing."

"No, don't—don't be annoyed. I'm going to encourage you now. I have to make up for lost time. You're like the opening and closing of a night-flower."

"Mother?"

"Night flowers are used as the middle note in perfume."

"No more gin for you."

"You're no fun. Broken—tell me about that. You know when something is broken?"

She was still tracking. "Once when I was getting on a plane, going to a publishing meeting in Montreal—the color drained away from everything. I knew there was something wrong with the plane. I got on-board and sat there, waiting. We took off. In six minutes the pilot came over the loudspeaker and said the landing wheels wouldn't retract so we were going back to the airport. The odd thing to me was, with such certainty, why did I get on the plane?" I realized this was also what had happened with the Potato Eaters, when the room drained of color—that grim gathering foretelling some breakage in me.

"Oh, you must always get on the plane," Sophia said.

"Why? That's nuts."

"It's your duty, part of your work."

"What if it had crashed?"

"Never mind. You did the right thing."

Her cock-eyed ethics was to fulfill a duty even unto death. "Sophia, I'm exhausted, you must be too. We really have to go to bed."

"It would work, wouldn't it, for us to live here together? We wouldn't fight, I promise."

"We'll see how you do."

Dogs were barking two doors down. "Why do they do that every night? I'm in your yard, near your house. I never see them; I never see their owners. It unnerves me."

"They're just city dogs."

I took her by the arm and, with difficulty, she climbed the stairs to the second floor. She wanted to take a bath, but I reminded her that the tub wasn't outfitted with support bars as it was at the mansion; we didn't even have a non-slip rubber mat. Sophia simply said that I could help her, that I would be her safety net. While she undressed, I ran the water and put in drops of essence of bergamot which I found in her medicine chest. The scent roused me from my alcoholic dullness.

She stood in the doorway, her bare feet on the tiled floor.

I had no memory of ever having seen my mother naked. The skin on her neck pleated down to the drooping sacks of her breasts. I came from that body. I hadn't considered that before. Had she nursed me or my sister when we were babies? I never thought to ask. Her dark nipples were erect because she was cold. She had no hair covering her pudendum; she was pre-pubescent, shorn and—naked wasn't a strong enough word to describe her state. Was this part of her illness that she had lost her pubic hair? I was born from that body, from between her legs.

She had been caught by the unflinching cruelty of a Diane Arbus camera.

What could I do to save her from this?

"Let me bring your dressing gown."

"What for? I'm getting into the bath." She moved forward, shuffling, and her legs were so thin, lacking any muscle, that it seemed impossible they could carry her. She held on to the side of the bathtub, leaned over and felt the water. The vertebrae protruded on her back. She was already skeletal. When she stood up, she turned to me. "Alicia, are you a prude? This is what I look like now."

I'd spoken not so much out of prudery but of prurience. I was awkward and guilt-ridden and I couldn't stop looking. I saw my future.

My eyes were like houseflies circling around her. Yet, I wanted to hide from the sagging crepe paper thinness of the skin on her arms. As though some issue of morality and rectitude were joined, I blamed her for standing there and being so old. People should never be seen this way, even if they don't mind. Her beautiful head, her thick auburn hair, did not belong to this body whose skin had started to melt.

"Get me into the tub."

WHEN SHE GOT OUT of the bath I covered her with a large white towel, helped her into her night-gown and then into bed. I had changed her sheets.

For the first time since Russell's funeral ten years ago, I was going to sleep in the room of my childhood, reclaiming a botched past where I hadn't belonged in the world. I took a sleeping pill.

The next morning, as we got ready to leave, Sophia said unexpectedly, "Don't keep your new family from me, okay?"

"Okay." I wondered what jealousy I had inadvertently kindled to fork out her affection.

As I took Sophia to the top of the steps, I carefully tipped the wheelchair on to the planks. The rake of the boards was too steep, and I had to use all my strength to hold her back. The rubber grips came off in my hands; she sped down the ramp and at the turn of the sidewalk careened onto the grass. I shrieked—I didn't want to lose her through negligence—and ran. The chair rocked but she didn't fall out.

She looked up at me with a crooked smile. "I sure wouldn't want to try that again."

18

WHAT A DUTY HE ASSUMED

The Lover [To Hart]:
I came to say you should have left the poles.
Hart:
They should not have been salvaged?
The Lover:
Salvation does not have such a stunting purpose.
They should never have been taken.

Alix's Lines for the Libretto

I slammed awake, as though hit by the bead from a sling-shot. All around me, the beating of helicopter wings, a voice yelling, "You're not going to come out in one piece," whipping my brain apart. "You're not going to come out in one piece."

Trevor Crane's warning, coming through my hypnagogic state, clinched my resolve to get someone to help me. I phoned Claire for advice, and she gave me the number for Miles George. He was a friend of hers, a chief in the Coast Salish Nation, and he taught medicine at the university. He had also known Austin Hart.

THE PRODUCER MUST HAVE received a call from his banker, because he was suddenly aroused from some apathy of the rich and wanted to get together with me "right away" about my progress on the libretto. "I've been writing a lot of checks." I hijacked his agenda and suggested we meet Miles George with a view to bringing him into the project as a consultant. "More checks?" was his closing riposte.

I arrived at Le Mistral restaurant a little late; they were already together at a table near the window. Sitting next to the robust and unassuming nobility of Miles George, the Producer seemed wan and diminished. The Producer's breath would seize up in weather made just for Miles.

"People go through an enormous struggle before they decide to commit suicide," Miles was saying to the Producer. Urging him to continue, I sat down. "Once they have decided, then it is as though they are pulled in to it. Suicides give in to something that is luring them—the not-being."

The Producer, eager to speak, was always on the verge of interrupting Miles. He finally took over. "This opera is bigger than all of us. It will happen even without us. It must." He seemed to think there was something inevitable about it, nothing depending on how well or poorly we behaved or wrote or composed.

I reminded him that the demands of the story also meant that it could easily go wrong. "Of course," he said, "I am always thinking of the responsibility I have."

There was a lull.

Miles continued. "My son has tried to commit suicide and my wife as well. There are always so many deaths on the reserves, the families are swilling in grief. Each one is like Hart's but there's a whole village of them. If you disconnect from your community or your family, you try to reconnect with something else. I think that's what Austin Hart did. He worked with my people in the early days. We have stories about him. I met him a few times. Through this opera there's a chance his death won't just be like any other."

I felt enlivened by the ease of Miles's wisdom and his self-disclosure. The Producer seem to be waiting for an opportunity to interject.

Miles talked of what it was like for him to live in a spirited world, to see things in the every day which others didn't see: to be influenced by something that has no regard for the distinctions between the living and the dead, the animate and inanimate. "Austin was in these realms. It must have been so difficult for him to be surrounded by people who didn't really understand him." The Producer was jovial, inclusive, laughing, saying oh yes I feel that, too, every day I do, laughing.

The Producer had to be off to another meeting. "Alix, the libretto, coming along well?" There was still food on the table when we left.

As we walked across the street, Miles touched my arm. "The Producer upsets you."

"Oh, dear. Is it so obvious?"

"He reminds me of the kind of white man who marries a native woman and comes to live on reserve. He's only really comfortable in himself when he's with us, because he thinks he's superior."

I sat in Miles's car. Although it was still summer, fall-time was pending in the air.

"When you walk into a room, people notice you, Alix. You don't realize it, and that's attractive, a little the way Austin was." I'd never heard such a thing before, yet when he said it, I believed what he said, not as a flattery but as a description.

"This is important work you're doing. There are a few things you need to know. One is understanding what it's like to be dominated by another culture. When the settlers came into our territory, we called them *kamina* which means 'people who are hungry' or 'people who need to be fed.' They didn't have any food or really have the technology to acquire it, so we fed them. Eventually, they took us over. It used to be that my wife would never speak her native language unless she was drunk because she was told by the priests that our language was from the devil. Whenever a white woman walks into a room, she said, whether a friend or not, she feels diminished. Eventually, you see, as a people we lost our ability to even speak about ourselves in an articulate way, especially to those who had power: the Indian agent, the school teacher, the judge who sits on land claims cases. The anthropologists have tried to do that for us. They're always taking someone's stories and reinterpreting them, speaking for someone's grandmother. We wanted them to do that. But it's easy for the anthropologist to become a usurper. There's also a danger of inflation because people tell you their secrets—you get to know things no one else knows. Do you understand?"

"You're talking about my work on this opera as well."

"Yes."

"Okay. I see."

"Hart came into my community. He cut straight into the middle of things. My people had been missionized—but they really didn't believe in anything any more. Here's this outsider in our midst, wanting to know about us, full of belief in what we are about. What a duty he assumed when he re-awakened our hope. Unlike the Producer, Hart was uncomfortable with the native people and that was a plus; it drew us to him, his discomfort. Because he didn't know his place—he had to earn his place. I figured he felt the same way in his own family. We were his family."

"He was trying to learn from you."

"Yes. To choose to enter another's culture—whether it's Austin or you—you have to leave part of yourself. He went a long way in. Anthropology is really an impossible profession because if you do it in good faith, you end up with people's souls. When you learn someone's secrets with a promise that you'll explain them so others can understand—your promise is to try to make sense of people's lives, and all they have lost. To go away, as he did, with important parts of what he'd learned still unwritten, unsaid, unfinished, it was a promise broken. You become a kind of thief."

"How did he let that happen?"

"He isolated himself. Extraordinary things have a way of working themselves out in ordinary ways, if you let them, so they belong to everyone. Right away when I first met him, I knew he was somewhat fearful because he trembled all the time. It was okay to show that. But the kind of fear Austin needed had to open him up. Something happened to prevent that. That's also the courage you'll need for this story, you know—exactly the courage that failed him."

"I don't really get this."

"No, that's why I'm here."

"Will you help me"

"I am. Some people, desiring enlightenment, think they need to go beyond the material world, get rid of it, transcend. The material isn't different from the spiritual realm. You'll have to experience what I mean. It's not just that the spiritual is engaged with the material but that the two can never be separated. This is why people collect things, because the spirit is incarnated in the physical. But it can become a fetish, and then it will get the better of them. Austin had an inkling of this. He wanted to gather works of art so that others could see god booming down into the physical. Something happened to him which is still a mystery. It's for you to resolve. You need to come to the longhouse, where the spirit dancing takes place. Austin used to attend them. I'm a dancer. Even though the society is now closed to outsiders, I'll arrange it. Then you'll be able to understand more what I'm talking about."

It was agreed.

19

IT'S BREAD

A deer offers himself to the hunter
is shot, is skinned, is scraped
becomes a hide
becomes a shield
stretched tight across a frame.
Becomes a drum.

Alix's Lines for the Libretto

I waited for Miles George at the Plaza International Hotel, North Vancouver, 7:30 at night. Men in tuxedos emerged from the cabs. They escorted women in long black dresses. Outside the restaurant there was "Private Party" marked on an easel beside a table with a large bouquet of assorted flowers.

As I sat on a couch in the foyer a mirror caught my image; my face looked flattened out, in a fish tank. A man came towards me, smiled as though I could be waiting for him, and sat on a chair beside the couch.

I got up and went into the parking lot.

"Excuse me." The cab-driver didn't respond. "Excuse me." I tapped on the glass. He rolled down the window. "Could you tell me the time?"

"Eight o'clock." He began to roll it back up.

"Do you know where the Capilano Longhouse is?"

"Hmm?"

"The Capilano Longhouse?"

He turned his head. "Down the road there about 500 yards." He pointed into the dark.

Then Miles pulled up in a large, red Buick which looked freshly washed. Beads of water were crystallizing on the back window. I got into the backseat.

"You had to wait," Miles said.

He introduced me to his wife, Ruby, who was sitting in the front seat. Her face was wide open, and shiny as a penny. "I know you already," she said, "from what Miles told me."

It was nice to be known already.

The noise from the hotel faded. I leaned back as the car descended the hill, and a real hopefulness nestled in with the comfortable silence.

We advanced into night. Miles turned onto a gravel road and in through a gate. Cars were parked at all angles around a long, low barn-like building which had no windows and didn't seem to have an entrance. The tires slumped in the mud. I couldn't see the hotel from here.

As we got out native women passed us, carrying things. I heard drums.

I had been staring at the building and, so unexpectedly, my courage edged backwards. "Don't be afraid," Miles said. Smoke was coming from the roof and drifting up the hill. "Come with me."

My foot slipped as I walked.

Part of the outside wall was really a wooden screen behind which was a cubicle, and the cubicle led into a massive space. Three open fires, twenty feet apart, were burning inside the building. A man carrying a four foot log across the earth floor heaved it onto the closest fire. The fire breathed and the current of sparks streamed into the high, charred rafters. There was a hole in the roof above each fire.

The sparks blackened like stars put out before reaching heaven.

Twelve drummers, wearing jeans and short-sleeved shirts, were beating batons against skins of animals taut across wooden frames.

Miles touched my arm. "Over there." He pointed to the rows of bleachers rising almost to the top of the walls. Ruby lay a blanket on the second row, towards the middle, and I sat there. I was the foreigner in their midst, being looked at by hundreds of people.

The building was long enough to contain the fires and wide enough so that from one side I couldn't make out the faces of the people on the other.

The only light was from the fires, and the only sound was from the drums. The native people moved slowly on soft earth.

Opposite the entrance and high in the bleachers, I made out three enclosures created by hanging blankets, open at the front. In each sat a figure holding a long staff. They were heavily cloaked, and their feet seemed to be covered in thick cloth. They shivered now and then with a rattling sound. More drummers came from somewhere and stood around the fires.

"Those are the new dancers." Ruby pointed to the figures rocking back and forth in the three stalls. "Each one has two helpers with them day and night for three months during the initiation. They look after the new ones. Gradually they help bring out their spirit dance and their song. They learn it once it's out, so then everyone knows it."

Sounds issued from the new dancers like birds weaving between the drumbeats in the air, getting caught in the sparks and swirling up to the rafters.

"They are crying?" I was sitting between Miles and Ruby; my voice sounded childlike.

"It's their spirits starting," Miles said. Two-toned cries slipped out of their throats.

"Are they calling to one another?"

He shook his head.

The men at the fires had black bands painted across their eyes and foreheads, but otherwise they were unadorned.

"Does the smoke bother you?" Miles asked. "It will stay in your clothes and in your hair for days. It might hurt your eyes."

I followed the sparks from one of the fires up to the roof where a young man was standing on the rafters. He had a hose in his hand. A fine mist of water combed the air even as some sparks escaped through the hole.

Someone was now at the center fire holding a shorter staff with a cluster of bell-shaped objects near the top.

"That's Walker Andrew," Miles said. "He's the elder of the longhouse. He's going to call the witnesses."

"What's on his staff?"

"Deer hooves."

The long staffs being held by the new dancers also had deer hooves clustered at the ends. When the dancers breathed, the hooves rattled.

The elder was talking to the crowd, speaking in Halkomelem, the native language of the Coast Salish. As he called out, people moved down from the benches, drawn by the incantation of his voice. When they reached the fires the men with black painted faces placed something in their hands.

"The witnesses are given money to remember what happens tonight. Other people will also be paid, the ones who gave something a long time ago. They will be paid back with more this time. We mark everything down so it lasts."

The song-filled sighs from the new dancers went back and forth above the elder's speaking. Miles went down onto the floor, talked to someone, and I followed the message from one person to another until it was lost behind a fire. I was warm in my trench coat.

Walker Andrew came towards us; the sound of the drums followed him like lights.

"Alicia Purcell," he intoned in an orator's voice, "Alicia Purcell I am calling you to witness this work."

I thought it was a mistake, my name being called, but Miles

was motioning to me from the floor. I removed my coat and went down. I just wanted to be an observer.

As I walked towards the elder, I could feel a force around him of astonishing magnitude, like the wing-wind of my dream but calmer, not generated by movement but simply his presence. Four feet from him, I hit a wall. But I wouldn't stop. I pressed forward and arrived inside his orbit. I was expanded in the crescendo of his wide, numinous self. It was like nothing I had ever known.

He spoke to the crowd. "We are opening this house now for the work that needs to be done tonight. There are some people who don't understand our ways and because they don't understand they try and stop what we are doing. Now we have someone here who might help us, because she is going to try to know what she sees. They won't be able to stop us. What we do helps our people when they are sick, when they are almost finished and no one else can help them the Indian dancing helps them. Now I want to thank this writer. I want to thank Alicia Purcell for being here to see the work we have to do tonight."

I was immobile. A man came over to me and shook my hand. He left four quarters in my sweating palm.

"That's all," the elder said quietly. He touched my shoulder, propelling me back to my place.

All the witnesses had heard my name, had heard that I would help. I had been thanked and paid.

As I sat down in the bleacher beside Miles, he must have noticed how razed I felt. "Keep watching. Stay with us." By motion of his head, he indicated the man who had given me the witness quarters. "He's the husband of the dancer who died last winter when she was being initiated into the longhouse. He is Stanley Joe. There was a coroner's inquest. Maybe the spirit dancing would be outlawed again. I instructed a lawyer." Miles was speaking above the current of noise from the fires and the clattering of deer hooves. "This time we could defend ourselves."

The drums increased. More people were gathering at the far end of the floor. My face felt furrowed and dry, my eyes smarting from the haze of smoke surrounding us.

"Over there is our son," Ruby said. "He's been dancing for two seasons." Her voice seemed disembodied, talking to me from just behind my right shoulder, or above it.

"Why is his face painted red when all the rest are black?"

"Because of his spirit. Spirits have different colors."

The sound of these drums—what was it like? The words of my thoughts were flat and punctured compared to the expanded dimension of this scene, which was in a frequency of sight and sound I had never known before. The percussion vibrated into the wooden planks of the bleachers on which I sat and on which my feet rested. They vibrated through my bones. What was this like?

There was no hunt, no urgency or desire. It was not a rhythm calling human limbs to move. It was pounding a certainty not an insistence. It didn't call death or anything newly created. It was a perfectly timed explosion which had already occurred.

Austin Hart had been here. He'd held Paige on his lap as she fell asleep.

How could anything not break under the weight of this drumming? How could any concussion repeat itself, surviving the last, without splitting up? I was being altered cell by cell. The sound did not come out of darkness or invite into darkness, or light. Opposites had nothing to do with it. It endured.

A man sitting on the lowest bench was rocking back and forth, the deer hooves of his staff rattling with the pulse of his movements. He was propelled to his feet. Men gathered around him, drumming and singing. He crouched over, legs apart, and went in long rapid strides down one side of the longhouse. The drummers lagged behind. Once he was beside the fire, he turned and, crouching again, was stopped by something. The thing that was in him vibrated, but he couldn't move.

"Something's wrong." Even Miles was disturbed.

The dancer limped back to where he began and, with the drumming starting his song, his huge strides took him in an instant past every fire. Then he was stopped. He didn't get it right. He was left shaking and inconsolable in the midst of the other dancers.

The first of initiates, startled as out of a sleep by the women around her singing her song, was brought down from the bleachers, an elder on either side of her. With tiny steps she began to go around the fires, pausing every now and then, taking small steps in one place, then forward again, her hands making narrow circles away from her body and back. Her movements seemed mostly internal.

This was as much of a dance as silence was a song, and her song was an agony up and down her spine, in her feet that seemed to ache with the excruciating detail of her almost stillness. She swayed. She was surrounded, protected, watched by the women. As she passed, older women came down from the bleachers and followed in behind her on the floor. They raised their arms in a celebratory gesture, and their hands vibrated like the leaves on a tree animated by the breeze.

She was learning to walk. Everything had to be done from the beginning. She came near me. I was afraid.

I wanted something ornamental only, a quiet ritual in a dead language, the sound of the organ not the drums, or the clinking of glasses, not the deer hooves, not the spirits and this difficulty she seemed to be in. The drums beat out her song. The native men with their strong, dark voices were a chorus to her. I leaned over as she passed close in front of me. The drums and the chorus were masking her wail. I wanted to steal her away, her cries were of such terrible sorrow for something larger than the world. I wanted to rock these sounds, hug them and rock them and stop them, make them go away saying no, it's all right, almost crying myself. It must stop. Please don't, shh, it's okay, okay, now breathe, quiet now, one hand on her wrist, checking her pulse.

She had gone once around the longhouse and still moved forward, but her sisters held her back. She was finished. They took her to her place. Her cries continued like the cries of someone who had dried up from the tears and had only convulsions left. The next dancer started.

"Her dance was strong," Ruby said.

Strong? I had watched someone being born. Strong? How could Ruby speak?

The man who had given me the witness money came over to us and said to Miles, "You should eat."

How could they talk?

"Do you want to eat?" Miles asked me.

"Eat what? Where?" I couldn't imagine anything like that in a place like this.

"We'll take you."

The ground was covered with tiny feathers that swirled over the earth as I moved in the wide circle around the fires. The sky was ribbed and slick with the blackness of having been burned. I followed Miles through a door and into a large room attached to the building. There was a feast laid out: rows of tables, the places all set with knives, forks, plates, glasses and steaming food in the center. I sat down between Miles and Ruby. Feeling like a child, I took the bowl of soup Ruby had ladled out for me.

Pointing to something on a plate, I asked "What do you call that?" Nothing seemed familiar.

"Bread," she said.

20

SPIRIT DANCING

Still smelling the pungent smoke from the longhouse, with its combined associations of hearth-comfort and primal fear, I went to the archives the next day, wanting to review Austin's files on Spirit Dancing. I was especially careful driving because there was something wrong with the steering on my car, or maybe the roads were slippery. I felt a little disoriented.

The cells that made my sum had been reorganized.

This was the first time I would be coming to Hart with any real experience of my own to help me understand him. I didn't call ahead.

Bernadette Verspoor was sitting in her office wearing the same dark clothes as always. She nodded to me. I handed her a photocopy of the permission letter from Paige. She took it as if it were a large sheet of flypaper and frowned as she read. Then her face cleared.

"This is a copy. This isn't an original."

"Oh, please, Mrs. Verspoor. I have the original. Here, you can compare them." I removed it from my briefcase.

"I don't know if this is the signature of Mr. Hart's daughter, now, do I? How would I know?"

"Do you think I would forge her name?"

She continued to stare at the letter like a lawyer trying to find a loophole, unembarrassed at making me wait. "What do you want to look at? I put all the boxes away. Do you expect me to keep them out on the table for you, in case you take it upon yourself to reappear?"

Instead of arguing with her, I wanted to tell her that I'd been to—where had I gone—to a beginning, before the Word? "I just want to see the Spirit Dancing file."

Reluctantly, apparently defeated, she said, "I'm writing on this copy that I have compared this letter to the original and I'm putting the date and time on it. Please go and sit down."

Verspoor, McNabb, the entire institution was holding time hostage, not letting me—or any inquiring presence—bring it into now.

Then, just-like-that, she returned with the file. She didn't bring the box. I should have asked her for the box.

A new vulnerability had set into me, a weepiness because of God-knows-why—more susceptible than before, noises louder, and Verspoor's antagonism brittle shale on which I walked. It hurt as though I'd misplaced my shoes and socks. I wanted to grass over her unnecessary dislike of me.

"Last night I went to the longhouse with a native friend of mine—to the spirit dancing," I said haltingly. She looked surprised, as if realizing that perhaps I was doing more in this opera than seeking illegitimate inspiration from tapping into Austin's thoughts.

"Do they still do such a thing?"

"Yes."

"I noticed an odd odor about you. I wondered if you'd been caught in a bush fire or something. But how many people get caught in a bush fire? Not many."

I hadn't changed my clothes.

"So, Mr. Hart will be telling you what it was like for him forty years ago." She seemed to have softened.

"I hope so. It's pretty upending. Pretty terrifying."

She raised one eyebrow, as she raised her guard, and pointed to the file, directing me to start my reading.

The word "terrifying" recalled Trevor Crane rushing to escape the crushing fear he had in the sweat-lodge. I wrote in my libretto notebook:

Our arms are weak from not carrying
Our spirits tired from not engaging
Will the masks sear us
like beauty we cannot bear?

The papers were fastened through a hole punched in the corner and a large metal button butterflied at the back secured them. The documents appeared to be typed and written notes Austin had made when researching the outlawing of the potlatch and Indian dances.

I learned that although the kind of longhouse dance I'd been at was outlawed by the same legislation as the feast dancing, the custom and purpose of the spirit dance was quite different.

> *These winter dances, practiced especially in the southern part of the province of British Columbia, are unlike the summer pow-wows, and indeed are unlike the ceremonial dances of the north. They are at the extreme outer places of the spirit.*
>
> *Native friends have explained that some of their people become what they call 'spirit sick.' It may be a general sense of illness, long bouts of excessive drinking, marked changes in behaviour. If the longhouse elder does an assessment and determines that the person has such sickness, and if the family wants the person to be initiated as a dancer because their spirit needs to come out, then a surprise taking—a kind of abduction—of the person is organized. Surprise is a necessary element. The person is removed from the community, sometimes forcefully, and goes into the longhouse to join other new dancers. The first winter they stay in the longhouse for the entire season, generally four months. Once initiated, commitment*

to being a dancer lasts a lifetime. The spirit returns annually to its human owner and is brought out during each dancing season. Those watching the dancing, who are uninitiated, might also quite suddenly become ill if their guardian spirit is restive. The solution seems to be to dance and to sing. This is a rite of passage, curing the main reason for depression amongst many native people, which is loneliness. This is not loneliness in the sense normally used in western society. It is a profound isolation that comes from experiencing the inexplicable and having no one who understands. Metaphorically it is the same as if the roots of a tree were hacked off under the earth. The tree still stands somehow, but barely.

It is this revealing of the inner spirit (as well as the potlatch feasts) which the federal government outlawed for 76 years. During all that time, from 1884 to 1952, the dancing went underground, practiced fearfully and earnestly in secret locations.

In pencil in the margin, Austin wrote:

It was a crime to participate in these rituals, even as a spectator. I could have been found guilty many times over in the past number of years.

I put my head back and closed my eyes. Miles George knew this kind of loneliness; it was what Austin Hart felt. The potato eaters had sent me to find them both.

When I opened my eyes, Mrs. Verspoor startled me, just standing there.

"You haven't done enough today. You could look at this." She handed me another file. I was on a drip-feed. "Mr. Hart was getting it ready for publication but he ran out of time."

I thought she'd said, "...he ran out *on* time." "I'm sorry I didn't hear."

"Ran out of time, to finish. I'm sure he wouldn't mind if you read it."

I thanked her.

The title page was "The Meaning of Home." It was dated seven months before he killed himself, the nearest writing to his death of anything I'd seen. I scanned the pages. It was an article about the first non-natives to voyage to Haida Gwaii. It started with an entry from the diary of Juan Perez written on July 19, 1774. Thinking that the land was uninhabited, Perez suddenly saw smoke coming from a hilltop on the island ahead.

> *The first thing the natives did when they approached within about a musket shot of the ship was to begin singing in unison their motet and to cast their feathers on the water... They opened their arms, forming themselves in a cross, and placed their arms on the chest in the same fashion, an appropriate sign of their peacefulness... They invited us by signs to come ashore, and we signaled that on the next day we would go there. But first, they sang and cast feathers in the air. All the rest of the afternoon 21 canoes of different sizes swarmed around. The largest of them, in which an old man came representing [himself] to be a king or captain... [he] carried his tambourine, jingling it.*

This was the other side of the story. H.S. had told Austin the natives' oral history of this event when he was in the Charlottes.

Because of foul weather Perez was not able to go ashore, which meant he didn't plant the flag to claim the country for Spain. Hart's paper was a detailed, carefully crafted argument to prove that Perez had lied.

> *There are legends of many famous explorers, for various reasons,falsifying the records, or, at the least, not disclosing all that happened, omitting certain significant events of shattering proportions.*
>
> *I believe Perez falsified the record. He did go ashore, where he was taken by the Haida into Ninstints Cove. He was ceremonially blanketed. He was fed. He was treated as a friend come home. Under the thrall of such people, under their charm and influence and*

transportment, a genuine uplifting occurred, as if into another realm. Why would he claim their land, seek to subjugate them, make them submissive. It would set off an almost immediate and catastrophic series of events that would wreck them. He knew such consequences would eventually follow, with other ships occupied by other men from other nations. He knew he was the first. If he didn't claim the land, there would be a postponement, some respite, however short. As it happened, the next ship to pass that place was in 1778, a reprieve of four years. Four years is a victory of sorts.

Is this bad scholarship? Forgive me. Is this rash conjecturing? I suppose. Do I believe it is possible? I do. Condemn me for that. Every day I feel my desire to hide the traces of where I have gone, to cover the stories the natives have told me and which I revealed. To let those stories be there, inside their communities, allowed to stay intact without the blaring, cynical and caustic eye of the outsiders who tear them apart. I exposed them. I did not have the courage of Perez, to be a silent witness, in awe. Was it courage I lacked? Simple humility would have sufficed to hold me back.

This was written seven months before he took his own life. I wondered if I could penetrate this scholarly calm, which hinted at his own wracked and ruinous state. I bet that was it. He was still talking in this slightly ponderous academic voice, practicing answering his detractors after the last lecture. He was going to publish this to acclaim, as he had done before, but he didn't finish it, because he couldn't. Why was that?

I could just make out the margin, printed in pencil beside the ultimate paragraph, the invective "poppycock." It was in his handwriting. He had given me an important clue.

Cracker-barreling through to me came the word illegitimate. I'd been illegitimate. Hugely, but by happenstance, I was connected to the people of Austin's story and they'd replaced my family, even my past—they were a substitute for it, answering what I lacked. Sophia had glimpsed this, but I now felt it full-throttle, almost embarrassing and guilty in its potency. I knew what Austin Hart meant in his essay. I just wished he were alive so I could tell him. Exiled from exile.

He worked on this in his last, reclusive year, fighting an unwinnable war with himself against the terrible scourge of the invective "poppycock." Yet Claire was mistaken that he was having difficulty writing. He was formulating his ideas with the cumulative urgency of a confession. He had lied to her. If only he could have told her the weight of his suffering, he might have lived.

Whatever had lock-stepped his decision to take his own life, it was after this time.

21

SEX

The Lover:

Cup your unanswered passion–
Meet it–
And take it down deeper
into want
into lack
into loss:
The words that open the throat.

Chorus:

Use your love;
use your desire–
use your need
as your horse,
and ride.

Alix's Lines for the Libretto

I finally told Sophia that Richard was going to be in town, and I'd try to see her the next day. I'd been dodging the topic because of her scorn; although the thought that I belonged to another family—that I didn't have to think of her as my mother—induced a new, relaxed feeling of kindness towards her. Instead of being upset, she talked excitedly about having watched the funeral of Ronald Reagan on television.

"It went on all day. Even Mrs. Griffin saw it on the big screen in the lounge without getting confused as to whether it might be her funeral she was watching. And Mrs. Askew, the one who sits near the door and clings to visitors, she left her post to see it. I never really liked that trite, empty man, but it's a credit to the United States that even the banal can be celebrated to great effect. 'The Gipper,' now what kind of name is that for a president? What does it mean anyway?"

"I think it was the name of a football hero who died young."

"What's the matter with men that they don't last? I've seen so many newsreels of wives walking behind their boxed-up husbands. The boots of the coffin bearers for this President made such a sound, they could have been marching on broken glass. Do you know that at funerals nobody applauds, no matter how rousing the song or the speech? At mine we should have someone sing, maybe something from your opera—and if the soprano is any good you just start clapping to show people they're supposed to. Mrs. Reagan patted her husband's coffin with the American flag draped over it—so sweet—she gave it a little pat like you would a son setting off to a place of higher learning. God it lasts a long time, this being old."

I told her I was sorry but that I had to go. She ignored me.

"You know when my friend Karen Dunant died, they had an open casket. I was so relieved the person inside didn't look like her."

"Mother—"

"—I could pretend someone else had died."

"Mother—"

"And all the flower arrangements in the church, she would have hated them, and hated the dress they put her in. 'Where the hell are my slacks?' she would have said. Her daughter looked like the widow, and of course she was getting all the money."

"Sophia, I really have to go. Sorry."

Finally she stopped talking long enough to make space for her sarcasm. "If you're too busy to see me, you're too busy to see Richard.

I'm not complaining, but you do have a lot of work to do on this opera. You don't know enough yet."

I explained that Richard was in town on business.

"I can guess what business that is," she said. When I didn't respond, she added, "So he'll be staying at a hotel?"

"Pan Pacific."

"That costs a bit of change. Nice hotel. The bilious sails on it look like they're pulling the city out to sea. He's clever to have booked a room. That way you'll be off-guard when he wants to sleep with you. You don't owe him anything, Alix, just remember that."

"The word is *billowing*. Why are you so hostile to him?"

"He's never liked me, that's a good enough reason."

"It doesn't matter now, it's over between us."

"He blames you for not being in love with him anymore. You can't really blame someone for not loving you, can you? And Alix, you always think you have to pay someone off to get what you want."

It was true that I had the habit of the illegitimate child, thinking I needed to purchase what was my due, whether it was affection or the end of affection. Yet I wanted to block her from taking casual possession of all corners of my life with the familiarity of an owner. "Sophia, you're making all these declarations about me." She'd become the traffic cop of my days: stop, yield, right turn, drive with both hands on the wheel, directing me as she'd never done before. I added, "Really, to be honest, you and I have not been mother and daughter for years." If she could claim me, she could also drop me again.

"What do you mean? There was a point in time when you became an orphan?"

"Don't you know what I'm saying?" Her's was a poisonous kind of claiming.

"I only know that you are on the last page of my life," she said.

And hit the bulls-eye of my heart.

RICHARD AND I ATE AT La Lumière Restaurant on West Broadway. We had the five course set menu, with the wines selected by the sommelier.

The conversation over dinner was geared to avoid the conversation we would surely have to have. The wine: Sancerre, Cabernet Franc, Meritage (with honey-dew melon in between to clear my debased palette) started to loosen my anxious tongue.

Richard asked me about my work with the composer.

"Brett's a bit worried. He's afraid of my being another dry writer, although the previous librettist certainly wasn't dry in the alcoholic sense." I was telling him things he wasn't really interested in. I was reporting, and to no one in particular. "I'm making notes, but I haven't got the shape of the story yet. Maybe after I've seen the unsighted mask in Ottawa next week."

"You can come to Toronto then."

I let the invitation pass. "What a terrible thing for Paige and Jason—the two kids—to live with a father who could at any time have killed himself. It would be like living on the top floor of a condemned house."

"Are you having an affair with Brett?"

"I think I'll use a condemned house in the opera, in a scene near the end."

"You didn't hear me? Are you having an affair with Brett?"

"This is an expensive trip to get an answer I could have given you over the phone," I said with more pique than I actually felt.

"Do we still have a deal that we'll tell one another if either of us is having an affair?"

"No we don't, and I'm not."

When the check came I picked it up; it was $370. Richard took it from me. I put my credit card down; he matched my actions. When the server arrived I made a sign with my hand, splitting the air. "Please fill in half the amount on his chit, will you, and I'll look after the tip."

We waited outside for the valet to bring my mother's car. I stared at the looming red and white cartoon face of Colonel Sanders on the fast food outlet across the street. The odor of spattering chicken fat mixed with and overwhelmed bouquet garni.

When the car arrived, Richard took the keys from the valet.

"What are you doing?"

"Driving you home."

"Not a discussion, just stealing a march on me?" He put his hand on my arm and maneuvered me into the passenger seat. Although I resisted, his strength won out. Had he always taken such control of me? I didn't seem to be, any longer, the person he thought he knew.

We sat in silence, not moving, our car in the line of traffic; other drivers had to go around us.

"You don't know where my mother lives," I finally said.

"You're not going to tell me?"

"Nope."

Richard put on the emergency lights and got out. He returned in a few minutes.

"What were you doing?"

"Looking up her address in the phone book. Getting directions."

The streets in Shaughnessy were serpentine and confusing to the uninitiated, but finally he found the house on his own. It began to rain.

I sat perched on the edge of the winged-back chair in the living-room; to my dismay the flowers he'd sent me were still in the fireplace, behind the chain-linked screen. I hoped he wouldn't suggest a fire.

"I'd like to stay," he said, sitting on the couch and then getting up. "I'll find us a drink."

Not even my coolness and the power play see-sawing between us could override my mother's training that, at all costs, I be a polite host. I led him into the solarium and poured two glasses of chilled Meursault.

"You didn't give me much warning—that you were leaving me," he said softly, his voice surprisingly tremulous.

"You knew as soon as I did. Although maybe—it's more complicated I guess. I used to wonder how we'd know when our relationship was over."

"Because there was so little going on between us?"

"Hmm."

"That's harsh."

"Sorry." I felt a little shame-faced that I was happier now than when we were together.

"You're distracted. What were you just thinking?"

"I was wondering if that's how Mary-Anne, Austin's wife, felt. His death mainly confirmed his absence."

"Are you saying... ."

"I was just thinking about her—"

"What about us?" he asked, interrupting.

I leaned back in the chair. We'd been unable to successfully negotiate the terms of our love; it seemed vain to try to negotiate why it was ending. But I'd give it a try. "I used to look at you while you were sleeping, seeing your leg uncovered by the sheet, your naked thigh, the curve of your hip, the hair under your arm. I liked the look of you. When we didn't make love I would start to fret and imagine the worst, that you weren't attracted to me any more, that we would have a sexless future. Eventually, that's what happened. The face wore off the currency we had."

"The face wore off—"

"Sorry, probably not a great metaphor."

"Whatever. It didn't have to."

"I want to have a different person as a lover; I want to be a different person as a lover."

"Why?"

This was all so serious and, I realized, quite beside the point even if true. My defensiveness felt unbecoming and unnecessary, and Richard undeserving of it. "I didn't mean to walk out on you. I was coming undone in some basic way, as if there was a dropped stitch somewhere and it was all going to unravel back to that point, maybe even quickly."

We sat drinking our wine in silence. "What else?" he asked.

"It's riveting, what I'm working on. Even Sophia is engaged.

She goes for long minutes without thinking about herself."

"Come back," he said.

"Oh, Richard, I don't want to. I'm here now. I was so afraid we'd end up living in a world of potato eaters."

"Potato eaters? What are you saying?"

"Don't you see it too? Forever playing it safe; coddling one another's fears, absorbing them, not facing them; becoming more and more narrow, less light to see by. We'd end up like Russell and Sophia, sleeping in separate, single beds."

"Wasn't I good to you? We could still have children, it's not too late. You could stay home and—"

The room felt airless. "It would be heartless for me to have a child. You need a wife. I'm no wife."

"It's your mother, isn't it? She has you back in her zone where she wants you, so you can continue your role—you're just her audience. I was your only hope for getting away from her and having your own life. I still am."

"I have more hope now. And I don't want to get away from her."

"You don't? This is new."

"She's changed."

"All right then, all right. So your mind is made up? You've changed too."

"I'm sorry. I don't want to be churlish."

"Whatever churlish means, I don't want you to be that way either."

I laughed. The garden lights came on. "Sophia's mind is starting to go. It's mainly in her language, her misuse of words. But she still remembers everything about tulips."

"About tulips?"

"Yes, and other plants—everything in her garden. She told me yesterday that even if I didn't water her garden, it would still be all right because some of the plants like being stressed, being denied what they need. I think it was her philosophy of child-rearing. It sends them into over-production, into florescence. They think they're dying."

"Let's sleep together tonight."

"Really, Richard—"

"One last time." He took my hands and raised me to my feet.

I hadn't really thought of sex since being in Vancouver. I'd been considering Sophia, illness, death—but not The Little Death. Before Le Petite Mort your heart rate doubled, high blood pressure was a worry and—I wondered when mother had last had sex. I was drunk. The Little Drunk. It would be unconscionable to sleep with Richard, to have a little death with him because—I realized with a slight sense of fatigue—he had treated me as Sophia used to: as a compliant child always ready to please. How can you love a man who treats you the way your mother did? It was very unromantic. No wonder the face wore off the currency of our sex—that wasn't such a bad metaphor. Why had I put up with it? Because I hadn't been there. I hadn't been anywhere. Nicely repressed and dutiful. Until the Eaters showed up with their little Potatoes.

"Alix, hello? Are you in there?" Richard was still holding my hands.

"All right we'll sleep together on the condition that you don't take off your clothes." I was being too clever for my own good. I revised my dictum. "Okay, you can only take off what you bought this week for this visit."

"And you have to take off everything you didn't buy this week in preparation for my visit."

"An apt response to the coy mistress. I didn't know you were coming until a few days ago. I didn't know about this game, otherwise I would have gone shopping."

I pulled the heavy lined curtains closed on the windows of my bedroom. I'd never fucked anyone in this bed. It was a little small for two.

"I bought underwear," Richard said.

This time I giggled. I never giggled. I was regressing. "No you didn't, Richard, you didn't buy underwear this week. Did you? Maybe you did."

"I have to be able to get to it in order to take it off." He undressed as I watched.

It would be unconscionable, I thought again as he was undressing me and—I could undress myself, couldn't I? I always had. He was a good, albeit intermittent lover, a little fast in coming and then it was hard to get his attention. Actually it was damn hard and—maybe I wouldn't try to please him. Moving over, shutting down, staying silent, claiming nothing. Not the way to everlasting life. I'd lie still and wait to be pleased. After all I'd paid for half the dinner and all the tip.

He made tiny gestures, small movements of his fingers on my cheek, my shoulder, the place below my collarbone. Everything was jet black, wet black, taut. Then he withdrew. I lay like a landscape. He worked me through absence, denial, yearning. I couldn't find his mouth. Was his head tipped back?

Then it was there, his tongue in my partly open mouth, then gone again. I never knew where he would touch me next, and so he seemed everywhere. My remote inner body, planning for love somewhere else, lost its future tense; I started to rise to the surface of my skin, to his fingers.

He touched my neck and my left breast. My cells lit up as if the breaker box for an entire city had just been flipped to 'on.' It hurt to be so wide awake.

All the dams along the main-stem of the Snake River were breached, drawing down reservoirs held back until even the spillways were submerged. He decommissioned all the dams. I had a full continent's response to the ending of a drought.

I started to chuckle because of the extravagant metaphor. "'Now barbarous in beauty, the stooks rise.'" I quoted the lines in the midst of laughing.

"What are 'stooks?'"

"Upright sheaves. Arrows in a quiver. Gerard Manley Hopkins."

He retreated. He got up from the bed and turned on the lamp. I hid under the covers. When I pulled them down to see what he was doing, he was standing there looking at me as if I were a stranger who'd stolen into his bed. His penis had detumesced. Such a fancy word for limp. I couldn't resist saying, "And lowly with a broken neck the crocus lays its cheek to mire." I reached out my hand to him but he didn't take it. "I'm sorry."

"I don't like being laughed at." He dressed.

"Really, I wasn't laughing at you. I meant it as a compliment."

"Stooks? Being compared to stooks?"

"Oh, Richard, please."

"Fuck off. Menopausal bitch."

"Stooks and stones will break my bones."

And then, even more threateningly, he repeated the horrid line he'd often said, the domestic turned poisonous, the cherished turned to contempt. "Some day: 'All the kings horses and all the kings men.'"

He called a cab and left my mother's house.

He wasn't kind. Neither was I. With settled regret, I knew I would yearn, but it wouldn't be for him.

22

GETTING TO THE WELL

Chorus:
Your spirit must strive
within the needs of the day
or your humanity is lost.

Alix's Lines for the Libretto

Being with Hart, looking through his files, was at the equator. The blank page I faced each night was the north pole.

Before going to Ottawa, I wrote a letter to the coroner's office, asking if I could review their file on Austin Hart's death. I enclosed the permission letter from Paige intended for access to the museum files, which I was now using for this different purpose,

I returned to the archives for inspiration. Despite Verspoor's prison-guard animosity, I would just keep turning up like a bad penny, as Sophia would say.

I had made my way through most of the Haida Gwaii journals, without finding any entries about his actual trip to Ninstints to assess the poles. I was in official and bureaucratic territory, detailing Hart's planned expansion of the museum which would house the poles. He was involved in all of this, from the roof line to the lighting fixtures. I nodded off twice.

At the end of the day, Mrs. Verspoor appeared at the door of her office to announce that the library was closing. I obediently packed up. She came to my table. I expected some kind of scolding for breaking a hidden rule in the rule-book she serviced and maintained.

"You have about fifteen minutes, during which you can look at this." She handed me a plain beige folder. "I still don't think you should be trying to find an opera in all of his papers, but I guess you're going to keep coming back, so you might as well get more of the picture."

I thanked her, careful not to presume this would be the commencement of a friendly pact between us.

She stood there as I read the first page, written in Austin's hand.

> *Diary—Austin Hart "for my eyes only"*
>
> *If these diaries are being read by anyone other than me, it is as a result of some mistake. Please read no further, as these are entirely private musings, not meant to be seen by others."*

I looked up at her quizzically.

"I figured you'd noticed something was missing. It gets a little grizzly for Mr. Hart." She pursed her lips and lightly touched my shoulder as she returned to her office. My defensive stance dissolved in a brush-stroke. This dry inhospitable termagant was a woman of sorrows. She was going to let me in.

The pages were 8½" x 11", larger in size than the notebooks, stapled together. Austin's handwriting was sometimes uneven, more difficult to read.

> *If I were to tell the truth, I am here not as an anthropologist but as a buyer. I am here, not to have the people tell me things so I can explain them to others; I am a merchant. The Haida probably*

know this. They are well experienced in having to deal with visitors who arrive with some kind of moral uncertainty, at best sincere, but always on the take. People like me have been here before.

As we were leaving the bar yesterday, Harold asked, "Will you encourage me, help me to show more of my own life and who I am." What a tender request. It is the appeal of someone naïve, innocent, asking help from a stranger. What can I do for him? Especially since my purpose is full of a double-cross.

Any chance I might respond in an honest, forthright manner requires that I rekindle in myself that same innocent place from which he speaks. It seems long gone.

Yet he has awakened in me an old longing, half-glimpsed now through time, when I was certain the world was good.

I walled that longing inside the inner room of an inner room. As a child I was only able to emerge from there by dressing in clothes not meant for me, too tight at the waist and long in the sleeves. I went about the world so absurdly dressed. No one seemed to notice this strange child's clothes. No one said, "My poor boy, you look so odd, whose clothes are these, surely they are not yours, they don't fit you, they belong to someone else."

If anyone had said such a thing to me, my heart would have opened beyond the confines of its small beating. Perhaps I wouldn't be here now. I'd be sitting in front of a painter's easel, or working in wood or stone, creating in an artful shape my inner life so that someone might recognize their own. Instead I carve my heart and toss it away, morsel by morsel, to the dogs.

Now, this plangent call: help me to show more of myself. I should, in all honesty, tell him to hide from me.

As contented as I had been with the formally dressed professor in his button-down shirt collars, and as gruesome his state, this was the man I had wanted to meet. I was going to get a true, fixed place on the map from which I could triangulate the other points: the taking of the poles, the ascending fame, the suicide. He would not be sorry that Verspoor had given me this access to him. Ethically, it was a feast.

I have come back to my lodgings. I sit here in the dark. Then, unmistakably, my father's voice, Charlie's commands: Buck up. What's wrong with you. You've landed on the wrong shore. His looming, ubiquitous presence blocks every view.

"You are not my son..."

Did he really say that? Or did I re-compose these words from a dozen splintered phrases of reproach. "What son of mine would..." "Who do you think you are..." Did I remain slyly content with that, as lonely as I was, because it gave me a certain amount of freedom. Freedom won at the cost of not being fathered by a loving man.

Buck up.

My purpose, my mission here, will put paid to all his doubts about me.

Poppycock, he would say. Poppycock. Be a real man.

So I come here, as a man, to answer a father's curse. For now, I am in a dusty room above a dirty bar, happy that I have met Harold. I don't feel quite good enough to be in his presence.

The word "poppycock", written in the margin of Hart's essay about Perez, was from his father's profanity. H.S., in the official record, is Harold.

Would Candice, two years younger than Austin, know about the source of these memories that beset him? She hadn't said much about the father except he was a limited man, jealous of his own children, particularly of Austin. His father's curse disowned him. Candice would have to help me.

I am making arrangements to travel to Ninstints. My father voice is still in my head, like the buzzing of this wasp that has come in through the open window and pesters me as I write on this tilted table. I won't kill it. I wave it away, like someone wafting a fragrance through the room. That is my intention but not my inner state. My inner state is murderous. The voice, disembodied, sickeningly clear, dark and dominant leers at me, says like a judge delivering a life sentence "you are a fraud." The voice attends my doubt. It accompanies my hesitation as I wonder whether or not this project to salvage the poles will ultimately help these people or cause them further harm. I am irresolute. "Where is your gumption?"

I imagine a time—did it ever exist—when my waiting was not an infirmity of purpose, not the loud tolling of uncertainty, but a small bell, marking a deliberate time of readiness. Now he banishes that blessed ringing calm, the quiet gathering in of details with "poppycock" and a fist smashed onto a plate of food. How I hated him then. How odious he was. I stood up and scrabbled to find a route through a great bag of loathing, to get away from him.

There is no space that isn't him or his voice or
his breath or his smell. Or a dream of all of that.

So he has, once more, come to find me here, the cunning bastard, so many years later, in this remote place of beauty and squalor. "I know what you're up to, fooling everyone. They'll find out you're a fraud."

I try to put his voice aside, urge it out the window,
shoo it away. Smash. It's a wonder that the plate didn't
crack. It's a wonder that I didn't crack it over his head.

So this was the hectoring curse riding herd on Austin. More calamitous, more debilitating than my mother's passive dismissal of my talents; his father had called him a fraud. At college in Halifax, I had longed to find the place of nothing. Austin, on the contrary, was being exiled from the source of his own inspiration.

I would do anything to rid my brain of him, would take an implement to my own skull and dig deep inside with a dull blade to take it out, scrape away the nerve endings that attach me to it, any small "you" or large "I," cut my name to be in peace again. Even if all I have left is blind silence, I would do it, if I had the knife.

Tears dissolved my face. The poor man. When I studied his

photograph, my sense of him as a surgeon didn't have this terrible, lacerating resonance.

Mrs. Verspoor was there to take away the files. "That's enough for today," she said.

I don't think she saw.

I didn't leave.

Mrs. Verspoor said, "I'm sorry, you'll have to go now."

She wasn't unkind, she was just strict.

I was composed now. "Do you mind my asking how you got his diaries?"

"They came to me after his death. He must have wanted me to have them." What a strange and extraordinary gift he'd given her. It was no wonder she guarded the man so jealously. "I can let you in early tomorrow morning, if you want. Seven. I'll be here. Come to the staff entrance at the back."

"That would be great."

As I walked out of the archives, I passed the towering Ninstints poles behind the glass showcases in the extension to the museum Hart had made for them. These animals, topped one upon the other, were no longer able to growl and snarl and fly. They looked inconsolably trapped. The Watchman's eyes were blinded; he'd been unable to warn the Weeping Woman.

I checked into the Empress Hotel, the Queen Mother of hotels overlooking Victoria's harbor. I trudged a wide, empty hallway carpeted by someone who now spent more on gin than on redecorating, and I got lost in the crossroad of corridors—looked forward to where I'd already walked and back to where I'd never been, and finally found my room.

The Empress had always had an imperiled presence, built by the great architect, Ratenbury, who was killed by his wife's lover.

The world seemed murderous.

Austin's story didn't end well. I knew that, but as with all tragedies, I still wondered how it would unfold.

I was glad my mother was alive. Caring about her would keep my feet on the ground.

23

TAKE THE POLES

The Lover:

[Speaking directly and intently to Hart]

You've cut them down
and now they are yours.
You arrested what belongs to that place;
The consequences fall.

Alix's Lines for the Libretto

Mrs. Verspoor was waiting for me at the back entrance to the museum. "He gets to Ninstints today," she said as she walked ahead of me up the back stairway.

"You knew him," I ventured.

"He always called me 'The Good Mrs. Verspoor.' He was so intelligent, so intense, so decorous. No one but the two of us knows his torment. Well, the three of us. I guess we count him."

To Claire, Miles, his family—even the mixed-up, water-logged McNabb—Austin was a sensitive, vulnerable man. Except for the inebriant Trevor Crane, all had perceived his suffering. His death itself delivered that conclusion. But Verspoor was right, no one had suggested a tormented man. I still had the chilling image of his carving up parts of himself and tossing them to the dogs.

I asked her if Trevor Crane had had access to these files. She said, "Who?"

When we reached the archives, she gave me more foolscap sheets. "Here's the last part. He's on the island now." She was handing him over to me.

> *Harold brought me ashore without any difficulty. He said I couldn't manage in my city get-up and loaned me a sweater and trousers of his own which he had on the boat. I'm swamped in his large clothes. Although I wanted to set up camp by myself, he insisted on building me a table by cutting down two saplings and bracing them against a standing tree. The table top was a piece of plywood he had on board. I wondered why he built the table so far from the shoreline. He said there'd be a 17 foot tide in the night. I smiled, knowingly. What that meant was that the campfire I made, and part of my tent, were gradually inundated with water. I had to evacuate under a moonlit sky and take myself to higher ground, near Harold's writing table, where I sit.*
>
> *The totems are before me.*
>
> *It's so quiet here. Charlie's voice is gone. He seems to have missed the boat. Blessed relief.*
>
> *I have lived on the west coast all my life, where the tide comes in and then, twice a day, recedes. Twice a day the world is changed, and I didn't observe it. We have built our houses with our backs to this change. Like a child discovering static electricity, the balloon stuck to my hair, I am in awe at how the tide alters everything. I think I have been put down in one place and then, when I look up, I have been transported to another. Where did these rocks come from? Then, eight hours later, where did they go?*
>
> *o o o*

Three days have passed, two nights. I don't write very much, and thought itself has been stilled. I walk. I sleep under the stars. I look up at the poles, lean against them, touch their spirited forms. I am afraid all the time, and yet not afraid. I am unknown and yet known. One morning, sitting on the ground under the poignant Weeping Woman pole, I heard a knocking sound, like someone at the door of a house that wasn't there. Raven was perched on the tree growing out of the Woman's lap. Come in, I said.

I've found a cave and the sites of many houses. One of the house posts still stands as an entrance. I walk through what seems to be a mouth, and, inside, above me, the sky. I had not thought I would be so affected by this place.

I want Harold to come and get me now. I want him never to come.

o o o

Why did the people leave this island? I have studied their art like an autopsy report, looking for the cause of death. What inner terror took possession of them and made this a place from which they had to flee? There are so many locations in the world where civilization suddenly packed its bags, loaded up, and got out. And here I am, asking: Why did you leave?

How curious his question looked, in his own handwriting, because it was the same one his family and friends had been asking, and which I had sought from him: why did you leave? Was he also overtaken by an inner terror? When I was eighteen, if I'd been able to acknowledge it, was fear beneath the flat certainty of my purpose?

Four nights and three days had passed before Charlie finally made an appearance at 2 a.m. I could hear him coming through the trees, and then he was standing over me. I yelled out loud "go away." He did. I slept. Then at 4 a.m. I awoke again. I heard another sound in the bush. I sat up straight, ready for him, but it wasn't him this time. I called out "who are you?." As clearly as if we were in a room together, I heard a man's voice—not my Dad's voice—another man's, coming from about 9 feet away. He said, "I don't know what your name is, but my name is Yahweh."

Amongst the thousands of gods I could have pulled, my luck was to get one who doesn't know my name. I laughed out loud and slept until noon.

o o o

I sit for hours watching the totems, waiting. . .

Masset Village

The only bothersome aspect of my stay on Ninstints is that it seems as if the geography of that place has lodged itself inside my head. At night instead of a brain I have an island with its long bays slowly altering with the ocean's tides, the gulls careening over-head and the raven in the tree, making that knock-knocking sound in its throat. When I wake up in this room, back at the hotel, I think I'm still there amongst those totems, the animals climbing up and out into a hole in the sky. I have had to wrestle with that place to try to dislodge it, to get back my mind. The sleeping tablets I have brought with me do the trick. Although I am somewhat groggy in the morning, it's only for an hour or two and then I am alert.

I know the building I will construct to house those poles; I am confident I can be its perfect architect. The poles will last forever. Surely this is how I can help Harold. Enough of diary-writing. It has led me away from my purpose, which is now clear. I am untroubled.

Actions speak louder than words, Charlie used to say. Now I am remembering that lesson instead of hearing him saying it in my head.

When Harold came to fetch me on Ninstints, he reached down into the long grasses, and like a magician, picked up something hidden at the village site which, despite my daily perambulations, had escaped me. I was awe-struck, shocked, almost repelled by its beauty and profanity. It is a Raven Rattle. Harold says it was made by Shawcroft, showing me the refined, exquisite detailing which led him to this belief. I am not yet familiar enough with Shawcroft's work to come to my own conclusions, but in due course I will. Then I must catalogue it and put it in the collection, on display in the new wing of the museum.

I must get home now, and as soon as possible.

Three dots indicating the gaps within which he'd made the decision to take the poles—without extending his visit, as he told himself he must—without showing me what had changed.

I WAS FINISHED READING. I placed the pages back into the folder. The ache in my back ironed its way up through my shoulders and into my neck. I had to think. I was rocked by his unblinkered assessment of the choice which had faced him, and then the choice he made.

I went to Mrs. Verspoor with the file and thanked her for her help. "I feel a little overwhelmed by what I read." She nodded. "I guess he didn't write anything about what happened the next year, on the expedition?"

"Yes, he did."

"I didn't see it in the file."

"No." She took an envelope out of her desk and handed it to me. "You can read it sitting here." She pointed to a chair.

The silence that takes hold as they have finished all the supporting and strapping and hammering. The silence as they tighten the winch and the pole starts to move in its descent, inch by inch. It has begun. I watch from a distance. Now Terry has taken an axe. He's chopping down another pole. It starts to fall. It's going to hit the sun, bring down the galaxy with it. Oh, calamity.

The forest is cracking and splitting. The poles rake through the trees in their descent, like someone dropping ten thousand knives all at once. I will hear that sound in my sleep.

Branches are showering down, with nests in the branches, and eggs in the nests.

Terry calls out to me. I say, "Take that one too, take them all." It is a gluttony of destruction.

Tom comes over to say, "It can't be helped," trying to comfort me. I want to stand in the way of these butchers I have hired to do this job. I am one of them.

They are cutting down the tree that supported the table Harold built for me last year. Everything falls.

I am someone who has come upon a house that is on fire. There are people inside with their priceless, fragile treasures. I have decided not to save the people in the house, but their treasures. I have decided.

"It's upsetting," I said as I handed the papers back to her.

She returned them to the envelope. "You'll keep this to yourself, please. I don't think people should know how he felt about taking the poles, especially the natives."

"Because?"

"It loosens the museum's hold on them."

"Oh, I see."

"That's all of it." For the first time, an expression in her face of—caring, I think. "So you won't be coming back any more. I got used to you."

"Maybe to visit." We had come a long way.

She nodded. "A question? Do you know who's going to play Austin Hart? I'd like to come."

"The opera isn't even written yet," I said, embarrassed at her shift in allegiance from Austin to art, especially given Austin's last entry. "Certainly you'll be invited."

I walked.

I walked for hours.

Austin was aware that creativity flourished on the islands because the natives knew that these invaders were systematically trying to wipe them out. They knew it. They had to carve at a faster pace, to erect poles which would tell the stories of their clans. Someone said Austin focused on the time when the people felt themselves to be dying. But they didn't have pneumonia; they had assassins.

What happened to him on Ninstints in those five days: between laughing that he had a god who didn't know his name, and then deciding to go ahead with the expedition? What the hell happened? Brett will say, "Alix, what does this matter to us? The opera is not about the gaps. We can't wonder in this opera, we have to make magic."

I was unnerved by the thought that Hart's question of the Haida was "why did you leave," and instead of getting an answer he moved the poles to a museum. I didn't understand why he quit us, and I was going to move his life to the stage.

I'd come to this work wanting to know why Austin Hart killed himself. I still had that question and also another: why did he take the poles? I could only write toward a reply, that's all I could do.

I thought of the edict "between art and life, choose life." It was a smug aphorism. Who first gave this direction anyway? Why this dichotomy? Between art and life refuse to choose, even if they hold a gun to your head. Tell them to go away.

In the room Austin had imagined, after the visitors had come and taken everything, even the children—in the corner of that room sat someone carving a stick, creating art. This work had to be achieved facing those atrocities.

24

PITCHED DARKNESS

Hart:
An ache has started in my throat.
I thirst—
I long for more.

I want to lay bare the very thing
this art is made to disguise—
where everything's wrapped in light.

I am excited
yet my moods disperse and gather.
They make this different light.

Alix's Lines for the Libretto

I waited for Sandra Mason in the reception area of the Museum of Civilization in Hull, Quebec; she would take me inside to see the unsighted mask. Miles had given me an introduction, and we had talked extensively on the phone.

All the doors leading out of this area were locked.

Finally she arrived and took me down the hall to her office. The clutter of her room was almost unsavory; there were piles of books and papers everywhere. She was harried, disheveled, absorbed in things beyond this realm: she knew the divinity of a basket, and when she talked, I began to understand the sacredness of the artifacts, but she hadn't attended to herself. Her brown plaid skirt was hitched high on her waist and twisted off center. Her hair looked like a home permanent, applied without assistance. She spoke the way people do when they are afraid no one wants to listen; she covered her mouth so that I had to lean forward to hear her.

We went to have coffee at the far end of the building. The restaurant's large windows overlooked the river and the bridge to Ottawa. Directly outside was a long stretch of tended lawn, and on it were three plains Indian tepees. The skins looked vulnerable, flensed, in the wide expanse of grass, in this manicured environment. They needed a dry and rough terrain.

The sky had a lowering, accumulating weight, putting at risk any sense of comfort one might have. Suddenly thunder bowled through the room and a great snake of lightening cut this heavy sky and touched the top of the tepees. The sound pegged into me. Only some thin, friable membrane kept us from these elements. The people in the restaurant went quiet, fearing and desiring another shock. Then everyone spoke at once.

Sandra and I shook ourselves free, left and went further into the building.

From the outside the museum looked beautiful, a place a worthy civilization would construct. But in here, in these hallways, the smell of hospital death was immediate, and it intensified as we moved through the interior corridors toward the center of the building.

Every step we took was towards a bend in the hallway, always rounding the corner, never arriving. Cluttering the corridors were huge garbage bags filled with plastic wrap needed for moving the artifacts from city to city or from one country to another.

We reached a door that was thick metal, and she couldn't open it with her card. To the right was doorbell.

A young woman came, smiling and welcoming. Compared to

her, Sandra and I were haggard, from a time that had aged us unkindly. Behind the attendant loomed a warehouse. The ceiling was forty feet high; shelves filled the entire space. The woman was wearing a white coat and clear rubber gloves. The place was antiseptic. Light burned from high, unreachable bulbs.

We moved inside.

On the shelves were hats, wooden masks, boxes, bowls, cedar cloaks, baskets—the things the natives had used in their daily lives. They had been borrowed or stolen, purchased, given away or collected and brought here.

As we walked down the aisles, another young woman would appear around a corner. There were half a dozen of them in the warehouse, all fresh-faced, wearing protective gloves. They were called conservators—friendly, soft-spoken, centered in their work.

On milliners' stands were hats created by Edward Shawcroft, looking for all the world like a display in a shop window, ready to be selected and worn out into the street. But the wooden masks on the next shelf unnerved me. I stopped in front of a row of them.

It was not that they were dormant or asleep, but rather they looked stunned, as though petrified and paralyzed in place. They were not staring at me but into a horrified beyond. That was what had been captured here, and what Hart had described: the moment of seeing the invader's face or feeling his hand or simply knowing that all the locks had failed. The moment of being taken alive.

As I looked closer at the cedar bark hats and asked Sandra if I could touch one of them and she said yes and I did—I realized that my physical intimacy with these objects was much less reserved than hers. I wanted to put on the hat.

These were things you would need every day. A bowl for soup; a cane for walking—now kept in scientifically controlled conditions. These were the things the visitor had hauled away in the truck.

Sandra had shown me a circular distributed by the Smithsonian Institute in 1880. It emphasized the need to acquire a "full series" of native American skulls "to be procured without offense to the living." But, other than that, no object was specially singled out. "Almost everything has its value in giving completeness to a collection." There was some urgency because "many articles are perishable and the tribes, themselves, are passing away." Franz Boas, anthropologist and collector, had watched an outlawed potlatch feast near Haida Gwaii in 1930. While the meat was being distributed, the host Chief made a speech. He said to his guests, "This bowl in the shape of a bear is for you and for you." The speech was the same one Boas had first heard 40 years earlier. The only difference was that now the carved bowls were not, in fact, there. They were in museums in New York. The Chief said "this bowl" to the empty space where it should have been.

Why hadn't they made more bowls to replace the ones that had been taken? Austin Hart knew why: "Each time your children come back, they understand less and less of what you say to them. Everyone sits alone."

I caught up with Sandra and the first conservator who had stopped ahead of me.

In a glass box on a shelf as high as the farthest reach of my hands I could see the stone mask. It was not so much a mask but the visible part of a body in repose. It was surrounded by startled wooden faces. That was the value then—perhaps even the purpose—of stone. The wood continued to carry the imprint of shock, but not this stone; this sleeping head dreamed, unconfused, uninvolved in the nightmare that had been absorbed by the others. I looked for a long time through the glass box at this mask. Then I noticed that there was another box beside it, exactly the same size, but it was made of wood, painted blue.

The conservator explained that there were two unsighted masks here, one was the original and the other a copy. She didn't know which box—glass or wood—contained which. She went to check her records.

What would Austin Hart think of this? That the duality of the mask was not, in fact, a question of there being two separate masks, but rather there was a doubleness in its essence that was always maintained. It was maintained here, even in the absence of the sighted mask. The twinness in front of me was represented by the authentic and the inauthentic. But now I was unsure if all the qualities in the mask had been identified. I had thought they were blindness and vision, even mystical blindness: self-inflicted, tragic, bringing insight. Until this other unsighted double appeared.

I was baffled. Yet I knew that the mask within the blue box was the authentic, unsighted one because I could not see it. The other mask behind the glass, which I could see, was a copy. The sightedness had to do, then, with me. The logic of the art, even the storing of the art, was that the original unsighted mask was the one kept in darkness.

The conservator returned to tell us that the records indicated the real one was in the blue box.

Sandra asked her to call an assistant. I stood, attending, as though waiting for the start of a ceremony. The assistant brought over a special ladder which she leaned against the wall and climbed.

At Sandra's direction the conservators moved the container out of the dusk of the shelf and over to a small white table. As they placed it on the table, Sandra said, "We'll need a small screwdriver." I smiled, recalling Claire's story of the party when Austin Hart brought the sighted mask back from Paris.

She handed the screwdriver to me as she pointed to the four corners of the box. I wanted to stop here—to go back again in the story, circle around, not have this, yet, be the beginning—because maybe there would be no foothold. My movements were slow and Sandra looked at me, confused at why I hesitated. I proceeded, and when the last screw was undone, Sandra started to lift the lid; I noticed that there was a handwritten tag, like a luggage tag, on the side of the box that said "for traveling."

Sandra took out the block of white styrofoam and placed it on the table. Removing the top, she reached in with both hands and carefully pulled out the mask. She placed it on the table. It rocked slightly with a bowl's center of gravity.

Something in me started to shut down. I wanted to shield my eyes against the sheer magnetic pull of its shape. And of one thing I was certain: all the representations of this mask—all the photographs, descriptions, articles—had not revealed the most essential thing. The mask was amphibious, a human being becoming frog, and at the same time the frog becoming human. In that thin membrane—bordering between the human and the animal, between air and water, between material and spirit—lay the raw space of ambivalence, the space that gave no comfort—where this one lived.

A green color had either been massaged into the stone or induced from it. It was not shown in any of the photographs, nor ever described. Red ochre was around the ears, as though the ears were sore.

This mask was not blind. It had closed eyes. If I touched them, I would feel the round orbs of the eyes beneath the lids.

I reached over and lifted the mask. It was so balanced and strong I had to hold it with both hands.

They were standing right beside me; they didn't want me to touch the thing, as though I might lick it, taste it, now, on the spot. I said to Sandra, may I put it on. But she didn't know. She shrugged. I raised the mask to my face.

So dark. It was not the darkness of the world out of which we were born; it was the darkness of the unborn world. It was terrible. I was going to be ill. And then I could hear the sound of water contained within the stone. There was an ocean. I had been inside this darkness. The faces of all the people who had worn the mask touched my own: Claire's face, Hart's, going back to the beginning.

I pulled it away from my face.

"The masks are about Raven stealing the light," Sandra said, breaking the spell.

I looked at the mask. I was sighted again.

Sandra reached for it and I gave it up. She put it back in the box and slowly covered it.

She called a conservator. The youngest came. She was putting on her gloves. She lifted the box to the shelf.

Everything I had written, everything I had thought, was an approximation. I had only been close to the target. The target had now hit me.

25

PARABLE OF THE UNWASHED HAIR

Hart:
[Waking up on Ninsints]
I step onto this shore.
I feel so released.
I feel so discovered.
I feel, holy—
I am afraid.

Animals were not in my dreams,
as though extinct in me

Alix's Lines for the Libretto

The phone rang. It was Sophia. She was upset and asked that I come as soon as I could. When I hung up it rang again. Brett said the Producer wanted the written report on my trip to Ottawa.

AS I WENT UP the steps of the rest-home, I noticed that the outer board on the fourth stair was soft, almost pulpy underfoot.

Mrs. Askew was asleep in her wheelchair just beyond the entrance, her arms crossed helplessly on her lap and her head doved onto her chest. It was unimaginable that a body with a spine could take such a position.

Mother's door was closed when she usually kept it open.

"What is it, Mother? What's happened?" She had her glasses on, but I could see that her eyes were red and bloated from unaccustomed crying.

"Mrs. Griffin died right after breakfast. I ate with her at the same table, like I always do, and then she didn't show up for lunch because she was dead."

I sat on the bed beside her. "Did she seem all right at breakfast?"

"As usual. She was batty, you know that, but otherwise pretty healthy. How can I stay in a place where people die between breakfast and lunch? I was asleep when they took her away, and I never heard a thing." I put her hand in mine, and she didn't pull away.

A tall man with a grizzled face was standing in the doorway. "No, Peter," she said, "not just now." His hands jerked suddenly and thrashed up to his face; I thought he was going to put them in his mouth.

"Who's that?"

"Peter Maybe, that's what I call him. All he can say, over and over again, is 'maybe.' He got here a few days ago. Put me in the wheelchair, will you, and walk me to the park. We'll get an ice-cream. Those boys still go by peddling the ice-cream in their carts, with that same tune playing. I need the sound of summer. It'll be worse than ever without Mrs. Griffin. I wanted to ask you to take me to Pine Street, but I thought you'd say no, so I won't ask."

"Next week. Let's plan for next week—"

Although it was mild outside, Sophia was so frail I opened her closet door to get her coat.

"Mother, whose dresses are these?" I flipped through the rack. "Most of these aren't yours."

"The staff are pretty busy. They say they can't keep track of whose are what's."

"Have you been wearing that same dress for days?"

"It's mine. If I don't put it in the wash, I don't have to worry about it not coming back."

"Oh dear."

"I never know whose clothes I'm going to get from the laundry. It means that the inmates seem vaguely familiar to one another—even for the ones who are far gone—because they recognize something about someone else, and it's their own clothes. I'm glad my shoes don't need cleaning. Poor Mrs. Griffin."

I looked on the floor of the cupboard. In and among the shoes were piled dozens of empty cans of tonic water. "What are these doing in here?"

"I don't know. I'm saving them. They're a comfort. I drink cans of tonic without the gin."

"What are you going to do with them all?"

"Keep piling them up 'til they all fall out I guess."

"I should take them away, don't you think? You never hoarded things. You never even liked leftovers for dinner. You threw food out."

She didn't seem embarrassed that I had discovered her new habit; in fact her mood brightened.

"Even if you take them away, I'll just save more."

"All right, you do that."

"Dear Mrs. Griffin. At breakfast she said—because she can't remember anything from one minute to the next—'I'm one crank away from enlightenment.' That's like one of those things I do, you know, a misanthropism."

"Oh, Mother." I sat down on the bed with her Burberry coat over my arm. I lowered my head and started to laugh. "Dearest, it's not *misanthropism*, it's a *malapropism*."

"Well, you can laugh. Lucky you. Probably I caught it in here from one of the others. Thread my arms through my coat, will you?"

I put her in her wheelchair. "There, are you comfortable?"

"Are you kidding?"

"What can I do?"

"Not a damn thing. Get me some ice-cream."

"Are you hungry? Did you miss lunch, with all the upset?"

"I'm not sure. I guess I've had an apple. I still have the taste of it in my mouth."

Mrs. Askew was awake, and as I wheeled Sophia past her, she reached out and managed to grab the hem of my mother's coat. She was stronger than I imagined and we were caught.

"Take me home," she said.

Sophia looked down at the hand fisted on the garment, and then looked directly into Mrs. Askew's stare. "This is my daughter. Isn't she beautiful? I'm going home next week. You can come too."

Mrs. Askew let go. "Next week," she said with complete certainty and calm.

When we were out of ear-shot I reprimanded her. "Sophia, you mustn't promise that. How can we?"

"Why do you call me Mother sometimes and Sophia other times?"

"I don't know. Look—"

"You'll figure out how to get the three of us to Pine Street. You're writing an opera about Austin Hart."

We were moving towards the top of the ramp when I stopped. "I want to go tell the manager about the front step, there"—I pointed—"it isn't safe."

"I wouldn't know. I don't walk on it anymore."

"What's the name of the manager again? Mrs.—"

"Are you testing me?"

"No, Mother, I've forgotten."

"Well, so have I. You know I've told them I think this joint should be renovated and that I would plan it for them for free. They look at me so kindly, as if I'm a real nutball. I hate that."

When I returned, Sophia had wheeled herself to the very edge of the disabled ramp. "It's pretty steep, Alix."

"I've had the grips fixed on the chair. It was a design flaw."

"Speaking of which, my glasses are failing me. I need a stronger perspective."

I let the malapropism pass. "Dr. Kniefel will come and check your eyes again. I'll set it up."

"You are a dear. I am so grateful."

There wasn't a walk-way down to the view-point from the mansion, and so I took her across the grass to the verge.

"God this is hard going." I heard most things she uttered as having a double meaning which she might, or might not, have intended.

"My friend, Miles, who is native, told me—"

"Are there really any native people around any more? I know your opera is supposed to be about them, so maybe that's a problem, haven't they all gone—been absorbed or something? Well, I suppose not, since you have your friend Miles. But does he look like an Indian?"

"I don't know how to respond to these assumptions."

She turned her head around to look at me, and I could only see her wide right eye. But she was more hurt than angry.

I patted her on the head. "Let me tell you what I was going to say. An elder from the Dogrib Band—don't comment—they're in the Yukon—"

"Dogrib. Amazing."

"Do you want to hear this?"

"Of course I do. Just because I'm ill-informed doesn't mean I'm dull or disinterested. What happened to the Dogrib person?"

"She was going to Ottawa from the Yukon, her first time on a plane; they were going to make representations to the government about their land claims. Anyway, she hadn't flown before and she was terrified. But she got used to it and eventually felt comfortable. At one point the plane began to really vibrate. She said, calm as ever, 'We must be going over an Indian reserve. The roads are always so bad.'"

"That's good. Yes, that's good. So I'm traveling over a reserve that's waiting for me, my hole under the ground."

"Are you feeling morbid?"

"If you want to live, you end up in my state."

We made it to the edge of the grass overlooking the beach, the ocean and the mountains; everything beyond that seemed irrelevant, if it even existed.

"I remember there used to be a house right here, in this very place. How nice of them to level it for us."

I sat on the ground next to the wheel of her chair.

"You know, Alicia, I was thinking this afternoon, just before you came, that I really haven't been a very good mother to you."

She had never made such a statement to me before, had never expressed any doubt about being a mother. Mrs. Griffin's death had probably brought this on.

"I think we've managed." It seemed too late in the day for such a discussion, and Mother too vulnerable.

"Tell me the truth, Alix—I really haven't been a great mother—maybe I was okay for Peg, but not for you, don't you think? Tell me. I can take it on the chin."

I turned so that I could lean against the chair. "Are you sure?" Then I did want to talk to her the way a daughter would, meet her in disclosure perhaps for the first time.

"Sure I'm sure. You can tell me. We're still in the game."

What could I say that would make any sense to her? I scanned the past as though looking at an ex-ray. "Well, I remember once, I guess I was seven or eight years old—you and Russell were going out, and you had on that purple cocktail dress with the chiffon top—"

"I loved that dress. And matching shoes, *peau-de-soie*. Great shoes. I still have them, don't I? I always looked good in heels. Could stride like a model."

"—You told me before you went out that I should have a bath and wash my hair. When you came back from the party, I was still up. You asked me if I'd done it—had a bath and washed my hair. I said yes. Then about half an hour later, you came up to me, leaned over and said 'Your hair smells like hair. Didn't you wash it?' I said no. I guess I was pretty mixed up because of my dog. You stood there, looking down at me, and said, 'Don't you know whether or not you've washed your hair; don't you know whether or not you've had a bath? Do I have to take you to a psychiatrist? Don't you know?' You repeated it all again. This was the day after you had my dog put down so—"

"Bosh—" she interrupted.

"—so I didn't—"

"Bosh."

I looked up at her from my place on the ground. "What?"

"Alicia, that never happened."

"What do you mean?" I didn't understand.

"Just what I said. That never happened, dear."

I stood. I could feel how flushed my face was.

"Sorry," she said, as though I'd lost a coin toss.

"What part never happened, Mother?" I moved away from her. I was afraid of her and what she could do to me, yet again. I had made a mistake.

"None of it. I never had your dog put down. It just didn't happen."

"Yes it did." I took another step back and then stopped. She was shaking her head, as if I deserved to be pitied. "It did happen. You had my dog put away. He was sick, once, on your carpet in the living room, and that was it."

"Alicia, this is ridiculous. I didn't do away with your dog."

"You did. Instead of taking him to the vet to get better like you said you would, you had him put down. That's what Russell told me."

"Russell? You believed Russell?"

"And—" There was more—I couldn't remember. "I also saw the veterinarian's bill, addressed to you, Mrs. Russell Purcell, for 'euthanasia services $25.00.' I didn't know what euthanasia meant, so I looked it up in the dictionary. It said 'gentle and easy death' so I was relieved. Then it said 'the bringing about of this.' Which is what you did."

A ripple of some emotion contorted her face. She looked almost gleeful. She was grotesque.

"If this really happened, as you say it did, why didn't you mention this to me before now?"

I went behind her and gripped the rubber handles of the chair.

"Not mention it before now? Why would I? So we could end up right here earlier in our lives?" I pushed her back over the grass towards the mansion. "You think you were a good mother to Peg?" I was wheeling her very fast. "You're kidding yourself."

"If this really happened, you would have said something."

"Why do you think Peg left, years ago, is sailing around the world, never comes home?" Finally I would tell her. "Because of you, that's why. She can't take the way you are." Telling her the truth, decades too late, was cold, mean comfort.

"Alix, stop. Why didn't you say something before now?"

Then I did stop. Then I went around in front of her. I looked right at her. "Why didn't I say anything before now, Mother? Because you would have told me it never happened."

"Oh, Alicia." She exhaled, a sigh dispelling the unacceptable.

Then I was crying. The walls of my *self* were being scribbled on with a child's crayon, the bold swinging colors of emotion or the eradication of emotion. Of sorrow for a stupid dead dog that had just died.

"If this did happen," she said, "—and it didn't—well then—I'm sorry."

That was as far as we could go.

I hated having to push her. I wanted to just leave her there, stuck on the lawn, unable to fend for herself; me, walking away, not knowing what was true. Maybe it had never happened. Maybe she had always been right. I felt like a blind woman standing in the middle of an intersection, ensnarled in traffic, waving a cane for eyes.

The apotheosis for all the confusion and despair of my life: a traffic metaphor.

Finally, we made it back to the rest-home and to her room. As I left she said, "Please don't be upset. I'm upset too. Mothers are always a tough deal. Only a mother could say such things to you. Maybe you could try to be thankful you have one."

26

A MUG'S GAME

The Beginning of the World
Chorus

Raven
being born
needs a mother
to be born
needs to love
being born
makes the light

[There is a brilliance, like the light inside a window getting brighter. It fills the theater.]

Then Raven steals what he has made—
like that—snatched.
[Darkness]

Alix's Lines for the Libretto

I'd been back in my mother's funhouse, where I'd been schooled, as she urged me into an open space that suddenly turned into a glass wall upon which I banged my head.

All of this pressed hard against my fear that I would never get the story right, not this one or any other, not about my life, not about Austin Hart. The roadway to my history was always under construction. The traffic cop looked like my mother, wearing an orange vest covered in reflector stripes and holding up a "detour" sign. I couldn't get a purchase on the past, and it addled the present. After Austin Hart's return to my life, I was less cautious with others, more trusting. However, Sophia and I had found a new fault line and I was staring into the wide fissure that went deep into the center of things. Never before had I advanced my version of an event, to be met not with a different variation from her, but a flat denial. I'd been a fool to answer her question about her being a good mother. She had played the shill to her own shell game.

There were too many metaphors and no solutions.

Unexpectedly, in the middle of the night, awake and inconsolable, I decided that Sophia was right, she could get to me in a way that no other human being could. It would have been hapless of me to hold that against her. I would waft it away, as Austin had tried to do when he encountered his father transformed into a wasp and a god who didn't know his creation's name.

She tested my resolve the next afternoon when I visited her, opening with the tease, "So, did you wash your hair this morning?"

"Actually, I don't remember. Maybe yes, maybe no."

She viewed me with satisfaction, as if finally being able to claim me as a worthy ally. A shame-faced, almost crooked smile crossed her face, ghostly, and then disappeared. Some large discounting was being done in her mind over her victory. The nasty phrases at her ready command which she habitually used to put me in my place: 'it's all bosh'; 'don't play the fool,'—she didn't say any of them. Some stick had been poked into her wheels.

She put the game aside. "Did Rachel Epstein's daughter call you?" she asked. "Jada I think her name is. Lovely name."

"She did call."

"I asked her to. You're going to get together? You don't seem to have enough friends, so I worry about you."

"I don't really have anything to say to anyone, except about the opera."

"You should go out with her, with anyone, enjoy yourself."

"I don't mind being alone."

"You didn't used to be like this, did you? I'll get Jada to call you again." Sophia handed me her new glasses. The frames were broken.

"What happened?"

"I loaned them to Mrs. Askew and she sat on them. There's no point in getting them fixed. They weren't any damn good anyway. I haven't been able to read. Read something to me, will you?"

"What about Emma Bovary?" I reached for the book from her bedside table.

"I'm tired of Emma. I don't think Flaubert loved her as much as Tolstoy loved Anna. It's important for a writer to love the characters they create. I hope you love the ones in your opera. What's the news? You can tell me things and we can bury the hatchet." She smiled.

"Brett is panicked. I have to see him tomorrow. Trevor Crane, you know, the previous librettist, called me and left a message, apologizing for being so 'scary' about the risks of working on the opera, said he was now in control of his faculties. Paige sent me a note saying she's struggling a bit in her 'cramped and narrow little house.' Asks if I can visit her—"

"Yes, you must visit her. You'll need your new family, especially when I'm gone." She was weathering an emotion just shy of self-pity. "I've been thinking how desperate Austin must have been at the end. But didn't anyone of his friends or family know he was going to kill himself? Claire—or even Mary-Anne—if these women loved him how could they not know?"

"That's harsh. Supposedly no one knew."

"Someone must have known he was in trouble. Someone must have called him. Why didn't he answer the phone?"

"Maybe people did call him," I said pointedly. "Maybe a lot of people called him. And maybe he didn't answer because he knew they'd have to do more than just telephone. They'd actually have to come over. When you save someone you can't just leave them. You have to feed them."

I was back in the outlet of the past, putting my finger in the socket; the electricity hadn't been turned off even though the account was closed.

"I fed you," mother said defensively. "Look, see, you're here."

Look look, see see. See Spot run. She was trying to teach me the basics. Yet these old mother-daughter misunderstandings had re-surfaced from the past, unbidden, like a rash.

"Tell me more about what you've been discovering."

I described the article on Perez which Austin had written. "It's such an interesting theory, so contrary to the established scholarship: that Perez did go ashore but didn't disclose it, in order to protect the natives, if only for a few years."

"This I apprehend," Sophia said approvingly.

"And comprehend, I hope," noticing, but not highlighting, her misuse of words.

"This is an important clue about him. I like the man Austin Hart has become. I understand wanting to keep something secret in order to protect it from others. Sometimes self-disclosure is a kind of mug's game. When did he write this again?"

"Just a few months before he killed himself."

"What a stupid solution for such a brilliant mind," Sophia concluded. "So, what else are you getting? You sit at a table in the village square and people come to you, like you're the only one in the whole place with a phone card, those new things so you can call long distance. They tell you things they hope you'll communicate, because they trust you."

She'd always been a little scornful of my accomplishments, and I wondered if she'd eventually call on an ancient fidelity between us, an early, unspoken pledge every daughter has to make: that I wouldn't venture beyond the limits she set by her own achievements. What she'd made of her life was paltry compared to her real capabilities. Out of low-grade allegiance was I now breaking the pact I would not go beyond her? I was failing her because people did confide in me. To speak about this to my mother, to seek confirmation of the dynamics between us, would be to acknowledge a secret system that kept the planets on orbit.

It occurred to me now, with uncertainty following like a contrail—maybe she wasn't calling on an old fidelity. Maybe she actually enjoyed my being at the center of the village square, responding to those who needed something, in a way she hadn't been able to respond.

"I'm proud of you, Alicia, and what you're doing."

She was knocking off my doubts like at a skeet shoot.

As if sensing my confusion, she added, "I'm not opposing you, I'm grooming you. It's never too late. We're like monkeys, picking the nits out of each others hair."

This mother who never really cared for me, caring for me.

"So tell me what more you got," she said. She was happy.

She settled her head back against the pillow and rested her legs on the bed with her feet dangling over the side so as not to soil the bedspread. "By the way, I hope you don't believe everything people tell you."

"Why would I doubt them?"

"I just want you to be careful. Sometimes you're pretty gullible. Well, innocent is a nicer word." Then she laughed. "Maybe you figure I'm a crook training you on thievery."

"More like a liar teaching me to distrust the truth."

"Touchee, my dear. None the less, you do need to be around people who are trustworthy." Then she asked, strangely I thought, "Am I going to be in this opera? Is my garden in this opera?"

"My lunch is probably going to be in this opera."

"I hope not."

27

MUSIC TRUMPS WORDS

Hart [on Ninstints]
I've been here
Here before
At first contact with this light
At first contact with this place
And I was afraid

Alix's Lines for the Libretto

Brett insisted I come to the island and show him what I had completed on the libretto.

As I entered the small cabin detached from the main house, where Brett did his composing, I heard his wife call from the porch. "The Producer just rang. Tom Price is dying. The Producer also wants you to know he spoke to the Kerner Foundation about money. Wants to see progress. He'll call again in fifteen minutes."

I listened as Brett talked on the phone. Goats were at the door. Brett leaned against the wall and then held on to the doorjam. He said "but" and then "yes, I know...but how is Tom...Tom, how is he?"

When he finally hung up, he said there were two views: Françoise wanted Tom to be put on life support and Tom wanted to die. It was uncertain who would prevail.

Of course I was disturbed by the news of Tom's health, but I also worried I wouldn't get a chance to meet him. He'd been on the expedition, was the narrator of the official version of the film, and was the man who had blossomed into the great Haida carver.

As I was showing Brett what I had completed, he stared at me and finally said, "God you look tired. You should get more rest." I didn't think I felt tired.

"Austin's been disturbing my dreams," I said. Brett didn't seem to want more. I understood the difficulty for anyone, other than yourself, being interested in your dreams.

I led him through the historical scene I had just completed, when Juan Perez meets the Haida. It would come at the commencement of the opera.

Brett was thumbing through the libretto. I spoke more quickly, not wanting to lose his interest.

Brett read aloud:

"They cast feathers on the water
for our bow to spread
to lay aside
to open—
They opened up their arms
As if expecting me.

Who's saying this?"

"Perez, about the Haida," I answered.

"Then you have the native chorus singing:

'Send the word back to the shore,
across the feathers we laid down,
spread the news:

They are just like us
They are people
They are just like us

Real people
We have discovered a new human race.'"

"And Shawcroft, you have him as a character? That's good. I like it." He drew a long breath. "So what's the theme here about first contact with the Haida?" He continued to page through the work.

I explained that in the beginning, the relationship between the Haida and the explorers and traders was one of mutual benefit. As the explorers gave way to settlers, the natives realized they were going to be taken over. "There was a surge of energy, a dark florescence. Art was created that had never been made before, new totems, competitive feasting. They couldn't take their future for granted any more." As I was speaking, it occurred to me that Austin's buying up of native art on the last day of his life was a truncated version of this strange florescence. "Austin understood what the Haida had been through. And he took the poles."

Brett sat down at his keyboard. "You mean Hart met a similar fate. Good, a tragedy, in classic terms. I can use this. Remember we have to end on an upbeat note. An opera can heal." He put the libretto beside the keyboard. "Let me tell you what I believe about this project." He played a few random notes. "We're not concocting a story as much as we're discovering what's there already. And it's not a local theme—it's universal." He sounded like the Producer, grandiosity masked as humility. He played a chord with his right hand. "The opera might open first in Paris. That's my belief and my dream." Two chords, right and left.

I wanted him to be less expansive, we were still at the beginning, but I didn't want to quell his enthusiasm, his most engaging quality.

I explained the next scene, set in modern times as the expedition lands on Ninstints and Austin "wakes up," as it were, on the island. And I continued, "It's like a first contact; the connection to Perez is strong. Austin sings 'I've been here before.'"

"Alix, good work. You've managed the reincarnation theme in just one line. Austin is Shawcroft."

I demurred. "Actually, his association is with Perez."

"Anyway, it's still reincarnation. Art has prevailed over family politics. But listen, Alix," Brett picked up the libretto again,"be careful not to write too many words. In the end they'll just have to be cut."

I was taken aback. "I guess you don't know that yet, do you?"

"I do. There mustn't be too many words."

"I'm not sure what you mean by 'too many.'"

"Think of it this way: music is a man; he is always constituted. Now he's hurt, now pleased, now triumphant, but always constituted. The libretto is feminine. No word has any value without the chord preceding it or the notes that follow. Your words are there to inspire the music, and they will. The magic and the music—that's just the way it is—they carry the libretto."

I almost laughed at the sexism embedded in his metaphor. "Is that really what you think?"

"That's the way it has been throughout the entire history of opera. Didn't you know that?" He was flat-footed and humorless, unnerving qualities to bring to a creative partnership.

"But the words provide the clarity. Don't they?"

"The audience wants transportment, not clarity."

"Subject closed?"

"Yes. Now what?"

I had been working alone amidst the great and insightful company of the dead and their artifacts, and so I felt a little giddy, revealing the lines they'd inspired. I'd wanted to have a little fun. I hadn't expected such a serious lecture and kind of ultimatum.

"The Calculators goad Austin about his hesitation in cutting the totems," I said, keeping on track. "Finally he says to the men, 'Fell these poles.'"

"Hold on just a sec. These people, The Calculators, who are they?"

"They're financing the expedition."

"Ah, so they're really the bad guys I guess. I'm not sure about 'Calculators.' What else could you call them?"

"They're collectors."

"Yes, we'll name them that. Let's go back."

I was newly alarmed at his autocratic decision-making. "Hold on, Brett. You're hardly giving the woman time to support the man," He didn't seem to notice my sarcasm.

"Alix, another point. Hart's feelings have to be clear. A lot of what is said and sung won't be heard by the audience. The audience needs help. Here there's in a line in the libretto, 'the poles are alive'—but if the singer has bad diction, then people miss it. So you have to say it a number of times to make sure they get it. Tell them what they're going to see, show it to them, and then tell them what they just saw."

"You're not giving the audience much credit."

"Most often they're just thinking their own thoughts. The music will help. There's lighting that could be fixed on the poles to make them seem alive for those people who still don't get it. Figures could come out of the poles, dancers, and then go back. Maybe it's outrageous but there's a lot of magic in it."

"The magic also has to be earned." We were approaching a stand-off. This was Brett's territory, the theater, but I was worried. "The opera isn't just about fantastical visions," I said. "Austin left on the journey, triumphal, and he ends his journey, a suicide. The opera has to answer why."

"Can you?" he challenged.

"Not yet, but I will."

"Okay, pressing on. What's Raven doing in the opera?"

"After Austin and the crew take the poles, there's a debate between Shawcroft and Raven about whether Austin is just a Collector, like all the rest. Raven argues that he isn't, that his humanity can be restored. He sings:

"If the human race is squandered
the sound of its going
will spread to the end of time
and back—

A billion years will pass

before people will come again—
a billion years of midnight—
and me, forlorn, and waiting,
as I waited, too long, before.

How alone I will be
Without a human friend
All stories put in a box—
Lights out—
Left watching a greedy old man."

"The future of the world is at stake. I like that."

"Raven gradually convinces Shawcroft to agree that if Austin manages to bring the twin masks back together to be danced he will have shown his humanity and the blight in the world will end. Raven says 'I will use Austin as a drum.'"

He was excited. "There should be a huge cadenza here. There is a sound. Drums. What's next?"

We worked through the rest of what I'd written until Brett stood up. He seemed even taller in this small space. "You have to catch your ferry. Been a good day. Do you think that people—natives and non-natives—will understand this opera? I mean I think they will. What will they understand?"

"Loss."

"Is that all?"

"All?" I repeated. His appetite for the dramatic verged on the vulgar. "What it's like to lose your home, the people you love—to lose them like losing parts of yourself: your speech, your hearing, your eyesight—bits of yourself taken away like the land you once occupied. You can only stand there and watch." I was talking about the Haida, Austin Hart, my mother, myself. "It's about our struggle with death. Or least that's what it's about today," I said, trying to downplay my zeal, so it would fit into the somewhat narrow space Brett Morris allocated to words. I'd need to enlarge that space.

"Yes, I think people are still in their seats. Anyway, my music will ensure that."

There was a cry from the house. I looked at Brett. He hadn't heard it. Another more urgent plea. "Your wife," I said as her voice finally registered with him. He took one step and was out the door. I followed. He was already across the yard, running in the dark; his wife was hollering through the window and then through the screen door. There was a fox in the chicken-house. One night they'd had a cougar.

28

WHAT DO WASPS HAVE TO DO WITH ANYTHING?

Hart

The past is not dead
it only seems inaccessible,
but just for now.

Alix's Lines for the Libretto

I needed Candice's help with my discoveries about her brother, to find out what had happened in his childhood which so plagued him years later on Haida Gwaii. I hadn't asked her enough questions about their father.

When Candice answered the door, she seemed pleased to see me, even though I had come unexpectedly.

As I followed her down the hall, I noticed that the family photograph she'd shown me the last time hadn't been put back on the wall. There was a noticeable blank space where it had hung.

I sat in the kitchen, looking out at the broad, precipitous view of ocean that had somewhat alarmed me. It now didn't seem like such a toppling expanse to me.

I'd brought a bouquet of exotic flowers, anthuriums, birds of paradise. While Candice was putting them in a vase, before I was able to pose my questions, she started in.

"I was thinking about Dad and his affect on Austin. You've really got me going now. I guess you need to do a kind of psychological study of Austin, to make sure you get him right, do you?" Her rotund figure was overly mature for the sprightly pink and green outfit she wore. Skort, that was the name for the style of shorts she wore; she looked a little comedic.

"Well, I've been thinking," she said, leaving the flowers in the sink. "I'm no brain, mind you, but I read a bit, listen to CBC radio, it's my favorite; try to take in what I hear, follow up sometimes. I'm not on the internet, but I've asked Bill to get me a computer. He says he has an old one at the office which I can use, good enough for me. He hasn't brought it home yet, but he will. There's lots you can find out on the internet without having to go to the library or even leave your kitchen. I'll have him set it up for me here in this closet." She opened a large door filled with cleaning implements and products. "It's a bit of a mess, but I'll sort it out, use the utility room for the brooms, the vacuum cleaner. This is where I'll keep my computer. So—" she closed the door "—just like that and no one will be the wiser about what's inside. What was I saying?"

"That you were thinking about your Dad's influence on Austin."

"I was, yes."

"His name was Charlie?"

"Charlie Hart. He was never called Charles, too fancy, although he could be quite formal. Supper was always the same time, had to be on the table at 6 p.m. sharp and we had to be sitting there, no exceptions. Dad would come home from the store—that's how he referred to the electrical shop he owned—he called it 'the store'—and he'd change into his 'evening clothes,' just a clean shirt and jacket really. Sometimes he wore a tie."

"In the Ninstints film Austin is quite dressed up, even though they were in the bush."

"Oh, yeah, that's my brother. Got it from Dad I guess. Austin was always well dressed. Quite dapper."

I told her I'd been reviewing Austin's diaries held in the archives, and I wondered whether or not there was some family difficulty, maybe a tragedy, that happened when Austin was young.

"Nothing that I can think of. Tragedy? Now that's a ten-dollar word. What does he say? I'd love to read his diaries. Do you think I could? Well, I'm not sure. Never mind. I'd probably cry. Austin was very sensitive, you know that by now. Something may have happened that affected him and wouldn't have bothered anybody else. Not that he over-reacted, I'm not saying that. He just felt things more than most people. I was glad I came second in line. Under the radar, as they say now."

"Did Austin and your father fight a lot?"

"Fight? Like I said, Austin wouldn't let me criticize Dad. Even though he deserved it sometimes. He'd hassle Austin, because Austin always had his head in a book. Then he'd come to the table and Dad would say 'What a surprise. Look who's landed in our midst.' That irked Austin. 'He's decided to land amongst us." Candice was a good mimic. "He called him 'my boy.' There was a to-do once about Austin getting a scholarship. Dad wouldn't allow it."

"Why not?"

"Pride. He said whatever we needed he would provide or we didn't need it. That was the measuring-stick of our family's need, whether Dad could provide."

"What happened, do you remember?"

"Now this I can help you with. It involved Mr. McNally, who was Austin's teacher in grade 11, and I also had him for English, grade 9. He was the best teacher I ever had—"

I was afraid I was going to lose her again. "The scholarship?"

"Okay, so Mr. McNally sends a note home with Austin. This—I later learned—was about accepting this scholarship for Austin to go away to a summer school for bright kids in the arts. Austin hands the note across the dinner table to Mom and says 'it's from school.' She looks at the envelope and then at Austin and says 'but this is addressed to your Dad' and hands it to him. She was pretty submissive I guess, not like now. I have a picture of it all in my mind, because of

Dad's reaction. This time he was downright nasty. You'll see. So Dad opens the envelope, unfolds the letter, reads it slowly and then folds it back up and puts it away, just continues with his supper. We all carry on eating. We never said much over meals, not like now when you try to talk to one another. No one mentions the note that's just been passed around the table." She was smiling. "I guess I shouldn't laugh. Well, lemme tell you, I sure didn't at the time. So we're having supper, there's a knock on the door. We all look up. Dad frowns. He doesn't like visitors at the best of times and sure not at meals. He gives me the nod and I go to the door. It's Mr. McNally. The teacher is embarrassed too 'cause he's come when we're eating. Dad gets up from the table, goes to Mr. McNally and starts yelling at the poor man. 'What's wrong with you? Coming here, in the midst of my family, while we're having our evening meal. Are you suggesting I can't provide for my own family?' He's yelling, saying Austin's sneaking around, getting McNally to come here, conniving, cheating, some pansy he says. I'm adding this part, but I know that's what Dad thought. Something like it. So the teacher kind of backs down the stairs. Then Dad goes over to Austin, just stands there towering above him, and then he says, you know like Jehovah, he says, with big spaces between the words, 'You are a fraud. Everyone will find out.' Just like that. It was awful. I didn't understand it. It was like he was crazy. Maybe Dad was under stress, I don't know. To have Austin's teacher see his father go bananas, for no reason. It's kind of a puzzle, isn't it, what makes any of us tick?"

"And after that?"

"I don't know, just carrying on. Austin didn't go away that summer, for sure. You'd think from the way I talk that I just sat around all my life watching what was happening to my brother, but he was older, and I was keen on him."

"And wasps? Was Austin afraid of wasps?"

"What do wasps have to do with anything?"

I was prepared to let it go.

"Oh, I know what you're saying. Yeah, Dad could kill wasps in his bare hands. We'd be sitting out on the back patio, at the picnic table in the summer. He'd raise his hands up, and put them around a hovering wasp, keeping his hands just so. Then whap, he'd slap his hands together, open them and the dead wasp'd fall onto the table. Mom would be saying, 'Charlie, for heaven's sake, leave them alone. Just shoo them away. I've made poor old dad sound too weird, haven't I—for the opera I mean."

"No, don't worry."

"Just clues, I guess."

"Important ones."

I had the renewed confidence that I could actually find out what happened, even to the point of knowing why Austin killed himself.

29

NO LIMITATION PERIOD

Hart:

I am trailing a god
who is looking for me.

Alix's Lines for the Libretto

Memorandum to: Brett
By fax
From: Alix

I have listened to the tapes of the music you sent for the first two scenes. I'm sorry we were a little at cross-purposes when we were going over the libretto at your studio. Having you put music to my words is like the moment when the thermal updraft arrives (as Austin might say) and we're borne aloft. Better than flying, it's the creation of flight. All our differences dissolve.

Paige will be here today. I'll go over the libretto and play her the music.

Call when you can.

I set the dining room table for lunch. Beside Paige's placemat I put the black binder with the synopsis and the draft libretto of the first two scenes, and Brett's music.

"Nice digs," she said casually.

She had a colorful cotton scarf around her neck, so large it might have hidden a wound. Hanging on a gold chair down the front of her shirt, resting on a confusion of velvet, was a single moon-shaped piece of jewelry. She seemed anxious.

She declared she didn't want to be a mother anymore. Once she intentionally became homeless, living at a friend's, so that her adult daughter wouldn't have a place to settle. When Paige moved into the one-bedroom house where she now lived, she described to her daughter the smallness of the room, the tininess of the single bed saying, "so if you need a place to land there's only a narrow ledge, and I'm on it."

"Is this like your father then?" I asked. Paige didn't seem to mind such a direct question.

"In the winter of his last year, I lived in the basement of his house. For four weeks. It was dark there, no windows. My daughter was just a baby, the father had taken off. Sometimes when I wanted to go upstairs, even though he was on the third floor, he knew. He filled the entire house so that when I started to climb the stairs, he could feel it." She spread her arms wide and then rattled her hands as if shaking tambourines. "He'd isolated himself at the top of the house. It was like a bad dream. So weird. I moved out in the spring and then he was alone. I told you I wanted to come back after that. I should have.

"When he killed himself, I went with my Aunt Candice—you talked to her again, I hear—she's afraid she's telling you too much. Aunt Candice and I went up there to his bedroom. He'd always taken something to help him sleep, but in the top drawer of his dresser—vials of pills, lots empty, some of them half gone. He saved the containers, god knows why." She paused, snagged again on the past. "There aren't words in our language for the cold horror of being in that room. It was as though I'd found his remains. I mean I didn't. They were on the wall of his office."

The place of the opera was irrelevant compared to that searing image. "I'm sorry."

"Yeah. I know what it is like to be greedy. You end up wanting more even before you are finished with what you already have."

"Meaning?"

"He didn't finish his life before he ended it."

Although still elusive, I didn't press her to explain. She was shivering and I put one of mother's shawl around her shoulders. "You all right?"

"Ask me something so I can get away from that bedroom."

"Candice mentioned that your father went on a buying binge on the day—"

"Binge? Is that the word she used?"

"Spree maybe. Anyway she mentioned that on his last day he bought up native art."

"And that I'm now selling it in order to live, is that what she said? Ah, this family. We sure do talk in our sleep."

"I didn't think she was being critical. It sounded as though the rest of the family was afraid of having any of the collection."

"So what if it was a binge. Dad had always acquired art for the museum, but not for himself. He didn't want people to think he was profiting, you know, from his relationship with native artists. So on his last day I figured he must have been pretty happy, going around buying things. Who could begrudge him that?"

"Was there something about Austin inadvertently creating a black market—"

"McNabb told you this, didn't he? Fuck him. He probably told you this in confidence just the way he's told anyone who'll listen the same thing, in confidence. He did create a market for this artwork. Why not? It all had real value; without a market these native artists wouldn't be paid their worth. You know why it was illegal? Because museums wanted to keep these geniuses in ignorance of the worth of what they were creating—brilliant, beyond anything the world had ever seen. Dad's friend, Levi Straus, said that any comparison to the dazzling creativity of Northwest Coast art couldn't be found until Picasso. Picasso's was the work of a single man, lasting his lifetime. Theirs was practiced by a whole indigenous culture for 150 years."

She was her father's daughter, spirited and articulate. I asked her more about Austin's purchases on the last day. "I've been thinking it was like—"

She didn't want to hear from me, and I really didn't mind. I had second-hand insights, and she had the indissoluble experience. "He drove over to the island and called on some of his old friends on the reserves, bought whatever they had. He hadn't seen these people for a long time. Fred Moody sold him stuff. He told me that in the old days my dad would come and buy for the museum and it was like he was being followed because a few hours later the black-marketeers would come along and ask what Austin had bought. He couldn't help that, could he? When Freddie saw him on April 7th, there wasn't any sign he might kill himself. He said Austin seemed okay, just hyper. When Dad opened the trunk of his car Freddie said it was already full of carvings, and this was like early afternoon—so Austin had him put things in the backseat. Then he came back to Vancouver. He got to Chris Clarke's gallery about 3:30—she knew him because of his reputation. He came into the store and just started pointing. These weren't the old works, they were by young artists he'd probably never met. He was there for a few hours. Then he asked Chris to call Tina Mullhallen—she owned the gallery down the street. It was closed by then. So they eventually get her at a dinner party, and Dad asks if she wouldn't mind opening up the store. Tina said he was excited, you know, talking a lot, saying 'it's all authentic, nothing's a fraud.' He had 'the eye', he knew what was real. By the time he was finished even the front seat of his car was full. Tina asked him who this was for, you know, and he said he was buying for a give-away. He spent everything he had. Some of the checks bounced so I returned things. Tina was really nice about that, taking some of it back." She shrugged her shoulders to take off the shawl, and finally unwound the scarf from her neck. She was hot. "Something had burst in him, and there was nothing to staunch the wound. Maybe joy had burst. All this stuff was still in his car in the garage. He must've walked out to his office at the university, carrying the rifle. He probably didn't want his car broken into. It was like him to care about that kind of thing just when he was about to kak out on us forever. Jason said the art spooked him—so I have it. He was buying for a potlatch of one—me."

I removed the dishes from the table. I made some tea. "Why, after all these years, did he choose to collect from new artists, without knowing them?"

She seemed surprised at my question. "You don't know this yet? He'd turned his back on provenance, on learning exotic facts to tell the story of the work. He didn't believe in that any more."

Claire had said the same thing. "This was because—"

"The provenance of the work is a digression. People always wanting to know who made a thing, what the biography of the creator is, where are they from, all that nonsense. The story of the work is a con. The meaning is there all by itself, alone in its impact on you." She smiled. "Or not."

"A tough standard, don't you think?"

"Not if the piece is considered an important work of art, instead of an old bone, a relic. Anyway, that's boring. Except—"

"What?"

"Except if you figure that's what happened to Dad. He lost his moorings in his own personal story. I mean, in his family. Anyway, are you going to show me what you've written for Dad's opera?" I handed her the synopsis and she read out loud: "'We see Austin Hart about to go on the expedition. Mary-Anne is there with the children."

She was reading about her father, about herself, about her mother—she was reading about her past. The transformative element had to take hold or I was sunk.

She skipped down the page. "I don't know. I'm not sure about showing a happy scene between my mother and father, with me, the happy child—the joyous little family unit. It wasn't like that."

"Okay, I understand." I explained the set-up for the scene on Ninstints and the removal of the poles. "When they've gone, there's a wager between the two characters of Raven and Shawcroft as to whether Austin can bring the twin masks together."

"I like this part. If my Dad can rejoin the twin masks then what will happen?"

"Well, we're taking on big themes in this opera, and I hope it doesn't sound too grandiose."

"Don't be shy."

"The reunion of the twin masks will save us all, because the masks dissolve the polarities—which are ruinous."

She said "ha!" like slapping down a winning card. "And then?"

I was bolder because of her response. "The expedition has returned. Hart has just given a lecture on ethnology at the museum. He goes back to his office. The Lover follows him."

I had been thoughtless. Paige put her head in her hands. I wanted to comfort her, but I was the author of her upset. Then she pushed back her shoulders and lifted her head.

"Paige, is this too much? You don't have to be courageous, you know. We can stop."

She was angry. "I don't have to be fuckin' anything. So what if my father had lovers. My mother wasn't around." She diverted her attention to a roll call of concern for others. "My brother, Jason, won't like this, though. He's a family man. Candice won't mind. She doesn't mind anything." She turned the pages and continued reading. "Endscene—Synopsis—People know of his death without being told. They look up, fear something, are disturbed. There is a tumult. Paige enters, then Jason. They are the children left behind." She couldn't go on. "I'm going to have to get tougher to be able to take my own story. How about music? Can we hear some music?"

For a while she was captivated but then something detached and she wasn't listening. She was a boat drifting away from shore.

I read from the libretto while the music played, but I couldn't catch her up. Finally she said, "Yeah, I've had enough now. I'm having trouble with the death of two parents. It's dumb to say you're an orphan after a certain age, but actually there's no limitation period. I'm an outlaw and an orphan."

I'd been climbing over the rubble of grief with a distraught daughter, and all my guessing as to how she would react to the opera had only been that. She was authentic. She was the daughter, and she belonged to a real family; I didn't. I'd been mistaken.

We both needed some air.

As we walked in the garden, she said, "You never tell me anything about yourself."

"No, this opera isn't about me."

"Of course it is. Who are you? Why are you doing this?"

"Ask me what you want to know." I meant it as a offer but it sounded so retracted, like agreeing to answer questions while under arrest.

"I just did."

"Okay. I live here now. My mother is in a nursing-home. I have one sister who is always away. My step-father died ten years ago."

"Five concise facts." She was coaxing me with a tease. "Really why are you doing this? I've read your stuff. I know you're a good poet. But why take it on?"

What was wrong with me that even though I wanted to, I couldn't respond to her? She wasn't asking me to jump off a cliff, throw myself into a cold river, or make a life commitment. Just a little disclosure. I could readily line up the usual suspects: that I wanted to know what led to Austin's suicide, to find out how he was able to rid himself of obligations—brainy, schematic thoughts which I'd make into some kind of mental construct, a diagram. I couldn't even muster the usual pitch I gave to myself.

We'd circled around all the flower beds and sat on the cement bench beside the pond.

"You're struggling. How come? Is it something bad?"

Figuratively, there was a large hedgerow in front of me, and I couldn't see over it. My feelings were on the other side. Tangled in the branches near the scrubby roots and dry dirt were bits of old candy wrappers, soft drink cans, tissues—really unsavory things the wind had pushed against this matted hedge. It had some green growth on the top but was messy and leafless at the bottom where there was all this garbage. That was my mind's image of what was getting in my way. How could I possibly describe this? Maybe to

Paige one day, but not now. I had no idea if anyone in the world would have a clue what it was about. It was about Sophia forbidding me to dwell on the past, an absolute prohibition. It was about memory.

"Your father?" Paige was trying to help me out. "Maybe you can you talk about him. I'm sick of my own."

"I don't really know anything about him. My mother said it was a one-night stand, just one of those things. Then she married Russell, my step-father."

"What was your father's name?"

"I don't know."

"Your mother didn't even get his name?"

I almost guffawed at the way she put it, as if it were a hit and run. "I guess not."

"Weird. Sorry, but that's weird. Must be pretty strange for you." She had her elbow resting on her thigh, and her hand on her cheek, looking up at me in her open moon-face gaze.

"It is, now that you mention it." She was a straight-shooter, and I wanted to acknowledge my affection for her. Why was it so damn hard? "Let's go, you have an appointment with the Producer."

"Yeah, okay. I seem to have too much of a dead father, and you not enough of one. Maybe yours is still alive. "

That had never occurred to me.

EVEN THOUGH THE CITY AIR smelled of tar, neither of us wanted to go inside.

On the sidewalk in front of the Producer's office was a hopscotch marked out with thick, white chalk and numbers in each square. We walked up and down, scuffing and smudging the lines with our shoes. Paige had on sneakers and was more effective. We collaborated in effacing the grid made by an unseen child.

Unexpectedly, Paige went to the beginning of the course. With agility, she hopped and skipped quickly over the squares, taking the small steps required of her. When I applauded, she bowed and said, "Your turn."

"Good heavens, I haven't done this in a few decades."

"Begin."

I stood at the line, moved my arms up to jump, and couldn't. I looked at Paige, less embarrassed than needing help; although I was a little embarrassed. She nodded, giving me the go-ahead to try again. My feet were leaded to magnetized ground. I swung my arms and still didn't get any lift off. How absurd this was, this child's game in which I couldn't even hop into the first square.

Paige leaned over like a coach, and clapped her hands. "Come on, Alix, you can do it. Go girl."

I laughed as I thrust my weight forward, hopped onto the first square, and kept going. Straddling two squares, hopping onto the next, then two, one, one, reached the end, then back again, made it to the finish, turned and did it over two more times. Each jump was a chop with the pruning shears, taking down the hedge.

"Ha!" Paige said. "Ha! Ha! You remembered how."

We sat on the curb, right at the edge of our game. I was thirsty and wanted lemonade.

"I'm going to tell you this, and I hope you'll believe me, even if it sounds bizarre." I had started. "Okay?"

"I'm in."

"I was eighteen, studying at school, away from home—and it was like this solution came to me. Subconsciously, it must have been that I thought my mother didn't want me to exist. I was part of her unintended past, and the past was unwanted. That's just how I figured it. So I was going to kill myself, for her I think."

"Really?" Paige looked at me, surprised, then unwrapped her scarf from her neck and placed it over my shoulders. "Wow. How self-effacing. I mean, you seem humble and all of that, but this is ridiculous. You were collaborating in your own murder. Right?"

"How do you mean?"

"Your mother was out to murder you—only psychically, I mean just a little psychic death, but you took it literally, which it was. You were going to help her out." The cadence of her voice rose.

"I suppose. I guess so." I could feel the warm spread of tears but my head was blotting paper and they were gone.

"Then what happened?" She chuckled. "Like with the synopsis of the opera—'then what happened.' Well, we know you made it. I'm glad."

"My mother phoned."

She laughed out loud. "That was it? Saved by a phone call?" I must have looked a little abashed. "I mean that's good. I wished I'd called my dad."

Both of us were laughing and crying at once, our emotions jumping back and forth across the thin divide between uproarious and tragic.

She took her scarf and put it over both of our heads. We leaned our shoulders together. We were two little old ladies, sitting on the curb, telling weird secrets to each other.

"I guess we're both kind of wrecked. Maybe you more than me, strange as that seems." She adopted a witch's voice. "But who'd want to win that one, dearie?"

I could feel that a force against me, like atmosphere, reversed itself. How strange. Something pressing onto me until now, full of need, full of lack, questions and not-knowing, what am I doing here, dozens of spiky why's—the pressure simply changed direction and went the other way.

In its place I had an entirely new thought: instead of wondering why I existed at all, I would show my purpose by a commitment to being here.

I stood up and helped Paige to her feet.

"Did you feel that?" she asked.

"I did. What was it?"

"I dunno. Barometric pressure, or something. Maybe it's going to rain." She looked at the sky and then back to me. "This'll be our new game."

"Good. We should get to the meeting." I was pretty sure she didn't want to go.

"What's it about again?"

"The Producer has formed a society to support the opera, and he wants you to be a member." I didn't much want to be back in the straight and narrow either.

She shook her head. "Just tell him you're my society. Catch you later. I'm going to buy some chalk." She turned and walked away.

"Do you want a ride?"

"No, but thanks a lot." She waved backwards.

I went up to the office and explained to the Producer, as best I could, Paige's reaction. Interestingly, he didn't seem concerned. As I was leaving, I noticed on a side-table a cassette marked "The Last Lecture." He had promised to give me a copy, but despite my repeated requests, he hadn't. I put it in my briefcase.

30

THE LAST LECTURE

Even thought I needed the tape of Austin's last lecture, it was theft to have taken it. I didn't want to ask the Producer for it again, like a beggar. I tried to justify it. I should have asked.

Feeling hungry, I checked the fridge, and it gleamed and glared, empty, nothing to eat. I stepped on the bathroom scale. Fully clothed I weighed 110 pounds, the same as I had when I was eighteen in Halifax. I had to eat more, even if not in the company of others.

I took the cassette into the library, broke the tabs on the back to prevent accidentally recording over it, and put the tape in the sound system. Austin Hart's voice would be in this room—his real voice, instead of the one in my mind boosted from his writing, sounding like my own. I so wanted to be transported back to him, alive 25 years ago. I was half afraid the tape would be blank, that I'd be left staring into an immutable rock-face of silence.

The lecture was given in May, 1964, three months before his death. I wondered if I would I be able to discern whether he had the intention, then, to kill himself. I picked up the museum catalogue so that I could follow the artifacts to which Austin would refer.

I pushed the play button.

"I have the enormous pleasure of introducing—Austin Hart." There was a thundering round of applause; they were greeting someone who would lead them to new truths.

He began quietly. "I apologize because I'm told there's a room full of people next door who will only hear me and won't see me, nor see the works of art I will show you."

I realized that the sighted and unsighted masks were, once again, reproduced in this theater, in the two auditoriums. I was behind the unsighted mask.

I rewound the tape and with restrained excitement, started it again. I searched for adjectives to describe his voice: rich, smooth, instilling confidence, self-assured but not arrogant, his tone in a slightly higher range than I had thought it would be, yet as familiar as a friend's walk.

He asked for the lights to be turned out. Austin gave his lecture in the dark, illuminated only by the projection on the screen.

"Anthropologists have gradually developed the vocabulary to describe Northwest Coast native art. Even though, at first, the forms may have seemed strange to the western mind, we know pretty well when an artist is depicting a bear or a sea wolf. We have learned the stories which fueled the art. But meaning has lagged behind our insights. The old words and perceptions are no longer sufficient for my purposes. I want to take you on a journey now. I hope you'll come with me."

A sound from the audience, like a sigh, an acceptance of his enticing invitation.

"This slide shows an episode from mythology. Raven has become voraciously hungry. He sees bait on a fisherman's hook, so he turns himself into a halibut, eats the bait and gets himself caught. After he's cooked, he emerges out of the halibut again as Raven. He goes from the raw to the cooked and back to the raw again. He is the ultimate Transformer. When you go outside and look around, think of him. He makes things the way they are.

"Now in these next artifacts, the artist is revealing to us what the spirits look like—otherwise how would we know? It's the same as with ourselves. We exist, but what is the meaning of our existence? This is the question that calls to us and which we yearn to answer.

"There are supernatural entities incarnated in these works. You won't be able to see them unless you shed part of yourself, become available to them, as vulnerable as a child. Then they will shock you—and you should allow them to do that—to strike you the way a stick strikes a drum. You've been asleep. You want to wake up now: to open your eyes and go from darkness to light; to splay open your very self, and go from silence to song. I'm asking you to be changed by these works of the spirit."

His beckoning us to go defenseless into spectral realms was somewhat frightening.

Hart always shook, with a slight tremor throughout his whole body, and I could hear that tension in his voice. I didn't believe it was nervousness from a fear that he would portray an unlikable aspect of himself, or that he would be less than he aspired to be. It was a real physical tension, as though he'd become taut, tympanic, in order to resonate like a skin or hide pulled tight across a frame that became a drum. Austin Hart was a drum. He was asking all of us to be the same.

"What has occurred to me recently is that although we have interpretations going back 80 years—saying this is a diving whale, and later, no it's a bear sitting on its haunches—there's also a different agenda at work. The dancing bear is dancing to a different tune. It's one which we haven't been able to hear before. Now we can."

He spoke less urgently. Members of the audience shifted in their chairs, as though relieved by his change of pace.

"I've been struggling with some new ideas and I am going to take the risk of jolting you with them. I've had to develop fresh terminology for my analysis, and I want you to know that I'm not quite happy with it. To get to these new terms, I've had to do the very thing I'm asking of you. I've had to lay myself bare."

Hart said it didn't really matter to him anymore where artifacts came from, or who had made them. "I've turned away from the little game of anthropology, which I now find no more significant than a round of scrabble. In the past, as an academic, I undertook studying the shamanic. I confess I did that, not to have the shamans' experiences but really because I wanted to gain power over their experiences. That is fraudulent. I have left that endeavor. What's important to me now is that the power-holder, the artist, embarks on the terrifying quest to mine the boundless primacy of spirit in the every-day world, in carving a bowl, a spoon, a mask. As I hold these objects in my hands, it's my calling to try to follow him there."

He was leading the way, exposing his back, and he was asking us to go with him into a dangerous place. I was braced by the knowledge that he hadn't survived the danger.

"I'm going to be saying some novel things about sexual symbolism that is so important in the arts of the world. Such symbols were frequently depicted in early Northwest Coast native art. However, in more recent times this depiction is conspicuous by its absence. This has led me to suspect that we might find this symbolism in metaphorical forms, below the surface. Next slide please. This suspicion is confirmed here. The work has been called the 'Sechelt image,' a carving in stone, fifteen centuries old. It's been described as a mother holding her child. I suggest it's more complex than that. The artist is also showing a big, strong male figure with a huge phallus in front. Yet the phallus can also be read as a vulva-form. I've given a great deal of thought to this punning. My conclusion is that this master-work shows the trinity, mother, father and child—all three."

Probably because he named these body-parts, so unusual to say out loud in that time period, the audience laughed, but it had a narrow, anxious edge. I could hear Austin take a drink of water. He seemed off-kilter. The pause was so long I checked the machine to see if it had stopped. Then I heard him again.

"This is phallic as well as vulvic." He was bold and he regained his voice. "You see, at first this stone sculpture looks wholesome and benign, even somewhat sentimental. But the thriving underwork is not that at all. It is challenging; it is the turgid sea of our most powerful selves that will not let us rest, because it asks who we really are. Next, please, the house pole slide."

A decided hush and quietude took hold. I found the photograph in the catalogue. It was of a totem pole which was at the entrance to a dwelling on one of the reserves in the Charlottes. In order to go into the house you walked through a large hole cut at the bottom of the pole. He told the audience, "The opening is through the labia and vulva into the womb."

There was a collective intake of breath from the audience as they were whacked with the blasphemous, out-of-bounds words. I could almost see the stunned look on their faces. Yet he continued in the same measured cadence. "The only way you can get into the house is through the female regenerative organ. That is how I see it now. You must enter and exit through the feminine."

He hesitated, as if thought had swamped his speech. I could hear a growing murmur, like bees in a capped jar.

"We must soon get to the depiction of the sexual act itself." I guessed he was trying to be reassuring but I doubted that was the effect.

I assumed his tone used in lecturing would be more assertive than the one he used with me, the more intimate voice of his official journals and, especially, his secret diaries. But listening to this tape, I worried he would be attacked for his certitude.

"Whether we like it or not, all around the world, through art, sexual intercourse is depicted. I'm not talking about the pornographic; I'm speaking of life and death and creation: chaotic, juicy, startling—the divine."

There was a single guffaw which came from the audience, as loud as if someone had stood to ridicule him.

"I hope you won't misunderstand me," Austin said calmly. "To give you an illustration, I'll use the Anasazi in Arizona. The artist creates a perfect bowl of the most consummate shape, and then pierces it—actually makes a hole in the bottom. The artist mars it to ensure the gods will know we still acknowledge and suffer our humanity. Do you see? It is the objective correlative for the sexual act, as is the phallo-vulvic opening to the world-box of the house. I know this is not easy to comprehend. Think of when you have a sexual connection. You might feel it is your most direct access to and experience of the divine. In that experience you also know, most deeply, your frailty. I want you to take on board what I'm saying. My salient point is that here, on this coast, the native artists stopped showing sexuality in their art. We must ask ourselves why. My argument is that this happened because their depiction of the erotic nature of the spirit made us, the outsiders, afraid. It was foreign. Through the church, through the government, we spayed and neutered the native people and their art, desexualized them as a kind of run-up to the ultimate dismemberment of their societies. It was the conquering salvo."

Sensing incredulity, he took on a more modulated tone: "Consider the natives you've seen in the east side of Vancouver, if you've been brave enough to go down there. Remember what you thought as you passed a woman leaning against the side of the Patricia Hotel, ragged and bleary-eyed. You'll have had many assumptions about her, but I doubt if you would have assigned to her the attribution of a sexually powerful being. Rather, she is someone to be used, and to be used up. We have destroyed her god-head. Next slide please." There was a disturbance in the audience; people were leaving.

Hart didn't stop. "Look at this totem pole near Hazelton. The human figures depicted on it are sexless. Now this argillite panel from a much earlier period. It shows the sexual activity between the bear husband and his wife. There is the joining of tongues and much interlocking and sexual play going on. What a contrast. You may think that western culture does not know this shocking, almost obscene connection between ourselves and the animal world, the chaos and strangeness of such couplings. We do, but on a different time scale. Darwin's theory of evolution has bestiality in its embrace. However it's stretched over thousands of years, instead of the space of a marriage."

Now he expressed a sharp determination. "I repeat: to never see something means it's gone underground; it is now disguised. To break through that disguise you must unmask the feminine, reveal it where it is. This has just recently occurred to me with great force."

McNabb had mentioned Hart's statement in an unpleasant way. Perhaps because of his defensiveness, the comment did seem strangely aggressive, as though he had to hunt down something furtive, in hiding—ambush it before it tricked him yet again.

"Finally, the Raven Rattle." He sounded relieved, having arrived at his destination. "You see we haven't understood this magnificent, enigmatic creation. But we will. And when that happens, we will understand meaning itself. We must turn it over and see what's on the underside. This is the most daring piece in all of Northwest Coast art. There is only one purpose, I think, for which a human being will assume that particular posture, on her back with her legs spread wide, her hand on her thighs to make herself more available, to further spread her legs. The beak of the Raven is clearly ejecting something into the reclining woman's open, accepting mouth. Unless you try very hard you cannot avoid seeing the sexual act in this reclining figure."

Sniggering came from the audience, but Hart talked through it. "It is the sexual act, yet it is so much more. It is a portal, this being available for piercing, for allowing in—" he hesitated "—for allowing in no less than enlightenment through a god." The background noise, the ruckus continued. "For me, this has become the meaning of these artifacts. If they do not mean this—if I am wrong about this—then my whole argument fails." He was stating a challenge, and in doing so he'd silenced them. But he also faltered. There was another pause in which I could hear loud noises, shuffling in the auditorium; more people were leaving. His words were singed by his voice. "If you think that the clang relationship between womb and tomb in our language is accidental, you are simply wrong."

Someone called out, "This is not scholarship, Dr. Hart," and then further commotion; it was an exodus. Austin kept speaking.

"I wanted to talk to you about the twin masks—they are the apotheosis of this art—" The disturbance was dying down, perhaps because the clearing out of auditorium was almost complete. "But there is a third 'mask'—the human face of the person who wears the masks and mediates between them both. This is the sacred."

The tape hissed. I turned off the recorder.

I sat in darkness.

31

THE BLIND

Hart:
Man took an animal
as a guardian spirit
to acquire the eagle's certainty
that its offspring would be its own kind.

Mary-Anne:
What is this certainty you need?
As a father, as a husband, as a man?
Are you so afraid of your seed?
How is the eagle going to help you with this?

Alix's Lines for the Libretto

While the workmen installed the metal ramp on the front steps of my mother's house to prepare for her promised visit home, I paced. Their pounding hammers rattled the living-room window and shook my thoughts.

Would I have known he was going to kill himself? The question was shy of the mark. Would *he* have known? I didn't believe he was at the crossroad yet, despite the debacle. Something led him there after that.

I listened again to the entire recording until his voice was locked inside my brain as its only geography.

How lonely Hart must have been leaving that hall and walking out passed the colleagues who were afraid to look at him—the crowd whispering, smiling sickly when he passed, as if he'd disrobed in public, a spectacle—those like McNabb who wanted the man they'd known, not the one still on the move with his brilliance and his destiny. Claire was away. Who was there to comfort him, give him perspective on this audience happily residing in a provincial outpost in the mid-sixties, now alarmed by what he said, the same words they whispered in bed to excite a lover—labia, vulva, womb—words Hart also euphemised into the innovative "vulviform"? It took decades, after that night, for us to catch up to his ideas, if we ever have. If only he could have waited for us, for me, he wouldn't have been so alone, again wearing clothes too big for him, feeling absurdly dressed.

After the troubled, disconsolate taking of the Ninstints poles, which ultimately were the foothold to his great success, Hart finally chose to answer for himself the plea from H.S. *"to show more of my own life and who I am."* He told the audience his new ideas—and then, once more, he didn't fit. I could have wept.

Leaving the academic study of the shamanic, he experienced it directly.

I'd been so terrified after the longhouse spirit-dancing that I didn't recognize the imbedded ordinary in the miraculous; I didn't recognize a loaf of bread. By simply putting to my face the unsighted mask in a sterile keeping-place in Ottawa, I'd nearly been ripped apart with fear. Trevor fled from the sweat-lodge and hid under the blankets for days.

Austin put to shame any attempt I'd ever made in my life to reveal myself to another, to be disclosing, to have the stakes be high and say they were.

Although he had stumbled—not stumbled, he'd pitched himself into the fracture between worlds—although he'd done that, his voice was my own now, giving me some courage which I'd been lacking, to be unmasked.

Austin was beating out a tune for bears to dance to when he longed to move the stars to pity. I would not let him go. I would find the tune to reignite the stars.

The ramp was finished. I had to pick up Mother.

WE SAT NEXT TO one another in the solarium eating Thai food because it was too cold for her outside. She said she had memorized her garden and it didn't trouble her all that much that she couldn't see it clearly any more. I wanted to believe her.

She closed her eyes, as if testing herself. "The branches of the Japanese maple suspended over the pond, a favor that never needs repaying, a love that never needs answering. Its leaves are kept fire. Nothing wants to go. We are all stragglers to beauty and loss—" She stopped mid-sentence and opened her eyes, giving me a foxy look. "How'd I do? I memorized lines from one of your poems."

I never knew she'd even read any of them. It was a compliment, but I was wary of her exaggerated state. And a lifetime of resistance was on the chopping block.

The neighbor's dogs started barking, and I looked up at the sound.

"I told you before, they're only the local dogs," she said, and then, "I actually think you're afraid of them."

"They bark every time I go outside. I just don't understand dogs protecting property from someone two houses away."

"Make sure you know what's dangerous and what's not." This gratuity was followed by reminding me, once again, I had now found an honest family. She was lurching about in her thoughts.

"Austin's family seem to tell you the truth, and I'm glad about that. But they know about dying and not about death. I mean they only know the brutal fact of it, imposed on them, but not the gradual really awful decline of the body."

I lowered my guard and I settled into enjoying the loquacious Sophia who was transformed by being back at her home. She'd even been so clever as to adopt my poetic voice. I smiled at the strange joke that I was becoming Austin Hart, and she was becoming me.

"I guess what you're meant to do in this opera, Alicia, is to get this family moving again. But you should make your Austin ordinary. It's not heroic to kill yourself because then no one knows the shape of your life, so they have to make it up." She looked at my face as if it were a geiger-counter. "Don't be anxious."

"Are you okay?" She'd probably over-extended herself, trying to maintain a false energy.

She pushed her plate of food away and raised her chin. "This business of secrets. What you were telling me the other day—what Austin said about that Spanish man—I've been thinking." Her familiarity with him was keeping pace with my own. "Sometimes people do that, keep secrets to protect what's most valued. Just before I wake up, my dreams reassure me I'll remember them and I don't. Secrets are like that. You have to really want to find them out, to go where they're kept."

She was zeroing in on something, but from such a long way off I couldn't quite understand it. "Mother, what's bothering you?"

"Austin's idea that the Spaniard didn't say anything because he wanted to create a breather from the destruction that would follow. I've done that."

"It's a pretty complicated idea."

"I'm up to it." She took another forkful of food from her discarded plate and then pushed it further from her. "There, I'm sufficiently suffonsified. So—you remember that awful conversation when I said I hadn't been a good mother for you? I hoped for an answer, but instead you told me the 'The Parable of the Unwashed Hair'—"

"Please, let's not go back there. I really can't bear it." I didn't want to lose the hard won ease between us.

"A daughter should know things about her mother that no one else knows. Like me and Russell."

"We've barely recovered from our last heart-to-heart. Isn't it better not to demand too much of one another?"

She looked a little insulted. “Oh no, dear. Maybe we’ve been unkind, but we’ve never been lazy. Be a good sport.” She forged on like an acolyte to a cause. “Russell’s parents were very wealthy. It was the sort of family with inherited wealth that the next generation tended to drink away. Russell was going through it at a good clip even before we married.”

I laughed. “This is what you’ve always said about him.”

“Don’t put me off course. So the day I’m going to tell you about—I’ve been considering this, and I think this was the day before your parable happened. Maybe that’s why I was hard on you the other night. It’s been bothering me. You’ll understand when I tell you. So it was in the summertime. You were about six years old—is that right?—and Peg was almost two, just walking; she was late. She walked late and talked early. And you, you didn’t talk early but—”

“Mother?”

“Sorry, I mustn’t drop the thread—”

“Summertime, I was six.” I had to help her.

“You remember how good looking Russell was—there was something unnerving about his looks, and even at the end because when he was dying, he was still handsome in a way that old men shouldn’t be. I’ve never said this to you before, have I?”

“You always said ‘he held his youth.’”

“I guess that’s one way of putting it.”

“Summertime.”

“By the end, though, he was so thin. I didn’t worry about his gaunt body, his good looks. So yes, it’s Saturday. Peg was having her nap, and you were with a friend at the movies just over on Granville Street. Those were the days when children could walk around on their own, even when they were little. Without warning me, Russell’s brought some of his business pals here for lunch after a meeting, so I’ve gone to the delicatessen. When I came back, I went out to the patio. We didn’t have the solarium then so the French doors led to the backyard right from the kitchen. The men are standing near the wisteria; it’s drooping with blossoms. We still have wisteria here, you know—you must have noticed it—I’ve had it cut back and trained to go the other way, to the east of the house. Then it was pulling against the trellis covering the side and top of the deck.

"Everyone is drinking. Russell is at the booze trolley he's taken outside where he's set a tray of glasses, bottles, an ice bucket. He looks up at me and smiles. He takes a fresh white wine glass, holds it up to the light to check for water-marks, and then starts to pour me a drink. I say no, I'll have a soda water. I'm not sure why I say it. The look on his face is of apprehension. He says, 'Come on, darling, have a drink with us. Be friendly.'

"In the five years of our marriage I was in cahoots with him, helped along by two glasses of wine, then three, then not counting the number. I tried to fall asleep on him before we argued. Sometimes I made it. By this time he figured we were going to succeed in destroying one another. It wouldn't be sloppy. It would be bloodless in the usual way."

I'd never heard her speak this way. "Destroying one another? How?"

"By being failed, unrealized, making less and less sense to yourself, using less air, imagining you don't need water—hoping no one discovers anything about us—that no one counts the bottles. There's something fascinating about it."

"Really?"

"But I shook my head, saying no to him. I didn't want a drink. As soon as I said it, I knew he'd try to get back at me. So he says, seemingly out of the blue and not relevant to anything—but he knows his pals can't hear him—he says, nonchalant, pouring himself a scotch, not looking at me, 'But you see the last laugh is on you.' I waited, because I was on new ground. He went on, still not looking at me, smug, 'The last laugh is on you because our daughter is just like me.' Of course, he meant Peg."

Sophia took a long drink of water. "Couples destroying one another are very clever. Most things are in a code only the other will understand. He meant I could never escape him, never get away from him, because he was part of her, my little girl. He wanted me to think that the more I hated him the more I would have to hate my child. He'd clinched it. He was saying I was stuck with him. I knew all that in a second. I didn't take long to respond. I said, 'You just played a card that should never be played.' Then I walk away.

"He follows me. I go to the back lawn under the trellis where his friends are. Coming up behind me, standing at my back he whispers 'You're the only one who knows me.' He's relying us being already doomed, the odds known, everything lost. But I'm there amongst his friends. I won't pretend any more. He's afraid everything he's done will be uprooted and known, even extending to things he didn't remember he'd done.

"In so many different ways we'd tried to kill one another off and suddenly—he didn't expect this—I'm moving beyond his reach. I'd tried before to break the spell. It was always the same deal: my refusal, his seduction, the threat followed by the capitulation, and then the small kindnesses. But something has changed. I could see the look of fear on his face that he showed just before striking me. So I said—right in front of his friends—'Hit me again, darling, be friendly.' To my utter shock, he slapped my face."

"I can't believe he hit you. He had hit you before? The bastard." He was long dead, yet the shock of her revelation made me want to protect her from him.

"He didn't know where to look. Neither did the other men. I walked back into the house, the sting of his hand on my cheek. I couldn't imagine what he was going to say to explain what just happened, maybe something about me—that I deserved this, didn't they ever hit their wives?—I didn't give a damn what he'd say. I reached the dining room—and there you were, just standing there. You were supposed to be at the movies."

Every day she managed to surprise me. Some things had to lie dormant for decades before words could be put to them.

"You said, 'Don't leave me. Don't leave my sister.' I didn't know what you'd seen. Of course I'd never thought of leaving you. Do you remember any of this?"

"Just being at the movies with my friend Janice and deciding I had to come home. I don't remember what happened when I got home." She looked drawn and haggard. Her hands trembled as she picked up her glass of water. "Mother, let's stop for a bit."

"Oh, no, we mustn't stop yet." She sat up straight and tried to push back her chair, but it was wedged against the wall.

"Let me help you," I offered, standing.

"No, please. Sit down. You startled me, suddenly appearing out of nowhere. You brought me to my senses. I didn't know what Russell would do next. An embarrassed man is dangerous. I resolved he wasn't going to get my children. That meant I had to be sure you never loved him or trusted him."

"But Mother, I didn't trust you either."

She raised her eyebrows, not in scorn but a kind of awakening. At the same time as she, I realized the real psychological horror of what she had done. "Oh, I see," she said. "Yes. Well, good heavens, now I see it. I thought I was protecting you, but I put you out in front of me, so you'd protect me from Russell. Not so good. All these things look so different now that we know things. Could we have a glass of wine, dear. Something cold."

She needed a break. I brought the remainder of the Mersault from my evening with Richard. "This might be stale." I poured us both a glass.

"Who cares." She held the goblet with both hands. "That was the night I told you to call him 'Russell,' not 'Dad'—from then on you did. He was furious. But I protected you." Gazing into the garden, she paused for a moment. "All of this cost us dearly. You knew to leave home as soon as you could, both you and Peg did. You've told me your unkind version of that. So maybe what I did wasn't a wholesale solution. We lost a few emotions along the way." She tried to smile but couldn't pull it off. "At least he couldn't hurt us any longer."

"You have to explain more." We seemed like a family of hemophiliacs who'd all learned to use red handkerchiefs to pretend there wasn't so much blood. "I still don't know what you mean that you were trying to destroy one another."

"I married him for security, for money. I was peeved when you reminded me of that the other day—or whenever it was. It doesn't turn out right if you marry for money. Through compromise and the hundred small expediencies that followed, we became servants to one another. That sets up a lot of hatred and eventually something's got to give." She was speaking rapidly now, the relief of telling the story urging her on. "It was the complicity which finally sickened me, and all the damage we were doing to you children. I had no stomach for it any more. So I took one step outside of it, but it was a good step. Then you were standing there in the doorway." She conjured the scene from so long ago. "Your wide, open and innocent face. To my amazement—you looked just like your father." She stopped abruptly.

"My father?" I was confused. "My real father? You didn't even know him. You said I was an accident."

"What an awful thing to say."

"Don't you remember that?"

"Maybe I do. I guess so. I was aiming for you to be whole by having you make it without a father. I didn't want you to be weak."

In this conversation of disclosure, opposites fell into one another. Deprivation was supposed to be wholeness. Lack was supposed to be plentitude. "What father?" I asked, persistent in the midst of my bafflement.

"He's the only person I've ever loved, except for you and Peg. And there you were, looking just like him."

"Mother, I did not have a father," I said slowly and clearly, as though to a child who had forgotten her lessons.

She merely shook her head indicating it was I who was unnecessarily muddled. "So the last laugh was on Russell." She returned to the detour of her previous theme. "He'd hoped to score a final victory over me, but he was foolish to try this. A father should never use a child against her mother. No parent should. And there you were—"

"What was his name?" I interrupted her.

"His name?"

"You told me you had a one night stand with a stranger during the war."

"No, that wasn't true. We'd known one another for over a year." I had a sense she hadn't said this to anyone, ever.

"What was my father's name?" I was nearly cracked open with a desire to believe her.

"Alexander, " she finally said, like a confession. Then added, somewhat brightly. "You were named after him."

"Oh, Mother, how many versions of this history do you have?"

"This one, darling. Keep this one."

"How can I know what to believe?"

"Why would I lie?"

"Because that's what you do."

"I think that's uncalled for—but it's different now between us, since you came back and started on this opera." I nodded. The fingers of my right hand had gone numb again and I clenched and unclenched my fist.

Sophia continued, "Seeing you there he came back to me—as if he'd been lost and now I'd found him again. He set my course through you. Do you get it?"

"But why didn't you tell me about my father before now?" I didn't remember ever saying the phrase 'my father' out loud, and now I had said it three or four times. Whenever I had wondered about him as a child, I created a blank space where our relationship might have been. "Is he still alive?" The questions were dammed up in me.

"Hold your horses." She covered her eyes with her arthritic hands, holding infirmity up to forestall the flood. Then she said, "I didn't want you to dwell on the past. It's not good for you. Better to feel absence than loss." I frowned. "I mean especially for you. Better to not have a father than one you longed for."

Was it possible that this harebrained code had cost me the story of my life? "I'm not sure it works that way," I suggested, more blandly than I felt.

"I was going to be an unwed mother, a disgrace. Then I met Russell, and he was handsome, wealthy—he knew I was pregnant and marrying was his act of gallantry. I had to forget your father and make him—well, non-existent. Things were different then. We made up a new life, everything legitimate and—false. Then you stood there, reminding me so much of him, and that I needed him."

There were so many gaps in this story, I couldn't follow all the runaway leads. "Why didn't you marry my father? Did he die?"

Ignoring me, she picked up the pace on her intended trek. "So when the men left the house half an hour later—I'm sure they didn't want to hang around this calamity—I was in the living room, waiting. I had sent you upstairs. Peg was still asleep. When Russell came into the room, I startled him, just sitting there on the couch, not hiding from him. He was in a drunk's self-absorption. I said to him, 'Peg is not your child. You have no children and from now on you have no wife.'"

"Isn't Peg his daughter?" Suddenly every relationship in our family was subject to revision.

"Of course she is. But he got my point, he understood me. I went upstairs. I had strength now. I could salvage what remained of myself and my crummy choices. It sounds strange saying all this out loud for the first time. Was I selfish, not telling you this before?"

She was like a child who had broken all the heirloom plates and then wondered if everything was okay. She really didn't know.

"I was so afraid you'd just dwell on the past. I didn't want to have to live there with you."

The truth went right through me, so cleanly I hardly felt it. "Mother, is he still alive? Can you just answer that part?"

She repeated my question as though buying time. My suspicious habit of mind left me impatient with the slow-moving vehicle of her story. I wanted her to barrage me with information and she was being cautious. "No, he did die, in the war." She was talking quickly again. "Don't be mad at me, but I considered terminating the pregnancy. It was dicey in those days. I'm so glad I didn't. But he knew about you. I wrote to him that I was pregnant. He was elated. He wanted to get married after the war. In the last letter I received from him he wrote, 'If she's a girl, we'll call her Alicia and her nickname will be Alix.' He chose your name."

I was speechless. Even the casual admission that she'd considered aborting my life seemed irrelevant given that I was finding out about my father.

She returned to Russell. "Gradually things changed. Russell started another business, recovered his fortune, was away a lot. In those days people kept up appearances. But we never again slept together in the same bed, or even the same room. When I had the solarium added to the house, I was so satisfied watching the workmen putting in the footings, pouring the cement over the place where it had all happened."

"What about my father—" I couldn't finish the question.

"He would have wanted to know you. He would have understood you and loved you. He was curious, just like you. With the same pull to darkness, which I fear in you—"

"Oh, Mother, this makes such a difference." In the course of minutes, with just a few sentences, I could feel the empty spaces in me being named before they were filled up, a rising tide, buoyancy, clemency.

"I had to manage it so you wouldn't blame Russell for anything. Blaming people isn't pretty. Still I wanted you to be wary of him."

"Why didn't you give me some clue about what you were doing? I was afraid of Russell. I had the idea that he had done something unspeakable, like injure someone—if I could have put words to it—but he hadn't been caught yet. That's the way he acted."

"Yes, pretty unforgivable. We both had."

"I still don't get why didn't you tell me this—maybe after Russell died—or even before, when Peg and I were out of his reach?"

"Why didn't I?" She contemplated the question and then answered in an almost dream-like voice. "You seemed to manage okay, without knowing the truth. I thought you were all right. I mean I know you always seemed to be looking for some sign that you belonged in the world, some essential go-ahead. I didn't give it to you, but I did the best I could, don't you think? Oh, Alix, please, I can't diagnose this."

"But it was such extreme a remedy, wasn't it, to build a family around distrust and uncertainty? And secrets. Why didn't you just divorce Russell?"

"Just divorce Russell?" She lifted herself awkwardly in the chair. "Just divorce him?"

The familiar mounting cadence with the repetition of a phrase reminded me how fearful I was of her anger, of her ancient unfulfilled love and sacrifice and deceit, and that, in this revelation to me, she might realize I wasn't worth the price she'd paid. Maybe I still didn't deserve a father.

"Divorce Russell?" she asked again, and then held her breath. "Because," she said finally, "I am a coward. That's why I married him."

It seemed an impossible answer, that Sophia were cowardly. As if hearing my internal puzzlement she said, raising her head with some difficulty, "I've told you this as if all along I knew the shape of it. I didn't. I still don't, not really. But I'm giving you what I've figured out. Maybe I lied to you and Peg but at least I kept both of you clear of Russell. And of me. I never struck either of you, ever."

"Of course you didn't," I said reassuringly.

"Not 'of course.' It wasn't a given. I had to make sure. Russell and I stayed together; we kept one another in check. You know what a blind is, in hunting? Remember how much Russell loved hunting geese. There were so many pictures of him and dead geese. After he passed away I counted twelve photographs before I threw out the entire lot. Well, a blind—I once went with him, just to see what it was like—the birds are coming into the lake just after sunset and before dark. Their seeing is very acute and so the hunters must hide. You hide in their midst. They're coming in to feed. They come in close. Then, you shoot."

"Now it's you who is talking in parables." I was freshly confused even in the midst of my growing elation.

"Don't you understand? I'm saying I called out to you and Peg. I shouted 'We're here, in the blind. Fly away. You're not safe.'"

"And am I safe now?" I was too hopeful for my own good. If

she were going to betray me I wanted it to be quick.

"You got away," she said, seeming not to understand my question. She closed her eyes. "Now you're back, and now I'd like everything to be forgiven." Then she paused for the longest time before saying, "We're the same in many ways: you are more beautiful than you seem."

I smiled. "That's quite a backhanded compliment."

"It's my fault you're that way. All of this nearly wiped you out. I know that now. There just wasn't enough love to go around."

"Peg and I seemed to be hungry all the time." Her perceptions emboldened my own.

"I know what you mean."

"We were fed just enough to stay alive. But we were starving."

"Yes, it was like that."

"As a child I never knew what was true. I thought I was crazy because I could never tell."

"I know."

"I have to say that I'm afraid you're doing it to me again, with what you've said about Russell. And my father."

"You could just choose to believe me, couldn't you, that I did love your father? That's all you need to believe. I'll believe you if you believe me. We could make a deal."

I knew this chance, with its large measure of grace—as strange and unbidden as it was—wouldn't come again. Yet, I considered what I had to lose if I accepted her offer to make a pact, to settle on an agreed reality. I would lose my self-righteous notion that I was alone in the world, a fatherless child; my self-appointed position as the triage-officer of truth; my sly self-aggrandizement that I was superior to those who were wanted and loved. I almost laughed. In some way I had been waiting a lifetime for this moment. "Yes," I finally said, my mirth condensing into tears. "Yes, let's make a deal."

She had told me much of this with her eyes closed. Then she opened them and smiled.

Unexpectedly, without planning, I said, "Do you love me?"

She had tutored me against asking such a question. Such

a question meant I might soon be disarmed, crying, needing her, incapable of walking. But it was out and I stood on guard for her answer.

"Oh, yes," she said with a fullness not to be denied. "How could I not love you? I have looked into your wide-eyes, innocent, unguarded, while I held you in my arms. I looked back at you, the same."

For the first time, I knew that she did love me.

"I mainly thought you wanted to get rid of me," I said quietly, trying to correct the past.

"I can understand why you would have been confused." She closed her eyes again as we continued to face the garden. We were almost whispering so as not to disturb the enveloping sanctity.

"That time in Halifax—"

"When you were in trouble."

"I was going to commit suicide."

"Yes, I know," she said simply. Something muscular was holding us up. "A year before Austin did it."

"You called. You interrupted my plan."

"What exactly was your plan, then?"

"I was going to take a train at midnight and travel back to you."

"You were going to kill yourself along the way?"

"Take pills."

She opened her eyes, but still didn't look at me. "Oh, Alicia, I'm so sorry. Yes, this is what I've been afraid of." It wasn't so much a regret as a rectification.

"I went out for dinner beforehand. I'd bought a new dress. It was purple chiffon."

"Like the one I used to wear."

"Oh, yes, I see." It hadn't occurred to me that the dress I wore was like hers.

"Why didn't you tell me all of this before? But—I guess I could have asked. Why were you going to do this?"

"I just wanted to disappear."

"But why?"

"I thought I was a mistake, an accident. Like you said."

"Oh, dear God. Oh, dear God. You thought this is what I wanted of you." If she'd had more practice, she would have reached out to touch me.

"I suppose."

"You've kept this secret."

"Yes."

"You must let this go. Will you forgive me?" She was genuinely penitent and it was a real question.

I couldn't answer too quickly. "Forgive?" I checked myself, needing to be sure. This wasn't a deal that could be agreed to, it had to be the state I was in. She waited, seemingly without expectation. "I do," I finally said. It sounded oddly like a nuptial vow.

"I love everything that has happened to you—" It was a strange declaration from the mother who seemed to have caused everything. "—because it has made you thus." A blessing.

Finally, she reached over awkwardly and put her hands on either side of my head. She looked at me square on. "Promise me you'll never consider such a thing again, even after I'm gone."

"I can't."

"Yes you can."

"I won't."

"I want you to."

SHE MOVED MY HEAD up and down, in an affirmation. Then I let her rest my head against her neck, as she put her arms around me. She gathered me in. Slowly she moved us back and forth, in the tiniest of motions. We were in a boat and the waves rocked us. I felt a kind of vertigo which then dissolved into comfort, which soothed me, and continued to answer the question I had never before asked.

"You should take me back, I guess."

"I guess so."

"I'm sorry you and Peg didn't have any children. I didn't create children who wanted to be mothers." She lifted my head. "Anyway, there's tomorrow," she said, with fatigue and contentment.

On the way out the door she looked at the photographs in the foyer. "Take all these pictures down, will you? Even the one of Oliver. Have the walls painted. And there's so much junk in the garage, chairs without legs, tea pots without spouts. Take it all away to the garbage; we don't need them now."

I waited for the inevitable parting line, the cap on the conversation which mother always managed to produce and which I wanted. "And play the piano in the library every now and then, will you, the way you did when you were young? To get out the moths. Or have your composer do it."

32

FINDING THE FATHER AND THE MOTHER

Hart and The Lover:
Between God and the world
is creation.
Between God and humanity
is redemption.
Between you and me
is revelation.

Alix's Lines for the Libretto

After I had returned Mother to Styx Mansion, I came home, removed Richard's flowers from the fireplace, and lit a fire.

I had a father. Not a cloaked, faceless figure, a man who came from the dark and went back into the dark. Not something on one leg, so unstable it fell over in the morning, a one-night stand, leaving me, accident, broken on the floor.

He had a name; he had given me my name. Actually, he had given me two names, one with a skirt, draperies, something to cover me, Alicia, and another name that snapped with clarity and certainty—Alix. I was named after him.

I would accept what my mother said, even if it was an exaggeration, a romantic overstatement. I accepted it with open arms.

Scaffolding. I had been trying to climb this rock face of my life using ropes and spikes attached to my shoes, and I had been afraid to look down and afraid to look up. Now I stood on scaffolding fixed properly to the ground, with level boards resting on tough metal poles. It was so much better than a ladder.

I didn't have to hold on so tightly anymore.

Me, once so careful with truth and stingy with adjectives, I was now Baby Jesus. Baby Jesus who was depicted in paintings as if childhood had been skipped, a fully developed person with a five o'clock shadow standing in the palm of my mother's hand, in gold so buffed you could see your reflection. I'm pointing with my two fingers upward, not to the heavens but to the man standing right beside me, the father, Alexander. Not a space, a dove, a ghost, an absence, a wish or hoax, a place-marker to avoid being odd and hurt. I had a real mother, too, one who eventually loved me, who didn't want me to get myself on a death train. The three of us had an endearing corona of light around our heads.

Calm down. Put another log on the fire.

There were so many questions I hadn't asked. Sophia had been with Alexander for a year; she must know everything about him; they were real lovers, going to get married. I could ask her and she could tell me. I didn't even know what color his hair was. Maybe it was black like mine. No wonder I didn't have my mother's legs, I had my father's. My smile, which I had never really liked, was his smile. It was a good one, shy but welcoming. What had he wanted to do in his life, where were they going to live? What friends did he have? If my mother could answer these questions, it would be an illumination. My mother would turn the pages for me and there would be a large gold letter starting the next chapter or verse or even the next thought.

How unlikely it was to find, at such a late hour, that in my devious mother's life there was love, the thorough-going, incessant and unyielding force in her every day. I'd never loved anyone in this way. It had never occurred to me I was even capable of such a thing.

My father's life had been a narrow band of light. Within that band there was room for me to stand—not on sufferance, but a real place reserved for me.

I had, until now, kept everything I owned packed away in a trunk, ready to leave. I started to unpack. Having a father made me rash enough to love my mother, even if she were still an unreformed liar on a bender.

I had to do everything again. I had to revise it all. How could I manage this?

I could dial the phone. I could phone everyone. I had limbs, arms and hands. I had a new capacity for—well, everything.

I thought to call Richard. Maybe I would, maybe I wouldn't. Oh, God, what would I say? I might say, "I want to see you." I'd have to tell him I was just unpacking my trunk and still had a blistered heart.

All right. I could make a fresh start. Not the dreaded, perpetual starting over: a new day, dawn, the beginning of the month, the New Year, the always-beginning-again which haunted my life, the new horizon, the possibility of reformation, expecting things would change just because it was Monday, hope at the door, the trash-man coming to get all the garbage piled in the corner.

I wouldn't have to wait any more for hope. It was a Wednesday, nothing heralded, nothing necessary. In this mid-week of my life, everything had altered. I was in a new country. I didn't know its history or why the streets had the names they did, but I knew why I had the name I did, why I had a round, open face. I had a father.

Filled up with all my blowzy hallelujahs, I would call Paige.

I had to think clearly why I wanted to do this. Was her father now changed with my change? Did I think, for some reason, it would help Paige that I'd found my own father?

Weeded as a widow, a broach of the moon on a chain around her neck, Paige was trying to hold up her head while a universe of stars weighed it down. The pin on her broach was unclasped. I would close it.

I CALLED HER THE NEXT morning. I woke her. I'd take the ferry over, and we could spend the afternoon together, perhaps have dinner.

"Sure, you bet, come on in, don't know how warm the water is but there's plenty of it."

Just as I was ready to leave for the ferry Mother phoned. She seemed always to call as I was about to depart for someplace else. She sounded confused. I told her I was going over to Vancouver Island for the day, perhaps overnight, but I would visit her tomorrow.

"Yes, that's nice. Now who is this again?"

"You mean who is speaking?"

"Yes. I'm sorry I've forgotten."

"Mother, it's Alix, your daughter. You called me."

"Good heavens. Sometimes when you're phoning someone and they answer, you forget, you're lost in thought."

"It's better to tell me you don't remember. Then you don't have to be anxious and pretend, at least not to me."

"Well I'll tell you what I don't remember, and I've been worrying about it. Where's the dog? I don't know when I last fed him."

"What's happened to you since yesterday? We haven't had Soldier since I was six. That's forty years ago."

"I haven't fed the dog in forty years?" The strangeness of the calculation released her laughter. "Okay so the damn dog isn't hungry. What about the car, I mean where have I parked it? How am I going to get out of here if it's been towed? Are you going to tell me I don't have a car either, not since we lost the dog?"

"I have your car."

"Thank heavens. I was afraid I'd have a windshield full of tickets, or that it was towed. I probably shouldn't drive much anyway."

"Sorry, darling, I have to go. I'll be over tomorrow."

"Not until tomorrow?"

"Tomorrow. I'll be there. You haven't forgotten to take your medication, have you?"

ON THE FERRY to Vancouver Island, I went to the ladies' washroom to looked in the mirror. So this was what my father looked like, made into a woman. I carried legitimacy like a crown.

I picked up a bottle of wine at the first liquor store I saw, about four blocks from Paige's in a somewhat rundown suburb of Victoria, a neighborhood in transition. Her house was as small as a garage. There wasn't a doorbell. I knocked.

Paige called out "hello," and then, as she frequently did, as if she weren't sure she'd said anything out loud, she repeated herself. "Hello, hello. Welcome to my piano box. One step inside and you're in the living room, dining room, bedroom all at once. Very efficient. The kitchen is separate. Hello, come in."

I handed her the bottle of Australian merlot. "Thanks for having me, especially on such short notice."

"Short notice? You're funny. You don't have to notify me. Don't you catch my Dad's formality—no more than you have already." She looked at the label on the bottle. "Nice. I'm drinking scotch." I believed she genuinely appreciated the wine. I'd never had to double-think what she said, feeling for the caustic vein.

"Sorry, I should have asked. I can go get scotch; it's not far."

"No, no, no. You drink merlot. I'll stay with the scotch."

"Are you sure? I'll be right back. What scotch do you like best?"

"Ni Plus Ultra."

It was the middle of the afternoon, and she was drinking scotch. Well, it was Saturday, a day off, a day for indulging.

When I returned, the door was ajar. I called out and walked inside. The front door barely cleared the bed. There was room for one chair with a small table beside it and a reading lamp. Paige had set out a tray with the wine bottle, a Waterford crystal wine glass and bottle opener.

On the walls, from top to bottom, was native art: masks, paintings, carvings. They were finer, more shocking and beautiful than I'd seen in any museum.

I heard the toilet flush.

"You okay?" I asked as she came out.

She looked up as if she hadn't expected me to be there.

"Oh, hi. Yeah. Hi, me, I'm fine." I gave her the scotch. "Great, thanks. I'll pour myself one of these." She then bowed her head and pointed around the room in a circle. "You've met my friends?"

"Yes, they're exquisite. 'Always amongst these savages, these hunters—their art.'"

"Is that Austin?" She smiled. "You're getting to know him so well you can use his words and sound like yourself." She pointed again at the wall, this time looking at it. "Dad's last minute purchases. They keep me alive." I knew the double entendre of what she was saying, that this art literally and figuratively kept her alive.

She poured herself a tumbler of scotch, and the ice-cubes cracked like nerve endings. "I've bought a year's worth of food by selling one Edenshaw. I've eaten the masks."

I was too happy and, at least for now, didn't want her to expose how the economics of her father's death had sustained her.

"Candice said your dad used to carve. Do you have one of his masks here?"

She removed the one hanging nearest to the kitchen and handed it to me. I held it on my lap. It was made from blond wood, probably fir, skillfully done but embryonic compared to the works by the natives.

"He called it a self-portrait." She sat down on the bed. "So, what's up, pal?"

This place seemed a little small for my newly found father.

"You're struggling. Why? Has something happened?"

I was going to start, that's all, just start on the narrative and trust I would end up where I wanted. "I told you that my mother is in a nursing home. Yesterday I brought her back home, where you came the other day."

"That's good. Is she with it? That must be the worst, when the mother doesn't even remember your name. Wow." She took a long swallow of the new scotch. "Good drink. Thanks. I get used to the crap I always have and then get a taste of what I really want."

"My mother is competent—she's pretty good most of the

time. In fact she's been telling me things she's not been able to tell me before."

"Oh, careful of that. Careful of what they say when the end is near."

"I think it's okay. I mean I understand her reasons for not telling me before."

"How trust-worthy is it, what a dying parent tells you, eh?"

"She wasn't used to telling me the truth when she was healthy. At least now she's trying. Paige, are you okay?" She seemed lost.

"I am, sure I am. This is good. Glad to hear this stuff about your mom."

"She told me of my real father. You remember I didn't know anything about him." I recounted some of what Sophia had told me.

She was sitting on the bed, looking at her feet. I wondered if she were bored with it all, figuring nothing could be said about any father which she hadn't already thought or puzzled through about her own. I looked over at the bottle of scotch which was sinking fast. I was losing heart. I wanted a drink of the stronger stuff, to join her in the muck of blank, but I had to drive.

I tried to rally. "It was like finding a missing piece to a puzzle."

She seemed to flinch. "That's what some people said about my dad, lots of times, about this and that. Oh, this is the missing piece, like when they re-read something he'd written. I don't know about missing pieces. He left pretty much a hole. But hey, tell me more about you, okay?"

"My mother said she'd always loved my real father, which is astonishing—especially since I didn't know I even had one."

"Yeah. I like a love story. That's way cool."

I knew she was trying to focus on me, be generous to me like a friend, but it was hard for her. The alcohol was swamping her.

"Maybe a month before he did it, he said, 'I'm starting over.'" She was unmoored, a boat set out from shore. "There is no starting over." She kept looking at his mask. I wanted to give it back to her to break this spell, but I couldn't seem to move. "He was careless as to whether we could even get up after his fall. What's worse, he didn't give a damn. A piece in a puzzle? Mine left a hole, a routed, gouged out landscape, splattered with his skin and blood. His bloody pieces." She raised her eyes and focused. "Answers don't come in shapes so violent we can't see the message." She seemed to be quoting herself.

The sight of me with her father's mask in my hands seemed to startle her into a realization that something was out of kilter in what she was saying. She began a raging soliloquy which I imagined she'd said over in her mind but never out loud. "He threw us back into a dark that has no name. Not raven's dark, fumbling around, bumping into things, but pitched into the gall of nothing, pitched into this gag, his murder." She stood and paced the short distance to the door of the kitchen and back to the bed. "Raven wanted to see a daughter's face, so he stole the light." She suddenly stopped, as though she'd walked through the wrong door and ended up in the wrong room. "This isn't right." She took another route. "Maybe Dad stole the light, okay, maybe, but not so he could see me. After all his fuckin' brainy insight he just turned away."

I was relieved she wasn't reciting from a nightmare.

She stopped in front of me. She was swaying and she was lost to me. "I have dreams now, but my dreams aren't of him. They're of women: Mrs. Fury, Mrs. Sorrow."

I was out of my depth, and she was drowning. "Paige, I'm sorry." She didn't want to hear from me. She wanted to be alone with her grief.

"He acted like a childless man, leaving me fatherless."

She was quieting down; maybe it was over. Her head slumped forward. I said her name again. She looked up at the mask her father had carved and addressed it directly, steadying her aim. "You were a mirror for me. You could hold me. You were there, present, you existed, you had a body, I could hold you." The directness of her speech was an effort to account for a cavalcade of loss. "What have you done?" Her voice was filled with horror. Then she looked at me. "You've taken the light." She was confusing me with Austin. "More than that, you've taken my compass. I'm howling. And I don't even know if the sounds are coming from me." She stepped forward, reaching for the mask and for me. "You bastard."

She managed to get one hand on the inside of the mask, near the jaw, and one hand on my right arm. "Paige, stop this."

She yanked my arm and the mask slipped from our grip and smashed against the wall beside her bed.

"Good. I hope it broke. I hope it didn't break. I hope it broke. I hope—" She sniffed the air. "There's a sour smell in here." The enthrallment snapped.

I was shaken. I looked hard at her. She wasn't joking or toying with me. She had really smelled something foul.

"Could you check? Maybe it's the garbage," she said.

I went into the kitchen. The plastic bin under the sink was empty.

"Paige, you know what? You're upset—I'm upset—this isn't fun. There's nothing in your garbage. I doubt if you have eaten today."

"Today?"

"I'm going to get you some food."

"You're going to get take-out?" She was limp and exhausted. She made her way back to the bed. "There's a Greek place beside the liquor store. Here's some money." She reached inside the drawer near her bed and pulled out bills secured with an elastic. "You can get them to wrap the food in this."

"I have money."

"You always pay."

"Please come with me. I don't want to leave you alone."

"I'll clean up. I'll pick up Daddy's head. I'm sorry. Sorry to you both. Good scotch is bad for me. You go. Don't forget to come back. I'll be waiting." She reached, trying to touch me. I moved forward so she was able.

I found the restaurant, ordered four meals for Paige, and waited. I felt like a door with bullet holes in it.

When I returned, she was asleep, holding a wooden carving in her arms, as if it were a comfort toy. I put the food in the fridge. She shifted on the bed and then looked up at me. "Hey, pal. I think this place has rats. Maybe that's what I could smell. I couldn't hear what you were saying because of the rats running in the walls." She put her head back down on the pillow, her eyes slits, half-closed.

It was after 7 p.m. when I finally boarded my ferry, in a state of shock and confusion. It had been impetuous for me to go to see Paige. She needed so much more than I could provide. How embarrassing my coronation was. I had ventured into her inconsolable center.

In the ferry cafeteria, I heard my name called over the loudspeaker, that I was to go to the ship's steward for a message.

It was from Dr. Hall. I called him on my cell phone. Apparently they'd been checking with every ferry that evening.

"Your mother, Mrs. Sophia Purcell, isn't in good shape."

"You'll have to speak up, Dr. Hall, I'm on the ferry, and we're going through Active Pass. The reception isn't that good." I was hollering into the wind. "What's happened?"

"We moved her to a larger room this morning and that has, unfortunately, confused her. Also her medication is out of balance. She's terribly afraid you might be in trouble and you don't know where she is. We all keep telling her that you've seen her every day and she says no, that she hasn't seen you for months. She says she urgently wants to talk to you, but when I hand her the phone and say that she should call you, I'll dial your number, she refuses. She says she can't reach you that way. She's frantic. She's refused her medication."

"I'll get there as soon as I can."

"She keeps asking about the dog."

"Yes. The dog is dead."

"Well, I'll leave that to you."

WHEN I ARRIVED, Mrs. Askew was not on duty.

Mother was sitting in her chair and Dr. Hall on the bed. She seemed strangely disinterested in seeing me.

"Hey, Sophia, what's happening?" I was being jolly when I felt despairing.

"I'm trying to reach my daughter, Alicia, and no one in this joint can help me. She doesn't know I'm here." She didn't look pleadingly at me, that I might be a source of relief or succor but rather looked at Dr. Hall in a harsh way. She sounded bone despondent.

I feared I might say something that would unanchor her even more, and so stayed silent watching her like she'd come around after a knock-out. When her head was turned, I looked at the doctor with as bland an expression as I could muster and nodded to him, trying to give him the go-ahead. He had to be the guide in this unknown territory.

He picked it up. "Sophia, who do you think this is?" indicating me.

"She's my mother." Sophia looked irked. "How can you people help me if you don't even know my relatives?"

"Sophia, I'm going to step outside just for a minute, do you mind, to speak to your mother? Would that be okay?"

"Don't talk to me as if I were a child. It's my child I want to speak to, not you. I don't care what the hell you do. You have to get her on the phone and tell her where I am. She doesn't know. What if she's in trouble."

"All right. Just hold on."

"To what?"

The doctor and I went into the lounge.

I launched in. "This is so bizarre. What the hell is going on? Yesterday she was completely cogent, articulate and thoughtful. This morning she was a little mixed up, but eventually she was fine. Who am I to her now? I'm her mother for God's sake."

He was covering his panic with doctorly calm. "She seems to be under some new stress. Moving her to a different room is part of it. It happens with the elderly, especially when they have multiple problems, diabetes, her hip, and probably the onset of Alzheimer's. Sons become husbands, and daughters become mothers. They believe the person in front of them, you, the daughter, is the mother, because internally they haven't aged. So you look the age her mother was. You really seem to be the mother to her."

"I only knew her mother when I was a little girl."

"How can that have a bearing on this?" Dr. Hall seemed to think I wasn't following this closely enough. I was just saying I didn't know how to act like her mother, but I supposed, that had nothing to do with anything. My reasoning was all useless and befuddling.

"Right." I was dutifully, but really I had caved. I couldn't keep changing shape to others, becoming Paige's father, my mother's mother. "I don't know how to act. Do you think that some of this mix-up was there earlier but lay buried?"

"There are theories."

"What I mean is, do you think there would be less confusion, in old age, about all these relationships if we cop to their dynamics earlier on?"

He looked at me as if I wanted to discuss the philosophy of war in the midst of bullet-fire. I did. I didn't want to feel anything. "Will I ever get her back as my mother?" I would not cry. I never cried.

I had an idea. I told him what it was, and we re-entered the room.

"Mrs. Purcell." Dr. Hall aroused her.

"Oh please, I'm Sophia. Sophia, wanting my daughter, not some marital status."

"Sophia, I'm going to call your daughter and tell her where you are."

"At last. Thank you." She looked at me and smiled. "At last."

He picked up the telephone and without even feigning dialing the numbers began to speak.

"Hello, is this Alicia?"

"Say Alix too, that's also her name," my mother counseled.

"Is this Alix, Sophia's daughter?" the doctor asked.

Sitting across the room, looking at the two of them, I said, "Yes, this is Sophia's daughter."

My mother seemed pleased.

"Alix, my name is Dr. Hall."

"I'm so glad to hear from you. I've been wondering how Mother was doing. I was worried." I looked out into middle ground.

"Well, she's doing fine. She has, however, been concerned you didn't know where she was, and couldn't find her."

"I'm very glad you called. Where is she?"

My mother was looking down at her feet, smiling, nodding, content with how the conversation was going.

"She's at Point Grey Lodge."

"Give her the exact address." My mother reprimanded the doctor.

"She wants me to make sure you have the exact address."

Mother interjected. "Ask if she has a pen to write it down. Or a pencil."

"Do you have a pen or pencil to write it down?"

"Yes, I do." I took a pencil from my purse and a piece of paper. "Okay, you tell me."

"Your mother's at 2672 Point Grey Road. I'm thinking that the two of you should meet tomorrow, would that work for you?"

"At breakfast?"

My mother nodded. "Right," said the doctor, "at breakfast. She usually eats at the first sitting, about 8 a.m."

"Tell her I'll be there."

"Fine, thank you. I'll let her know." He hung up the telephone. "Well, it's all settled."

"At last I'll see her after so long. Thank you very much. Now I'm worried about Alix's dog. I don't think I've been feeding him, and she'll be sure to ask me. She really liked that dog."

"I can take care of that," said the doctor.

"Oh, good, that's good. And my car. I have to be able to tell Alicia that I've been looking after things while she's been away, that I am a competent mother for her, and I'll help her if she's in trouble. Let me know about the car so I can drive out of here."

"I will."

"The other thing—there are so many things—my husband's socks. When he died he left two drawers full of socks. This is my second husband, not the first. I don't know what to do with them. I used to give to the Diabetes Association, but who wants to wear a dead husband's socks? They're in the garage, in a bag where I've left them all this time."

"I'm sure the Diabetes Association would appreciate whatever you could give them."

"Even a dead husband's socks?"

"I'm sure they wouldn't mind."

"Good. There's also something about the dog that I don't have to worry about, but I can't remember what it is."

Tears came to the very brim of my vision. Poor dear. She settled into bed. She was calm. I wanted this to be the last time I looked at her as her mother.

What to do with two bags full of a hated husband's socks and a dog that needed feeding after 40 years.

And Baby Jesus.

33

HAPPINESS IS IN THE BANK

Hart

The gods want me to sleep
and not remember.
Or to fly, not knowing that I am.

Or have I found another kind of god?

Alix's Lines for the Libretto

I was exhausted. I was late meeting my mother for breakfast.

She was sitting alone, and I hoped it was me she was expecting. Despite what had happened the day before, I was on the look-out for good signs. If my happiness were a bank account, my parents had just made a large investment and I was determined to spend it lavishly.

I stood in front of my mother like an offering. "Good morning."

"Hello, darling. They told me you'd be coming." She turned her cheek for me to kiss her. She was strangely rested, more rested than I felt, although it wasn't a competition.

"Alicia, did something happen last night? All I know is that I feel slightly guilty, as if I offended someone. My brain is giving me the slip. But Dr. Hall came with medication this morning, and I downed all those nasty little pills."

I took her hands in mine and touched them to my lips. Her hands were bony, and the skin slid around as if I could pull it off like a glove.

"You're thin. You're not eating enough."

"Here's our opportunity." A rotund Latino woman delivered to us two plates of a soggy crush of scrambled eggs attended by a slippery, cherry tomato. Although unappetizing, I took a forkful to show a good example.

"You know they have an expression here," Sophia said. "I've overheard the nurses use it as a diagnosis. They say so-and-so is bed-seeking. You'd want it to be about looking for someone to love, but it's not, it's wanting to sleep all the time. Alix, I don't want to end up as a bed-seeking person. Okay? I don't want to die in a dump like this. I'm on third base. You've got to hit me a home run."

"We don't need a home run. Even a bunt will do." Then I realized I had missed her pun on 'home run.' "I'll get you out of here."

"You've come to your senses."

"I'll arrange for a full-time nurse for you at Pine Street."

"We might have to spend all the money I have—you left with nothing when my very reason for marrying Russell was to avoid that. You're frowning." This time she took my hands in hers. She closed her eyes and slowly tried to work through the logical steps of a difficult problem. "Can you stand to live in financial uncertainty, no support from me—hell, you never asked me for money but I wanted you to be secure after I go—so—" She squeezed my hands tightly, redoubling her effort—"Could you manage the way you have, not depending on me, because I've drained the coffers by being even more doddering than now, all the money spent on supporting a brain-dead me? Could you—" She started to cry. She had been valiant, funny, forceful and then she crumbled. I held her awkwardly in my arms.

"Well, we're decided." She lifted her head. "You'll take me home to Pine Street. I don't mind if my brain goes, but as soon as I start to drool, pass me the pills. I've been saving Tylenol 3 for the occasion. They're in my jewelry box. If I can't put them in my mouth, help me, will you, when the time comes?"

I couldn't imagine a future which would call on such a promise. "Okay."

"I want to go to the beauty parlor." She was cheery. "I'd like them to put in hair lice."

"Hair lice?" I was once more alarmed.

"Hair lice? I mean—oh god—hairlights—highlights—highlights in my hair. Oh, Alicia, do you see? You can't have me asking for hair lice. Let's have a good time, spend all the money and never have hair lice for any occasion."

"Right, no hair lice. Eat your eggs."

"You eat yours."

I had a back-sliding, habitual fear that perhaps she had staged the entire event, a charade to get me to take her home. "About last night—"

She didn't look at me straight on but shifted her head the way I remembered her doing when I was a child, as if she could get a better measure of me through one eye, her right eye, which seemed to widen with readiness and suspicion.

"Last night," she repeated, keeping a neutral tone.

"I wondered if it were possible that you were—" I finally asked her directly. "Were you faking it, Mother?"

"Faking it?"

"Did you?"

"Did I what?"

"Oh, Mother, sometimes you can be a tricky one."

"Tricky? Alicia I'm an ailing woman. I'm all tricked out. The jig is up."

"I'm sorry."

"That's okay. You can trust me now."

"You said Russell was your second husband?"

"I did?"

34

THE DOG IS DEAD

I finally reached Paige. She asked me cheerily why everyone was so worried about her, that her Aunt Candice had called as well. She said she didn't remember much about my visit and asked how the opera was going.

"But are you okay," I persisted.

"Don't keep asking me, right? I don't want a grief counselor, I want art."

I was reluctant to tell her I'd taken her drunken episode—transposed it, transmuted it, transformed it—all the euphemisms for "used"—I was using her life to get me to the words I needed for the opera. Was I, like Austin, sincere, but always on the take?

I summoned the nerve to tell her I had written more of the libretto after my night with her. I read the lines which crescendoed in Hart throwing the mask he'd carved against the wall.

There was silence on the other end of the line. I wondered if she would finally call halt to my ransacking her life for what I needed.

"That's what happened, didn't it? I threw his mask across the room."

"Yes."

"It's strange. It's like an instant replay, not of a game but of my story. It feels weird. I guess this is all right. I use my dad's death in my poems, and you use my sorrow in your libretto. Put another nickel in the nickelodeon. You're pretty ballsy to write this and tell me about it. But this is what I'd been hoping for from you."

"Do you want me to send you this part?"

"No, you just keep telling me, like this. It's better when you tell me than when I read it."

DR. HALL ADJUSTED Mother's medication and it helped. She could remember who I was, that the dog was dead and that I had her car. She hadn't again thought I was her mother.

One day I called and said I would be by in an hour. When I arrived, she was sitting in her wheelchair just inside the front doors in the place where Mrs. Askew normally sat. Like Mrs. Askew, she was alert and ready for visitors.

"What are you doing out here?" I put my hand on her upper arm as I wheeled her, and she reached across her shoulder to put her left hand on top of mine.

It occurred to me that she was stationed at the front door because she knew someone was coming to have lunch with her, but she couldn't remember who.

"Mother, a question—were you sitting out there near the door in the hope that you would recognize who was coming to have lunch with you?"

Without turning around she said, "Yes, that's right. I just couldn't remember who had called. I hoped it was someone I liked a lot. And it was. You don't mind that I am beginning to live entirely in the moment, do you? No matter what they say, I don't think it's that enlightened."

"We'll make the best of it."

We sat alone at the special table. Mother was especially friendly to the other residents who passed by. Everyone acted that way at the mansion when they had a guest, proud to be noticeably loved;

they all dressed up in their best clothes and looked as if they were ready to be discharged, get a job, jog around the block.

I was afraid that Sophia's mind had gotten snagged in strange places partly because she didn't have enough stimulation at the mansion. If she remained stable, a private nurse would come next month to be with her at home, one who could administer her medications. Why I hadn't thought of this before, I feared, was because I loved her more now.

As the servers came, Mother looked at her food. "I don't know what they've done to the schnitzel. Maybe they dropped it on the floor. You don't have to eat it, I won't mind. So, tell me more about your work on this musical."

I laughed. "I hope you're not expecting *Hello Dolly* or *Fiddler on the Roof*."

"They were both very good. I saw them in New York in 1964 with Russell. Ginger Channing played Dolly. I've still got some dates left." She paused. "I don't mean date-dates, but times when things happened. I'm beyond dating. Although some people in this joint aren't. You'd be surprised at what goes on in here. I don't object, of course, why should I? But I gave up on intercourse long ago."

I'd never heard my mother say the word "intercourse." It sounded strangely interesting and heartening coming from my aged mother, as though she thought it were a still useful but somewhat antiquated means of transport, getting the right trains onto the right tracks for the right destination.

"By the way," she said, "did you take down that ghastly rogues gallery of Russell's family photographs from the front foyer? When I get back home, I hope they're gone."

She remembered, then, our conversation about Russell. Still, the old fear that had looped around me like a vine, when I was a child, found its roots. Maybe Sophia invented the story about my father. Even if she hadn't made it up, he might absent herself at any moment, no longer capable of telling me where I came from. I couldn't risk her being befuddled or, worse still, saying none of it had ever happened.

"You remember a few weeks ago now," I said, "when you came back to Pine Street, and we sat in the solarium? I brought food from the delicatessen, and we ate on the TV tables which we've had since—"

"God, since you were a kid."

"You told me about Russell and what happened on that summer day in the 50s. You ended up telling me about my father."

She looked alarmed. "Did I tell you about him?"

Stay with me, I thought, don't turn me into your mother, don't be mistaken about who I am.

"You did. I wondered about his family, and what he wanted to do with his life after the war, a profession or something?" My questions seemed inept.

"Yes, of course you need to know that. Let me see. He wanted to travel. He was very clever at languages, very artistic. But his family was poor, and being an artist in a poor family is a crummy deal. I was so—ambitious, I guess." It took effort for her to dig into the gravels of the past. "I can't quite tell what you're thinking, my eyes blur everything—but I guess you want more."

"As much as you have, not more than you can give."

"Darling, you're on the right track at last. You've got a loaf of bread under each arm. Don't go down that old rabbit hole. Tomorrow. Maybe tomorrow." She closed her eyes. Soon she was breathing heavily in her chair, her food barely touched.

35

THE WORLD IS AS SHARP AS A KNIFE

Tom Price:
I lifted a board
and underneath
a totem pole, ten inches high in slate—
It crumbled in my hand.

A god fell apart in my fingers
before my eyes
that weep.

Alix's Lines for the Libretto

Miles asked me to come and see him at his office at the university.

I looked through the glass-fronted door. He was leaning back in his chair. I thought he must be watching a television, but he was looking at something that didn't seem to be in front of him.

I knocked and entered. It was as if my presence pulled him away from a place of such absorption and enticement that he was reluctant to leave.

"You're in trouble," he said, as he looked up.

"What's happening?" The unexpected panic in my voice caught me off guard.

"I received a call from Violet Clayburn, a Haida elder who lives in Skidegate. Apparently your Producer called up to the Band office looking for what he termed an 'authenticator' for the opera, which set off a slough of questions and concerns. The Producer told them I was involved, so Violet called me."

"An authenticator? I haven't heard about this."

"He used the unfortunate description that he wanted 'a Haida who could make the libretto sound authentic.' Not the happiest way of putting it. He also said that because I was helping you he wanted to hire 'his own native.'"

"What a repellent idea."

"My guess is that this work is going to start to change shape on you because everyone's confronting their own fears, and probably their own greed." Despite being in his late thirties, his voice had the calm and gravely tone of an old man. "Violet Clayburn will protect what she considers to be the stature and reputation of the Haida Nation as if it were her first born. She's understandably suspicious of outsiders. The Producer is saying this work will happen even without any of you because you're not creating a story but discovering it. I'm not sure about that. Most of us don't feel worthy enough to accept all the bounty we receive, so instead of being simple and straight-forward, we make up these grandiose ideas. We don't really want what we're given, because then we'd be beholden. Gratitude is enough. When you need to thank someone God is useful then."

I didn't really understand why he was saying this.

"What should I do?" I asked.

"I have a university education; I teach medicine. My brother, Arthur, is the head of the longhouse. He can't read or write. Recently there's been a dispute about protocol over the taking of a new dancer to be initiated—a question of what should be done and when. Arthur is there to resolve it. One of the dancers, a man older than my brother, has other ideas about it all. He's opposing Arthur in many ways, subtly, every day. Finally Arthur goes over to this fellow and stands in front of him. He asks him one question: 'Who am I to you?' The older man answers, 'You are my father.' The dispute is settled. That's all it takes. Humility."

"How do I find humility? I'm not even sure what it is."

"Ah, then you'll learn. There's a Haida saying: 'The world is as sharp as a knife.' That's where you'll start. Violet wants you to consider some practical things."

I said that, of course, I would. "Who is this person? What is she like?"

"Violet Clayburn—how shall I describe her? She moves as if she wears a cape—which she sometimes does—and it's one that sweeps things off the table as she passes."

"I see."

"The name Shawcroft has to be changed in the opera because it's a real family name. For the Haida, and the Coast Salish, names are places and the people belong to the places. Violet's point is that if, in the opera, you put people on Ninstints who didn't own Ninstints, you're going to have trouble because some natives will think these families have a claim because you've written it down. Shawcroft didn't have an hereditary place on Ninstints, that's your invention. White folks can still define what's real for us, I'm sorry to say." He told me that stories were objects within the longhouse. "It's as if stories are picked up and moved around, and then they are set down. At the end of the story-telling, people say, 'Throw it away, throw it away.' The story needs to be released again. But Violet said very firmly, 'It also means this writer can't take this good story and tell it to the next person she meets, even if she claims it's a universal story.'"

I felt hedged in and censored. "What story of the Haida have I taken?"

"Only you know that. She's concerned. And it's also attributing stories to them which don't belong."

"Isn't it the same with Hart's family? Do I have any right to tell the story about Austin and Paige and—his other relationships?"

"That's for you to answer. Undefensively, if you can."

I laughed. "Okay, I don't have a right to it. So far they want it told."

"You're the one taking it on the chin because you write the words, and words can be attacked where the music can't be."

"That's what Brett says, too."

"Well, there you are. You should be mindful of your production team. My hunch is that the composer assigns to others things that should be a function of his own character."

"Like what?"

"Caring."

"Oh, dear."

"Also, your Producer isn't a good decision-maker. He's too interested in how he's doing. He hates himself, but he's still the most interesting person he knows. Alix, listen to yourself."

"All right."

"You might call Violet. Suggest that the grandfather needs to let Raven transform the world. You can go now."

I was gently dismissed as from a tutor.

I went to Styx Mansion to see my mother. To my great relief, she wasn't stationed at the front door and seemed to be in good form. After I told her about the developments with Violet Clayburn, she was ready with her opinions about everyone. "You're the writer whose neck is on the line, don't you know? I keep thinking of when you were little. You did everything wrong at first. You tried to walk before you crawled."

"I'm worried there isn't enough time to make so many mistakes."

"Keep your eyes open. Don't get on the plane if there's something wrong with it."

"Ah, you've changed your position on that."

"Because I see I've taught you to ignore what's best in you."

"Which is?"

"Your lovely self. You are dutiful, and duty can bring missteps." Sophia had her eyes closed as she advised me. "You're also not sleeping very well. You look tired. I'm not sleeping well either. We could be awake together. While you pace about you could be wheeling me around the house."

"Stay stable for a month and then come home. I am worried I have to be away quite a lot."

"Have everyone come to us."

"Paige called me. She said she'd heard there was trouble."

"That's the word everyone uses, isn't it, 'trouble.' It sounds like a thing, a figure that's entered the room."

"Yes, I think her name is Violet Clayburn."

"What did Paige say?"

"She said, 'I don't need to know a lot of the details. I just want to make sure you're all right.'"

"Like a sister," Sophia said, satisfied. "She's releasing you from duty. I like her. Call Mrs. Clayburn, get her on your side. Actually, I think I'll call Mrs. Clayburn. Have a mother-to-mother chat."

"No, Sophia, I don't think that would be appropriate."

"You don't want me to be part of your village square?"

"Not if you feel competitive about my having a phone card."

"Touchee, my dear."

36

FIGURING OUT THE FORM LINES

[On Ninstints]

Hart:

There is someone else here
whom I have known
an attended silence
a watchful eye
watching me.

In his presence
I realize my soul is bruised,
my vision the cross-hairs
of a gun

There were to be no boot prints in the sand.

Alix's Lines for the Libretto

Françoise had prevailed in putting Tom Price on life supports. He'd made a recovery.

Brett and I were invited to their apartment for dinner at 7 o'clock. I bought a bottle of wine and a container of purple tulips. When I met Brett outside their building, he noticed what I'd brought and seemed churlish. I suggested they could be from both of us.

Something was again changed in Brett's appearance, but I couldn't quite tell what it was. Perhaps he'd lost weight. He looked leaner, more angular and rougher than when I had last seen him. Maybe he was growing a beard.

We took the elevator to the fourth floor, struggling with Brett's sound equipment. The door to the apartment was wide open.

On the wall facing us, and covering its entire surface, were native masks. A vault had accidentally been left open. I knew from my research and from talking to Miles that some of these masks were supposed to be kept hidden until they were used in a performance.

I could have stood there for a long time, staring at this multitude, but I heard someone moving inside.

Brett leaned forward and called out, "Hello?"

In a very deep, but faint voice, a man said, "Come in."

Tom Price was sitting at a round, cluttered table near the window in the living-room. Although the long summer light filled the room, it was fading behind him so that he was backlit, and it was difficult to see his face. He was holding a pencil or a carving tool poised in his right hand. His huge form, hunched and bowed as it was, was roosting over his work.

He looked up, said "hello" and looked down again. His voice was as flat as a 2x4. We were set adrift.

He'd emerged from a cavernous place so quiet and kept apart it seemed unkind to have disturbed him. Then it was unkind of him to have left us. He became so completely recessed and private, it was almost beyond describing.

Tom Price was barefoot and wore a flannel dressing gown, one he might wear in a hospital to show he intended to go home soon. It had gray and mauve braiding along the edge of the cloth. He seemed not to be wearing anything underneath.

His state of undress was part of the composition of the room and his influence on the room—which was as a forceful old man. We would have to make do, just as he was. His dishevelment was a public thing, something presented to us and to which we were expected to give our understanding, but not much of our curiosity.

I looked for a place to put the wine and flowers.

I had come to his apartment a week earlier, in the afternoon, to give him a copy of my notes showing how I was going to portray him in the opera. I stood in the living room amidst a muddle of activity. No one paid much attention to me, nor did they seem to mind that I was witnessing this native man, a member of the formidable Haida Nation, and a highly educated artist of genius, being dressed by an array of people. His dressers, after managing to put his legs in his trousers, removed his gown, exposing his pale and weakened chest. Then they struggled to put on his shirt. Because of his Parkinson's disease, every now and then he would shake uncontrollably, but his helpers adjusted their movements to his and were finally able to capture him in his clothes. He was being readied for a ceremony at the university where he would receive his fourth honorary doctorate degree.

In his living room now, in the fading light, I felt even more uncomfortable than the first time; this embarrassment was again entirely my own.

He began sketching with the pencil directly onto the slab of wood.

Brett and I were both trying to decide where we might sit. This simplest of things required a strategy. All of the chairs in the room were oddly placed, so that sitting in any one of them would mean being far apart from each other and facing in different directions. Finally Brett announced to me, "I'll get you a chair," thinking that might be the organizing principle for this malaise. He moved two chairs near the table, creating a semi-circle around the master carver.

I handed Tom Price the working draft of the libretto. He looked at the cover and put it on the table beside the block of wood.

We were back in awkward silence. At the same time the uncertainty and unease created by this man was intriguing. I'd never met anyone so entirely careless of social conventions.

Brett spoke again. His mouth seemed dry and the words had a tactile quality. "Is there a better time when we might—"

Tom interrupted and, not looking at us, said slowly, "I hear you're having trouble with this work." It took physical effort for him to speak, like hurling heavy stones. "You're having trouble with Violet Clayburn."

"We were," Brett said. "But Alix spoke to Miles George and we've solved—"

"She won't want you to do it."

"We've agreed to what she wanted," continued Brett.

"Yes." He implied that concessions were irrelevant. "She once wanted to be head of the Haida Nation. She was treated poorly, very unpleasant. She deserved it."

As if single-mindedly intent on delivering a message of good cheer—because it was impossible not to understand what Tom was saying—Brett went on, "I think we've patched everything up."

Violet Clayburn posed a threat to us. Unlike Brett, I would not have kept talking because we only knew our own strategies and had little real understanding of the opposition. When Brett said to me, "Don't you think so, Alix?" I didn't want to answer.

"I doubt it," Tom said. "Not for long, anyway."

"It was a mistake, how it all happened," Brett offered.

"There'll always be a mistake."

He said other things, but I had difficulty hearing him. It wasn't just that Tom mumbled. He talked covertly, as if he wanted listening to him to be hard-won. Despite his fame, his intelligence and wry humour, there was something leaden and burdensome about him.

And he was grumpy. He had invited us to dinner, but really he wanted to be left alone.

After a long pause he continued in the same monotone, "The trouble with this place is the dinner hour always changes." It was proprietary, the way he said it, while at the same time mocked his assertion of authority. I decided it had to do with his having a beautiful and stylish wife who was much younger than he. He liked to say "the trouble with this place" even if it didn't mean anything, or even if it really meant "I am a cuckold."

He looked toward the hallway, as if Françoise might enter. If she had, it would be his magic as well as hers. She failed to appear.

Tom's mention of the evening meal was a relief, a minor confirmation that we were not completely at cross-purposes with our host. Still the comfort left much to be desired. It wasn't clear where dinner was going to come from. Nor was it clear whether Françoise would show up. Brett had told me they might have separated.

As a young woman, Françoise had studied with Claude Levi-Strauss. The story, first told to me by Brett and confirmed by others, was that when Françoise was 19 years old Levi-Strauss sent her to Canada to work with Austin Hart. It wasn't until after Hart's suicide—it was because of Hart's suicide—that she met Tom. Distraught by Hart's death, she searched out his brilliant and difficult friend.

Tom picked up the libretto. He slowly moved his carving tool above the paper, as if tracing a design he was imagining.

His movements created a trance. I tried to free myself by remembering what we had come here to do: discuss the opera, consider Tom's views on my portrayal of his character, listen to some of Brett's music—none of which had been advanced. Just when I decided I would never escape from this senseless place, when I decided this was, at best, a meditation on the awkward, Françoise was coming across the room towards me, her coat over her arm, carrying an abundance of purple tulips. Brett and I stood up.

"You are Alix," she said as she kissed me on both cheeks and then went to Brett. She trailed light refracted through cut glass.

Nothing had happened until then.

After kissing Tom, she turned and saw the potted tulips which I had brought, "Ah, we love the same flowers."

How meager mine were compared to hers. The coincidence of the flowers seemed not to be a sign of harmony between us so much as an object lesson for me.

Her French accent was still strong, and she charmed me like royalty. She wore an off-white silk suit with a long tailored jacket, which she removed and tossed onto the couch. If she and Tom had separated, they were back together again. Or perhaps there was another explanation: that this was her performance, something that she—that they both did—as required. Yet if that were true, their way of being together was so complex the phrase "not together anymore" could explain little about the present or the past.

Without any apparent signal from Tom, Françoise left the room and returned with eight vials of pills which she placed on the table and started dispensing to him. She gave him a handful and said "all at once"; he opened his massive, cupped hand, tilted his head back and swallowed them. She gave him a glass of water.

"It is dark in here?" She looked around as if we had been forgetful, then turned on both lamps near the couch. "And some wine, I think."

Eventually, she looked at Brett. "You are talking about the opera?"

As Brett perched forward, readying himself to respond, Tom answered. "I'm asking them if they have figured out why Austin killed himself."

Had Tom looked at me he would have seen my face so actively startled that it was a form of caricature. He had not asked us, even indirectly, why we thought Austin had killed himself. We hadn't mentioned Austin. I couldn't find this question buried anywhere in the parched terrain of our conversation. It was a stated question now, a first-test, the answer to which informs the master whether you have any hope of succeeding at the next tasks, which are sure to be even harder.

Brett gestured to me that I should respond. While it seemed polite and gentlemanly, as the librettist, I was learning that there was an ethical burden that went with the words which the music could avoid. For the first time it also occurred to me that Brett might be cowardly.

I felt as if I were searching out pieces of ribbon and string, trying to make a nest of my ideas. Françoise and Tom were Austin's friends. How absurd for me to explain Austin to them. "I've been asked by people who knew him well, why he killed himself."

"You are an investigator," Françoise said. "People tell you things that are secret, so you might get at the truth. But in fact we don't really want to know, because we all feel responsible. You might name any of us. And about the Haida—please just carry on with your work. Forget about everyone else, even us."

Françoise was putting on her coat. "I've ordered some Japanese food. I'll pick it up." At the door she said, "Tom, you feel strange about being a character in the opera who is different from who you actually are, is that right? You and the character Alix has created would argue." She left the room without waiting for Tom's reply.

She would have waited for a long time.

Finally I said, "You believe that it was acceptable to cut down the poles? One of the young Haida carvers has written that she woke up to find the islands empty of totems."

"Rubbish." He took the synopsis. "'Tom Price was likable, well balanced.' I'm not well balanced. I've never been well balanced in my entire life." I started to laugh. "It's true."

By the time Françoise returned, Brett was playing music he'd written for the first scene of the opera. The room was dark with the isolation of the remote Ninstints island and the haggard poles. Once again, Françoise turned on more lights, placed trays of sushi and sashimi on the table, and brought us back to life.

She stood in front of Tom and held out her hands to him. He raised his heavy arms. "Ah, you're stiff." As she pulled him towards her, he rose slightly, and then rocked back. She pulled again. I watched the two of them move almost delicately with his huge form, the arc of a pendulum, the most basic of movements: of a boat rocking in the water, of a scythe, of a pole, cut, hung up on the trees. He was a crippled giant.

They jostled with balance and gravity until there was enough momentum to hoist him onto his feet. She seemed to align him or sort him out in some fundamental way.

I felt happier sitting at the table, eating sushi and drinking white wine. It couldn't have been worse and suddenly it was better.

"Austin Hart was a very troubled man," Tom said. "We suffered from the same despair. That's why we liked one another. But Austin was Prince Charming."

Françoise laughed. "Ah, you like to think of him as Prince Charming. That's what you like to say about him."

Maybe Tom's leaving the table and showing us that first necklace, bringing it out in an unselfconscious way, maybe it was that which started the unexpected tumble of impulses—Françoise getting the treasures Tom had made for her—all of us to moving in unguarded places.

When he first got up, Tom went down the hall, hunched in his great form. He returned and held out a gold and diamond necklace. "I made this in 1971. Worked for months on it. It would take me hours. Then at the end of the day something would go wrong and I'd have to start all over the next morning."

Françoise turned to me. "I'll show you more."

I stood at the door of a room which I knew was hers alone. As Françoise opened the closet, she looked back at me and said, "Come in, Alicia."

She brought down a metal case from a shelf and opened it. Trays and drawers unfolded like an ordinary fishing-tackle box. They were filled with gold brooches, gold bracelets, earrings and necklaces.

This was her room and she had the jewels.

"Try this on." She brought out a pendant which I had seen in photographs. It was called the Dogfish Woman. "You have to look at it in the mirror in the hall. It's too dark in here."

As I went out, Tom was standing there. He must have taken a short-cut through the kitchen. This infirm man had become sprightly, maneuvering himself down the corridor and turning on the light so that I could see what he had created. I looked at my face, and I looked at the Dogfish Woman with her round, moon-shaped head. "Isn't it beautiful?" Tom said, "Yes." Françoise was putting a necklace on Brett, working from in front, so it became a kind of embrace—not seductive but enchanting. Brett stood beside me in front of the mirror. With this one piece of jewelry he had regained the androgynous quality I'd first seen in him. Then there was The Woman of Wealth, the hinged silver bracelet in a bear design, the inlaid abalone shells in the shape of a hawk. And more. Tom kept calling to Françoise "Bring the other one, bring the other one. Bring everything."

Françoise held up a necklace. She'd worn it to the unveiling of Price's massive sculpture in front of the government buildings. "All the women said, 'She's wearing the one from the book.' They wanted to buy it."

Françoise left the room. Tom left the room. They both came back with more pieces. We tried on everything.

Then it all stopped. In the fist of her right hand Françoise held a bouquet of metal stems. We stood, attending. Slowly she opened her hand to reveal carving tools. They were miniature, delicate, sharp. We looked at them as into a pool.

"They are Shawcroft's," Tom said.

"Edward Shawcroft?" I was dumbfounded, seeing the instruments of this genesis.

"Have you carved with these?" Brett asked.

"I've tried. I can't." A deep laugh issued from him, the first. "It's true, I can't. They're too small."

"You did once," Françoise corrected him. She brought out a bracelet. "This is the only piece of jewelry he wears. You're not supposed to wear your own art. Shawcroft created it. Strangely—it must have been mistakenly—a former owner polished down all the hatch-lines. With Shawcroft's tools Tom retraced the lines."

She spread out a small piece of blue velvet and set the tools and the bracelet on the cloth. The objects looked startlingly clear, lit from within.

Tom wanted to show us more. He found the small black box painted with the killer whale which was becoming frog becoming man—the maze of interconnecting lines almost a description of all possibilities contained in a collapse of time.

"I don't really understand this." Without thinking, I added,

"It seems so sexual."

"Oh, yes. It is entirely sexual." Tom nodded his huge head.

We all laughed.

It was then that I said to him, "You take all your energy and put it into the material you are working with, whether it is stone or silver, gold or wood. You put it in to express the spirit—"

"I don't do that." He was abrupt. "I'm a craftsman. I have a certain skill. But I'm just a technician. Don't try to search for spirituality in my work."

It didn't seem possible he was serious.

He lowered himself into his chair at the table. "The Haida lived in a difficult world. But they had abundance, everything they needed, in the ocean, on the land. Out of that they created their art which was ordered, subject to rules, completely defined. Then the traders came, then the settlers. The Haida didn't have a clue what they were up against. How could they?"

I moved around Brett and pulled my chair beside Tom but didn't interrupt him.

"For these guys—Shawcroft and others—to respond to the traders by making beautiful, sought after things, with form and no function? It was a disaster. They were working against their art. I had a dream that I would go up there, have the young kids apprentice to me. Show them how to create again, within those rules. But our societies are in a terrible state."

"What was it like when you went to Ninstints with the expedition?" I'd only had Hart's perspective.

"The first hours on the island were the best. We could forget why we were there. Then we started. We took these massive totems down from the air. Austin was undone when the pole got away on us and smashed. I figured he was going to call it off. I reassured him, told him we had to do it. We handled a ton of wet rotting wood like you would a piece of fine china. We finished. It was dark. We somehow managed to collect the rest of the sections from along the beach and boomed them up. No one could sleep so we sat there on the crates, not saying much, just waiting for dawn. We couldn't even see one another—no moon, no stars. I remember saying, 'We won't see such mastery again.' Austin's voice came over the others and across to me. 'It's not just that the people died, but they had a fire illuminating a civilization that could live artistically on the earth. That's gone. We are the losers.'"

"Life is so ragged," Françoise said, joining in. "His life was ragged. We may be making it fit now more than it ever did."

We weren't melancholy as she said this but there was a silence which suspended us in an unfinished life. There was also an opulence to our state.

Tom said, "He left his wife, he left his children and he left his family, long before he left the world."

No moon, no stars, and it was time to leave. Tom wanted to show us his sketch for a new invention that he had made while in the hospital a month earlier. Françoise said, "You'll never find it." He searched and came out empty-handed. Without the prologue of the five hours we'd spent together, the comment might have been domineering. Instead it was the pendulum swinging: his brilliance, and her caring for his brilliance. By this time, I loved them both. I loved us all.

We had Brett's sound equipment to cope with, and so we looked around the room to decide how we could get it down the hall and to the car. We spotted Tom's wheelchair.

The chair loaded with the gear as its passenger, Françoise wheeled the edifice out the door as we called to Tom "good-bye, good-bye."

At Brett's car Francoise said to Brett, "I'm sorry, I have to take this from you." He was still wearing the necklace. "It looks so good on you."

The building was constructed like a star. If I forgot the center's relationship to the points on the star, I would be lost.

37

ANY FONT IS TOO LARGE

Hart
[Absorbed in himself]

A rampant beauty invades my soul.
As though a lover has been waiting all along
her house arranged,
the table set,
everything wrapped in light—

Alix's Lines for the Libretto

The singers were hired, the forty-five piece orchestra booked. An hour of the music and the libretto for the opera would be performed in the Great Hall of the Museum of Anthropology with three hundred invited guests—corporate sponsors, federal government officials, reporters, friends, some of the Haida and the Coast Salish—all seated in and amongst the salvaged Ninstints poles housed in the museum. This was also the place, in office number 121, where Austin Hart had shot himself.

I noticed a problem with the invitations Brett had prepared. They announced an opera by Brett Morris, libretto by Alix Percell.

I told Brett it should have said music by him and the libretto by me, because we had created the opera together. He said it was never done like that. I said it should be. He said it was too late.

The day before the performance, after the rehearsal with the orchestra, I went for a drink with the composer and the Conductor.

"We should think about the guests," I suggested, still on organizational duty, concerned about the anxious family who would be behind the fourth wall. "I'll spend time at the reception beforehand with the Hart family. Brett, could you talk to Tom and Françoise? We'll share the Haida and the Coast Salish. Miles will be there. He's invited Violet Clayburn." They both nodded.

We were buckling with fatigue. Brett cheeks were dark with stubble. I hadn't realized how really short the Conductor was; probably his whirling arms extended the illusion of tallness.

"I'm not sure if Austin's son, Jason, will make it. This is hard on them all. The dead will be brought back to life. I'm going to try to get my mother here."

"I didn't know your mother was still alive," the Conductor said with genuine interest. "I guess I don't know much about you." He was bemused. "Father?"

"More complicated story. Basically, he's dead. I live on my own now."

"Easier. I have a wife and two children. We're probably going to separate."

I consoled him in a trouble about which I knew nothing. It was the eleventh hour, and we were on the lip of a kind of artistic cauldron. Self-disclosure was a relief, like parting wishes.

The Conductor and I both looked at Brett because it was his turn.

"You know me; family life fine. Nothing to report." Despite his denial, Brett seemed wistful.

"You must be thinking a lot about your mother." My empathy was thoughtless. I'd forgotten he never told anyone about her suicide.

He gave me a cold, unforgiving look; I'd crossed the line.

"Is your mother still alive?" The Conductor was mining for needed intimacy.

I shook my head, trying to deter him from further questions, but it was unnecessary, as Brett drained his glass of whiskey and said, "Nope. We should be going. Anything else?"

"We can't be undone by our private lives." The Conductor retreated with an aphorism specially made for the theater. Brett stood up to leave.

"Oh, I forgot to mention—" the Conductor motioned Brett to sit down—"just for a second. I had a call from the Producer. In order to actually use a chainsaw, orchestrally within the piece, we had to have permission from the university. Apparently there's a regulation."

"What about a sound recording at that point?" I suggested.

Brett scotched the idea. "I don't think it would work. We'll get a permit when we open in Paris. Okay? Done?"

Despite Brett's earlier refusal, I wanted the libretto to be available to the audience. "Sorry to raise this again, but the libretto—"

"Nope," Brett said with the same decisive rancor and then, his anger mounting, "I will not have the rustle of pages while my music is played."

I figured he was out to punish my insensitivity about his mother.

I said that without enabling people to follow the words, the story line could be misunderstood, adding that the libretto could be printed in small font so that it would fit on fewer pages.

"Sorry, any font is too large."

"Careful," I warned. "Don't wreck what we've done together." He didn't look chastened; I shifted to purely rational ground. "In most theaters now operas have surtitles above the stage. You know this. It's not a sacrilege to have the words physically present. This is the only way we can do it in this venue, by providing a script."

"Sorry, Alix but no one really pays attention to the words."

"Why you are so adamant and insulting. People want to hear the words so that they can also ascribe meaning to the music."

"That's just wrong. We've had this argument before."

"Well, we have to have it again." The bile went deeper than in a marital dispute.

Brett and I had had our disagreements before, mainly about the relationship of the music to the libretto, but our arguments had always been shepherded into a conversation of ideas. Now something was baring its teeth. I had felt with Brett that we were swimmers, each with different skills but moving in the same element. On the eve of the performance, we would let the other sink.

Finally the Conductor intervened. "You really want the libretto there, Alix, and I understand that. I don't know how you're going to do it—we're twenty-four hours from the performance—"

"What about the disruption, the noise of the pages?" Brett insisted.

"If the audience can hear the words clearly—or if they don't care about them—they won't need to look at the sheets," I offered.

Changing tack, Brett said calmly, "Sorry, Alix, I'm against this." He looked at the Conductor, who shrugged.

If music, as the man, was always constituted, the woman with the words deserved to be constituted as well. I was going to get them there.

I spent the rest of the day and into the evening trying to sort out the way the libretto would fit on the page. Finally, at midnight I had it ready. It looked so different in this form, as if dressed in clothes I'd never seen before.

After sleeping for four hours, I awoke and took the original proof to Kinko's Printing House near the university. I explained to the attendant that I needed three hundred copies of the twenty pages of libretto, and I would pick it up at five in the afternoon.

After the operatic team met at four o'clock to review with the orchestra the last minute changes, I left for the printers. The opera was soaring through my head, the chorus singing "jubilance." As jubilant as I.

When I arrived at the printing house I asked at the order desk for my copies.

"Here's your original. The work hasn't been done. Machines are down."

"What do you mean?"

"Just what I said. The machines have been down all day."

"Why didn't someone call me? This has to be ready in half an hour."

"This is Kinko's. Machines break down, right?"

I was murderous. I reached across the counter. "This has to be done," I shouted, waving the sheets in his face. The employee lurched back.

"I'm going to call security."

"This can't be true. This can't be happening."

As he picked up the phone, I fled from the building like an outlaw.

With the libretto in my hand, I parked my car in the disability space and ran into the museum. The first person I saw was the Producer's assistant. I told her of the problem.

The Producer came up beside her. "What's wrong?"

"I want the audience to have the libretto. All of the machines broke down at Kinko's."

He smiled. "Bad luck."

With his underslung mouth, I thought of a shark trying to look forlorn at the smell of blood. I turned away.

"Where are you going?" the Assistant asked.

"Will you apologize to the family? Do what you can."

I walked down the sloping corridor ramped between the Ninstints poles, now so stunted that the wide eyes and long teeth of the totemic figures were all that remained. Floor lights blasted up the silvered cedar and hollowed out the face of the Watchman.

The administration offices were to the right of the hall. I went into the photocopying room. The sorter didn't work. I laid the pages on the floor and then onto tables and finally spread them into the adjacent room. The copier ran out of white paper so I used green, then pink, then yellow. I was collating by hand. What had started as an intention had now become an unassailable fixation.

After an hour, when I had finished copying and sorting two thousand pages, I returned to the reception. All but a dozen people were already seated. I went into the audience and started handing out the libretto.

"Sorry, this is late," I kept repeating, passing the pages down the rows. "Share this, one to two people, would you? The libretto, so you'll be able to follow the words." I felt ashamed by my urgency.

Finally, I saw Brett. He was clean-shaven; he looked quite altered.

"Where the hell have you been? The Hart family has been wandering around as if they were homeless."

I knew he'd never thought to help them. "Here's the libretto." He looked stunned, as if I'd slapped him in the face.

As the orchestra was tuning up, I phoned a cab to pick up my mother. When I returned the Producer was on stage. He welcomed everyone. He was excited. He said so. I stood at the back of the museum, looking at the audience, looking at the poles, trying to find Paige and her family, my hands shaking.

I calmed. I had done it. I watched. I listened.

Brett went on stage. I now saw that he was wearing a new blue suit for the occasion, and his hair had been cut so short his black curls had all but disappeared. Any sense of effeminacy I had perceived in him when we first met had been eradicated. He looked tough as nails.

"There are so many people who need to be congratulated for bringing this off... ." He did the right thing, he thanked people. "I especially I want to appreciate the librettist I worked with early in this project, Trevor Crane. We conceived of this together. He's here in the audience." Trevor stood up to a resounding applause. I had never met him in person. He looked thin, corpuscular, like someone too long on a bus.

Strangely, I felt embarrassed for Brett that he had forgotten me.

The Conductor spoke next. He said that in this excerpt the audience would be launched into the midst of the work. He read what I had written for him. Then he apologized, "We have been remiss." I stood. "I want to acknowledge our government and corporate sponsors. Without them—"

I sat down.

The lights went out. The music started. My habitual awkwardness at others' rudeness—even annihilating rudeness—was felled by rage: clean, sharp, appropriate. My rage was then quelled by art.

IT WAS NIGHTTIME. Austin Hart had just landed on Ninstints Island.

"Pitched darkness.
Never born.
Death smothered against my head
And crushed upon my eyes.
I am extinguished
I never was
I am not now."

PAIGE AND HER BROTHER saw their father revived as Benjamin Stewart, tenor. They witnessed their dead mother, Mary-Anne Hart as Jane Napier, soprano, holding hands with their father, Paige at her side. The aged Tom Price, hunched in his place in the audience, raising his head with difficulty, saw the youthful Harold Johnson, baritone, picking up a 10" slate carving and, in the space of an aria, it disintegrating in his hands.

The poles were taken. The expedition returned home. The Lover challenged Austin. Then it was over. There was a standing ovation, and someone, ignorant of the form, called out "Author, author." With an audible 'click' my back aligned, my insecurity vaporized. When I stood, I felt like a colossus. Trevor Crane walked down the aisle and, taking Brett's arm, they went onto the stage joined by the Producer and the Conductor.

I left the hall, afraid to look at anyone, a spectacle. The crowd seemed to be snickering, smiling wanly as I passed.

IN A SHADOWY CORNER of the thoroughly seedy Cecil Hotel, I ordered round after round of scotch on the rocks. I hated scotch. I hated rocks. Then I ordered beer for the rowdy students sitting at the three tables beside me. To their chorus of inquiries, I said I was a stranger, new to city, unknown. A lanky no-bummed boy wanted to fix that, but I rebuffed his advances and left. I descended into the unkindness of the downtown eastside, ending up at The Drake, no jubilance, lacking capacitance, an extended blank.

WHEN THE PHONE RANG the next morning, I remembered my terrible neglect. Sophia hadn't arrived for the performance. But it was Brett on the line.

"Wasn't that wonderful? What an evening. Where did you go afterwards? We all went out to celebrate—" I didn't respond. "What's wrong?"

"It was pretty difficult for me."

"Difficult? Why?"

"Really, you have no idea?"

"Oh, about Trevor. Yeah, that was a mix-up. He shouldn't have come back on stage when it was over."

"I was humiliated."

"Humiliated? Didn't you see the review in the paper? It was all thumbs up. Here, listen: 'Although still a work-in-progress, the new, fledgling opera, *The Dual*, is stupendous. At last a libretto by—" He hesitated and then went on. "This could be staged anywhere in the world.' Now that's a rave review."

"Does it say 'a libretto by Trevor Crane'?"

"Sorry about that. I'll get in touch with the critic and have that corrected. But look, we're going to make it with this thing. We're going to hit the world's stage. Nothing can stop us."

"You forgot me." I felt like weather, cumulous, threatening. "You remembered your pathetic friend who barely knows which end of the bottle to open. You wiped me out." I had never spoken to anyone like this before.

"This is crazy."

I couldn't swallow the bile in my throat from a sleepless, drunken night. I started to cough.

"Alix?"

I hung up. I wished I could have been grander, but I had no grand to give.

I had to call my mother but instead called my friend. "Oh, Miles, this is so awful."

"I know. 'The world is as sharp as a knife.' Terrible to actually experience what the saying means. But even Violet Clayburn loved it. Humiliation and humility are also twin masks."

Miles's perspective was restorative enough to enable me to phone Paige.

"I'm so sorry, because of the botch-up with copying the libretto, I couldn't be there with you at the reception—"

"Congratulations, my dear, you have a hit. It was almost unbearable to see my father alive amidst those poles, seeing my mother again. Even my brother Jason was teary. And man, did you get fucked over. I tried to find you. I told Brett he was a jerk, but he didn't get it. I'm really sorry."

I thanked her.

"Keep talking to me, okay? Don't get dunked by this."

I thanked her again.

Holding on to some form of serenity, I called my mother to apologize. She'd been taken to the hospital.

38

A PENNY FOR YOUR THOUGHTS

Hart:
I walk amidst these amputated poles,
my purpose blind.

Sometimes I didn't keep track of the sun;
my eyes adjusted.
Now this sudden darkness has left me felled.

I've lost the trail of the god
who was looking for me.

Alix's Lines for the Libretto

Sophia had developed a small aneurysm in her brain, and it had ruptured. She was in and out of consciousness.

I sat beside her in the hospital, holding her hand. Sometimes I massaged her feet, gnarled like a geisha's from wearing tight-fitting high-heeled shoes most of her life. I watched her like the television. On the third day, I went home to shower and change. I ate standing up.

There were four messages from Brett on the answering machine. His tone of voice had changed. Usually, he sounded somewhat artificial, self-possessed and looking for an advantage. He was now simply ambitious. He'd been contacted by a number of people interested in the project who'd read about the opera in the press. We were going to hit the big times. When could we meet.

In the second message, he said he had decided that the Producer didn't have the competence to take the work forward. He was seeing a lawyer.

The third message was that he'd received legal advice on his contract with the opera company, and mine as well. Why wasn't I returning his calls?

This man who was just a nice guy with ducks in his backyard and goats at the door, he was very savvy.

I erased the fourth message without listening to it. I went back to the hospital.

Sophia was awake but didn't seem to see me. She had the eyes of a dead fish. I kissed her on the forehead; her skin was cold and clammy. I found her another blanket and covered her. She was drooling. I wiped her mouth. This didn't count; the promise I'd made to her didn't extend to this moment. She'd had a stroke, for God's sake; come on, she should be given a chance to recover. I was pleading with the gods who kept track of pledges between mother and daughter.

"Alicia?" She could talk, she knew my name, she wasn't really drooling.

"How are you, Mother?"

"I was with your father."

"Stay with me. I'm not ready to let you go."

She moved her tongue around the inside of her mouth. "My teeth are mossy. Can you brush them?"

I had never brushed anyone's teeth other than my own. I brought water and an empty cup from the bathroom, put some toothpaste on the brush, dipped it in the water and put the brush in her mouth. Her mouth was so small. "Open as wide as you can." She tipped her head back. "Rinse now. Just swill the water around and spit it out here. You're not supposed to drink anything."

She almost cooed with pleasure. "Oh, that's so nice."

It was impossible not to love someone when you have brushed their teeth.

The phone rang beside my mother's bed. Somehow Brett had found me.

"I expect an apology," he said.

"For what?" I kept my voice down.

"For yelling at me."

"Why are you getting legal advice about my contract?"

"I want an apology from you."

"Before you'll answer me?"

"Yes."

"To hell with you." It came out as a kind of growl.

"What you wrote, it was great. But I told you not to give the audience the libretto. I could hear them turning the pages."

I hung up.

With her eyes closed, her speech slightly slurred, Mother said, "I was waiting for you to come and get me so I could see your opera."

"I'm so sorry. It was inexcusable. I sent a cab for you, but you must have taken ill before it arrived."

"What does your composer want?"

"I yelled at him and he wants an apology."

"Men are afraid of a woman's anger, especially if she doesn't have children. Could you get me another blanket? What's happened to me?"

"You've had a slight stroke. The doctors are going to operate."

"On this old body? In that case, I'm even happier you brushed my teeth."

"You have to rest now. I'm here."

"Maybe your composer won't play the piano to get the moths out after all." She smiled as she drifted away.

About an hour later, she said, "A penny for your thoughts?" She used to ask that all the time when I was a child. I never wanted to answer. A penny didn't seem like money now, the smallest amount of money; instead it represented a real desire to know and be known by her through a currency that had no equal.

I told her I was thinking about the first meeting Brett and I had with the Producer—

"Mr. Brett, he has his eye on the ball," Sophia managed to say, her voice as sweet as a child's. "For some reason you don't realize that others consider you in their strategies. You're like some Canadians who don't think they have an accent." She had a crooked grin. "I'm trying to divert you."

"I know. Thanks."

"You're down in the dumps."

"The opera is coming undone."

"Why is that?"

"Greed."

"You're not greedy, are you?" Before I answered she fell asleep on me.

Even though she probably wouldn't hear, I said out loud, "I'm always hungry now, not for food but in my face, in my eyes. Hungry in my feet, my legs, my fingers. I look around as though someone might snatch a bone from me."

I went home but I didn't bathe. The phone rang. If it wasn't the hospital I didn't answer.

I called Miles. I said there's something wrong with me and could he help. He came.

He approached like a space-walker, slowly coming towards me where I was sitting at the desk in the library. He said I was absent, someplace else altogether. Like a conductor of smoke-clouds, he smudged the house, wanding a fist full of burning sweetgrass through all the rooms. He said I was spirit sick. What should I do? Your work isn't finished, but you need to find yourself.

Again, the sharp longing to disappear, as though remembering a destination marked on a map in a vast, undiscoverable continent where all the lights were out except that one location, a concentrated nothingness, absolute zero, a black hole.

"You must not yield to this," Miles said, knowing. His voice was elongated, flattened out, distorted.

It wasn't a real memory of being at the university in Halifax which was aroused in me, but a physical sensation—a pull, with a gravity so strong I didn't think I could resist it: being sucked back to that time until I was on the cusp of an event horizon, no path capable of leading me out, no possibility of escape. Home became this impacted zero.

"You have to go away by yourself." His deep, warped voice stuck on the skin of my face. "Use your skill, your language, describe this strangeness, its singularity, the sublime." He kissed me on my forehead. "Do what I say."

He was gone.

The sweetgrass on the plate in the solarium continued to burn. I was hungry.

Someone irredeemable. Someone fallen. Me, fallen. Mother found, Mother lost. Everything misplaced.

I was exhausted. I was lost.

One train had left the station. There would be others.

I SAT WITH MY MOTHER in the hospital. That was where I belonged. I didn't sleep. She got better. I didn't want her to die. It was too late for that.

I went into the garden with its nameless flowers. I went to the library, its fire unlit.

Austin Hart our bright star, our golden boy, we loved him so. Austin Hart, our boy so dead. Alexander, dead again.

I listened to the message from the Producer as it was being recorded on the answering machine. He said Brett had broken his contract with the opera company "so my lawyer advises me that my contract with you is terminated forthwith. Brett thinks he's going to carry on, using Trevor Crane as the librettist. I don't know where he's going to get the money. I have the money. I have a new librettist. We'll see who wins this one."

My creative partners had rushed to lawyers and emerged as bully-boys ready to scrap. I felt only a despondent lassitude.

And a feeling of corruption, as though I'd done a terrible thing that could never be amended or forgiven. I felt shame, not of something visible and known to others, but the original sin of some irredeemable, inner wrongness. I was back at the beginning.

This was how Austin felt after his last lecture.

Outside the window it was a beaming day, the garden riddled with light—and I tried to marshall adjectives appropriate for an enthusiasm which had entirely vanished. Oh, the emptiness was so much worse because I had known another state. I was once more excluded from the scheme of things, more fallen than an angel. My heart was singed, my arms scalded; I could smell burnt hair.

I thought of Richard. I didn't want to go back to that place seeing chimneys dripping with the toxic waste of a lifetime, reading my poems to Potato Eaters in a cafe at the end of the world.

Mother's operation was successful, and she was discharged to the rest-home.

BECAUSE OF SPENDING so much time at the hospital, and because of exhaustion, I caught a flu. I had a temperature, awake forever and then not awake at all. I lost track of everything. The numbers on the clock beside my couch-bed meant very little except a designation of either day or night. With the drapes drawn in the library, I was never sure which. I sweated; I washed the sheets twice a day, and then simply went through all the ones in the closets. I managed to phone Mother. I'd get there as soon as I was able.

Lying on the couch, I looked at the space between the desk and the wall. The intention to inhabit that emptiness, which had so compelled me when I was a teenager, was back and, like a failed resolve, was even stronger in its force and clarity.

The fever took me over.

THE SOUND OF A VOICE woke me. It was Austin's.

You made a mistake, don't you see now, trying to avoid your fate.

You once thought you didn't belong, but you do, it's only in another realm, not the one you've struggled so mightily to inhabit. Oh, how I've watched you, hoped for you, and you've done well. But it was not meant for you, don't you see? Nor you for it.

I stood. His alluring voice was outside my brain, in this black room, silent except for him.

As Sophia would say, your part in the opera "just didn't happen." It was a trick. Trevor Crane did it, not you. You were fooled again, as you always will be. Don't feel bad about it. Don't question it. You'd always end up in a fun-house, bashing your head against glass walls that don't seem to be there. I'm sorry to say this, but you had it right when you were young. You gave it a try, good for you. Now it's over. Come with me.

I recoiled, hitting against a chair which smashed the side of the desk.

This was just some mischievous, self-torment which had hijacked me because of the humiliation of the opera. Not Austin in the room, not his voice.

I lifted the chair from the floor and placed it back at the desk. Order was needed, that's all. I was feverish.

I was scared.

His presence would split off a part of me which would then assassinate the rest of me.

I called his name: Austin Hart. We were in an echo chamber—Austin Hart. I have put life back into you—propped you up both on stage and off. You are now healthy and I am worn out.

You can change that, as simple as flicking a switch from on to off, click, there, just like that. Click.

I can't even lift a finger to do it. I can't hoist a purpose.

Click, that's all.

The ringing of a phone isn't nice to hear for so long, going on and on. There was my mother, not knowing why she was calling; there was me, not knowing why I was answering. Now you—

You think she's a real mother to you now. You're wrong. The purpose of your work on the opera has been to get you back to this place of knowing how to reclaim the place of nothing. Brett and Trevor were doing their duty. You understand it clearly again, and you can correct this error, your accidental being, once and for all.

My mother's too sick to dial the phone. Have pity. She can't even find the phone.

That's right. The phone won't ring.

Don't say that.

It won't ring.

I was only eighteen, I'd barely touched the ground. Now, I've scuffed and marked it. Isn't that some kind of commitment? Shouldn't that be a protection against you?

I was crying.

Please go away, I whispered.

I raised my hand to fend off God knows what, and in doing so knocked the corkscrew off the table. I bent down on one knee to reach it and then, half way, I paused. This was almost the stance for prayer; I was in half a prayer.

I swung my leg around and put my other knee on the floor. All over the world people adopted this position in order to experience the divine. It felt so awkward. I was too large; everything in me protruded; my bones were showing through.

Maybe I could bow. As I let my head fall, the top of my spine ached.

You don't belong here anymore. Look at yourself: your hair is disheveled, your clothes don't fit. Nothing fits. You've landed on the wrong shore, that's all, just like me—a simple mistake. There's no one and nothing to blame. You've always understood that. There is no space now that isn't me—or my voice—or my breath. You're not lost, I'm with you. You no longer need to hope for the best or try so hard. In the place where we're going there is the continuous sound of singing, as in the old days.

You are silent. Admit: you have no prayer other than me.

May I please not assume I know you better than anyone in the world, when you are not in the world. May I please not take you as my guide, when you are lost.

Not enough of a prayer to resist me. You know it's almost time. Take down the pictures in the front hall, renew the house insurance, just a few things to do. Then click.

I found the bed again. I sank into an enormous, unalterable blank.

39

FORGIVE ME SUCH EXUBERANCE

Hart:

[Thinking of Shawcroft]

Sometimes I see his face;
Sometimes I hear his voice.
If I reach down inside a well

I am thirsty
there is water to drink.

Alix's Lines for the Libretto

When the ringing was about to fall into the well and be put out like a drenched torch, I caught it in my dream. I answered the phone.

"Hey, Alix, what's up? I've been trying to reach you for two days."

It was Paige.

There were six messages on the machine.

My fever had broken. I was alert, awake, wide awake. I was released from that other gravitational pull, on the ground, no more my sweating self.

At last, air. In my mother's garden the buds of the Queen of the Night were plump under the ground. I looked up. The first leaf on the tree in this almost spring day was a bird.

I could have shouted for joy.

I knew the days would stretch out again, stretch down to the equator—that the black Indian rubber ball of night which had encased me would get taut, bounce, would bound away. I'd find my north. The days would make me sane, put light on the subject and on me.

I went into the house. I had things to do. Like a breeze finding an open window and swirling through it: a decision. I would write a libretto in which Austin Hart did not die. That was my line of resistance to his tethering voice, the answer to my prayer.

Of course. A suicide wants saving, and I would save him as no one had been able to do. His insistent, seductive voice, which had been in my fevered head, would be dispelled by my giving him eternal life. The mistake was his, in killing himself. That mistake began my world, and that world needed to continue. I'd save him.

I searched for the word to describe my state. I needed forgiveness for being so exuberant.

I WROTE TO THE PRODUCER with a copy to Brett. It was brief. "Whatever you do with the opera doesn't concern or involve me. However, you'll have to create another libretto because the words I wrote belong to me."

I had a vast sense of certainty and confidence; my brain almost sizzled with the power of knowing what to do.

Following Miles's suggestion, I'd go away to complete the opera. Peg was coming home to stay with Mother. Finally Sophia would be back at Pine Street for the rest of her life.

That day a letter came in the mail from Deborah Taylor of the Coroner's Office, in response to my request to see Austin's file. The documentation had been kept for the length of time prescribed by the regulations and had been destroyed the previous year. Only the

Coroner's Report was on file, and a copy was enclosed.

REPORT OF INQUIRY AS TO CAUSE OF DEATH

DECEASED:	Austin Alexander Hart
WHERE FOUND:	Office at the university campus, moved to Vancouver General Hospital—doa
WHEN FOUND:	11:55 p.m. April 8, 1976
POST-MORTEM FINDINGS:	Aspiration of blood and gastric contents Laceration and contusions of brain Gunshot wound of head, apparently inflicted through mouth
OPINION OF CORONER:	Investigation and autopsy into the death of this fifty-one year old Professor of Anthropology, of Canadian racial origin. He had apparently shot himself in the head with a 22 calibre rifle at his office at the University of British Columbia. No suspicion of foul play. Death by suicide.
ITEMS SEIZED:	.22 calibre rifle, retained by R.C.M.P. University Detachment. Pages of a diary, apparently written by the deceased, with a note attached indicating they were to be given to his daughter, Paige Hart. Native ceremonial rattle to be returned to Clarence McNabb, Victoria Museum, as per deceased's request.

I HADN'T KNOWN his middle name was Alexander, the same as my father's. More importantly, there'd been a mix up. The diary had been sent to the museum, which must have been how Verspoor ended up with it. Paige was given the ceremonial rattle. What ceremonial rattle could it have been? Surely not the Shawcroft Raven Rattle which had gone missing, that Paige had this priceless object and that her father—

Austin would not have taken the rattle. Even Clarence McNabb had recanted the idea. There were lots of ceremonial rattles in the world.

Still, it was strange.

Subconsciously, I'd been hoping the coroner's file would have a last letter from Austin, seized by the police and mistakenly not delivered to the family. Paige had said the family was still grieving, as if his body had never been found. A final word from him would have given them some kind of comfort, or at least closing.

She wanted the opera to complete her Dad's work. My finishing the libretto would help to some extent.

Maybe he did leave letters, which had now been destroyed. It was entirely possible. Everyone thought he must have. I knew him so profoundly, even to the extent of his delusional visitation. No one else could recover his voice on behalf of those who had only his vast, incomprehensible silence. Paige, especially her—she would be quieted by receiving a letter from her father.

I called a pawn shop on Hastings Street and asked if they had an IBM Selectric typewriter which would have been in circulation in the 1970s. I bought it and returned to the house late in the afternoon. In order to incorporate the cadence of his way of speaking, I listened over and again to his last lecture; I reread his Perez paper; I started to type out the suicide notes he would have written.

The numbness in my hand returned as the objective correlative for my—whatever—I didn't even care. I could still type without feeling in my fingers.

> Dear Sis
> What I'm going to do will seem incomprehensible
> to you. Please forgive me. You have a good husband
> and a good family. Your creativity is there, and
> that is worth everything. Believe me, I don't want
> you to stop me and that's why I've kept my plans
> hidden from you. Roll away this sadness in the way
> I know you can. We had glorious summers together.
> Remember me in one of those summer afternoons.
> Love, your brother

Dear Jason
Insofar as I have known happiness, a great part of that has come from you. You are my boy. I reveled in your beauty and perfection. That beauty and perfection will remain. I am so proud of you and always have been. Forgive me for failing you now. But I have completed my life. In the future, when you think of what you have lost, find instead our good times together.
Pop.

Dear Paige
My brilliant daughter, you are the most sensitive one. I know this will fall the heaviest on you. It would have come sometime, no matter what. I blocked you out, because we are so similar. I was trying to protect you from me. That's why it was so awkward in the spring when you wanted to come and live with me. You have a daughter now. Give her the love I failed to show to you.

Don't follow me, I beg you. You have a duty which you can fulfill, both in writing and to your child, dual purposes under which I collapsed. Know that you are the daughter whose face I have seen and I have loved.
Dad.

Dear Claire
You, of all the people, will understand my sense of paradox at writing this note when I am, in a minute, going to commit suicide. If I can write it, to talk to you, why can't I go on living? But I needn't spell out this perplexing equation which, like all the others, cracked my head.

I am remembering, not our last abrupt talk at your house—but another time. Did this really happen or is it delirium? Taking a sailboat out into False Creek in the midst of the summer fireworks we saw from the deck of the boat. Standing beside you, watching you glow with excitement at each shattering explosion of color—in my vision you said 'look, you can

almost see the sound traveling up all the streets.' You are so vitally alive. Your life will balance my death. Some equilibrium will be maintained by you. Even if this was only a dream, it was a dream I really had.
Love Austin

I believed that anything in the created letters which didn't seem to them like his voice would be generously and silently excused, because of his state.

On my computer, in script that seemed so clear and contemporary compared to the typed notes I had created, I wrote a cover letter to each recipient.

I'm sorry I have been out of touch with you. As I think you know, my involvement with the opera has ended. But a surprising and exciting thing has happened. I had contacted the coroner's office some time ago, asking to see whatever material they had for Austin. I wanted to review it on the off chance there might be something important.

Because of the lapse of time, the file was just about to be destroyed. The file contained the missing letters. They'd been collected by the patrol officer but not forwarded to you. The coroner's office gave them to me on my undertaking I'd make sure you received them. The agonizing mystery has been solved. I am enclosing Austin's farewell letter to you.

I am leaving shortly on an extended trip. I wish you all the best, and hope that you are well.

40

LAYING DOWN TRACKS

Chorus:
What has happened to our love—
florescence—
our mutual song?
What has happened to the news
of a human race
coming across the waves
on feathers we set down
for them to lay aside,
to open?

Alix's Lines for the Libretto

I longed to drive into the country, knowing the elementary fact that one rotation after another of the tires in contact with the road was taking me forward, mile after mile—no gap, not one single inch missing in the continuity of my path.

I rented a car. Summoning good cheer, I said goodbye to Sophia and Peg, not saying where I was heading because I didn't really know.

After two days, driving east, I decided to call home. I hadn't expected Sophia to answer.

"Mother, hello, it's Alix calling."

"Who?"

"Your daughter."

"I'm sorry, my daughter has gone out to get groceries."

"This is Alicia, honey, your older daughter."

"Oh, Alix. Hello."

"I'm in Keremeos."

"And I'm sweet on you, too."

"No, Keremeos, I'm calling from Keremeos, a city. In B.C."

"Gosh, I couldn't hear you very well on this line. Where are you?"

"Keremeos. It's in the south of—"

"I know where it is. When are you coming home?"

"I'm not sure. Where's Mrs. Close, your nurse, is she out with Peg? You aren't alone, are you?"

"We had to let Mrs. Close go. She was getting into the cooking sherry. I didn't mind, but only after breakfast. She was more unstable on her pins than I am. Peg's going to find a nurse in AA who has climbed all the steps and isn't falling down." She laughed at her joke. "And guess what? We've bought a dog."

"A dog? Why did you do that?"

"Why not?"

"Well, how you are you—going to look after it?"

"The nurse will look after me and the dog. In that order once the dog is trained."

"This was your idea?"

"I kept thinking about Soldier, and Peg decided we should just forget him and get a new one. He's darling, a pup, chocolate lab. You know how I love chocolate. He ate most of the telephone book this morning. We call him—what do we call him? Soldier, I think. Well, that's what I call him, and the others will eventually come around. What the hell are you doing way out there? So we had to bring Peg back so I'd get a dog and finally come home. Then you vamoose. You're not sore at me are you?"

"No, not at all. You sound good. How are you feeling?"

"Tip-top shape for a half-blind woman whose marbles keep falling out of the jar. What's new with you? Except I think maybe the dog and I have a cold. Neither of us is feeling well."

"Do you think you need to have the doctor come?"

"No, it's just something I caught from the dog. This must be costing a pretty penny, and I'm using up all the money at a good pace what with the Mrs. Closes and the cooking sherry and the dog. Peg will be sorry she miffed your call—miffed that she missed your call. Oh, God, what a state." She sighed. Perhaps she, too, was mounting false cheer. "Peg put me out on the chaise in the garden with both the dog and the phone on my lap. When the phone rang, I reached for what turned out to be Soldier's ear. Poor thing. He doesn't bark yet like the rest of the dogs, but he'll learn. This is expensive small talk. Is this on your dime?"

"Sure. Mother a quick question before you go. About you and Russell—"

"That old cad? Oh, Alicia, you expect too much of me. You never used to, and now I'm not up to it. Sorry, the soufflé's fallen. Any other questions should be submitted in writing." She laughed again. "Okay dear?" She raised her voice indicating she was going to end the call. "See you soon. Don't take any wooden legs."

"Okay, I won't. How's yours."

"My what?"

"Your leg, your hip."

"Thanks, hon, I do try to stay with it. Goodbye."

"I love you."

"And I love you. Oh, listen, Peg's just walked in. Here, Peg, it's your sister. Talk to her."

I asked her why she bought Mother a dog—and not a little lap dog but one that would grow up and be like a small horse in the kitchen.

"Mom said you wanted a dog."

"Why would I want a dog?"

"Because you were spooked by the ones you could hear barking at night when you sat in the garden. Mother said you were afraid of the neighborhood dogs."

"I wasn't afraid of the dogs. I just didn't know why they barked all the time. Now Mother thinks she's caught a cold from her new pet."

Her breathing quickened and I could hear that she was walking into the kitchen, the heels of her shoes clicking on the tile floors. "Listen, Alix, Mother's not going to live long enough for this dog to grow up. For now it's doing her good. We'll figure out the rest after she's gone."

I told her I was sorry for badgering her.

I DROVE, MINDLESS, the geography my only thought. I was finally expelled from the Rocky Mountains into the flatlands. In a barren, soulless motel room surrounded by trucks, I brought out the draft libretto. There were rings of wine stains on the front page where I had set my glass, apparently having used it as a coaster.

To try to complete this work felt like going back into a battle from which I had defected. Miles had said to describe this strangeness, its singularity. I would write from there.

A scene well into the opera took shape, and I wrote, not knowing what came before or after. When I had finished, I opened a bottle of wine and sat staring at the script.

My cell phone rang, startling me into the present.

"I received your letter," Claire said. "And the one from Austin. Your sister said you were on the road. You'd better come and see me."

41

ETHICAL SACRIFICES

Hart

God cannot do without me.
He is contained
by me.

Bend the wind
Bend my box.
I am ready.

Alix's Lines for the Libretto

I checked out of the motel and asked for directions. I would be at Claire's in an hour.

The hot colors of the day were buried in darkness; the moon, come before its time, was routing them again.

When I turned into her yard, I could see her, backlit, standing at the front window. She didn't come to the door for a long time, even after I knocked.

She was much older than when I had seen her last, diminished, almost wasted. Some essential vitality I thought was her essence had withered. Silently, she ushered me into the sparsely furnished living room. She had the letters in her hand.

The rocking-chair creaked slightly as she raised and lowered her slippered heels on the carpeted floor.

"You're obviously upset. Have I—"

She interrupted me. "'You, of all the people, will understand my sense of paradox at writing a suicide note,'" she said dryly, quoting from the hoax letter. Then her voice became more agitated. "This business of watching the fireworks together from a boat in the harbor. 'Each shattering explosion of color.'" The scorn in her voice was unconcealed. She was on to me like a prosecutor. "Why did you do this? Fake up these messages from him—fooling around with life and death."

"How did you know?"

"You've moved onto dangerous ground. I'd like you to answer me."

I sat up straight and squared my shoulders, prepared to expose the raw center of myself, exuberance and all. "I believe you and the family needed to receive something from him to give you hope."

"Hope?" she said with derision. "How banal."

I was not prepared for this sour cynicism, yet I couldn't be undone by her querulous stance. I would lose the hard-won certainty that writing the letters was the right thing. I pressed on, as into sleet.

"His death has been misunderstood, and I'm trying to rectify that." She frowned. "'Were my objectives not laudatory my method would put me to shame.' The letters were an ethical sacrifice. I'm glad I sent them."

"You're quoting him, are you?"

"Yes. It's how he justified what he did in Haida Gwaii."

"I wouldn't join him in that excuse, if I were you. It was a nasty business."

My behaviour was incomprehensible to her but my convictions would ultimately dispel her scorn. I was sure of it. "I've come to know Austin better than I've known anyone. I've lived with his secrets, his fears, his desires. I've been inside his brain." I was ardent. "The reason why his death continues to have such a hold on you, and all those who loved him is that he didn't say goodbye; he was never really buried; he's still going to come back. The letters will halt the endless, unrequited grief." I added, "I want to rehabilitate him."

She didn't wait a beat. "Through trumped up messages containing feelings he never expressed?"

What I wrote on Austin's behalf had worsened his neglect of her. "I don't believe that. I want to convince you otherwise."

"Alix, don't you see, the feelings in the letters are yours, not his. You no longer have to be the proxy for a dead man."

This usually soft-spoken, articulate and passionate woman was heart-broken at her core. I had to help her.

"How did you know what I'd done?"

She shook her head to fend off my question. "Is this the extent of your plan to rehabilitate Austin?" The derision had emptied from her voice, now flat and disembodied. She resumed rocking, calming herself.

"I'm going to complete the libretto, and in it he won't die," I said simply.

She stopped the see-saw motion of her chair. Her whole face widened with disbelief. "He won't commit suicide?"

"I don't want him to." My statement sounded befuddled. "It seems unnecessary."

"That Austin die?"

"Not in the opera."

"But he did die." She turned my head to face the unassailable fact of the matter. "He did really, truly, actually, kill himself."

The rocking-chair pounded back as she stood, and it continued to mark time while she paced the room, searching for new resolve. Finally she placed herself directly in front of me.

"So it's all for you to decide? Whether Austin lives or dies; whether I grieve for him or not. You decide?" She was focussed and tough. "Don't you understand that's no answer?" Because it was apparent I didn't understand, she modulated her tone. "You said in your letter that your part in the opera was over. Something didn't go well. Please don't tell me that was also a ruse."

"No, it wasn't." I was stung by her distrust and it also resonated with something—she sounded the way I always used to, with Sophia, never trusting anything she said. "I'm sorry you think I'm just out to fool you. The composer and the Producer—we've gone our separate ways."

"You had a good review. A friend sent it to me, although Trevor Crane was named as the librettist. What happened?"

"Something wrong in the very beginning was finally revealed."

"You're a detective who's off the case, and you're still looking for clues? What are you after?"

I was almost flattened by the accumulation of bracing challenges, yet was able to summon, as from a separate self—words. "In the beginning I discovered, in two different films, two versions of what happened on Ninstints. One showed the heroism of salvaging the artifacts, the other showed the confused elder, the smashed pole, the totems all cut up. I found two separate Austins, in his journals, the dutiful man, and then in his diaries, his torment. It was proof of the duplicity I thought shaped the world. This time I had a ticket into the back rooms. I saw the make-up artists at work. I could find out the real story. It was intoxicating." I was afraid she'd find all of this penny thoughts, which had no value.

"Alix, all of what you've said just now—that was at the beginning." Her right hand marked in the air, point by point, what she was saying. "This is now. You've found those you really care for. Why do you keep forgetting that? People like me."

Her face showed the frayed-ends of sorrow. No, I was mistaken, it wasn't sorrow. I had to think—actually, it was—I didn't know what it was, except, that she knew these were high stakes, and for both of us.

Then, as if the question had occurred to her afresh, she asked me why I thought Austin had killed himself.

There it was again. I wanted to find out from her what she was seeking from me. What I knew about truth could thread through the eye of a needle.

I started in. "He killed himself because he was afraid of death, or there was a wasp in the room, or because he took too many pills—" It sounded like a list of the laundry on a line. I closed my eyes, trying to summon all I knew. "Because he didn't answer the phone. Because—"

She crouched on the floor close to me, leaning against the couch. "You don't have it."

"No? What then?"

She spoke quietly. "I told you he brought my manuscript back. I told you we were out of touch. Not so." She held up her hand against any interruption. "Austin had been calling me. I was away. He left a message saying he needed to see me. I phoned him back early in the morning of what was to be his last day. He was excited—just the way you've been tonight. He had all these revelations about the poles, a new understanding of their meaning. He was going to begin again. I remember so clearly he said, 'There are fish in the rivers. To catch one, I hold out my arms. To explain what I mean, I release my voice—' His confidence was unbounded. Of course I was glad. The way he'd been treated after his public lecture was really tough on him. He seemed to have recovered. But I was also bothered. If he was going to start over it had to be grounded. He said he realized 'with great force' that the taking of the poles was a mistake, and he asked me to forgive him." Her voice sounded young, almost plaintive. She shook her head. "There was no God in the endless expanse of the universe who could say to him 'I forgive you.' Certainly I couldn't. He had to forgive himself. I knew he would never make it if he still held on to the Raven Rattle. He'd found it on Ninstints, put it in the museum's catalogue, of course, that was proper, but he borrowed it and had never put it back."

I was dumbfounded.

"That's when it happened," she said.

"What happened?"

"I told him, 'I want the best for you. But until you give up the Raven Rattle and return it to where it belongs, your newfound joy is a sham. I told him being sorry wasn't enough—You'll be a fraud." After quite a long silence, he said, 'It would have been better had I died in a burning house, rather than salvage the poles.' He hung up on me."

The weight of her disclosure dropped inside me like a stone. "You said that?"

"He wouldn't answer the phone again. I went to his house; he wasn't there." A mass of tears streamed down her face. "So when I received the letter I knew it wasn't from him. The last time we talked wasn't at my house, that's only what I told you. Also he would not have written such things to me after our conversation." Her voice became calm and factual. "I've shirked my responsibility for his death, but not any longer. Really, I have you to thank." She was genuinely grateful.

"You didn't realize what you'd said—repeating his father's cruelty. You didn't know."

"Yes, I did. Lovers know each other's stories. I wanted to shake him up." Like a marionette dropped by its puppeteer, her body seemed to cave.

I went behind her and put my hands on her shoulders, moving her as on a swing, rocking her. "You were going to help him." I was trying to map her profound bewilderment.

She looked up at me. "Don't you see what's happening? No, you don't. You're confused. You don't understand why I'm so upset with you. Come and sit here." She pointed beside her. "Listen to me. Please listen."

I said okay, not having a clue what she expected of me and afraid I couldn't fulfill the willingness I felt.

"He wanted to keep the poles alive when they were meant to die, and then he killed himself, meant to live. The letters you wrote show you're in the same ruinous mix-up as Austin."

"No, I don't get it."

"You can't relieve our grief through giving us letters he didn't write. You can't change his death by reincarnating him to another fate in the opera—just as he couldn't give the poles eternal life, or be forgiven for what he did." She spoke with rigorous clarity. "As for my part, I can't take back what I said. But I am certainly not going to repeat the mistake I made with him." With a muscled resolve she said, "I am claiming you right now. He blew his brains out, failing to be a god. And you know what? When you peel back his heroic desire to save the poles, it was a desperate, false bid for eternity—and underneath that, a weeping nostalgia." She had unblinkered courage and finality. She was describing Austin's suicide, and—I realized—my own state. "I am not going to allow you to suffer the same delusion. I am not—" she spoke slowly and deliberately, "I will not let you follow him." She put her fists on the couch and raised herself with difficulty. "Austin has become your totem. Now—" as if it were her last thunderous breath, "—now, you must let him go."

From a distance, coming closer, something arrived that had been traveling for a long time and, but for Claire, would have passed me by. Two distant points were triangulated to locate, not Austin's suicide, but me in this room with her.

"Yes, I think I get it. I finally understand."

"The living are more important than the dead."

She had just saved my life.

She went to her chair, a teeter-totter, shedding all regret. I moved around in front of her. It was I who knelt. "You didn't kill him, and I can't revive him. We'll both let him go."

"It's done." The rocking became her boat, caught on the rocks in a low tide, then raised afloat.

I could feel her arms trembling as she embraced me. We'd made it through the needle's eye. I felt glad to be alive, the sudden, doltish miracle of the next breath of it.

AS I SWITCHED ON THE LIGHT in the guest-room, I heard the "click" from my afternoon with Austin. The click of a switch; the click of a trigger. The clicking of my sister's shoes on the tiled floor of the kitchen. Click click.

I returned downstairs and in the darkened house I called my mother. The phone rang without answering. Why didn't someone answer? Then I lay on the couch, the receiver next to me, and dialed the number again. I counted the rings. Twelve, thirteen, fourteen. Searching through the vacated rooms, down the empty hallways, into closets, carrying a light whose beam ran up and down the walls, over the ceiling, into every corner. "Mother, I know you're there. What's happened?" No answer.

I left a note for Claire, shoved my things into my bag, got in the car and turned back. It was past midnight.

42

BRING ME ONE OF EVERYTHING

I drove into the gun-metal dawn, into the space between things.

I drove the car like an ambulance; I talked to my mother like a lover. It was an incantation: I see you're in trouble and I love you, and I'm going to come and get you. I know you're there; I don't care if you don't answer the door, I'm going to break it down and get you and keep you with me. The joker's in the tulips. The living are more important than the dead. Please wait.

At a truck stop with a phone booth outside, the door leaning off its hinges, I called her again. Still no answer.

I went in for breakfast.

The waitress was haggard; if she'd slept at all, it was in her clothes. As she came towards me, she seemed to be far away and then, without progressive movement, was beside me. Not only time, but distance, was now on the fiddle.

She handed me a large plasticized menu with photographs of mounds of iridescent food. "Just you?"

I nodded. As she started to remove the meagre place setting on the opposite side of the table—one fork, one knife, one spoon—I held up my hand.

"You expectin' somebody?"

"No, but leave it. Thanks."

She looked at me as though I had a tooth missing. "Okey-dokey. Whatever." She clanged the cutlery back onto the Arborite surface.

Some childlike sorcery from decades earlier, played out in a restaurant in Halifax, was repeating itself but in such a changed way. The unused table-setting across from me would cast a spell on time itself, to make it stop until I could get back home.

"Whad'll it be?"

I returned the menu to her. "Just some toast and—would you by any chance have espresso?"

She frowned. "You kidding? Like how about regular coffee, like diner coffee, right?"

"Fine, thanks."

The father in the booth behind me talked to his daughter as if he'd just met her that morning. "How do you like your eggs, Carolyn? You don't want eggs? What do you like for breakfast then?"

I found it difficult to listen to this stilted parenting of a muted child, as if I were overhearing the submerged voices of my own past. I was afraid they were the ashen Potato Eaters coming to thrash the buoyancy of my resolve to get back home, and so it was with great reluctance, I made myself turn to look at them.

They were in full color, pink-skinned, alive. The father had red hair, as did Carolyn, who was maybe five years old—they both had bright red hair. Contrary to fashion rules, she was wearing a purple sweater.

It was okay. It was okay. It was going to be all right.

As I approached the cranky waitress, she moved behind the protective cash register. I apologized and asked if she could make my breakfast to take-away.

"No skin off my teeth." She shrugged.

I set the brittle paper bag down inside the phone-booth with the broken door. This time Peg answered.

"Oh, thank heavens. I've been calling and calling."

"You have to come home now." Her voice was a crack in a cup.

"What's happened?"

"She wasn't feeling well, so I took her to the hospital. Yesterday she had a headache, today she has liver cancer. Come home now."

"I'm already on my way. I'll be there tonight. Is she—"

"She's sitting out in the garden. The doctor says she's going to go fast, but she's coherent, even cheerful. I don't think she understands—"

"Tell her I'm coming. Ask her to hold on."

Twenty minutes away from the restaurant, wanting coffee, I realized I'd left the breakfast bag in the phone booth.

IT WAS ALMOST ELEVEN o'clock at night when I pulled into the driveway at Pine Street. There were three large bouquets of flowers on the table in the front hall, under the place where the family portraits had once been. Already, flowers.

I went upstairs to Mother's room. In the ash light of the vigil candle, two figures. Peg, in her pajamas, was sleeping beside our sleeping mother. Who opened her eyes.

I had shaped myself in relation to her even in opposition. She'd set my course.

"Hi," she said softly. She could see me.

"Hi."

"I've missed you."

I wouldn't cry.

"Me too. I phoned. I let it ring for a long time."

"That's nice dear. I wonder where I was."

I picked up her limp, unresisting hand. Her skin slipped on her bones like hardened Jello.

"You came back. I'm so grateful."

I wouldn't cry.

Peg awoke. I took her place in the bed without removing my clothes. I held my mother's hand, her left hand, large, competent—tethered.

"I guess we've got a deal," Mother said sleepily. She sounded drunk.

"A deal? What's the deal?"

"You know." Did I? Some incalculable reciprocity was working itself out in our lives, but I wasn't certain of its dominion. "It's okay, honey. I'll remind you tomorrow. You're tired, get some sleep."

She was comforting me. How extraordinary. Her eyes closed.

Just to watch her breathe a little longer.

SHE COULDN'T REMEMBER how to suck. I put the straw in her mouth, and it just rested there on her lips. "Suck, Mother." She smiled at the word but didn't know how to do it.

I brushed her teeth.

"Now gob."

She smiled at the word gob. "I will if you bring me Cadbury's chocolate," she said through spittle.

TWICE THAT MORNING she pushed pills out of her mouth with her tongue, pills I thought she'd long since swallowed. She didn't just let them fall, she spat them out, and was pleased.

Alarmingly, she would bank her breath for a long time until she suddenly exhaled. Followed by no breath. She was the billows for a fire going out.

The nurse came and gave her a sponge bath. Then Mother—Sophia had now become Mother or Mom and never Sophia—the original childlike appellation actually signaled a contorted evolution of our relationship rather than a regression—Mother asked if Peg and I could wash her from now on because the nurse was too rough. Peg didn't want to; she seemed afraid of this bloated, dying body. The long-standing, unspoken pact between my sister and me—that we would stay armed against our mother's annihilating narcissism—had been broken. I had broken it. It was with the unhappy result that Peg and I were isolated from one another, like standing in a clear-cut.

"This is pretty hard going," I said, mustering the obvious. "I think it's especially hard on you because you haven't seen her decline, but only the shock of her present state."

"Are you blaming me for not coming home earlier? Both of you told me not to."

"Gosh, no, I'm not blaming you at all." I felt like a goalie trying to prevent my own team from scoring a point on me.

"Then why'd you tell her I left home because I wanted to get away from her?"

Had I said that? "Peg, that was so long ago now, or it seems. I said it in a pique of anger. Everything's changed."

"I'm left out of it, I guess."

"Well, you're here now. You don't have to be left out." She was my former self, chewing on an old bone.

"Alix, it's too late for us to get a new mother. She's done too much harm. Me, I'm saying goodbye to that mother, the bitch, the one we really had in our lives. I suggest you do too, and not live this—ridiculous fantasy, as if she's different now. She's not."

It was almost blasphemous to hold such a grudge. Her hurt had been paid out on a chain still anchored deep inside her. I stepped towards her to embrace, or at least touch her. She moved back. "I don't think it's too late, Peg."

She closed the door, but I went after her. She wouldn't listen.

THE DOCTOR CAME with his stethoscope and his false cheer.

"She wants chocolate. Is that okay?"

"Give her what she asks for. It doesn't matter now."

"Her breathing is so strange—"

"Cheyne Stoking respiration. Happens near the end."

The doctor left. Peg came back. Peg said she didn't want to stay. She wanted to sail away on the water element which had served as the habitat of her detachment and her isolation for all these years, her part in the family's system. The unfathomable deep was less dangerous to her than our mother's dying. Our mother: this elegant, private, glamorous woman, always so well dressed and refined, was now encased in a flaccid, demanding sack of organs, unmentioned before in the entire history of the world. What earthly conspiracy had kept the eventual decrepitude of the body unknown to her children? The pleats of skin between her legs, once her labia, were wrinkled flabs enfolding erotic secrets long gone—there were no names for these body parts that had become her sum and to which I attended, sometimes flinchingly. This woman, once treacherous to me, devious and lying, was now as guileless as a child, and as trusting. Her jellied thighs.

Somehow holy.

She had stopped caring about the beauty of her body: what she had once most coddled, adorned, preened—she'd stopped considering it. She didn't mind that her daughter wiped her bottom.

Once, after I'd managed to get her off the commode, she slung her arms around my neck, raised herself and seemed to hang as though on a chain. Her chest rested against my own, her heart pounding with the exertion, a twin pulse.

"Mom, what is it?"

"I saw myself in the mirror. I'm as bald as a coot down there."

"When you first came back to Pine Street and had a bath—"

"I'm pretty sure I had some pubic hair then, didn't I? Even a few. Where've they all gone?" She released one arm and ran her fisted hand over her head, like a worry. "Still have some up top."

"Lots."

THEY CAME TO THE DOOR without calling or they called and then didn't come. So many friends I'd never met who thoroughly loved her. She let them see her, wasted.

The purblind Shirley Lang arrived with the palsied Wilmet Peters. Oh how they looked. Decked out with matching everything, belts, scarves, earrings. They carried their house shoes in dark blue Segrams bags.

Shirley stood, waiting for me to say hello because she needed to locate me in her blurred horizon. The sighted Wilmet pointed her friend's embrace in my direction.

Oh, Wilmet Peters with her large costume jewelry, or perhaps it was real, a ruby in the center of a gold rococo setting on a necklace; her ochre-colored earrings were so big they must have blocked her hearing. A red and yellow scarf to go with it all. Her face was long and thin, an El Greco figure, the bones of her jaw protruding. She nearly fell over when I took her coat, and grabbed for her cane. She leaned on the curved antler grip, trembling a little.

They both had a fresh feeling of grief.

I escorted them into the library and went upstairs. "Put your arms around me, mother. Now, on three. One, two" and three was long and slow as I lifted the heavy, emptied out jaundiced body. "Gentle," she said. I pulled her up but she could hardly move the few steps required to get her into the wheelchair.

"I think we should have another plan," she said.

"I'll bring them to you?"

"That's it." She was pending in the air. "Will you put me back in bed?" I cocked my head, wanting her to change her mind because of the bruising effort to move her. "You look like Soldier when he's trying to understand me. You look like the dog."

"Be nice, Mother."

"I am." And then, "Sorry about the dog. Sorry about the euthanasia."

"Oh." The truth will out.

We managed to maneuver her into the bed and under the covers. By the time Wilmet and Shirley made it up the staircase, Mother was asleep. They sat in the two pink chairs I'd moved near the bed, trying to talk to one another, stealing glances at mother's placid face, her mouth open and drying up with each breath.

She didn't know they'd come into the room. She didn't know they'd gone.

WHEN HER FRIEND, Eunice Daily, was to arrive on the bus to see her for the last time, Mother asked me to give her eyebrows. I marked them on the slightly mounded place where they used to be. I also put lipstick on her because Eunice had been her friend at school and Mother wanted to look her best. Somehow during the day the eyebrows rubbed off. In the evening the lipstick was crusted like blood.

Her fingernails kept growing and in the night she scratched her forehead.

Peg slept in the spare room. I slept with Mother. Her death was lasting forever.

One night she squeezed my hand. I didn't know whether or not I'd been asleep. "What's wrong with me?"

"You have liver cancer, Mom."

"Oh. Will I get better?"

"No."

"Oh. Are they pretty sure?"

"Yes."

"Oh."

"I'm sorry."

"That's okay, dear. You never call me Mom. I must be close to the end."

I wanted to say: Mom, Mother, Sophia let's go out together, unbounded. We'll look at things close up that will never again look the same when far away.

But the earth had no sky. I didn't know where it had gone. There was no outside.

I wrote thank-you cards for all the flowers people sent. They started with oh, and oh.

This one
so independent
so strong
now didn't want to be alone.

"Don't leave me, okay? Where's Peg? Is she mad at me?"

In fact, Peg was going back to Cambodia. Jeremy had called. Unable to sail without her, and having stayed too long in the country, their boat was in danger of being impounded by the authorities. She said she'd return to Pine Street as soon as she could. Of course. Of course Peg didn't, any longer, want to watch her die.

HER HEMORRHOIDS BLED on the swaddling diaper pad I put on her.

I kept expecting her to smell. Her breath wasn't sour; her skin smelled like nothing. Even her shit didn't smell. Her breath, like nothing. Her gnarled feet had become ginger-root, her hands, tethered claws. It was the living who smelled. I smelled. When I showered, the fragrance of soap overlaid the stench of my fear.

But her eyes were terrifying. The pupils were black holes through gummy yellow liquid. She blinked rapidly, trying to capture a glimpse of everything before her eyes rolled back and were closed for an eternity.

I put sunglasses on her because I didn't want to look at them.

Or see a stone mask open and shut its eyes.

THE DAY BEFORE PEG was to leave the neighborhood, Rachel Epstein, arrived with her five-year-old grandson and a macaroni casserole the size of the flat-bed on a small truck. It was late afternoon. I adjusted mother's sunglasses.

I could hear Mrs. Epstein whisper to Peg, "I don't think your sister should do that."

"Do what?"

"Put sunglasses on her."

"Why is that?"

"People will think she's blind."

"People? What people?"

Oh, if only she were just blind, I'd jump for joy and more; joy would jump for her. Let her live forever, blind.

Mrs. Epstein's grandson must have gone into the fridge on his own because he went up beside Mother with a small lettuce leaf in his hand. He put it to her lips. "Here," he whispered. "You're thirsty."

"Wonderful," Mother said as the child fed her a lettuce leaf.

SHE HAD NEVER TAUGHT us anything about the insides of our bodies. All its needs were to be overcome, never admitting too hot too cold too tired too lonely. Now the body prevailed, dominated, exerted its bullying demands. Some days she'd had enough. "I want to go. I'm a mess." Later the determination, the folly, returned. "I want to get better." In the middle of the night, again, the question: what's wrong with me, Alicia? Are they pretty sure?

"Never mind," she said, seeming to revive. "I don't want to be good, I want to be gorgeous."

She couldn't make it go away. Death was coming at us like a boulder down a hill. Only her heart was strong. Everything else had collapsed, lock stock and barrel.

SHE TALKED OF HER mink coat—not "talked of" but said the words "mink coat."

"Do you want me to get your mink coat for you?" I asked.

"Sure."

After looking through all the cupboards, Peg and I finally went down to the cedar room where Mother kept her off-season clothes. I was going to wear the coat into the bedroom but worried she'd think I was claiming it. Then I thought "bosh," the way she would say bosh, and so I put it on, vamping before her, opening and closing the front of the coat, letting it slip off one shoulder like a tease, priming her until she laughed. Then laying it over her like a blanket so she was covered in mink.

I applied makeup to an almost corpse.

Peg was efficient. She arranged for the medics to bring an hydraulic bed which they set up in the library. Because of our denial, this most practical arrangement had been deferred.

PEG STOOD IN THE DOORWAY, going. "I'm sorry."

Mother had heard. "We'll have no weeping and wailing and gnashing of tears." Her voice was clear. "My dears, it has been a privilege to know both of you."

I helped Peg put her bags into the cab.

There was nothing more to say.

I SAT WITH HER ALONE, watching her trying to breathe.

Her arms were crossed against her chest. She raised them up, fledgling, and then they plummeted like millstones, her body pushed from a nest. Again, they rose as though involuntarily, almost fluttering, then plunged, no thermal uplift to wing her away. What a terrible defeat, those dead hands dropping. They rested until strength was summoned for some internal flight only she could navigate. I tried to let her go. Go, I'm letting you go now. Who does not consent? I looked around the empty library. She crashed against the cage of her life.

She was speaking. I made out the words: "It's too late, my dear."

"Too late for what?" I asked.

"It's the punch-line of a joke. But I can't remember the first part." Then silence.

I STARTED WEARING her clothes. It was a mere convenience. I spent so much time in her bedroom, looking after her there, that I would go into her drawer if I were cold and put on a sweater; then a blouse underneath. We were almost the same size. It was easier than returning to my own room. Besides, the laundry was piling up. Eventually, I was wearing her jeans, her long skirts, her shirts. As the days passed, and I never went outside, my stomach felt doughy and bloated with all the starchy food brought by the friends. I was entwined in her decline: sleeping together, losing day to night, waking when she did a dozen times in an hour, wiping her, wiping myself. I lost my sexuality to a slow and repugnant alteration. I didn't want to have a body. The body I had was my mother's.

As a strategy, I began to dress up for Sophia.

I walked the way she had before her fall: a kind of model's catwalk, not swinging my arms, leaning back a little, strutting. I spoke to her the way she used to speak to me, almost languorous, not afraid of pauses. If she were going to get better, it would be my doing. I was out of my mind again.

As though I were being reabsorbed by unbirthing, I gave myself to her. Miraculously, I stopped my anticipatory grieving. I would block the path of this boulder. I would cook a real meal, invite people over—return a few favors—cook food that my mother couldn't eat but I could if I tried. I had the butcher on Granville Street deliver a 12 pound turkey.

"I'm going to cook a turkey," I announced to her, standing at the door to the library. She didn't hear me. "Mother?"

"Wonderful, darling," she said as if she knew what it meant, a 12 pound turkey. Able to say "wonderful" beneath her breath at God knows what to God knows who. I wanted to ask how long I should cook it, how much butter to use in the stuffing, what spices I should add—I wanted her to comprehend everything again, and tell me. The details of a vivid life were important to get right, so wrong was this state she was in. Why not eternal life?

I wished I could trade in her liver for one from some black-hearted mother, as she once had been, who spread less light than she did now.

When the turkey was delivered, and I took a knife to the plastic cover fitted as tight as a thief's mask, the slimy feel of the flesh was nauseating. The color, a pallid grey, looked like my mother's neck. I went into the bathroom and vomited.

After I had washed my face, I returned to her bedroom. From the clothes-closet I pulled out a turquoise sequined jacket with a fringed cowgirl skirt Mother had worn once when she and Russell went to the Calgary Stampede. I put it on, found the matching hat, applied make-up in her bathroom and went downstairs to the library.

Her bed was pushed over to the couch where I slept beside her. I took the dirty dishes to the kitchen and returned with chocolate Ensure, the only thing she could eat.

With the electronic switch, I raised the top part of the bed. Although late afternoon, Mother still had on her sunglasses.

"Hello, dear," she said.

"You're feeling better. Time for some food, my love."

"How 'bout a drink before dinner?"

"The doctor says you can have whatever you want."

Her eyes focussed on me. "You look swell. You going out with a beau? To the rodeo?" Although she spoke haltingly and with a kind of dry, throaty croak, she was revived. "Pretty good figure don't you figure?" It was a relief to have her either joking or mis-choosing her words, no matter which.

"Whose figure, yours or mine?" I asked.

"Ours."

"Yes, m'am." I circled my arm in the air as though to lasso her.

I cooked the turkey and fed most of it to the dog.

EVERY DAY I TOOK from the closet a different one of her outfits, trying to remember how she put them together and doing the same. I even wore the priceless brocaded Japanese kimono, although the long sleeves impeded my service to her.

NEAR LUNCHTIME ONE DAY, Rachel Epstein came to the door holding a pan of food in front of her. "I've brought knishes and—"

The way she looked at me I knew there was something wrong. Her eyes snaked down my clothes to the shoes. I was wearing mother's purple satin dress with the chiffon top and the matching *peau-de-soie* high heels. "Alicia, isn't that your mother's cocktail dress?" She angled her head, "Aren't those your mother's old shoes?"

I looked to the left of her face and then to the right. I didn't want to look at my feet. "They're not so old are they?"

"Yes."

"I was just trying on everything, to show herself to herself, so she'd see she was alive." My chest filled to breaking.

"Alicia, are you okay?"

"She always loved this outfit." All I had left in the world was my granite purpose, my careful, uncomplicated plan to bring her back to life, to prevent her death, to create a miracle. I had been caught in the act. Although I made no sound, I couldn't stop the tears. "There's only her heartbeat now. Everything else has quit."

"Honey, you look so strange."

She handed me the aluminum container with the foil over the top, and while my face was distorted with crying, she turned and walked back down the stairs.

I had scared her.

I went to the long mirror in the dining room. I was dressed in purple: for a coronation, for a graduation, for a first date, for a rape. My entire self was held there at eighteen when I bought a similar dress for a last dinner in a fancy restaurant in Halifax: unsmiling, resolute, lonely. My image streamed down the mirror like a sheet of water and was fixed again, replaced by my mother coming back from a party, asking me if I'd washed my hair: haughty, self-assured, lonely. Flowing down the glass into me, now: a bleary-eyed madwoman, ragged, full of love for someone I couldn't spare.

I reached around my neck and unclasped the hooks at the back. I pulled the top over my head and then unzipped the skirt, letting it fall. I took off the nylons and underwear.

I stood. I'd never before looked at my body full on, naked. I looked newborn.

I dressed in my own clothes which I found tossed on the bed in my room, a pair of jeans, a sweatshirt. I came back to the mirror. I was myself; I was my mother's daughter.

"TAKE A PICTURE of the sunrise, will you?" Her voice in the dark as I lay beside her. "Then you can show it to me." She wanted to live.

"Why don't I take you to the solarium?"

"Better still." She slurred her words, but I could understand them.

The doors were wide enough for me to push her in the metal bed through the living room, the dining room, the kitchen and out into the glassed solarium, the route I had taken when I first returned to Pine Street after her fall.

The bed-frame hit the liquor trolley and nearly toppled all the bottles.

"I wouldn't want to try that again," she said. She was referencing the time the rubber handles came off the wheelchair; she was making me laugh.

I angled her to face her garden, still in darkness, and then clicked on the switch that illuminated the yard. From off to on. Click. Just like that.

I leaned over to try to hear her words. "We didn't know until now," she said softly.

"What?"

"How much—"

"Yes."

"—of a disappointment—"

"Disappointment—"

"Austin Hart was."

I hadn't expected to hear his name. "Because?"

"He squandered—"

"Yes."

"—what I now want most."

"Which is?"

"Another day."

After the billowed holding and release of her breath, she said, "Call out."

"Now? Call out what?"

Barely audible: "Call out to the universe until it answers. No less an effort is required from you. That's our deal."

"I get it."

The darkness was lifting; the dawn, a promise. Six a.m. The clock on the wall measured not time but depth: the thickness of the membrane between life and death, the thin raw space.

The garden seemed to rouse itself with our looking at it, made an effort to recover from its autumnal decline.

"You won't follow him now."

"Who?"

"Your father," she said.

"Alexander?"

"No, Austin Hart."

I smiled at her metaphoric insight. "He has been like that to me, in a way."

"I thought you'd figured it out."

With a befuddled shock, I repeated the idea: that Austin Hart was my real father.

"It's true." A fine sliver of a smile animated her mouth. "Put on some music, will you? But not Vera Lynn."

"No?"

"Well, okay. Let's go out in sentimental style."

"We've always tried to avoid it."

"Successfully, I think. Time to be done with success."

"Where's the CD?"

"You can find it. You're writing your father's opera."

Triumph.

I put the disc on the sound system which connected the whole house and out to the garden. I pressed repeat.

As I sat down beside her, my hand on her shoulder, the strings began and then the sweet, concise voice of Vera Lynn.

"Let's say goodbye with a smile dear, just for a while dear, we must part. Don't let this parting upset you, I'll not forget you, sweetheart."

Mother's eyes were slowly closing. Her head rocked slightly with a bowl's center of gravity. Something in me started to shut down. It was everything I could do to keep looking at her, not to avert my eyes. This was what had happened to me in Ottawa, when

I saw the unsighted mask, and when I put it on.

"We'll meet again don't know where don't know when but I know we'll meet again some sunny day. Keep smiling through just like you always do, 'til the blue skies chase those dark clouds far away."

"It's a primer on farewell." Sophia could still talk. She was using her last breath to tell me things. "He loved this song."

"Who?"

"Austin."

She started to sing, broken, along with the words. "'And I will just say hello to the folks that you know, tell them you won't be long. They'll be happy to know that as I saw you go you were singing this song.'" It was almost more than I could bear.

She tried to raise her head, but the effort was too vast. "I squandered him, just like he squandered himself. Still, I got one of everything."

"We'll meet again, don't know where, don't know when. But I know we'll meet again some sunny day."

Strangely, and with deep satisfaction, the wide circle of my lifetime's search swung resolutely closed. It was all right if I didn't know my real father, whether it was Alexander, Austin Hart, or anyone else. I was not fatherless.

Holding in air; releasing it; holding; releasing. The gurgling sound of water contained within stone, her breath. She turned her head toward me but hadn't the strength to open her eyes. Her sight had gone.

I didn't know what it was, but although we were separate, we were part of something whole.

I looked out at her garden.

"Darling, can you hear me?" she asked.

"Yes, yes."

"I can't see anything, not any more. I think I'm blind."

"I know. I'll be your eyes."

"Oh, that's all right then."

At last, the exceptional, a miracle, in an unexceptional exchange: she and I were the twin masks.

Clearly, painting each word, I named the flowers which were gradually being illuminated by the dawn. "Mille-fleurs, lily-of-the-valley, The Queen of the Night, the Angel's Trumpets." Then more slowly, "Wisteria, magnolia. Under the earth, everywhere, tulips, ready to bud and break, feather and flame." I faced her.

"I sure got to love you." She spoke with difficulty, drowning.

"Oh, mother." My tears were heaving inside me. I put my head on her breast. A child on top of her heart.

"Wonderful—with nothing to forgive."

Oh gentle beating, resounding in my ears. Her life.

This was the first sound I had ever heard.

Oh terrible beating, coming to an end. A countdown.

Seeing for her, the last; seeing for myself, the first.

The song looped around again. And again. 'Just for a while dear, we must part. Don't let this parting upset you, I'll not forget you, sweetheart.'

She wasn't a bird, caged. Her lungs were filling up with water. Water in the locks so that her boat could go through.

"I've gotta get out of here." Miraculously, she spoke again. She twisted her head and shook it. She stopped thrashing, her breath, shallow.

"Let me go," she said.

I had an observing self, a child without breasts. I didn't know anything except the pulse of her heart beneath my hand. Her mouth, her lips not breathing. Then again, air. One, two, three. Nothing. Beat, beat. Nothing. Any moment, within moments, within the scope of this song, within the time of my attention, her life was going to, was bound to end....Waiting for it beat by beat by beat waiting on her, for her, counting fifteen, waiting, nothing.

Beatitude. Her body was: letting her go, beat by beat by beat by beat.

Clearly, quietly, not struggling, she said the words, calmly, not begging, stating: "Let me in."

And
then
waiting
not another.
Waiting.
Not another word
not another beat.
Waiting
Done
No
more

43

THE POLE IS RAISED

To feel the rise of day not dark. The pull upwards, gravity-light. We are unmired. The blessed ground gives up the weight of us, the fallen-down of us, released with each beat of the drums. The ropes hoist and heave and lift us all, all at once, inch by blessed inch, no gap, not one inch missed, the ground pulled back, pulled away, as we tip upward, this slow ascension, awakening. Remembering being aloft, desiring aloft, all desire rising. Pardonable what was done. What we are bidden to keep, to hold, a promise, re-engaged, given back, the promise kept, heartbeat again, drumming us inch by inch, the stringed wind unbowing, teeth unbared, all fleeing fled, the hint of song, of stories told and telling. The ground again below. The forest reaching to hold us, towered, aloft. Piercing the pinnacled sky. Awake to sight giving in to blindness and back to sight, the blink of an eye.

Let the soul in,
to begin again,
blessed beginning.
To this place
belong once more.

ACKNOWLEDGMENTS

THE WRITER DOESN'T MERELY IMITATE LIFE but creates an accessible world. My friends have had the access code and they have made this book possible. As with Harold Bloom, I believe literature is a way of life. Even more, the writing of it is a destiny and a destination. I hauled my friends there.

While the characters in the book were brain-mates for me, they were nevertheless close at hand for my friends. They viewed them over the back fence and, like all loving neighbors, had valuable opinions about how the characters should behave; worried about them; wanted to be sure, as we do with people we like, that their voices were authentic, that they were true to themselves. Conversations would often begin, "Now why would Alix do that?" If I couldn't adequately explain, I went back to the drawing board. We happily discussed Alix Purcell's motives; considered her mother's treachery; wondered about Austin Hart's suicide. Without all of this I would have been on a desert island, grumpy and alone. So, thank you: Kim Baryluk, Hugh Brody, Megan Close, Louise Mandell, Clarine Ostrove, Lorita Whitehead. All of you have believed in this project even when proof of its merit ran thin.

Along the way, others have commented on the manuscript, and I am grateful to Carolyn Forde, Carolyn McCool, Anthony Sheil, Carolyn Swayze, Bruce Westwood. Judy Globerman and Krista Hunt advised me on the medical problems and dementia of the mother, Sophia. More generally, the book started from a long way off before it found its course. In circling into its orbit, I owe so much to the insights of Marnie Duff, Andrea Laforest, Karen Mulhallen, Jada Pape, Steven Point, Bill Reid, Martine Reid, Robin Riddington, John Smyly, Hilary Stewart, and the work of Bruce Ruddell.

Peggie Merlin has given me her friendship, unstintingly.

You have all delved deep within yourselves to help me find the truth of these characters, their lives and the story they have to tell. It was a good destination. Thank you for getting me here.

NOTES TO CHAPTERS

Chapter 1: Taking of the Weeping Woman Pole

The description of the felling of the pole is intended to be reminiscent of Gerard Manley Hopkins "Binsey Poplars" (when a stand of poplar trees along the Thames towards Oxford was felled in 1879).

Chapter 7: Things that Disintegrate

When Austin says "spiritually, it is a feast," in that entire passage he is consciously drawing from Frank Cushing (the inspired enthnographer who lived amongst the Zuni in New Mexico in the 1880s). Alix also chimes in with this reference in Chapter 22 when she receives Hart's secret diaries. She says, "Ethically it was a feast." Cushing's letter to Professor Baird says of being amongst the Zuni: "Ethically, theoretically, a feast, a peace of mind unapproachable in all my previous experience."

Chapter 14: A Glaucous Time

The phrases that attract Alix in reading about plants and flowers are mainly taken from "Shocking Beauty" by Thomas Hobbs.

Chapter 27: Music Trumps Words

Some of Brett's views about the relationship of the music (the man) to the libretto (the woman) are derived from *Opera; or, The Undoing of Women* by Catherine Clement.

Chapter 30: The Last Lecture

The inspiration for some of the thoughts in this chapter is the lecture given by Wilson Duff as reported in "The World is as Sharp as a Knife," although the ideas are changed and are those of the fictional Austin Hart. See also *Bird of Paradox, The Unpublished Writings of Wilson Duff,* edited by E. N. Anderson.

Chapter 42: Bring Me One of Everything

Sophia's statement to Alix, "Call out to the universe until it answers," was remembered from a science book, but I've been unable to find the quotation.

Chapter 43: The Pole is Raised

In the final chapter, when the Weeping Woman Pole is raised, the lines "to feel the rise of day not dark" are a play on Gerard Manley Hopkins's "I feel the fell of dark not day."

ABOUT THE AUTHOR

LESLIE HALL PINDER has written short fiction, non-fiction, and two widely acclaimed novels. *Under the House* (1986) was published in Canada, the U. K., the U. S. and Finland. *On Double Tracks* (1990) was published in Canada and the U. K. and was short-listed for the Governor-General's award for literature. She litigated in court on behalf of the natives' rights to their land for 28 years. She lives in British Columbia, Canada.

COLOPHON

This book was typeset using Garamond, a classic 16th century typeface interpreted by type designer Robert Slimbach and released in 1988. Originally, Claude Garamond created the roman form and Garamond's assistant, Robert Granjon, designed the italics face. Together, this font family is considered to be among the most legible and readable serif typefaces because of its fluidity and consistency.

CPSIA information can be obtained at www.ICGtesting.com
Printed in the USA
LVOW111103020212

266605LV00002B/5/P

9 780983 490012